the BUS RIDE

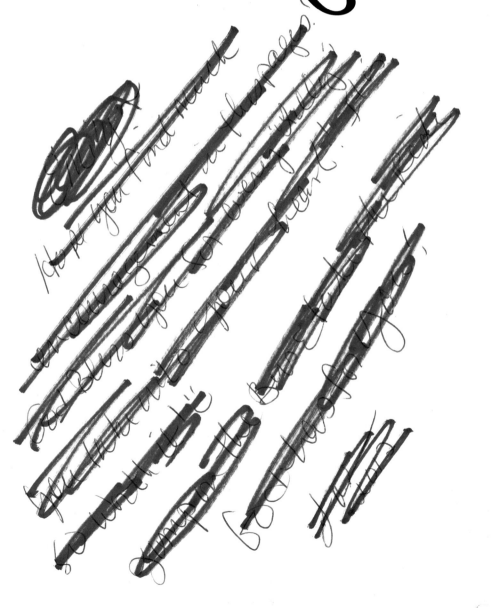

the BUS RIDE

LAURA WIGGIN

ORPHANED AT HOME

TATE PUBLISHING & *Enterprises*

Published by Tate Publishing & Enterprises, LLC
127 E. Trade Center Terrace | Mustang, Oklahoma 73064 USA
1.888.361.9473 | www.tatepublishing.com

Tate Publishing is committed to excellence in the publishing industry. The company reflects the philosophy established by the founders, based on Psalm 68:11,
"The Lord gave the word and great was the company of those who published it."

Book design copyright © 2011 by Tate Publishing, LLC. All rights reserved.
Cover design by Amber Gulilat
Interior design by Sarah Kirchen

Published in the United States of America

ISBN: 978-1-61777-625-0
1. Fiction / Christian / Romance
2. Fiction / Christian / General
11.06.08

To every child who goes through the day with
arms wrapped around an empty stomach.

To every child who covers up the scars and bruises of abuse.

To every child who cries himself to
sleep, wanting to be loved.

To every child who wears the label
"destitute" day in and day out.

To every child who faces another day alone.

To every person who takes one of these
children into his heart and loves him.

To every person who works in the Bus Ministry.

ACKNOWLEDGMENTS

The most important acknowledgment is to my LORD, Jesus Christ. I would never have been able to do this on my own. I've no doubt that He laid this on my heart to write, and I laid myself at His feet, completely undone, that He would ask me to do such an immense task. He gave me the strength, the endurance, the courage, and the power to begin, struggle through, and finish His will in these pages. May He alone be glorified for any encouragement that might be gained through the reading of this book.

To my friends who encouraged me along the way, who challenged me to keep on track for the glory of God, thanks is so small. May you be richly rewarded for your hearts of love and care for neglected and abused children.

To Charlotte Miller: Thank you for your eagle's eye in editing and suggestions. Thank you for believing in this project. Your red pen made this part a joy.

To my boys, who have relived many memories with me as we have journeyed along in life. I really hadn't realized just how much of my childhood history they had pieced together. Though this is a fictional book, they know what parts are taken from my heart and what parts are taken from my imagination. They were my biggest cheering section, whether by sitting over my shoulder, reading and laughing, helping me get the "green lines" off my computer, or by sitting next to me, letting me read it to them with great eagerness. I love each of you more than you know, Samuel, Joshua, and Zechariah.

To Sherman, the "Petah" of every book I write. I love you more than an ocean full of words could say. You're the love of my life, even though many years have passed. I love you even more today than the day we married. Thank you for helping me in any and every way to follow God's leading in this assignment. You're a man after God's own heart, and I'm blessed to be your wife.

TABLE OF
CONTENTS

INTRODUCTION

You're about to take a journey through the land of make-believe, traveling piggyback on the reality of life. It's a beautiful story with a happy ending. But the beauty comes from the ashes that the main character lives through. As you enjoy the story, my heart's prayer is that you also see the reality that many of these children might live right next to you. It's my hope that this book will awaken the hearts of adults and teens to welcome these needy children into their lives and share all the love they have to help, encourage, and point them to Jesus Christ.

It's my deepest prayer that any lonely, unloved, abused, hungry, destitute, or neglected child or teenager who reads this book will be encouraged, that you will reach out for help, and that you'll know that Jesus Christ died for you. He's the author of happy endings. It's for you that I wrote this book.

This is the first book of the series entitled Orphaned at Home. This was very much the phenomenon while I was growing up. It blossomed quickly and spread like wildfire, leaving in its wake children and youth scarred for life. These books are not about orphans in the truest sense of the word but orphans in the reality of life. Join me ...

CHAPTER 1

Lilly, balancing as best she could, made her way to the living room.

"Here you are, my dear. Your favorite hot tea, just as you like it—red raspberry with a teaspoon of honey."

She set the precious teacup down by her aunt, who had saved her life by taking her in two weeks ago when she had no other place to go.

"So where did you get this cup, Aunt Maureen?"

"Lilly dear, you are so kind. Someday, some special man is going to catch you and never let go. And what a prize package he'll have. He will, I tell ya."

That was Aunt Maureen's comment each time Lilly brought her tea. She enjoyed a long sip before she began her teacup story. Lilly, being very attentive, laughed at all the right places.

Lilly was just that way. Kindness was the work of her hands; caring, the work of her heart. And there was no mistaking that Lilly had the sweetest heart Aunt Maureen had ever known. She still shook her head at the very thought of her sister, who was always in trouble. She never had a good man, and her older girls were always in trouble too. But Aunt Maureen had never really gotten to know the youngest. She just assumed that none of her sister's kids would ever amount to anything. But when Lilly walked into to her life, everything changed.

She could still remember the very moment of stunned silence as she opened the door to the eyes of this lost and lonely puppy the day Lilly arrived on her doorstep. Suitcase in hand, shaking nervously, she stood, dressed in mere rags.

Surprised, though, she was to find her estranged sister's youngest daughter reaching out to her for help, Maureen offered Lilly a hot meal and a place to stay. Before deciding to make the arrangement permanent, Maureen had to find out if Lilly was anything like her mother.

"I ain't got no money, so don't be asking for any iffin you're in any money troubles. And I don't want no men comin' around here all the time a-lookin' for ya. Are you by any chance running from the law? I ain't gonna keep ya if that be the case! The first bit of trouble, and you're out of here. I'm too old to be putting up with all that chaos of that no-good sister of mine!" she sputtered.

A look of shock registered on Lilly's face. "Oh no. I … um … I'm not running from the law. And I um … I'm not in any financial trouble. Well, I guess I sorta am. I've no money and need some food and a place to stay. I won't ask for any money. I can assure you there are no men in my life to be coming around here." Lilly was shaking terribly.

Aunt Maureen instinctively knew she was telling the truth, so she began to relax.

"You're different, aren't you?"

"What did you expect?" Lilly asked, turning innocent eyes on her aunt.

A bit embarrassed and not sure what to say, Aunt Maureen briskly said, "Well, I guessed you'd be like the rest of them and bring a string of trouble with you that you want me to help ya out of. But maybe my judgment of you was too hasty. Time will tell. Just don't see how anything good could come from that messed-up family of yours."

Lilly locked eyes with her aunt and said, "Yes. Time will tell that I am indeed different." Then, promising to answer any questions in the morning, Lilly bade her aunt good night, leaving Aunt Maureen to wonder just what she'd gotten herself into.

"Good morning, Aunt Maureen."

"Grab you a cup of coffee and come tell me what you're up to today, my Lil," Aunt Maureen coaxed, having fallen more in love with Lilly every day.

"Well, after I fix us some blueberry pancakes, I'm off to find a job. I circled some possibilities in the Sunday paper."

"You've only been here three weeks and you hardly eat anything. I can take care of your simple needs. It's not a problem," Aunt Maureen said, hating the thought of losing her Lilly.

"Well, now that would be a nice thought, and thank you. But I'm planning to start college in just over a month. So I best get to looking for work, or I won't have any money to go."

"What will you go to college to be? Do you know?" Aunt Maureen was suddenly very curious

"Actually, I do know what I'm going to do. I don't want to see other children go through what I've gone through. So I'm getting a degree in child psychology with a minor in public speaking. I'd like to start giving speeches in schools and other such places, anywhere that will give me a voice to help children in abusive or neglected situations. This is what I feel God is leading me to do." She got up to flip the pancakes. "Does that make sense?"

She turned to see Aunt Maureen's eyes suspiciously wet.

"What is wrong?" Lilly knelt before her aunt.

"Oh, nothing, my dear. I just have never seen such suffering as you've been through. No child should have to suffer like that. Yet you seem to have forgiven and even have compassion for your folks. I don't understand how you could do that. That's all," she said as she blew her nose into a tissue and dabbed her eyes dry.

"Aunt Maureen, you see, I can't rely on my own strength or will. I must rely on the strength God gives me. It helps me persevere through even the hardest memories, knowing that God commands us to forgive others, even my mom and dad. He showed us just what forgiveness was when He died on the cross. I'd be glad to show that to you sometime if you're interested."

"Thank you for sharing. Maybe some other time. I'm not much on the Bible. But if it helps you, I'm happy for you, dear." Changing the subject back to Lilly's job search, she said, "Well, honey, I just know you'll find something."

CHAPTER 2

"Lilly, my dear, you're home at last." Aunt Maureen greeted Lilly with a hug and a smile. "How was your day? Did you find a job?"

Lilly beamed one of her adorable smiles at her aunt. "Yes, Aunt Maureen, God did provide me with a job. I begin Monday at the Stuffed Goose! Have you ever eaten there?"

Aunt Maureen stopped in her tracks, alarmed, looked Lilly square in the face, and asked, "Lilly, how did you get all the way down to the Stuffed Goose? I thought you were going to check out places in these few blocks. Please tell me you didn't walk all the way there!"

Lilly made a strong effort not to rub her aching feet but to cheerfully answer her aunt's questions and put her at ease. "Well, I did do a lot of walking today. But I didn't walk all the way there. I took the city bus downtown. Though it's not close by, I rejoice in what God has provided even though it's on a trial basis." She didn't tell her aunt that she'd already checked into most all the businesses that were within walking distance but nothing was available.

"Lilly, you're not going to walk to work. Do you understand me?" Aunt Maureen objected. She was still shaking her head as Lilly spoke.

"Oh, I don't plan too. I'll take the bus. I might have to borrow five dollars for the fare before getting paid. I hope that's not a problem." Lilly was shaking now. Seeing the look on her aunt's face, she gulped before going on. "I'll pay you back double as soon as I get my first check."

"No. I won't give you no money!" Her aunt was adamant. The look on her face was resolute.

Lilly was crushed. She slumped in defeat. *What now, Lord?*

She was praying and didn't hear her aunt speak. "I'm not going to have you riding the bus, young lady," she said stubbornly. "You'll drive my car, and that is that. No ifs, ands, or buts. Do you understand me?" She hurriedly continued on as she saw Lilly wanting to protest. "I don't drive anywhere most days, and there is just no sense in you taking the bus with a good car right here." With a wave of her hand, she concluded, "That is that."

With tears glistening in her eyes, Lilly expressed her deep gratitude for yet another act of love from her heavenly Father through the hand of her aunt. "Aunt Maureen, I'm deeply touched by your caring and concern. I'll do my best to take good care of your car. And, should you need it at anytime, I'm more than happy to take the bus." Lilly touched her aunt's shoulder as she continued. "You have blessed me once again. I can never repay you for all you've done."

By now they were in a tender embrace.

"Ah. Now stop that gibberish," her aunt said as she released Lilly. "I'm needin' to check the chicken afore I burn something," she said and excused herself before she got too emotional.

It was day number three, and Lilly's arms were aching for relief. For two and a half days, she'd washed dishes for eight hours straight. Huge pots and pans, almost too heavy for her to lift, came one after another until she was exhausted. She never realized how many plates, saucers, and petite cups an upscale establishment used. She didn't want to complain. God had given her this job. There wasn't a bone in her body that did not cry out for relief. But with a smile, she continued. The boss did come by and watch her from time to time. She flashed him her best smile and greeted him each time. She always got a quirky smile before he walked off.

I wonder if he's making it extra hard just to see what kind of material I'm made of, she thought to herself driving home that evening.

As she did each evening, she greeted her aunt, she wolfed down the food her aunt set before her, took a hot shower to ease her aches, and collapsed in bed only to have the sunbeams peer into her window to start it all over again.

"Well now, you did surprise me. You got more in you than I thought," the owner of the Stuffed Goose said at the end of the week. "I guess you win." He choked down his pride and then said, "As a matter a fact, I have a waitress opening coming up and wanted to offer it to you. You'll have to train, of course, and you will be on trial to see if you're good at it. But that was in our bargain, and I'm wagering that you'll be a good catch after all."

Lilly was beside herself. In just one instant, all her aches and pains floated away. With the LORD's help, she'd succeeded in getting this man to give her a try. *And no more dishes!* She almost shouted aloud but then, realizing she was being stared at, gathered herself under control.

"Thank you, sir. Thank you so much. I won't let you down," Lilly blurted out.

She was about to leave when he stopped her.

"You'll be working with Alisha for training. You be here when she is here. You do as she does. You'll be her shadow for one week. I usually don't pay my waitresses in training, but I'll offer you half your pay if you stay two hours each night and do the dishes since I'll be out of a dishwasher now."

She agreed, keeping her disappointment in check. "Have a great weekend," Lilly said as she turned to go.

Again, he stopped her. He handed a check across his desk toward her. She'd forgotten. She timidly took it after he shook it at her again.

He stared at her to see what she'd do. After a few moments, she looked her boss straight in the eyes, and proceeded to tear up the check.

"Mr. Bowman, a deal is a deal. I'll not accept one penny more than half the pay for this week's work," she said humbly as she put the pieces of the check for a full week's work into the wastebasket. Then she turned to leave. "Good-bye, and have a nice evening. I'll see you Tuesday." She was at the door when she heard his voice once again.

"Hey, hey! Wait a minute!" He knew this kind of material was worth every cent that was on that check. He felt a sudden rush of guilt since he'd purposely made it extremely hard for her at times just to see if she'd quit. But she'd stuck it out. She was always polite, never had a bad attitude, and was always smiling when he saw her. He couldn't deny she'd been a diligent worker.

"Yes, Mr. Bowman?" She moved back to his desk and faced him.

"Uh, yes, Lillian, could you have a seat for just a minute?"

A few minutes later, he handed Lilly another check. He smiled and said, "I still know a jewel when I see one. Here, Miss Parker, is your hard-earned deal." He chuckled and assured her, "You drive a hard bargain; but this time, I think we both win. Lillian, have a nice weekend. I'll see you Tuesday."

CHAPTER 3

Aunt Maureen sauntered into the kitchen, surprised to see Lilly up so early. She had been working at the Stuffed Goose for two weeks now. Aunt Maureen dreadfully missed her in the evenings, but the mornings more than made up for it. Lilly was a good cook and prepared breakfast every morning for them, along with good, strong coffee that was a perfect start to the day. While eating, they chatted like old friends.

The only thing that bothered Aunt Maureen was that Lilly often gave mention or credit to God. It made her uncomfortable. Lilly seemed very different from her own family as well as herself her aunt thought. She also noticed that Lilly seemed to have a calm assurance even when things seemed gloomy.

"Oh. Good morning, Aunt Maureen," Lilly said as she looked up from the paper in hand. "How did you sleep?"

"Why, honey, I slept like an old lady! Gets kinda boring after all these years! A lot of things changed when James left me," her aunt said placidly. Lilly perked her ears instantly at the name of her ex-uncle. She barely remembered him. Not sure what happened, but bitterness had consumed her aunt over it. Lilly decided it was best not to comment.

Maureen turned her attention to what Lilly was doing. She didn't recognize the paper her niece was reading, so she discretely inquired about it.

"What are you reading?"

"This is the Shaftner State Community College catalogue for this term. I need to select my classes and register today. I'm already past the normal registration deadline," she stated. "As it is, it looks like I'm going to have to take a TBA English class." She went on to explain what that meant.

"When do you start?"

"Depending on what I end up with, it could be Monday or Tuesday the week of August twelfth."

"Why, that's just over a week away, my dear. How will you work this around your schedule at the restaurant?"

"Well, it won't be easy. School never came very easy for me. I have had to study very hard to make good grades. This is truly where I have to rely on God to work out the details."

Lilly was delighted that she had ended up with a three-day schedule, enabling her to get her studies done and to get to work on time. She felt that God had blessed her once again.

She was nervous and excited at the same time. This was her first try at college. She'd spent much time in prayer that morning as well as soaking in the book of First John. As she prayed she slipped on her special necklace from Jeff and Jenny, her dearest friends. It was like having them with her on this very special occasion.

Oh, Father, help me love these people I meet at college with your kind of love. May they see you in me. May they not be confused in where my affections lie, Lilly prayed.

Lilly found her math class without a problem. Before she knew it, her first class was over and she was on to her second class. Most of the seats were taken, so she slipped into the back row. The professor had his head down in some paperwork when Lilly came in. From the back, she couldn't see him but heard his instructions.

"Good morning. I want to welcome you to my English composition class. My name is on the board. If you have any questions or difficulties at any time during this semester, please feel free to speak with me." Still seated, he continued, "My favorite way to start a class is by asking your name and your favorite piece of literature. It's been my observation that if you know what kind of reading diet someone is on, you find out what kind of person they are." Then he said, "I'd like each of you to stand and state your name and your favorite piece of literature. Let's see. Let's do things a little different and start from the back. Let's just start at the end desk in that last row there. Sorry. I can't see you," he stated.

The first person stood and stated his name and favorite piece, but Lilly didn't hear him. She was next.

She sat mute, trying to take in what was before her eyes. *Peter Collins! Peter Collins!* Her mind was racing. *My dearest childhood friend, Petah? Can it be? My English professor is good ole Petah!* She was so stunned she couldn't think.

The guy next to her bumped her arm and said, "Hey, it's your turn."

Lilly came back to herself just in time to hear the professor say, "Who's next?"

Lilly stood on wobbly knees and cleared her throat. In the smallest of squeaks, her breath barely audible, she spoke, "My name is Lillian Parker, and my favorite literature piece is *The Hedge of Thorns* by John Hatchard."

Peter stood staring at Lilly in total shock. *Could this be?* He shook his head in disbelief. It sure sounded like her voice. But it was those eyes that gave her away. It most definitely was his little Lilly.

Both stared, not believing what they were seeing. What seemed like hours were only moments.

Still not taking his eyes off Lilly, the professor said, "Class, I'm passing around the syllabus for you. Please take out your English books and read the first chapter. I need to run to my office a minute. I'll return briefly and we'll pick up where we left off." His eyes still riveted on Lilly, he spoke softly, "Miss Parker I need to see you in my office." When he saw she was still standing there, stone still and white as a sheet, he said very firmly, "Now!" Then he walked out of the room.

It took a few heartbeats, but Lilly finally moved forward on wooden legs. Out the door she went, but Peter was nowhere in sight.

Her mind was a whirlwind. She still couldn't believe this was her dearest friend on earth, now a grown man of course; and, she must say, very handsome at that. There was no mistaking his tall, thin build. The smooth skin on his face made his masculine jaw line stand out which made him all the more distracting. She used to tousle that jet-black hair when they were younger. But now it was all neatly combed and under the strict guard of hair cream. She remembered her Petah as that silly, sweet youth that took an interest in her welfare as a nine-year-old girl. All these thoughts and many more came whirling at her as she nearly walked right into the closed office door of the very person turning her world upside down.

The man behind the door was in no better shape. He'd run his hands through his hair, forgetting to keep it in place as he paced the floor, gesturing his hands wildly. His thoughts were going crazy, keeping up with his wild hands. He couldn't calm the beating of his heart.

He kept saying over and over to himself, *My Lilly? My Lilly? I can't believe it. I thought she was gone forever. Now she sits in my very own English class! How can that be? And the name change. Maybe she's married.* His thoughts whirled. *And wow, she took my breath away. Gone is the dirty face and matted hair. Gone is the kid with mismatched clothes.*

Lilly was breathtaking. Her hair was a lovely, dark blonde color, a little darker than he remembered, flowing around her shoulders and partway down her back. Her simple dress showed she had grown into quite the young lady. But it was those eyes that had always torn Peter up. He was in the midst of the heated conversation with himself when the knock came.

Peter opened the door and nodded for Lilly to come in. He shut the door behind them. They stared at each other for what seemed like forever. Then Lilly spoke ever so softly.

"Sorry, Peter. I mean, Professor Collins. I'm a bit late. I had to go get directions to find your office."

Peter gently grabbed her upper arms and looked into her face. He wanted to pull her into his arms now that he found his long-lost Lilly. But with much strength, he refrained from doing so. He had so many questions. But her tardiness wasn't on the list.

"Lilly, that's the least of my worries. I'm sorry I didn't think about you not knowing your way around. I only have a minute, as I need to get back to my students. But I just can't believe you're one of them! I have so much to say." He stared into her periwinkle-blue eyes. "What are you doing here?"

"Professor Collins, it's a long story," she said, sadness filling her eyes.

"What was I thinking?" he said as he hit his head. "Please, Lilly. I can't stand you calling me Professor Collins. I'm just old Petah to you." He said his old name exaggerated like he had heard her call him so many times. "I need to go," he said. He had to tear himself away before falling completely apart. "Can we meet for lunch? I have so many questions," he pleaded.

How could she refuse him? "I brought my lunch; and since you obviously know the campus better than me, you name the place. I'm free after your class until noon," she said with a smile.

"How about meeting in the south parking lot by the three oak trees? Do you know where that is?"

She nodded.

"There are some benches; and since it would be early, perhaps they'll be free." He walked to the door, put his hand on the knob, and turned. "By the way, Lilly, I just have to know, are you by chance married?" he asked so seriously and with such anxiety it was pitiful.

"No," she whispered.

She left as quickly as possible. "Take a deep breath, Lilly. Breathe slowly," she said to herself as soon as she hit the fresh air.

Lilly wasn't sure what happened to the rest of class. She was so distracted that she couldn't keep her eyes off Professor Collins. Though looking right at him, she didn't hear a word he said. Thankfully, since the class did most of the sharing, Peter only had to speak at the end of the class. He dismissed class with a homework assignment. Before she knew what was happening, chairs were clattering and voices were talking, all in a rush to leave, taking Lilly with them. Lilly went to her aunt's car and stashed her books and got her lunch bag. She proceeded to where Peter had told her to meet him. She spotted him right away on a bench under a huge oak tree. She was a bundle of nerves as she sat on the edge of the bench.

Seeing that someone needed to break the silence, Peter spoke. "Lilly, I just can't believe you're here." He continued when she smiled at him. "You've no idea the pain that I suffered when I found out that you were gone. Do you understand?" He paused and rubbed the back of his neck. "You've always had a special place in my heart, and it literally felt like something had died when I heard you were gone and no one ever heard from you again," he said, searching her eyes.

"I'm so sorry, Peter. I never wanted to hurt you. You were everything to my little world. I owe you so much." Lilly began to cry.

"Hush now, Lilly. You don't need to cry," he said as he gently touched her shoulder. He had to be careful. There were rules about professor and student relationships, yet this was a special case. This was his Lilly in much need of tender care. He wanted answers, but not at the expense of Lilly's tears.

Gaining control of her emotions, Lilly sniffled and thought lunch would be a good distraction right now. "Peter, you didn't bring a lunch," she said more as a statement than a question as she began to unpack her simple brownbag lunch. "Here is a sandwich. Can you believe it, like old days, a PBJ," she said with a chuckle as she tore it in two and gave him the biggest half. She gave him half of the rest of her lunch as well. Peter's thoughts were torturous. *How can I tell her I'm not even hungry, at least not for food but for answers? Not to mention that I usually just grab something hot to eat and go to the faculty lounge and eat with Veronica. I wonder how I'll explain to Veronica that I ate a PBJ with an old friend.* It nearly killed him to take food from her, but to refuse would have crushed her. He'd always known her to be simple hearted, sweet, and giving. She wouldn't let anyone go without if she could help it. She wasn't a complicated girl. She was always honest, at least after they told her lying was wrong. He chuckled out loud at the memory.

"Are you laughing at me or my PBJ, Professor Collins?"

"Why, Miss Lillian Parker, I would never make fun of one of your famous PBJs," he teased. "Actually, I was thinking about a sweet memory of you. By the way, thank you for sharing your lunch. It reminded me that some things don't change."

Lilly put her hand on her hip and said, "You've got to tell all, Peter! What were you thinking? What are you hiding in that silly head of yours?"

"Well, I was thinking that we are running out of time," Peter said, glancing at his watch.

Before Peter could say anything else, Lilly said, "Sorry, Peter. I mean, Professor Collins. I've got to go. I'll be late to my next class." She didn't even stop to look at him.

Before she shot off, he grabbed her arm. "Hey, can we get together tonight so we can talk for a bit longer about what all has happened?" he asked quickly.

"Um… um… let me think." She thought about her schedule at the Stuffed Goose. "Yes. That'll be fine. I'd like that," she answered, still in disbelief that she was staring at the face of her Petah.

"How about I pick you up at five for dinner?"

"How about I meet you here at five? And we don't have to go to dinner. I'd be glad to bring something, and we can have a picnic," Lilly suggested.

"Why, you're too kind, Lilly. Let me treat. I know just the place. Perhaps then we'll have more time," he pleaded with a smile, hoping she'd agree. He didn't want to take the chance on another PBJ. He wanted this to be special.

"Okay, Peter. I'll meet you here at five. I really have to go," she said. She nearly ran to her car and grabbed her books. Then he watched her go off into the east wing of Winston Hall. She got to her biology class on time, thankfully. She was breathing hard by the time she got there. She tried her best to pay attention. But it was difficult, to say the least.

By the time she was in her aunt's car, she was shaking.

Oh, LORD, I can't believe Peter is here. You're more than amazing. Only you could have done a miracle like that! She cried hard this time. *And to think how he was pained at my disappearance. LORD, bless him the rest of this day. LORD, help me not to hurt him tonight as I share. Help me glorify you tonight.*

She finally calmed down and started the car and drove home, continuing to praise God.

When she pulled in the driveway, she wanted to go straight to her room; she needed her bed and her Bible. Not to mention, she knew her eyes would certainly give her away, as they always did. Her aunt would be able to see right away that she'd been crying and would want to know why. How could she explain it all plus still get back to the campus by five?

"How was your first day, Lil?" Aunt Maureen called from the kitchen.

"Hi, Aunt Maureen! It went great!" Lilly said, trying to hide the tremble in her voice, but to no avail.

As her aunt met her, she immediately saw the puffy eyes. "What in the world happened to you?" Aunt Maureen asked with great worry. "Why have you been crying, my dear?" She put her hands on her hips. "Lilly, did someone hurt you? If they did, why I'll—"

"Oh no. No one hurt me. But I had quite an amazing day!" She smiled at her precious aunt.

"But you have been crying. What's wrong?" her aunt persisted.

"Well," Lilly began, thinking how she was going to put her aunt off, "Aunt Maureen, you're just not going to believe how God blessed me today. And it's so special that I want to have enough time to tell you everything. So I'm going to ask you for a big favor. I need to spend some time reading my Bible with a cup of tea and take a rest for a bit. I don't have time to share with you because I'm going out tonight," she said with excitement. She could see she'd shocked her aunt. Her eyes were big, and the expression on her face was a mix of worry and curiosity. "Here's the favor. If you can wait for me to share until the morning, I'd appreciate it. I'll probably be in late tonight, and I'm a bit tired after such an exciting first day at college. I promise to be very quiet. But I don't know how long this meeting will be," she said, looking to see if her aunt would agree.

When she saw some hesitation, she coaxed on. "I'll fix your favorite blueberry pancakes, and we'll have all morning before I start my homework. It'll be worth the wait, I assure you."

What could her aunt say but, "Alright, I'll wait, but I don't see what the big deal is. I don't like the fact that you've been crying and won't tell me why," she said. "To top it off, you're going out at night with someone you evidently just met."

But Lilly was resolute. "Like I said, Aunt Maureen, I'll tell you all about it in the morning, including the details of this meeting I'm having tonight; and this will all make more sense to you then anyway. Please trust me," she ended, convincing her aunt into compliance.

Her aunt reluctantly agreed, and Lilly retreated to her room.

Grabbing her cherished Bible, she went to the book of Colossians. This was one of her favorites. Colossians was filled with encouraging prayers, admonishments, and instructions on how she should live.

Lord, I want you to fill me with the knowledge of your will and give me wisdom and understanding. You said in James that those who ask for wisdom will receive it. Father, I desperately want to live a life worthy of you. Lord, I think how my aunt, who as sweet as she can be, will go to hell if she doesn't come to know she needs a Savior and realize that you're the only way to salvation. I lift her up to you. Use me in her life. Father, help me when I'm weak in my forgiveness to my mom. Lord, help both my mom and dad wherever they are. Lord, be with the father I never knew too. Lord God, have mercy on me.

On Lilly prayed until she fell into a much-needed slumber, only to be awakened by a slight knocking on her door.

"Lilly, are you awake?" her aunt called. "I thought you might want to be getting up."

Lilly, not realizing she'd fallen asleep while reading and praying, glanced at her watch. "Oh dear." She gasped, jumping out of bed. "Thanks, Aunt Maureen," she yelled at the shut door.

She quickly readied and hit the door. It was already four thirty, and she had to walk the two blocks to the bus stop and then three blocks after she got off the bus to reach the campus. She walked as briskly as her sandals would allow, praying Peter wouldn't leave, knowing she'd be late.

Peter looked at his watch. It was 5:00 p.m. sharp and no Lilly. Peter's heart beat wildly. He tried to calm himself by telling himself not everyone's watches are synchronized. His heart telling him not to worry did nothing for his pacing, so he tried for a distraction. His thoughts went back to the afternoon and his miserable attempt to explain why he hadn't shown up at lunch with Veronica as planned. He shook his head.

What a mess, he thought as he recalled what happened.

After he'd watched Lilly leave, he went back to his classroom, sat there, and stared at the seat Lilly had been in. He really needed to think. His mind was doing crazy things to him. It wasn't long until Veronica came in and sat on the edge of his desk, effectively jarring Peter from his whirling thoughts.

He glanced over to see her leg hanging halfway over his desk. She was a sight for sore eyes, to be sure. After seeing Lilly, however, it somehow took the spark out of her appearance.

"Hey, where are you, Pete?" she asked. "Hello?" Her soft, suggestive voice questioned him as she placed her hand on his arm.

She was rewarded with a smile as he sat back, letting her hand slip off his arm.

"You were a million miles away. Care to share? Was your first day that bad?"

Peter quickly tried to think of what to say yet kept coming up empty. He couldn't possibly explain to her about Lilly, at least not yet. She wouldn't understand. He wasn't sure he understood. How did he excuse himself for not showing up for lunch? "I must say, Veronica, you don't look as though you had any trouble today," he said, hoping to avoid answering her.

"Well, I do try to look my best," she boasted as she smoothed out her already-smooth skirt and touched up her hair that had so much hairspray it couldn't possibly be out of place. She smiled a coy smirk at Peter. "But I was wondering what happened to my lunch partner?"

"Ah, yes. I'm sorry, Veronica. I was tied up with a new student asking some questions about transcripts, and time just left me." He said what was mostly true. "And I must say I'm the one who lost out since my stomach is growling and I have my next class in five minutes." He smiled, hoping she wouldn't ask any more questions.

"Well, you could always make up for it by taking me out to dinner tonight," she said, sounding like a wounded kitty.

"Uh ... well ... uh ... I can't tonight, Veronica. I'm really sorry. I have a meeting I just can't get out of," he said. "And Wednesday night is church. Hey, you could always join me."

"No thanks. You know that Wednesday is my sorority meeting night." She was a bit frustrated that he'd forgotten.

"Well, how about I take you out for a nice dinner on Friday?" He had a plan forming in his head. "We can sort of celebrate a new school year at the Stuffed Goose." He hoped she'd take the offer; it was her favorite place to eat.

"That sounds wonderful!" She smiled. "I'll look forward to having you all to myself. I will feel like a queen." With that, she hopped off Peter's desk and said, "Tootles, Pete. See ya tomorrow." And she left.

Not one minute later, his class began to fill up.

CHAPTER 4

Peter was all wrapped up in his thoughts and emotions when he was startled out of his reverie. Peter squinted, looking to the far parking lot. It looked as though he saw Lilly. Surely that was not her. *Where is her car?* "Why, sure enough it is Lilly," Peter spoke aloud to himself as his long legs began to eat up the distance across the empty parking lot.

Concerned something bad had happened, the temptation to run was keen. He went in her direction. They met in the middle.

"Hello, Peter." Lilly was the first to speak, greeting him with a charming smile "I'm so sorry to be late. I hope I didn't cause you any trouble," she said as she looked up into his intent face. She thought he seemed irritated.

"Oh no. It was no trouble to wait. I was just worried about you. That's all." He kept looking around for her car. "Didn't you drive here?"

"No. I didn't want to ask for my aunt's car since she lets me use it for class."

"Well, it sure was nice of her to drop you off," Peter acknowledged.

Lilly, not thinking, said, "She didn't." She continued to walk, not realizing that Peter had stopped dead in his tracks.

Instantly, Peter grabbed her arm. "What did you say?"

"I'm sorry. I said my aunt didn't bring me here," Lilly restated.

Peter, not liking the sound of this, inquired further. "Who did you catch a ride with then?" Peter asked, hoping she'd met some friends.

They'd begun to walk forward at a much slower pace.

Thinking this was none of his business, she tried to make it simple. She said, "I walked some and took the city bus." She didn't look his way, for she didn't want to see his expression. "I've not usually had a vehicle to get places, so I'm quite used to taking the city transportation. It's not a big deal."

He tilted his head back and closed his eyes. How did he say he didn't want her using the city bus when it was her life? "Lilly, why didn't you just let me come pick you up?"

"I didn't want to inconvenience you. You were already taking me to dinner. The least I could do was get here. And really, Peter," she said, placing a hand on his arm, "It's not a problem."

"Well, next time, please let me do the honors and save you some tread," he pleaded, for he knew she had to have walked a good piece just to get to the parking lot from the nearest bus stop. He was not about to let her ride the bus home. But he would approach that problem later. "Here we are. Not a fancy town car, but your chariot for the evening, Miss Parker." Peter opened the door for her to get in.

Lilly noted that the Toyota Corolla was fairly new, forest green with a cream interior. Of course, it was immaculately clean.

Just like Peter, Lilly thought.

"So, Lilly, what do you feel like?" Peter asked. He wanted this evening to be perfect. He still couldn't believe his Lilly was sitting right next to him. "There are two places I was thinking of. One is a nice, fancy restaurant called the Stuffed Goose, and the other is called Round the Corner. It has gourmet burgers and the best fries in town." He looked over at Lilly. "Both are great places. You choose."

Lilly tried to keep her face from revealing anything about her workplace. The last thing she wanted to do was draw attention from the people she worked with. So she immediately answered.

"Burgers and fries sound wonderful," she said with a lick of her lips. "But whatever you would like is fine. It's really up to you. You're the driver."

"Round the Corner it is," Peter said. *That was easy*, he thought. Peter wasted no time in gathering information. "How long have you been here?"

"Oh, let's see. A couple months," Lilly simply answered.

"Have you found a church to go to yet?"

"I've been walking to a small church just two blocks down from where I live for the past three Sundays. It's a lot different than First Baptist Arlington." She looked over with a smile, remembering the church in which they had met and shared so many cherished memories together. "So until I get to know my surroundings better I'll just go there."

Before Peter knew what he was doing, he was inviting her to come to his church, not thinking of the snare he set for himself when he did. Totally caught up in the moment, he forgot about Veronica.

"I go to Grace Community Church over on Hearne Avenue. It's a big church much like the one back home. There are only a few minor differences. You're more than welcome to try it out. I think you'll like it."

"I just might, thanks. I've found it's hard to find a good church. I don't feel like an expert or anything, but it seems like most places either make the Bible so complicated or they don't think about the Bible at all." She was concentrating on her words. "I went to church after my mom resettled, I was never really comfortable, but I still went. I don't know what I would have done without the Bible that Jenny and Jeff gave me." She said with tears threatening as she held her hands close to her chest as though she were hugging her Bible.

What a beautiful Christian she's become, he thought. Peter would have never guessed that the Bible he'd given her through Jeff and Jenny would've meant so much. They were almost to the restaurant, so he tried to lighten the mood. "Yeah. Jeff and Jenny were awesome. I've never met a more devoted couple. I learned a lot under their kindhearted wings. Working with them in the bus ministry was the best thing that ever happened to me."

"I must agree. If it weren't for them, no telling where I'd be. Their kindness and love for me told me more about Jesus than all the Bible stories I learned. I'll never forget them. They were the ones who told me I needed a Savior. I pray that I will have a portion of their zeal and fervor in serving the LORD, kinda like Elisha asked for a double portion of Elijah's Spirit."

He turned off the car, turned to face Lilly, and softly said, "From all I can tell, He answered you."

Lilly was stunned as she understood his meaning. *A compliment way undeserved,* she thought. *I'll never be the Christian Jenny is.* The door opening made her jump a little, as she was lost in her thoughts. "Oh. Thanks, Peter. You didn't have to do that."

"I know I don't have to. I wanted to," he said as he smiled into the face of his sweet Lilly.

Peter had them seated in a cozy, quiet booth. He looked into her eyes and simply said, "Thank you for coming, Lilly."

It was then that he noticed the cross necklace she wore. He closed his eyes and tilted his head back at the remembrance. He'd given this to Jeff and Jenny to give to her the last Christmas he saw Lilly. He'd given her a gift every Christmas, only she thought the gifts were from Jeff and Jenny. And that was what he wanted her to think. He thought that perhaps his gifts would be more appropriate from Jeff and Jenny, his close friends and the bus captains of the church bus he helped with. He had no idea what effect seeing that necklace would have on him. It was striking on her. This grown up Lilly was so simple yet beautiful all the same. Peter couldn't calm his thoughts.

"Hi. My name is Caron. I'll be your server today," the waitress said, jarring Peter out of his private thoughts. She continued with the specials of the evening. "May I have your drink orders?"

"Lilly, what will you have? They have great raspberry tea here," Peter said.

"Oh, I think I'll just have a glass of ice water with lemon please."

She took off to get their drinks.

Lilly studied the menu with big eyes. She was very intent for some time. Then she laid down her menu, only to find Peter's eyes on her.

"Did you find something that looked good?" he asked her. He didn't have to look at the menu, for he'd frequented this place with Veronica and knew what he wanted.

"Yes. I think so. There are a lot of selections," she said, slightly overwhelmed.

"Lilly, I'll be honest with you. I want to just jump off and interrogate you until my quest for answers is satisfied. I have so many questions it's unbelievable." He ran his hand through his hair.

Lilly chuckled at his boyish antics. Lilly found watching him distracting. His handsome face was well defined in his sage-green, button-up shirt, with a yellow square tie to accent the look. The hint of aftershave accented his attractiveness all the more.

"However, because I care about you, just take your time and share with me from the time you left Arlington to how you got here." Peter sat back intently waiting for Lilly to start.

She wondered how many times the waitress would come to her rescue that evening. She arrived at the table to take their orders right as Lilly was about to speak.

Peter motioned for Lilly to go ahead. She ordered the smallest and cheapest burger they had, and that was all.

Lilly's order wasn't lost on Peter. He ordered his usual with house fries for two. After the waitress left, he questioned Lilly about her order. "Why did you choose the cheapest thing?" he asked as he put his napkin in his lap, his eyes kind but demanding an answer.

"Peter, when you're used to McDonald's, everything is bigger and better."

Peter, feeling a bit rebuked, had nothing to say. *When will this girl—no, woman—quit surprising me?* he thought but said, "Thank you for answering me. I hadn't thought of it like that before."

Lilly, taking this as a cue to start sharing, said, "Peter, are you sure you want to hear all of this? It's a lot to share." Even though Peter was nodding his head, Lilly knew she wouldn't be able to share every detail. "I'll do my best to share all the highlights and as much detail as time will allow. I'm afraid that I'm going to just babble your ears off," she said, slightly laughing.

"I don't think that's possible," Peter said as his eyes twinkled at her, giving her the courage to proceed.

"If you recall, you went off to college the year I turned thirteen. I was there at Arlington for one and a half more years. You came home that first summer and we spent a lot of time together. Those were the best memories of my life."

She paused for a moment as tears threatened to overtake her. "Peter, I don't think you'll ever know how much your friendship meant to me. I know what a pitiful sight I was. And I'll never forget the times that you stood up in my defense when other kids made fun of me. You didn't have to do that, but you did. I know you lost a few friends over it." Lilly had become quite passionate as she reminisced.

"They weren't really friends if they thought it was funny to tease anyone for any reason. That taught me a lot, and I don't regret it for one moment," Peter said.

"Anyway, then you came back at Christmas, and I saw you a few times. Remember when it snowed and we went sledding? That was a lot of fun until we got all wet in the snowball fight. I didn't know it then, but that would be my last Christmas there and the last time to see the "Cradle to the Cross Pageant." She continued with a dreamy expression. "Do you remember the first time I saw it?" She looked to see if he remembered.

"Yes, Miss Parker. It will forever be engraved on my heart," he said softly.

"Ah, it's easy to live in those lovely memories. But I don't think that's why you bought my dinner tonight, is it?" Lilly stated lightheartedly.

Dinner arrived just at that moment.

"Well, saved by the bell. Sorry, Peter. I guess I'll have to leave you in suspense until I've eaten." She smiled mischievously. "Or are you the kind of cruel date that'll hold a lady's hamburger hostage until the goods are delivered?"

It was evident Peter was not happy. He was totally into the story, as he too had been taken back to some of the fondest memories of his life. He'd play along with Lilly's game, at least until she was done eating.

"Do you like your burger?" he asked.

"Yes, I do. As a matter a fact, I think it's the best I've ever eaten. No wonder they do a great deal of business here," she said around a mouth full of delicious burger.

There she goes again, being so thankful for the little things in life, Peter thought. "Well, if you think the burger is good, try the fries. They're the best, and there is no way I can eat all these," Peter encouraged pushing the basket toward her.

As Lilly finished her burger and some fries, she began again. "Before I start, I must say that I worry you'll feel sorry for me or that you won't like what you hear. But above my fleshly fears, I want God to be glorified because He hasn't allowed anything in my life that wasn't for my good. I want Him praised for the good and the bad that, in the end, has resulted for my good and His glory."

Peter was blown away at her maturity and desire to please God. His complacency in his own spiritual growth became very apparent.

"Lilly, I'm just blown away by your heart." He continued, shaking his head. "Your testimony of God's goodness and grace has me a little awestruck. And just for the record, I'd never let anything from the past get in the way of our relationship now or in the future." He said the last part with raised eyebrows, letting her know how much he cared about her.

"Thank you, Peter. Your words mean so much to me."

"Sometime in August, my mother was at work and my dad wasn't on a job at the time. The school registrar called and requested to see my birth certificate since it wasn't on file and I was entering high school. My father thought it odd, but he looked for it everywhere he thought it might be, to no avail. When my mom got home, he asked her about it." She took a sip of her water.

"My mom avoided answering my dad. But my dad wasn't a man to be put off. He began to think my mom was hiding something from him. He pursued her relentlessly for hours. Then he hit the bottle really hard. But he still wouldn't let it go. My mom was yelling that she would take care of it and to leave her alone. My dad was yelling back at her. They went around and around. I was scared something terrible was about to happen." Lilly licked her lips and went on. "My dad was the maddest I'd ever seen him. He'd always left the house before getting abusive in the past. But this time I thought my mom had pushed too far and she was afraid he was about to hurt her, so she gave in. She screamed, 'Okay, okay. I'll get it.' She went to her room and dug around in her drawers and produced the birth certificate."

Lilly was crying softly now. Peter's heart didn't think he could take any more when Lilly continued.

"It had my full name, but the last name wasn't Beckler, but Parker. Then everything just fell apart. My dad was screaming at my mom, calling her all kinds of names I'm too ashamed to repeat. My dad wanted to know every detail of her infidelity and if there had been other men. Of course, I knew there had been. My mom often had men when my dad was away on month-long job sites, 'friends' she called them. As I got older, I caught on… I'm not stupid. She wasn't hiding anything from me. I just never thought it would be a good idea to tell my dad for the fear of that very thing. He came so close to hitting her. But he hit the wall instead. He immediately left in a rage. I never saw him again. Now I understood why after hearing how she hated the man who had part in my conception, my real father, why she couldn't stand me."

Soft sobs could be heard in Peter's ears. He so wanted to tell her to stop, but he must know everything. He waited.

"In the middle of the night, my mother came in, woke me and my two sisters up, yelling 'Pack your suitcases and anything else you might be needin' for school. We're out of here.' She was slamming things and pretty tipsy herself. I was groggy from crying myself to sleep, but you don't keep my mom waiting. I woke up with a headache out of this world. I'd just found out that the only person in my family who ever cared anything about me, who I thought was my dad, was not really my dad after all. That was a hard blow. While we were packing up, Delilia decided to tell my mom that she wasn't going with us. That sent my mom over the edge. She'd never struck either of my sisters, but she raised her hand to strike Delilia. My sister ducked and screamed, 'Don't! You'll hurt the baby!' That took the wind out of her sails. My mom brought her hand down in shock. My sister told my mom she was pregnant and that she wasn't going to leave that she'd move in with her boyfriend. My mom, seeing she wasn't going to change her daughter's mind, mumbled some obscenities berating how could she sleep around like that. I shouldn't have done this, but I rolled my eyes and said, 'Like mother like daughter.' To myself, of course. It was a hot night, and emotions were rolling high."

"So Chasity and I got in the car and left, never to be in that town, much less the state, again. After we were well over two states away, my mother said that Johnny—I still call him my dad—had been arrested for drunk driving, which was his fourth conviction, and he'd be spending some time behind bars. She went on to say that she was not staying in that a-few-choice-words town. She would drive as far as she could, get a divorce, and start over. Boy did she rant and rave for nearly two days as we drove. Let me tell you, that car got small real fast, those were some hard few days stuck in the car. We finally stopped and settled in a small town called Farmington in Nebraska. She saw a 'Waitress Needed' sign and got a job at another greasy spoon."

"I can only imagine that trip was no vacation!" Peter said, in shock of what he was hearing.

Lilly chuckled in reply. "To say we got there on fumes would be true. If you could have contained my mother's angry fumes, gas wouldn't have cost so much." Lilly then continued. "After we started school, things fell quickly in place. I was a freshman, and Chasity was a junior. My mom worked every evening, and I stayed by myself. My sister was hateful to me, so I stayed away from her. Sadly she fell into the wrong crowd and was on drugs about six months after starting school that year. And by the next summer, she was three months pregnant and wanting to drop out of school. Things were a mess. My mom did get a divorce. I never heard from my dad again. It was as though he literally dropped off the face of the earth." Lilly took sip of water and a breather.

"Shall I order some coffee?" Peter asked, thinking he was going to have a hard time getting to sleep no matter how much caffeine he drank.

"I think I'll have a cup, if you don't mind," she said. She glanced at her watch. "Oh my, Peter. You need to get home. You have to teach every day, don't you?"

"Well now, missy, do you think I'd sleep a wink if I went home right now with you leaving me hanging?" He chuckled as he caught their waitress and ordered two cups of coffee.

"Are you sure? We can finish this another time. I don't have to get up real early, but I know you do."

"I stay up late grading papers, remember," he said. "But," he continued, "I might need to borrow some of your makeup to cover the bags under my eyes in the morning."

She threw her napkin at him but then continued. "My mom had a string of men. I didn't like the way they looked at me; I always tried to hide. I hated it when she had her male friends over. Her hatred for me grew even more. But I still tried to honor her like you, Jenny, and Jeff had taught me. God helped me through. I'd pray and cry out to Him when I didn't think I could take any more. He'd always make a way." She looked up to the ceiling, silently praising God for being there for her.

Peter was having his own struggle with anger against her mom that she would allow men to drool over her teenage daughter. He tried to remember Lilly's wishes to praise God in all of the story, the good and the bad. But he was finding it hard.

"As soon as I turned sixteen, I got a job at Taco Bell. My mom often either harassed me until I gave her most of my money or she stole it for her cigarettes and nights on the town. But I did manage to scrape together enough to buy a beaten-up old—and I mean old—car. I took it to school and work. My grades suffered, but you know I was never that great a student anyway. I often stayed at work to do my homework, sitting in my car even through the freezing winter because my mom loved to have me so busy I didn't have time to get it done. I often thought she did that on purpose just to see me flunk. Now I'm thankful for all those freezing nights doing my homework, or I wouldn't have gotten to see the most handsome professor that Shaftner State Community College has."

"I'm delighted more than you will ever know that you persevered and that God had a purpose for all those cold days and nights you spent in your car, freezing," Peter said as he took a drink of his coffee.

"I continued on through high school doing the best I could. I did have a few friends, but mostly I lived a very lonely life, often crying myself to sleep at night. But God was always there to comfort me. My loneliness turned into His loveliness. My relationship with my mom got worse each year. I'll spare you the ugly details. The abuse got so bad until at times I feared for my life. I only got relief when she was gone. But I usually had to pay for her evenings out. We barely scraped by. I had to put all that you, Jeff, and Jenny taught me into practice many times during those difficult years.

My mom didn't even show up at my graduation. I don't think I ever felt so alone as I did that night." She shivered.

"After graduation, the man my mom had living with us gave me the creeps. I found him watching me several times when getting ready for bed, and it just made me really uncomfortable. And the fact that my mom was practically announcing that I was now available just told me it was time to go. I had to get out of there. I wasn't sure what to do, but I remembered I had an aunt that lived in North Carolina. So I sold my car for five hundred dollars and bought a plane ticket to my Aunt Maureen's house. She lives here in Shelbyville. I came with a suitcase in hand and no money. She wasn't expecting me of course. But again, God took care of me, and she let me live with her. So that's the story. My aunt is not saved, so I try to share God's grace and goodness that He has poured out on me with her. That about sums it up, Professor Collins," she said, surprised she'd made it through her story.

Lilly looked like a limp rag. But Peter just had to ask one more question.

Peter rubbed the back of his neck, which Lilly was becoming well-acquainted with when Peter was nervous. "I have a curiosity question. But if you would rather not say, that's fine."

"Go ahead," she encouraged. "I've nothing to hide."

"Well, you never mentioned any dating or special guys in your life. Were there any? I mean, are there any?" He stumbled over his words, feeling like he'd just intruded way too far.

Lilly, not expecting this question, was sidelined. She didn't know what to say or how much to say. So she said, "Peter, if you'll excuse me, I need to use the restroom. All that water is wanting out!" and quickly exited for the restroom. Lilly, as frantic as could be, simply went into a stall and prayed. As she prayed, God began to calm her.

When she returned to the booth, she felt ready to answer Peter. "I must say that this is a very personal and sensitive subject to me," she said as she nervously fiddled with her coffee spoon. "It's obvious that my example of relationships was not exactly great. I've not had much Christian influence in that area. Jeff and Jenny were the only people I knew well who seemed to have actually loved and cared for each other in their marriage, but that didn't tell me how to act in an unmarried state." She took a sip of her water and continued. "There have been some situations that I wouldn't be proud to share. I've had a few broken hearts, sad to say. Being so hungry for love, I allowed guys to blind my discernment to their end goals. But it wasn't all their fault. I was just as much a willing partner, allowing my flesh freewill. I struggled a lot in this area. But eventually, I managed to end the relationships before they went too far." Her shoulders went limp. "I'm embarrassed to admit all that to you. But I want to be honest and upfront. After a while, I decided that loneliness wasn't as bad as heartbreak. Did I answer your question?"

Peter wanted desperately to hold her, wipe her tears away, and tell her he would never let her be hurt again. But he couldn't promise that, and he couldn't hold her. So he did the next best thing.

"Give me your hands, Lilly," he commanded her.

She complied, not sure what he was going to do. He reached across the table and took her precious hands into his.

"Look at me, Lilly. I wish with all my heart that you hadn't been hurt so badly. I wish that you hadn't been so lonely. I wish I had been there for you. But just as you said, we have to trust God with our lives every day and trust that He knows best. And I'm going to trust Him with all that you've told me." Having said that, he squeezed her hands and almost let them go. He rubbed the ends of her nails and asked with a wink, "When did this happen?"

She pulled her hands away with an impish smile and said, "When I came to my aunt's, she helped me with some cream that has healed them up very nicely; but the habit is a hard one to kick. After biting my nails for many years, it seems weird to have nails of any length. But thanks for noticing my effort of change." She glanced at her hands before putting them in her lap.

He glanced at his watch. "It's ten, and obviously we're the last couple in here and they're closing up. We better scoot." He looked at Lilly and said, "This has been the loveliest evening, not so much because of what you shared but because of who you are, and you let me see the precious person I remember so well tonight."

She didn't know what to say. He put down a twenty-dollar bill for a tip, paid the check, refusing to let Lilly help with any of it then, gently touching her elbow, escorted Lilly out to his car.

As he smoothly pulled out into traffic, he asked a few more questions. "So am I to understand that you want to go by Parker?"

"Yes. That's my real name."

"Why, yes. Of course. And what is with the Lillian part?" he asked, looking over at her briefly.

"Well, I guess I just want to leave my childhood behind me. And though it's forever in my mind, I just thought Lillian sounded a bit more grown-up."

"Have you ever given thought to trying to find your real dad?"

"Yes, I have, especially when I think that he might need to hear the Gospel. It gives me a great desire to find him. Yet I shrink back every time I think of having to ask my mom for information in order to do so. I guess for now I'm stuck with not finding him." She shrugged her shoulders. "But I do pray for him."

"So why didn't you ever contact Jenny after you left?" he asked. He wasn't sure why she hadn't told him this information, but he did want to know.

"Oh, I forgot to tell you about that."

"Hey, how about telling me on the way to your aunt's house?" Peter butted in before Lilly could answer.

"Oh, it won't take that long, and I don't mind walking. You've already gone out of your way with dinner."

"Lilly, it's not a bother. I want to drive you home. It's late," he insisted sternly. "So tell me how to get to your aunt's before you answer the other question, and I'll whip us over there."

"Well, I guess if I don't tell you how to get to my aunt's then you can't take me home," she said, acting hardheaded.

"Look, Lilly, don't make it hard for me. I care deeply about you. If you're going to be stubborn, I can be more so. I'll spend the night in the car rather than let you walk one inch by yourself this late in the evening," he said seriously.

"Take me to the parking lot at the school, Peter." Lilly laughed.

"Are you serious? You've got to be kidding me!"

"Why yes, Peter. You must because it's the only way I know how to get home!" She was really laughing now. "Remember, I just arrived here. I'm not the avid navigator you are."

"You little ragmuffin. You had me going on purpose." He playfully pouted.

"I just wanted to make sure you were awake! That's all," she bantered back.

They'd just pulled in the parking lot, so Lilly told him how to get to her aunt's house. As they rode along, she told Peter about one of the most difficult trials that God had ever asked her to do.

"When we got to Nebraska, my mother told me I was to never, ever contact anyone from Arlington. No friends from school or church could I ever speak to again. I asked her about Jenny. I pled with my mother to let me keep contact with her. I told my mom she had nothing to worry about. But she slapped my face and said no. I ran to my room and didn't eat or come out for the rest of the day. Peter, it was the hardest thing my mom has ever asked me to do. But as a witness to how much I wanted to obey God, I knew I had to obey her on this no matter how it hurt. And let me tell you, Peter, it hurt like a knife cutting out my heart," she said. "There were many times I was severely tempted to disobey and write Jenny. But God helped me, in my lowest times, to keep my word to my mom."

"Wow. That must have been brutal. I know Jeff and Jenny took it really hard when you were just gone, never to return. They went to your house for months to see if you returned. Eventually, another man and son moved into the trailer. It took a long time, Jenny told me, to quit crying over missing you," he confided to Lilly.

"You're not serious, are you?" Lilly asked in disbelief.

"Why, of course. We'd all fallen very much in love with that lonely, little nine-year-old girl whose beautiful, blue puppy eyes stole our hearts with her sweetness and pure honesty." Peter had turned onto the road that Lilly's aunt lived on and chuckled. "At least after a bit pure honesty," he said, looking at Lilly with a sly smile of remembrance about her problem with lying when they had first met.

"Ugh! I remember." Lilly laughed, "How humiliating. But through all that, y'all kept letting me ride the bus! I'll never forget those years. Here is her house on the right."

Peter turned into the driveway.

"I'm so sorry I caused them such heartbreak. Believe me. If it were in my control, that would've never happened. It was actually all the things they taught me about obeying my parents that caused the separation. Funny how God works, isn't it?"

"Well, I've certainly seen God's amazing work today, and He does have ways that we cannot comprehend, but they are always, 'Wise, right, and good,'" they chorused together, remembering the one theme the pastor at their old church always nailed home every message in some way or another.

"Have you thought about writing them since you have left your mom's place? I'm sure they would be ecstatic to hear from you," Peter said softly.

"Are you sure they would even remember me or care to hear from me after I just disappeared like that?"

"Oh yes, I'm sure," Peter said, knowing they would jump for joy.

"Well, I have thought of it, actually, many times over, I'm just not sure how," she said.

"How about I bring Jeff and Jenny's address with me to class?"

"Oh, I hadn't thought of that. Thank you! Thank you so very much. Yes. I'd really appreciate that," she said with much excitement as she got out of the car.

"The pleasure is all mine, Lilly. Trust me," he said, having the feeling he'd just handed her the moon.

"Thank you for bringing me home. I'm glad you did so we could finish talking," she said as she leaned into the car to say good-bye. "Good night, Peter. Sleep well."

Staring into his face she spoke her heart, she said, "I'm afraid I'm going to wake up in the morning and find this was all a dream."

"Well, Miss Lillian Parker, it's not. But a dream come true to get to see you again!" His smile shining in the moonlight. "Now go on to bed and sweet dreams Lilly."

Peter waited until he saw that she was safe inside the door before leaving. On the way home, Peter recalled their conversations, including the blunder about inviting Lilly to church with him. "What a mess you can make," Peter said aloud to no one. His thoughts were a circus and he was the clown. Between the memories, what Lilly shared, and his anger, he was overwhelmed.

It seemed as though everything was spinning faster than he could control.

As he unlocked his apartment door, the word *control* lingered on his tongue. He went in; took off his shoes; and sat down on the couch, elbows on his knees, deep in thought. He began to talk to the LORD.

That's just it, LORD. I've been in control of my life. I took over and decided to do things my own way. I haven't left much time for You in my life. I go to church and all. I even study my Sunday school lessons. But I've lost my first love. I've lost my love for You and reaching the lost. I've become complacent in my spiritual walk. What happened? When I first met Lilly, I was so steadfast. I was sold out completely to You. I did whatever You asked me to. You used Lilly to teach me that You hold no prejudices. Actually, You illuminated my filthy rags through her. But when I left for college, after a few years, I let my agenda dictate my days instead of letting the Holy Spirit guide me. I let the thought that I don't really do bad things be an offering to You. Oh LORD, please forgive me!

Peter was crying now. He'd gotten so far from the heart of God that this release and confession overwhelmed him and poured out in his emotions. He cried with his head in his hands until he was spent.

After Peter was completely cried out, he readied for bed and actually fell asleep as soon as his head hit the pillow at 2:00 a.m.

CHAPTER 5

"Good morning, Aunt Maureen," Lilly greeted with sleepy voice.

After she put the first pancakes on, she poured a cup of coffee and pulled up a chair at the table.

"Good morning to you, my dear. How was your evening?" her aunt wasted no time in asking. "I thought I heard you come in around eleven, was it?" she inquired. "I 'bout never went to sleep last night trying to think about what all had happened to you. I want to hear every single detail, ya hear me?"

Glancing occasionally at the stove for the evidence of burning pancakes, Lilly started her story. "Before I tell you about yesterday, I have to go back a few years earlier. When I was nine years old, a couple came to our trailer one Saturday morning and knocked on the door. The couple, Jeff and Jenny Singleton, invited me to ride the church bus with them the next day to church. I said if I could, I would be outside waiting. They gave me a piece of bubble gum and left. The next day, I rode the bus to church, I must say ashamedly, without my parent's permission. But my parents didn't really care what I did as long as I stayed out of trouble and was home by dark, so I didn't think they'd mind. I enjoyed it so much it became a regular thing. The couple became like parents to me in a lot of ways. They also had a special friend named Peter, who was their bus helper. We all became very close. As the years went on, Peter and I became very special friends. He taught me many things and was a friend to me when I had no one. He taught me a lot about the Bible. He took up for me when other people made fun of me. He was my father, brother, and friend all rolled up in one. The year I turned thirteen, Peter went off to college. I thought I'd cry a river when he left. We had a blast during those short times he came home for holidays and summer break. When my mother snagged us up in the night to leave, I never saw Jeff, Jenny, or Peter again."

Lilly's aunt was already in tears. "Oh, Lil, I had no idea. The only good thing in your life taken away. Didn't you write?" her aunt asked.

"Please don't cry, Aunt Maureen. I want to try to explain something that you might not understand but just have to take my word for. During those five years under their wings of Christian influence, the most important thing I learned was my need for a Savior. They showed me my condition before the Almighty God, a sinner bound for hell, and that Jesus Christ came to earth and died on the cross to be that Savior, to be my Savior. So when I was twelve, I cried out to God to save me. I repented of my sins. I was baptized some few months later. Everything was so different. I wanted to do what was right because it pleased my heavenly Father. I still struggled, but Peter was patient. It seemed to be his delight to teach me the ways of the LORD. He was a real rock for me, and so were Jeff and Jenny. They were so ecstatic when I told them I'd asked God to be my papa, they cried."

"I don't understand what this has to do with yesterday," her aunt said, looking especially confused.

"Well, I just needed to give you those details for you to understand the full impact of what I'm about to tell you and to answer your question as to why I didn't keep in touch. After we left Tennessee and got to Nebraska, my mom forbade me to write or contact anyone in Tennessee. I begged with tears to be able to write Jeff and Jenny, but my mom was stubbornly determined to end all contact with that 'horrible hell hole,' as she called it. With all that Jeff, Jenny, and Peter had taught me about the importance of obeying my parents, I had to obey my mom no matter how bad it hurt. And believe me, Aunt Maureen, I've never known such pain as losing those three people from my life. But that was God's plan for me. Although I didn't know it then, He blessed my obedience in a way I never dreamed of," she said, beaming.

"That was just awful of your mom to do that. I would've done it anyway," her aunt said rebelliously.

Not wanting to comment on what her aunt had just said, she spent the next hour telling her aunt every detail of the day before.

Her aunt had been bawling. She dabbed her eyes and said, "Well, I guess you'll be moving in with him now and I'll be a lonely old lady again. Though he sounds like a knight in shining armor for my Cinderella, I'll still miss you."

"Oh no, Aunt Maureen! You've got it all wrong!" Lilly gasped. "You don't understand. I'm not moving anywhere. It's not like that."

"Well, he's a fool not to snatch you up. It sounds like a match made in heaven." She sighed. "But you just never know about men. My James made it clear that none were to be trusted." She stared off into space. "Come to think of it, James mentioned something about that *saved* thing to me. I didn't want to hear about it." She continued. "He came to me about four years ago, seeking forgiveness for the awful way he'd messed things up. He said something about getting saved or some kind of religious thing I don't remember." She wrinkled up her face at the memory. "Then he had the audacity to ask if we could reconcile our marriage." She banged her hand on the table. "After all these years, he wants to jump back in the bed with me! Well, it ain't gonna happen, I tell you. And I told him so." She was quiet for a moment and then went on. "He tried for about two years, asking me out on dates, bringing me flowers, calling me on the phone. And if I speak the truth, he was the perfect picture of kindness." She was winding down now. "But I ain't gonna have nothing to do with it. I just can't get past the pain of what he did to me."

This time, Lilly was in tears. She grabbed her aunt's hands and spoke as tenderly and lovingly as she could. "Aunt Maureen, the reason you can't forgive James is that you don't understand the forgiveness that Christ had on the cross for you. And if you never come to understand your own need for forgiveness from a holy God and how He provided a way of forgiveness through Jesus's death on the cross, you'll never be able to forgive James," she said passionately.

"I'll think about that, Lilly, but let's not let that dampen your wonderful news of meeting this Peter. I can't believe he's your teacher. I'll want to meet this fella. So bring him to dinner," her aunt demanded.

"I'll try, Aunt Maureen. It's not that I don't want you to meet him, you understand; but you know how full my evenings are. My work schedule usually has me working every evening. But like last night, I occasionally have a Monday or Tuesday night off. I'll do my best to get him over here," she said as she got up. "I already have some homework to do before I go to work. I better get it done." Cleaning up the few dishes, she said, "Call me if you need something." Then she headed to her room.

Lilly sat in the back row again for class. The front was too close to Peter, and she knew she'd be so distracted she'd never get anything done. And she didn't want to ruin his reputation by forgetting she was Professor Collins's *student*, not friend, in this classroom and on this campus.

Peter, calling out the roll call with his deep, smooth voice, said, "Lilly Parker."

"Here. And if you don't mind, sir, it's Lillian," she said softly but firmly.

No one would've ever guessed the dinner and conversation they'd shared the night before. Where she got the nerve to correct him, she didn't know.

"Ah, yes. I'm sorry, Miss Parker. I'll try to remember, it's Lillian," he said, stealing a glance at her. He continued the roll call and then proceeded to teach his class. This was going to be harder than he thought, but as long as he couldn't see her, he could function fine. Before he knew it, his watch beeped the five-minute warning, he wrapped up the class, giving them their first writing assignment.

Lilly was on her way out the door when he called her.

"Lilly-an, Lillian," he tried again.

She turned to his desk. All the other students filed out of class. He reached in his pocket and pulled out a piece of paper.

"Here's what I promised you. I'm tempted to call Jenny myself and say, 'You'll never believe who is in my class,'" he said, beaming. "But I want you to have the joy of the surprise. Just, if you don't mind, let me know when you do so I won't spill the beans."

"I'll post a letter by the end of the week, so give me until next Wednesday and then you can pick up my spilled beans." She squealed, holding the piece of paper. "I can't wait. Thanks so much, Peter, for remembering!"

"Really it was nothing, Lilly—I mean, Lillian." He rubbed the back of his neck. "It's going to be hard to quit calling you Lilly."

"I understand. You'll always be my Petah. Now not only are you my Petah but also Peter and Professor Collins too." She smiled at him, trying to explain it wasn't easy for her either. "So, Peter, I don't know who's got it the hardest." She gave him a cheeky smile of triumph.

"I guess you got me there, and I can't stand you to call me Professor Collins. However, I guess in class that would be best, though it grates on me."

"What are you doing for lunch?" he asked her.

Not that he could have lunch with her but he just had to talk to her some more. He ignored the fact that Veronica was expecting him in the lounge right that very minute.

"I brought yet another grand PBJ, and I plan to go and enjoy it under the big oaks. I've some special people to pray for right now." Her eyes twinkled at him.

"Prayer is an awesome privilege that shouldn't ever be taken lightly," he said. "Hey—" he tipped up her chin with his finger, barely touching her— "thanks again for last night. Your transparency was a treasured gift." He looked deep in her eyes. "You'll never know how special our talk was to me. As a matter a fact, thank you is way too small to express my heart." He moved to break the spell between them and to let Lilly go.

"Anything for my Petah." She smiled at the use of his nickname, and she scooted out of the classroom. She glanced back at him, and saw that he was shaking his head.

On his way to the lounge, thoughts of how much he took for granted plagued him. Going into the lounge, he found Veronica had not waited on him but was over halfway through her salad.

"Glad to see you could make it," she said snidely.

"Sorry I'm late," he said. Suddenly, he realized he hadn't even gone to the cafeteria to get anything to eat before coming to the lounge. *Am I ever going to have my head screwed on right again?* he wondered.

"Not eating today, or did you have lunch with someone else?" Veronica asked coldly.

Seeing there was no help for it, he said, "Neither one. I'm just not hungry at the moment." He tried to change the subject. "So how's class going?"

The distraction worked, and they talked about their classes for the next twenty minutes. Some of the other professors also stopped by for a chat before they both had to get back to work. As Peter got up to leave, he glanced out the window and saw Lilly sitting on a bench, writing. It was a priceless picture. He would've loved to read what she wrote describing her version of this miraculous reunion, but he'd have to let it be. She was way in the distance, shaded under a big oak, baring her heart, he was sure.

Friday was much the same. Peter knew he was going to have to quit detaining Lilly after class. But it was so hard not to check on her personally. He was glad she'd chosen to sit in the back because if she was going to sit up front, he just didn't think he could make it through the semester.

The students turned in their assignments that day. Professor Collins had made an assignment to assess each student's writing style and ability. He liked to do that so he could see the improvements throughout the semester. He watched Lilly leave. He wanted to ask how she was doing and about the letter to Jenny. He wanted to know what was going on in her little head. He wanted to share with her what God was doing in his life. He had been getting in the Word and praying throughout every day. What a difference it was making. He was praying that God would set him on fire once again and put needy people in his life. He was trusting God to lead the way daily. But how he was going to go about this new addition to his life, he did not know. It was sure a problem to be solved, but he had not a clue to the answer; however, he was praying.

"What a lovely night out, Pete," Veronica said as she placed a cloth napkin in her lap to keep any food from getting on her suit. "Dinner at the Stuffed Goose is a perfect way to start the year, I must say." She looked at Peter. "And we do have a lot to celebrate, don't we, Pete?" She flashed her eyes at him longingly.

"Well, yes, I suppose we do. It sounds as if we both have great classes," he said, not really sure what she meant. He thought perhaps she was meaning a more personal message, and he didn't want to go there. "I actually think this will be a year to remember." He, of course, was thinking of Lilly. It already was the best year for him. "I think there will be some pretty profound things happening this year that will dumbfound us, excuse the pun," he said with a half smile as he took a sip of his iced tea.

Veronica was more than interested in what he meant. She noticed that he'd not directed any of his comments to a personal level. She was keenly disappointed. "What exactly do you mean, Pete dear?" she asked pointedly. "Do you know something you're not sharing?"

Thankfully, Alisha arrived to take their order and Peter didn't have to answer. Veronica ordered her normal dish, but Peter tried something new off the menu, reflecting his new commitment to follow hard after Christ, moment by moment, empowered by the Holy Spirit.

Meanwhile, in the back, there was quite the panic occurring. Lilly was frantic as could be.

"Hey, girl, what's with you?" Alisha asked after she returned from taking their order. "Why did you want to switch sections?" Most waitresses didn't give up their tables, because tables meant tips. "Hey, don't get me wrong. I don't mind the extra cash, and from the looks of that guy, he'll pay good!" She whistled. "My area is smaller so you'll probably lose money tonight."

"Yeah. He'll pay good all right," Lilly slipped out then covered her mouth in embarrassment. "I just can't believe he's here!" Alisha listened, trying to understand.

"And who's that attractive woman?" she asked, staring at the table where Peter and Veronica sat. "Why did I just assume he wasn't attached to someone? For all I know, he could be married." She had to look away when Veronica reached out and touched his hand, though she looked long enough to see he didn't pull away.

"Girlfriend, you gotta do some explaining here. But I got to get back out on the floor. This favor is on me, uh-huh," she said. "And let me guess, you don't want someone at that table to know you're here. Am I correct?" she asked as she left.

Lilly was so glad to have to work the private rooms for business dinner parties. Some nights it was agonizingly slow and others overburdened. This night, she didn't care what happened as long as Peter didn't see her. She just wasn't ready. She prayed, *Lord, why am I so scared? Why does this bother me? Why am I so upset to see Peter with another woman?*

Peter and this woman stayed for what seemed like all night to Lilly. Every time Lilly came back to the kitchen, her eyes gravitated to the table where they were. Their smiles and demeanor certainly didn't make them mere acquaintances, Lilly deducted. She watched as they readied to leave. Peter placed his hand on her back, guiding her to the door. Hot tears threatening, she fled to the bathroom. She buried her head in a towel and had a hard cry. When she was done she washed her face with cold water and returned to work with a smile for the rest of the night.

Alisha came back after clearing their table with a grin. "Sure enough, that guy tips big. So what's with this guy that you're not telling me? Come on, girl. Give it up," she demanded of Lilly.

"It's a long story, Alisha, a very long story." She sighed. Suddenly, Lilly thought this could be a witnessing opportunity.

"Hey, look, I know someone's hurting when I see one. Come on and spill it, Lillian," Alisha said.

"I tell you what, Alisha. I do owe you an explanation, especially after such a great favor. You saved me from something I wasn't ready to do. But I still have a group in the back room to take care of, so how about I share after closing."

"Okay. I'll stick around a bit," she agreed. Alisha usually didn't stick around after work; she headed home to her kids. But she was very curious, and this gal did need a friend.

After closing, Lilly, true to her word, met Alisha outside and they went to McDonald's for ice cream.

As they sat at a table, enjoying their ice cream cones, Lilly shared briefly the whole story, sparing a few extra details to get through quickly. But she slowed down and spoke carefully and clearly the Gospel message of her own salvation. She continued, emphasizing that God had been her keeper and her strength during that time. She then shared in great, excited detail about meeting Peter on Monday, the inquisition dinner, and the drive home.

Alisha's mouth was wide open, and she had tears in her eyes. She said, "And let me guess. That was your Peter at that table tonight?"

"Yes it was."

"And let me guess. Two things: He doesn't know you work at the Stuffed Goose. And you didn't know about the other woman." She had summed up the situation perfectly.

"Yep, you got it. It took me off guard, for sure. But it's nothing God can't take care of," Lilly went on. "But at times, my flesh is weak and I forget to take all my cares to God immediately and to trust Him every second."

"You are a zealous thing," Alisha stated. "Well, being a single mom of three kids, I just don't have time for church stuff," she said with a wave of her hand.

"I don't know how you manage without God," Lilly said softly, not as a rebuke but as a thought-provoking question. "I would have never made it without God seeing me through every day and knowing He will carry me through tomorrow too."

"You've given me something to think about, Lillian. I've never thought of it that way," Alisha said thoughtfully.

Lilly thanked Alisha for listening and for being such a kind and caring friend. They ended up staying for an hour, but Lilly was glad.

CHAPTER 6

It was late when Lilly laid her head on her pillow. She'd exhausted her tears on the way home.

LORD, you know me. You know my heart is hurting right now. You know I'm confused. I just have to think back on how you carried me through the wilderness like the Israelites, so to speak, how you provided their every need as you have mine. LORD, there were days that I thought my sorrow would consume me or that I could take no more suffering. But You, oh LORD, put your arms around me and dried my tears and bore my wounds. LORD, help me glorify you. Help me understand. And most of all, help me in my weakness to not fill in the blanks of this situation with supposition. I love you, LORD. Help me love you more tomorrow than today. Amen!

Saturday started out with a sweet time in the Word and prayer. Lilly prayed for the many people on her heart: her parents, sisters, aunt, Jeff and Jenny, Alisha and other coworkers, her neighbors, and Peter. She prayed a long time about him. She beseeched the LORD if she should drop his class.

LORD, I don't want to, yet I don't think my heart can handle seeing him walk out of my life again. I know that is selfish. But then, on the other hand, maybe it's better for Peter too. He seems all bamboozled these days in class. Guide me in this decision. I'll have to make it by Monday in order to get my money back.

She continued to pray a bit longer before going to fix breakfast.

"Have you set up a time to get that young man over here yet?" her aunt asked. "I need to size him up to see if he's good enough for my Lilly," she said with a smirk.

"No, ma'am, I haven't yet. It might take a bit more time."

"James stopped by last night while you were at work."

"He did!" Lilly said excitedly.

"Yeah, he did. He'd noticed that the car had been gone several times he'd driven by. He thought I was gone," she said with a little smile. "He caught me taking out the trash and pulling a few weeds. He was very nice. I've been thinking a lot about what you said, Lilly. So I decided to be nice back to him for a change. He nearly fell over at my kindness." She laughed. "It was kinda funny to watch his reaction."

"What did y'all do?" Lilly was dying to know.

"I invited him up on the porch for some lemonade. We sat in the rocking chairs while I explained all about you."

"You did?"

"Yup." She nodded her head. "He was real happy for you, he said." She was beaming. "He smiled real big when I told him about your God. He said it's one and the same."

"He did?" Lilly's eyes got big. *Thank You, LORD!* she said to herself.

"Well, I'd like to meet him sometime, if you're up to it, of course. " Lilly looked at her for signs of the normal bitterness.

Before her aunt could get mad, she had agreed. Then she said, "What have I just agreed to?"

Lilly put her cinnamon rolls in the oven and fried some ham while she thought of an idea. "How about inviting James over one morning for breakfast on a day that I don't have class? I'll do the honors of cooking and serving, and we can get to know each other over a pan of coffee cake. How does that sound?" Lilly coaxed, "You can pick the morning."

"That don't sound too scary. Okay. The next time he comes by, I'll do that," Aunt Maureen found herself saying.

This is really weird, Lilly thought to herself. *This brings back such strong and wonderful memories.* Here she was, outside, waiting for the church bus. Lilly thought she would try Peter's church. So instead of keeping her aunt's car tied up on Sundays too, when she had called the church office to find out service times, she happened on an idea. She asked if they had a bus ministry. They did, so she asked if a bus came close to her aunt's address. As it turned out, there was one not two blocks from her aunt's place.

She then shyly asked, "I know this might sound strange, but I was wondering if the bus could pick me up at the entrance of that subdivision on Sunday? See, I'm new to this town and don't have a way to get to church. I know I'm not a kid, but I do need a ride and don't mind at all walking over and hopping on the church bus when it comes by. Would that be a problem?" Lilly asked hesitantly.

"Not at all," the woman told her and then proceeded to tell her what time to be waiting and the driver and workers' names.

So here she was, waiting for the bus like a kid. She was thinking of days past when the bus drove into view. She climbed on and sat by a girl who looked to be about nine years old.

After Sunday school, Lilly slipped into the sanctuary and sat in the third row from the front on the piano side. She was a bit late, as she'd gone to check on the little girl she'd sat next to on the bus. Plus, she wanted to see all the kids' Sunday school classes. She peeked into the rooms as she went down the hall.

The service was about to start, but did Peter really see what he thought he saw? He blinked twice. *Yes! That's Lilly!* he thought to himself. He kept looking her way. He knew she couldn't see him, as he was sitting toward the back on the organ side. Veronica was next to him, but he wasn't ready to make any introductions yet. Veronica was reading her bulletin and finally looked up when the service started. Peter got a hold of himself and joined in worship through singing. He only looked over at Lilly once to see if she was okay. He tried to pay attention and learn what God had for him. Before he knew it, they were singing the last song and Lilly had slipped away.

He was about to lunge forward to find her when he remembered he wasn't alone and Veronica was speaking to him.

"Are we still on for our usual?" she asked.

They usually ate out for lunch and then went back to his apartment to check papers together.

"Oh, sure. That sounds great," Peter said. Heading out to the car, he asked Veronica where she wanted to eat. He hoped his voice sounded normal.

Veronica wondered at his distracted demeanor but just shrugged it off. "Oh, how about Round the Corner?" she said as she got in Peter's car.

Peter quickly scanned the parking lot, but no Lilly. *Where did she vanish to? Of course, there's more than one parking lot,* Peter rationalized as he left. He needed a distraction from thinking about the last time he was at that restaurant. So he asked Veronica about the sermon.

"What did you think of the sermon?"

"Well, I think it was dumb on Jesus's part to put up with such imbecile disciples!" she said. "I don't know why Jesus always taught in parables. Why couldn't He just spit it out?" The pastor had been going through the parables one at a time for several months now. Peter thought it was great and had learned a lot, especially now that he'd asked God to pull him out of his complacency.

Peter was taken aback by her answer, "Well, Veronica, God's ways are not our ways, the Bible says in Isaiah fifty-five nine. They're much higher, better than ours," he said carefully as he continued to drive. "So we have to trust that He knew what He was doing when picking out His disciples and teaching the parables." He tried another subject. "Did you like the two new hymns we sang today?"

Veronica was checking her makeup in the visor mirror while answering. "They were fine. I just don't really see why we have to stand so long and sing so many songs." She put away the visor and smoothed her dress. "Hey, did you hear that Joe and Nancy are dating? That's what Rob said. Can you believe that?" She shook her head. "Why, Nancy has the most dreadful, homey case I've ever seen." She continued her berating. "I mean, she fell out of an ugly tree and hit every branch! What do you think he sees in her?"

Peter would've normally laughed at such a wisecrack, but not anymore. Peter prayed, *Lord, help me be faithful to You right now. Help me be worthy of Your name as I answer.* "Well, just like God says, He doesn't look on the outside but at the heart, I think that's probably what Joe sees." Peter didn't look at Veronica, or he would've seen shock on her face, but he went on. "It's what's in the heart that reveals the true beauty of a person." He paused, wondering if he should continue. "Joe probably sees what I see: a very thoughtful, kind, godly woman. And Joe realizes that these godly characteristics will long outlast one's outward appearance." Peter sighed inwardly. He thanked the LORD for giving him the words.

Whatever had come over Peter, Veronica didn't know. But she just dropped the conversation. They were at the restaurant anyway. Peter couldn't believe the hostess sat them in the same booth he and Lilly had shared. That night was powerful in his mind and heart.

"Hello there. You were daydreaming," Veronica stated. "Want to share, Pete?"

Peter was saved by the waitress coming to take their orders, Veronica ordered her usual. Peter surprised her by ordering the smallest hamburger on the menu, the very one that Lilly had ordered, and fries for two, though Veronica said fries ruined her figure and he usually ended up throwing them away.

Veronica wondered at the sudden change. *But then why can't he change his mind?* she asked herself. It wasn't worth bringing up. So she talked about her classes and sorority. She babbled on about what all was going on in her world. Peter didn't comment much, especially if it was hearsay.

Peter wondered when lunch would be over. He noted the vast difference in the conversation he was having now and the one he had with Lilly in that very booth.

"You're awfully quiet today," Veronica stated more as a question than a fact, flashing her eyes at Peter, waiting for an answer.

"Oh, I'm just listening to you. That's all. You seem to have a lot to share," Peter said in all truthfulness.

They continued the one-sided conversation until they were through eating and then left and went to Peter's apartment.

Peter had just tossed his keys on the table and was taking off his suit jacket and loosening his tie, when Veronica came over and put her hand on his chest. "I must say you're the picture of handsome today." She put her hand softly on his cheek. "And thank you, my dear Pete, for a lovely lunch," she said with a wink.

This was often what made Peter melt into his shoes. He put his arms around her waist, looked into her eyes, and simply said, "You're welcome." Then he walked off to get his papers.

"Pete, I sure thought I could earn a kiss from you," Veronica said with her lip stuck out.

Peter wasn't sure what was going on. He needed some space to think. This was the first time he'd ever been this involved, and he was a bit scared. He didn't want to go too far. And with Veronica's looks and forwardness, it was easy to get carried away. They'd gotten carried away before, but not to the point of no return. Peter was fully aware of how appetites could be awakened by a lot of kissing. He, being the man, knew it was his responsibility to not allow things to get out of control. In all honesty, in his flesh, he enjoyed letting go of all restraint. But with his new commitment to follow hard after Christ, he knew he needed to pull back the reins and be much more careful. He wasn't sure he really knew the boundaries himself. But he'd heard sirens going off in his head before with Veronica, and he didn't want to go there again. Even though he was serious about Veronica and they were both adults, he knew even if they married, he wouldn't want to have regrets.

"My dear Veronica, you make me doubt your compliment if all you wanted was a kiss from me," Peter said as he moved to stand in front of her.

He lowered his head and placed a sweet kiss on her lips. She put her arms around his neck and kissed him again. Peter, seeing where this was headed, reached behind his neck and removed her hands and stepped back.

"What is it, Pete?" Veronica asked, confused and hurt.

"Um … well … it's just that we need to be careful how we handle ourselves," he said, not sure where these words or the strength to say them was coming from. He went on. "Especially since we're here alone. We don't want to do anything we will regret."

"Well, Pete, we are adults, and I haven't regretted anything so far. Why, I think you're the nicest guy I've dated," she said, putting her hands back on his chest.

"I think we better get to checking papers."

He smiled at her but was determined to put some distance between them, knowing that even this area of his life needed to be captained by God. They both moved to get their papers and pens. They plopped down on the couch, shoulders touching, and got down to business.

Peter thought, *This is good. It feels good to have her next to me yet not too close.*

They'd been working about an hour when Peter came to Lilly's paper. His eyes were riveted on the name. He'd momentarily forgotten he'd have to grade her papers. With his eyes glued to the paper, he read Lilly's very heart. He wasn't sure he could do this. He was having trouble separating the content with errors. He put his head back and closed his eyes. Here in this paper were both the little, nine-year-old Lil and the now-adult Lillian. She wrote about her childhood. Then she wrote about her passion to get her education so that she could begin to make a difference in the lives of abused children. She planned to have as many speaking engagements in schools as was possible to heighten awareness and to encourage children who had worn her shoes. She wanted them to know they didn't have to suffer. She wanted all children from young to teens to know there was help available to them. She planned to pass out literature and helpline numbers for those kids who found themselves in abusive situations. Basically, she wanted to pour out her life on those who didn't have much hope.

"That's my Lil," Peter said ever so softly, his eyes closed as he envisioned this.

"Excuse me, Pete. Did you say something?" Veronica asked. Looking over at him, seeing his eyes closed and head back, she asked, "Are you okay, Pete?"

He blinked open his eyes. "Oh … uh … yes. I'm fine. I was just reading this paper, that's all," he said, trying to sound untroubled.

Before he knew what was happening, Veronica had grabbed the paper, curious as to what had transfixed Pete.

"Here. Let me read it," she said as she snatched it from his hands.

Peter tried to get it back but to no avail.

Veronica read the paper, tossed it back in Peter's lap, and said, "Oh my. What a horrible paper. Glad she isn't getting a real grade. She'd get an F. She writes as though she's never been in school a day in her life. She sounds like some of the kids I went to elementary school with whom I wouldn't be caught dead sitting by." She snorted with a derogatory air. "Where do they pick these people up from? Don't they test them before letting them enroll? I can see why you're so upset. You've got your work cut out for you," she ended with a laugh. "I'm glad she's in your class and not mine." She then went back to her own stack.

She'd completely missed the precious content. Peter didn't know when he'd been so mad. No. *Sick* was a better word for what he was feeling about Veronica right at that moment. How could she say that about Lilly's paper? Was she so cold-hearted that she couldn't see the spirit of the writer? The cause Lilly was pursuing went right over Veronica's head. And he couldn't stand anyone to say anything unkind about his Lil.

He re-read the paper. It tore out his heart to see such suffering; yet, it blessed his heart to see Lilly's desire to help those in difficult circumstances. Again, God used Lilly to bring conviction to his own heart. *What do I do for those who suffer? Well, I mean, I did a lot with Lilly; but what about now? Did I just check a box "job done" with Lilly and think I didn't have to care about others for the rest of my life?* He was asking himself all kinds of questions. It was just too much to grade the paper right then. He put it at the bottom of his stack and thought it would be easier to grade later, when he was alone.

He continued to grade the other papers. It wasn't long before Veronica's head fell over on Peter's shoulder. She snuggled close to him.

"Mmm. I love the smell of your aftershave," she said as she put her arm through his.

"Are you all done?" Peter asked her, surprised that she could be through her stack so quickly.

"No. Just taking a break to cuddle with you. That's all," she said, getting comfortable.

Of course, that meant that he had to stop grading papers too with her hanging on his arm.

"Is that okay? Or is it forbidden too?"

She was being ugly, all the while wanting attention from Peter. Peter wondered if he'd been this blind in the past. He didn't know, but he didn't like seeing this manipulative side of Veronica.

"Of course not," Peter assured her, ignoring her snootiness.

He began inattentively to caress her hair when she spoke.

"Could you stop that? You're messing up my hair."

Peter leaned forward to get away from her. In doing so, she had to sit up. This just wasn't working well.

How come she's so touchy today? Peter wondered. "Well, I guess we better get back to checking our papers," he said, hoping for a distraction. And he did need to get it done. "I'm planning on going to church tonight. They're starting a new Bible study in the book of Jeremiah, and I want to be there," he stated as he gathered back the stack of papers he'd laid aside. "Were you going to go with me?" he asked, looking at her with all sincerity. "It would delight me greatly if you joined me."

"Isn't Jeremiah in the Old Testament?" She completely sat up, smoothing out her hair and gathering her stack of papers.

"Yes, it is. He was a great prophet. He's called the weeping prophet because of the many tears he shed over the destruction of Jerusalem," Peter continued, hoping to convince her to come. "I think we can learn from Jeremiah's uncompromised preaching in the face of many life-threatening situations."

"Well, I think I'll pass this time. I really don't like much in the Old Testament. It seems so out of date to me," she said, thumping her pen in her lap. "But I'll miss sitting with you," she admitted.

Peter didn't know what to say. "Well, you can always join me anytime if you change your mind," Peter said. "That's one of the great things I'm learning about Pastor Ron in that he makes the Old Testament come alive and shows us how relevant it is to us today. He seems to be really blessed that way. And, of course, I'll miss seeing you too."

CHAPTER 7

Peter, with briefcase in hand, came through the main office to check his inbox. He usually had a few drop slips by the first Monday of the second week. This was the official last day to either switch to another class or drop a class for a refund.

He went to his office to read over his mail before his 8:10 class arrived. That's when he saw it.

"Lillian Parker dropped."

"What?" he said out loud. "Why in the world would she drop this class?" Peter was very upset, curiosity about to drive him mad. But sure enough, by the time his 10:10 class was in full swing, there was no Lilly in it.

After class, Peter was determined to find Lilly. It wasn't a small campus, but Peter banked on finding Lilly under the big oaks that she often enjoyed. However, he walked briskly around the campus in search of his ragmuffin to no avail. But he knew where he was headed when he left for the day.

Lilly decided to check out the library now that she had more time. She'd considered changing her English class to Veronica Hughbert's English 100 class, but it was full. So she opted just to keep the timeframe empty.

She knew Peter wouldn't understand why she dropped his class, but she thought he'd thank her later for making it easier for him. She did admit to herself that she missed seeing him terribly.

She made it through the day and had decided to get some yard work done. She'd taken it upon herself to up keep her aunt's quaint, little yard. Not that Lilly was a green thumb, but she knew how to pull weeds, mow, and trim. She loved to plant flowers even though she often didn't have that luxury growing up.

Lilly donned her worn-out jeans. They had a few holes but were comfortable. She threw on her old, white t-shirt and put her hair in low, shoulder-high pigtails.

"Let me guess," her aunt said. "You're going out to work in the yard?"

"You got it. How could you tell?"

They both giggled at the silly way Lilly looked when she worked in the yard. Her aunt had let her have her way about taking care of the yard, sensing it was important to her.

She'd mowed and trimmed first. She was humming a little tune as she weeded around the flowers she'd planted earlier in the summer when she heard his voice.

"Hey there! I need to talk to you!" he hollered out his window.

She stood up and looked around.

There was Peter looking at her from the window of his car. Smiling back, Lilly walked to the edge of the yard and leaned on the fence that enclosed her aunt's front yard.

He'd gotten himself into quite a rage while driving over, trying to figure out why in the world she'd dropped his class without even telling him. But with one sight of her, all the anger drained away. She was the picture of what he remembered. He chuckled at the sight. He was sure Lilly didn't know she had two streaks of mud on one cheek and a big blob on her forehead. She had grass clippings all over her shirt, and she was barefoot. She was in pigtails, just like he'd seen her every Saturday when they lived in Arlington, when he came by to see if she was riding the bus on Sunday. She was a mess! But he cherished the look. The flood of memories overpowered him, and he simply couldn't remain angry.

He got out of the car and walked over to the fence where she was standing. "Hey, ragmuffin. I missed you today in class."

He waited for a response, but she looked away.

"What is this?" Peter asked as he showed her the drop slip.

"Well, Peter, I didn't think you'd understand." She was softly speaking, but Peter wasn't listening. She was playing with a blade of grass, her nails black with soil.

"Why, Lilly? What is going on in your little head?" he inquired, trying to get her to look at him.

"It's Lillian, Professor Collins. Please." She shuffled her bare feet around, not wanting to have this conversation.

"Yes, it's Lillian; but don't call me that," he said, agitated. He put a stray hair behind her ear. "I can't stand you to call me Professor Collins when I'm just old Peter to you," he said, trying to calm down. "Come on. I want to know why you dropped my class. Have I done something to offend you?"

"Oh no, Peter. I'm really just thinking of you mostly," she said, a half-truth. "It seems that my coming here has really made your life more complicated," she looked away she just couldn't face him right then. "We can't just pick up where we were five years ago." She paused. "Plus I don't know about the rules here, but it probably raises eyebrows to have such a close friendship with a student." Then she just blurted out, "It's just plain too hard."

He could tell she was trying to hold back tears.

"Lilly-an, I just don't know what you mean." He was desperate for her to look at him. "Lillian, will you look at me?" he demanded, and she complied. "I admit I've been like a crazy man since you arrived in my life a week ago. I can't deny that I'm thoroughly distracted with you in class." He rubbed the back of his neck. "But I think I'll be even crazier if I can't see you every day," he admitted.

"It's not that easy, Peter."

"What is it that makes it so hard?" Peter was desperate.

"Oh, Peter, I never thought this would hurt so much," she continued, seeing no use in hiding the truth. "Peter, you never gave me time to ask any questions. You only interrogated me." She didn't want to hurt his feelings, but she must be truthful. Peter, just now realizing how selfish he'd been, looked up and closed his eyes at how he had treated Lilly.

"I'm sorry, Lilly. I didn't give your needs a second thought."

"I've prayed as to what to do. I just don't think I can handle the changes that I never considered were very probable." She was blundering, she knew, for the look on Peter's face was complete confusion.

"I don't understand."

Lilly finally gave in and just spit it out plain. "I hadn't considered that you might have an attached relationship. For all I know, you might even be married!"

Understanding dawning on him like a bomb, he began to speak, but Lilly cut him off.

"Hear me out, Petah." She had used his nickname in her frustration. " I don't know why this would bother me so, except that it would alter our relationship." She looked down. "I realized when I saw you with another woman Friday night at the Stuffed Goose what a selfish, wicked person I am." She continued with tears. "I didn't want to share my Petah with anyone. Even though our relationship was never a romantic thing, I knew that you having someone special in your life would greatly change our closeness."

She was crying hard now. "And I was jealous of her. It makes me even more upset that I had displeased God with this whole thing." She looked up, her face a mess. "That's why, Professor Collins, I dropped your class. So you could be free to continue your life as it was before."

"Oh, Lilly. Oh, Lilly." He reached out and hugged her, even though it was awkward over the fence. He held her until he heard her sniffles calm down. He patted her back, all the while soothingly saying, "I never meant to hurt you, Lilly. In all the world, I wouldn't want to hurt you."

Finally, Lilly pulled back and wiped her tears, which, combined with the dirt streaks and blobs, had made a river of mud all over her face. Peter cracked a big grin.

"I know I look a mess, but you don't have to laugh," Lilly teased.

"So tell me, my dirty-faced little ragmuffin—" he paused for the full effect of how he'd described her and to get her attention— "how did you come about seeing Veronica and me at the Stuffed Goose?" Peter was dying to know.

"I work there." She was trying to repair the damage on her face, but Peter thought she might as well give up without a mirror. She was making things worse. He thought, not for the first time, how different Lilly and Veronica were. Veronica wouldn't have been caught dead looking like that. She wouldn't have been out digging in someone's yard. But then, this was his Lil. He had to quit thinking of her as his, because this was part of the problem she was trying to explain.

He was processing all these thoughts plus how to explain what he wasn't sure of himself. He switched his feet back and forth. "I didn't know you worked there. Why didn't you tell me?"

"Well, number one, you didn't ask. Number two, it just never came up."

"It's not like you didn't have a bunch of other questions you wanted answers to," she said, making her point again.

"Well, you got me there, Lilly … I mean, Lillian. It's really my fault," he admitted. But he knew he had some explaining to do. "I'll be glad to answer your questions. Just shoot."

This was a lame attempt to rectify his mistake, but she took it.

"Peter, please come up on the porch. Let me go in and get some lemonade for the two of us, and if you really have the time, we can have a chat." She moved toward the gate to let him in. "But don't feel like you owe me anything. You have your own life, and I just came waltzing in and ruining everything."

"I don't want to hear you talk that way, Lillian Parker. You are very special to me, and I certainly don't feel like you ruined anything." He wanted her to understand. "If anything, God has used you to make things in my life clearer," he said firmly with a smile, thinking about how much closer his relationship was with the LORD since she waltzed back into his life.

"Who are you talking to?" Aunt Maureen asked as Lilly came in.

"Oh, you'll never guess," she said with a sigh. "It's my friend, Professor, Peter," she said calmly as she got out two glasses, filled them with ice, and poured fresh lemonade.

"What?" her aunt said, jumping out of her recliner. "Your Peter is right outside?" She was moving toward her. "Well, I gotta get out there and meet this guy." She put on her house shoes and headed out the door.

"Here you are, Professor, I mean Peter," Lilly said as she handed him a glass of lemonade.

"Thank you, Lillian." He took a sip. "Ah. This is very refreshing on a warm August afternoon."

"Professor Collins, I'd like you to meet my sweet Aunt Maureen. This is her home. She's the picture of kindness to me." She winked at her aunt. "Aunt Maureen, this is Professor Peter Collins. He is, I mean, was, my English professor and an old friend."

"What do you mean *was?*" Her aunt turned to her, forgetting all about Peter. "What happened?"

"I'll tell you later," Lilly said in a whisper, hoping her aunt would let it go. She didn't want to discuss this in front of Peter.

Peter stepped in to save the embarrassing situation. "The pleasure is all mine," Peter said as he shook Maureen's hand. "And please call me Peter."

"Peter it is," her aunt said with hands on her hips. "When Lilly told me all about you, I told her I wanted to meet you. This wasn't the way I'd planned it, so you'll have to come back." She said what was on her mind. "I told her then that if you didn't snag her up you would be a fool," her aunt said candidly.

Lilly wanted to crawl under the rocking chairs. She'd never been so embarrassed. But Peter saved the day by saying, "Out of all the times I've been called a fool, this one would be the most worthy cause." He knew she was terribly embarrassed. "You have obviously been victim of Lillian's tender kindness to have such an opinion," he said, looking at her aunt. He then moved his eyes to Lilly. "I must say I'm jealous of you, Maureen. It must be nice to get nonstop victimizing from such a blessed niece." He winked at Lilly.

"Oh, stop it, you two," Lilly said as she moved to sit down. "You'll have my head so big I won't have room for my studies! I need all the skull space possible!"

"From the paper I read yesterday, that can't possibly be true," he leaned over and said softly in Lilly's ear.

Sensing their need for privacy, Aunt Maureen said, "Well, do come often, ya hear? The door is always open."

"Thank you for your gracious offer. I'll try to indulge in it often, especially if I can't talk Lilly back into my class," he said, looking at Lilly with raised eyebrows.

After her aunt shut the door, Peter sat back down in the rocker he'd been in. "Your aunt is very nice," he said as he sipped his drink. "And, very, uh…" He chose his words carefully.

"Very direct," Lilly interrupted smiling.

"So what do you think about me hanging around here all the time with you barefoot and mud on your face?" he asked, trying to break the ice.

Lilly looked at her feet, only to see in horror how filthy they were. She didn't know why this bothered her, but it did. She tucked them as far under her rocker as she could get them. Her face, she knew, had been a mess, because when she went in to get the drinks she washed her hands and saw her muddy Mississippi River face. She was humiliated that Peter had seen her that way. But what could she do?

It's only dirt, and it washes off, she thought to herself. "Well, it depends on if you are always going to come when I'm digging in the dirt."

"If I recall correctly, I believe this is the way I saw you most every Saturday for years, Lil."

"Well, it's one thing for a child to look like it's playing in the dirt. I probably was," she mumbled, "but quite another for a grown woman to be caught dirty handed, enjoying herself!" she teased. "Maybe since you are getting old you will be completely gray headed by the time you get home and forget you saw me this way!" She laughed.

"Okay, okay, I give! Quit calling me old," he said, waving his hands in surrender. "And please don't make me gray headed when I don't have long to wait. I just found my first gray hair this morning!"

"Told ya you were getting old, Petah," she said, using his nickname. "It's all downhill from here."

Suddenly, they got quiet, both knowing some serious issues needed to be discussed.

"I'll make you a deal," Peter said.

Lilly was looking at him, curious as to what deal he wanted to make with her.

"I won't come around and catch you dirty handed as often *if* you'll come back to my class," he said with his eyebrows raised in hope.

"Now, Peter, that is playing down right dirty without playing in the dirt!" she said with a flip of the hand. "That's not playing fair. And, dirt or no dirt, I'm not going back to your class."

"Please, Lil. Please come back. I just can't bear the thought that you dropped the class."

"I don't know if I could get back in even if I wanted to. I think there was a waiting list for your class." She continued, "I tried to change to Professor Hughbert's English class, but it was full," she said, swinging her feet, obviously forgetting they were filthy.

Peter nearly gasped when she said that she'd almost enrolled in Veronica's class. What a disaster that would've been. He shook his head at the thought. Recalling the hateful attitude Veronica displayed about Lilly's paper.

Peter tried another tactic. "You know, Lilly, I mean, Lillian, when I graded your paper Sunday, you blessed me tremendously by what you wrote. Your passionate spirit was all through that paper." He smiled, hoping this would work. "And I must say I'd be disappointed as an English teacher not to get to enjoy your writings." He added, "I think not only I, but the rest of the class could learn a lot from having you in there." He could tell she was thinking carefully about this. "Not to mention, you need this English credit."

"Well, like I said, it's probably too late. I already dropped the class, and they're giving me a refund. Even if I did change my mind, things are already set in motion."

"Let me ask you, Lil, if I could get things reversed, would you be willing to take my class?"

Lilly was really in a hard spot. "Professor Collins, you're making this very hard for me," she stated with a frown. "Going back to your class isn't going to make things better for you," she reminded him. "Maybe not seeing me in class will help make our relationship more easily severable."

"Why do you say that?" Peter asked, totally lost as to what she was meaning.

"Peter, you just don't get it, do you?"

"Get what?" Peter was baffled. He rubbed the back of his neck, irritated at his own lack of following her train of thought.

"Peter, Peter. No woman wants to share her man with another woman. She was trying to make it clear. Your fiancée… wife, whatever she is, isn't going to appreciate our close relationship." She was shaking her head at him. "And I don't blame her. I wouldn't either," she admitted. "So it's best to just leave things the way they are for the sake of your relationship with this special lady."

It was becoming clear now. Lilly did have a point; it was time to explain about Veronica. Even so, he still couldn't stand the thought of Lilly disappearing from his life again.

"First off, Lilly, I'm not married or engaged. I am dating someone, which is who you saw me with. Her name is Veronica Hughbert. She was your other class choice. So if you'd gone to her class, it wouldn't have helped any with our situation. But I know you didn't know that."

Lilly's eyes were sad. Peter had to look away while he shared. He felt as though he was betraying Lilly, and his heart tore apart at the thought.

"We came here at the same time, both just a year ago and we sorta just hit it off with that in common." He stopped, thinking how very uncomfortable this was. "I don't know that I'd say I'm ready to ask her to be my wife." He stole a glance at Lilly. She was quietly listening, no malice in her demeanor. "As a matter of fact, I don't know what I feel or think as I consider this. We've been dating for about nine months. I think Veronica would be glad to move forward with a real commitment, but I'm holding back. It's a serious thing to consider a wife," he said, feeling like he was going to start mumbling any minute. He especially did not know what to think about the things he was seeing for the first time in Veronica that he didn't find becoming for his wife. Her spiritual state was becoming more apparent every day.

"Thank you for sharing your heart, Peter." Lilly placed a hand on his arm and looked into his eyes. "I know that wasn't easy to tell me. But that's the very reason we need to keep our distance, so the two of you can grow closer together without any hindrances from me," her eyes saying more than her lips.

Peter knew she was crushed inside. But she still was the picture of sweetness and wanted the best for him.

"Lil, I want to share what happened last Monday night. If you'll listen I'll bare my soul to you."

"Why, of course, Peter."

"I hate to even tell you this for fear it'll dishearten you. I would never want to cause you to stumble in your walk. But that's exactly what I've done." He was so ashamed to be telling her this that he lowered his head. "When I met you, I'd been saved for a few years. I was on fire for the LORD. Everything was fresh, and I was ready to go to the ends of the earth for Christ. Everyone thought I was crazy, and I guess I was. I was crazy about my love for God and obeying Him. God used you many times over to reveal sin and selfishness in my life. That is one of the reasons I bonded like glue to you. For God used you mightily in my life to grow me in ways I never dreamed possible. You challenged me in so many personal areas. God put me through the fire over prejudices I had. He used you to engrave on my heart Jesus's message: 'This is who I came for.' God taught me all about the true meaning of love for others and dying to self through our relationship."

He continued on even though Lilly was revealing total shock on her face at this confession.

"You probably have no idea how much time I spent in the woodshed where God was carving off chunks of my life that didn't belong, sanding the rough edges and carving a new heart that was like His." Peter chuckled. "When I think about it, I'm not sure who was more the project, you or me. And when you came to the understanding of your need for Christ, it seemed to seal our relationship to depths I didn't realize were even there." He took a long sip of his lemonade. He leaned back in his rocker. "I shared all that with you, Lilly, so you could understand what I'm about to say. Now that you know where my heart was all those many years ago, you will know how very much I care about you and how your coming back into my life has caused great change."

He could see fear in Lilly's eyes. You could literally read Lilly's heart through her eyes. But he'd come this far. He must go on.

"After I left to go to college, I didn't have my Lilly to keep me seeking, so to speak. I didn't have someone watching my walk as closely as you did. Your life was like a walking accountability to constantly ask me, 'Is Christ your treasure? Is He what you claim Him to be in your life?' I'm not trying to place any blame where it doesn't belong. I was so lonely for you that I thought I'd go crazy. I thought of writing, but I feared it might get you into more trouble. Jenny kept me posted, and I devoured each letter she wrote to me. Do you remember how I constantly hung around you when I came back on school breaks? It was so hard to be away, so I got myself involved in everything at the school that I could so I didn't have time to think about you. The pain of our separation affected me greatly. Then when you disappeared, it was torturous. I felt like my woodshed tool was gone. I began to lose my zeal for witnessing. And because I was so busy, my relationship with the LORD quickly disintegrated until I was just doing church and not much of that."

"I guess in a lot of ways, I felt as though the LORD had left me. I didn't get into trouble or do horrible sins. But I left my first love. Even Jeff and Jenny noticed, and we talked about it. But I just seemed to get more and more self-centered. I made my world all about me. You can't have God on the throne of your life if you are sitting there. And that is just what happened. I became complacent. And, sad to say, I stayed this way up to graduation. Then, when I moved here with my cousin and got the teaching job at Shaftner, I seemed to have lost all discernment and continued to live for myself, the only difference being my cousin kept bugging me about it. He was and still is a thorn in my flesh. He doesn't like compromise."

He looked over at Lilly. He saw only love and concern for him in her eyes. A breeze blew her loose wisps of hair. Peter continued.

"So I guess the point of sharing all that is that my dating choices were very blurred by my own lack of spiritual condition and discernment. It's so hard, to admit to you that I fell so far away from the LORD, especially in the light of how God has protected you, not to mention how much you depended on Him to get you through those years. It's obvious that your love for God never waned. I was supposed to be the example for you. I was supposed to be the faithful one. It seems almost as if I was as far away from God as you were close to Him. Does that make any sense?"

"Oh, Peter, I'm so, so sorry. I didn't know," she said softly.

"Which brings me to the end of what I want to share," he said. "After I took you home last Monday night, I fell on my face before God Almighty and cried out to Him. I cried a long time as I repented of my sin. I sought His face and begged Him to change me. He used you again to show, just like before, my lack of devotion to Him. Your devout loyalty to Christ alone really illuminated my unfaithfulness to Him. I'm ashamed to say that I was loyal only to myself and what I wanted. I was spent when I finally went to bed. But it was with a completely restored relationship with God. Moment by moment, I'm seeking the lover of my soul, and as I do, He has poured out His grace upon me. Since then, God has been revealing things to me that I hadn't realized I'd become so uncaring about." He reached over and put his hand on hers. "That's why I need you in my class, to keep me accountable," he finished at last. He looked at her, wondering what she would say.

"Peter, I'm so touched by you baring your heart so completely with me." She paused a moment. "I'll come back to your class if you can finagle the arrangement. I praise God for bringing you back to His heart." She smiled at him and continued. "But it needs to be the Holy Spirit that convicts you, not me. I hope I haven't said anything that would make you think you don't measure up, for I'll always love you no matter what." She said the last part in such a hush that Peter barely heard her. But what he heard brought a huge smile to his face.

"Thank you, my Lil. Now you've a better picture as to why you mean so much to me. I know it might make it awkward with Veronica, but I must walk down that road with all the twists and turns God puts in front of me. I've asked God to be in control of that area of my life as well. So we will see what He does with it." He looked over at Lilly. "That's also why I don't really know what is going on there myself."

Lilly, sensing that Peter was finished sharing thought it was time for lighter conversation.

"How did you get this teaching job?" Lilly asked.

"My cousin knew I was finishing my degree and had looked up some openings at the college and invited me to come for a visit. His family, my aunt and uncle, live about an hour's drive into the country from here. And as God would have it, I got the job. Willy and I decided to split an apartment when I moved here last summer," he explained.

"It must be a treasure to have a cousin who is like a brother for a roommate," she said, excited for him. "Not everybody gets that opportunity."

"I need that reminder often so I don't sit on him while he's asleep on the couch," Peter said dryly, thinking of Willy's crazy room arrangement. He'd set up his bedroom as a studio. He had a full, eight-piece professional drum set, two acoustic guitars, one expensive electric guitar, and an amp loud enough to blow down a brick wall. Due to all his equipment, there was no room left for a bed, so he slept on the couch. Peter was laughing pretty hard and said, "You'll just have to see sometime."

"So tell me about this wild cousin of yours," Lilly said in a silly tone.

"Oh. Willy, he's a crazy one," Peter said, shaking his head. "You'll see what I mean when you meet him."

"So, Mr. Collins, when are you planning the fabulous meeting between the crazy and the dimwitted?" Lilly asked with a glint in her eye.

"You, Miss Parker, are not dimwitted. You've the loveliest heart I've ever known. And in the things that really matter, in the spiritual realm, it ain't so smart to not have a heart," he said pointing his finger at her.

"I was thinking that my aunt will want you to come for a visit to interrogate you, and she'll probably nag me until it's accomplished." She smiled at the thought. "I usually don't have many free evenings, and you don't have free mornings; so I was thinking that if you're free Saturday you could come for breakfast. That's my favorite time of the day. That's, if you're not scared I might fix your breakfast with dirty hands," she teased.

"Shaking in my shoes!" he bantered back. "When do you want me here?" he asked. "I'm sure I'll like whatever you make. Even if it was mud pies, I'd eat them with a smile," he winked at her.

"You know, Mr. Collins, you always know the right thing to say," she said, thinking how often Peter's words had either comforted or encouraged her. She was truly thankful for him. Lilly, noticing that Peter had been out of drink for a while and it was warm outside, asked, "Peter, can I get you something else to drink?"

"Actually, I need to go so you can get back to digging being dirty," he joked. "This is one of the areas I need discipline in. I love your company so much, I'd hang around all the time until you were sick of me."

"To be sure, I would treasure every moment, but I'd surely flunk my classes. Then where would I be, *Professor Collins?*"

"Well, to make sure it's not my fault, I'm out of here," he said. "I'll see you Wednesday, Lilly—ian." He was walking down the steps. "If you wait just outside the door before class, I will let you know if I was able to get you back in." He said good-bye from his car window. "See you later, my little ragmuffin!" With a wave, he was off.

Lilly went back to weeding around her flowers, humming a tune, and thanking God for bringing Peter back to His heart. *What joy inexpressible!*

CHAPTER 8

Lilly waited just outside Peter's class as planned. After all the students were seated, he stepped out and stood very close to Lilly so she could hear him.

"I got you back in. I thank God it worked out." He smiled at her.

"Me too," was her hushed reply as she looked briefly into his eyes. Unfortunately, Veronica came breezing down the hallway at that very moment.

"See ya at lunch today, Pete?" she interrupted, not caring that he was in a private conversation. She continued walking, so she would not be late for her own class, but turned her head for an answer.

"I'll be there," he called back. He was rewarded with a smile and a toss of the head from Veronica.

Lilly had silently slipped around him and was back in her original seat.

Peter came in the classroom and looked to see if Lilly was all right. He knew she'd heard the interchange. He taught the class with his mind much more together than it had been. Lilly hoped that this was indeed the right decision.

The rest of Lilly's week went rather smoothly. She was having a hard time in biology and needed to spend every spare moment in study. But so far, she was keeping her head above water. Fridays were her hardest days. She usually didn't have time for a nap, but she always read a few psalms and had a cup of hot tea before heading to work. But today, a letter from Jenny had arrived, and she was ecstatic. Her aunt had left it on the nightstand in her bedroom. Her aunt was just as excited as Lilly was.

She was not long into the reunion letter when the tears began to flow. She could picture both Jeff and Jenny as she read the loving words. Lilly devoured every detail Jenny shared about how they'd missed her. As well, Lilly could picture the excitement of them both when they received her letter telling them of the sweet reuniting of her and Peter. Jenny ended with encouragement for her to keep walking with the LORD and to not grow weary.

Lilly re-read the letter three times. She handed her aunt the letter on her way out.

"Thought you'd like to hear from my friends I told you about. I gotta get to work. I love you, Aunt Maureen," she said, kissing her on the cheek as she went out the door.

Breakfast was in full swing Saturday morning when the doorbell rang. Peter came in, greeted Maureen with a huge smile, and gave her the paper he'd picked up at the end of her driveway.

"How are you today, Maureen? It's a lovely day to behold, only better on this side of town," he said with a wink. "I do thank you for having me in your home."

"Ya might not be after I'm done with ya," she said pointedly. "And I ain't supposing Lilly has anything to do with your jolly mood?" she asked, knowing he couldn't wait to see the face of the very one they spoke of.

"Well, really, I've starved all week, and I just came by because of the smells wafting from the kitchen."

"Well then, my son," Aunt Maureen said, "I'll just go fill you a plate of those yummy smells wafting from the kitchen and you can be on your way." She turned Peter toward the door.

"Okay, I give, Maureen. You play a hard game," He laughed. "Where's Lilly," he asked. She pointed toward the kitchen with a wink. He made a beeline in that direction.

"Well, good morning, my little ragmuffin. How are you this lovely day?" Peter greeted Lilly.

He had stopped and leaned on the entryway, watching Lilly take the last pieces of bacon from the pan and scrambling the eggs at the same time. He'd never seen Lilly in the kitchen cooking before, so this was quite the entertainment. After Peter had greeted her, she was even more a mess. He was trying to keep his chuckles under control.

Lilly licked her fingers and yelled at the bacon piece that threatened to slip to the floor, all the while balancing as she walked over to the table and was finally able to mumble out, "Just what has your laughter bucket overflowing, Mr. Collins?" She had run back to grab the eggs off the stove and, shaking her head, mumbled, "I almost did it," to herself. After getting everything to the table she said, "If you think you can stop laughing, Mr. Collins, you can join us. Here's your seat," she teased while pulling out his chair.

"It's my pleasure," he said as he joined them.

After Peter had prayed, Lilly jumped up, almost knocking over her chair. "The coffee cake, the coffee cake," she said as she ran to the stove. "I forgot the coffee cake." She banged open the oven door and fanned the smoke. "Well, I think if we pick off the nuts and just eat this end it'll be okay," she said, deflated, as she placed the half-burnt coffee cake on the table.

"I'm sure it'll taste wonderful," Peter said with a wink.

"Ain't nobody gonna starve at my house!" Aunt Maureen said harshly. "Go on now. You the man. Help yourself. Lilly always cooks a great breakfast! Don't know what got in her this morning, but she don't normally burn things."

"Peter, would you like coffee to drown your cake?" Lilly asked while rising to pour herself some.

"Yes, please. But I would never drown the best coffee cake in town. It's delicious, Lilly," he encouraged.

After Aunt Maureen had taken her last bite, she began the interrogation, to Lilly's embarrassment. "So tell me, Mr. Collins, where'd you grow up? What brings you here? How long have you been living here? Where do you live? Are you married or divorced? How much money do you make? And what are your intentions with my Lilly?"

She rattled off all these questions in a row like a semiautomatic weapon. It took Lilly's breath away. She wanted to crawl under the table. Her aunt was just sitting there, waiting to be answered, and not so patiently after firing off her rounds.

Peter let out a low whistle while shaking his head. He didn't know what to say. He'd never been fired on in such a way. And he did want to answer carefully.

"First off, Maureen, thank you so much for the lovely meal and—"

Aunt Maureen cut him off, "Don't try to butter me up, boy. Just get to the facts," she said, staring him down. "And you better tell me the truth iffen ya wantin' to be comin' around here anymore."

Lilly was beet red in the face and was staring at Peter.

Lilly intervened, "Aunt Maureen, you know I've told you a lot about Peter already—"

Her aunt interrupted. "Lilly, I want to hear it from him," she said, not taking her eyes off Peter.

Peter cleared his throat and began. "I grew up in Arlington, Tennessee. My dad is the high school principal in town. My mother is one of the local dentist's secretaries. They've been at their jobs for as long as I can remember. We all attended First Baptist Arlington, where I met this here ragmuffin, Lilly, when I was fifteen. We became great friends. I think Lilly must have told you some of this, so I'll move on." He took a sip of his now-cold coffee and looked at Aunt Maureen to see if she was calming down. Thankfully, she was. "I graduated in the top ten of my class. I then proceeded to start college in Lynchburg, Virginia, on a full merit-based scholarship. I finished my teaching degree in short order. Then my cousin called and told me about an opening here at Shaftner State Community College. I came, applied, was accepted, and started right away that next semester. That was exactly one year ago, and I've been teaching there ever since. My cousin and I share an apartment over by Centennial Square." As he ended, he sat back, glad to be done with that, and crossed his legs and looked at Aunt Maureen for approval.

What Peter found was a big frown. "Okay, Peter Collins. What are you hiding?" Aunt Maureen asked, her hand on her hip, her lips tight. "You didn't answer all the questions."

Peter shook his head and pulled up close to the table in disbelief. He was irritated at this grilling. But he said, "What else was it you wanted to know, Maureen?" He had used his napkin to wipe his already-clean face and hands.

"Well, you know, have ya been hitched up yet? How much money you makin'? I got to know whether it'll be enough to take care of my Lilly, ya know." She was outraged that he'd forgotten the important stuff.

Peter thought she was crazy and that he didn't have to sit there and listen to the likes of this woman. His mind was spinning as to what to say and if he could even speak without losing his temper at this line of questioning. Then he looked over at the astonished look on Lilly's face. So he put aside his not-so-nice thoughts "Since I'm not a horse, I can't be hitched," he said with a twinkle. "And my pay is more than hay." He said all this to try to lighten the mood. And it worked.

Lilly's aunt howled with laughter.

"Normally, Maureen, I consider those my private affairs that I don't feel the need to discuss with people. However, because of Lilly, I'll tell you I haven't ever had the privilege of being married. And let's just say that when I do, I have adequate money for my bride to be happy," Peter said politely.

Aunt Maureen was pleased with what she heard. But she still lacked the answer to the other question. So she went about getting the answer. She said a bit more kindly but directly, "And when were you planning on taking my Lil away?" She almost had tears in her eyes.

Peter didn't know how to answer this one. A look of total shock resided on his face. Lilly knew she needed to say something. Lilly moved forward and placed her hand on her aunt's arm.

"Oh, Aunt Maureen, please. Remember. I told you it was not like that." She desperately looked into her aunt's eyes for understanding. "Um … Aunt Maureen, Peter and I are not … um … our um … relationship is not that of romance." She stumbled trying to explain what a peculiar bond it really was.

Her aunt gave the strangest face of disbelief. So Lilly tried again.

"You see, Aunt Maureen, I desire for God to bring into my life the person He'd have for me. And I think Peter feels the same way," she said, looking at Peter, who gave a big grin and a nod of approval that she was doing fine. Lilly went on to say, "Peter and I are very dear friends, and hopefully, no matter who we marry, we will remain close friends."

Peter jumped in to punctuate the conclusion by saying, "Lilly is a cherished treasure to me. That is for certain. But as to who God would have me to take for a wife, He hasn't revealed that to me yet." He looked at Lilly to see if he'd said the right thing to comfort her aunt.

But her aunt said, "I don't know about all that God stuff, but it just seems like you two were made for each other." Both looked at each other, but neither replied to the comment.

Peter was the first to speak. "Thank you again for your lovely company, Maureen, and the breakfast too. It was the highlight of my day. No. I take that back. The highlight of my week."

"I'm doing the dishes. You two scat," she said firmly.

Lilly began to argue.

"You work all week, Lil. You go spend some time with our guest. Take a walk or something. Let me do this. I want to," she said with determination as she began to gather the dishes.

"Okay," Lilly said, clearly defeated. She looked at Peter, who shrugged his shoulders.

"Actually, Lilly, a walk sounds delightful, if you'd escort me since I'm the new kid on the block and I might get lost," he said with a grin.

"Oh, you wouldn't get lost, silly. But I'll join you if you insist."

"Your aunt is quite a hoot," Peter said with a chuckle after they'd walked a distance away from the house.

"I'm so sorry, Peter." She put her hand on his arm, slowed down a bit to see his face, and continued her apology. "I had no idea what she was going to say. And she can be, well, let's just say, kinda rude in her mannerisms," Lilly said lamely, not wanting to say an unkind word about her aunt. "Yet she is the picture of kindness in letting me live with her." She continued, "I just don't know what got into her this morning."

Peter, knowing full well what was going on with her aunt, decided not to comment. "Don't worry about it, my little ragmuffin," he said as he pulled her rubber band out of her hair. "She is just being protective of this sweet, little niece who came waltzing into her life."

Lilly ignored the fact that her hair was now loose and asked, "Do you think I should move out?" she said with concern.

Peter looked up to the sky and let out a chuckle. "Why no, Lilly, you shouldn't move out. She needs you." She still looked worried, so he said with a serious look, "Besides, who'd share Christ with her?"

"Yeah. That's been my prayer since coming here: that she'll see how much I love my LORD and inquire about Him." She looked up and pointed. "Just two more blocks and there is an old park. You wanna go there?" He nodded.

When they got to the park, Lilly headed for the swings. It was an old, rarely used park. The concrete walls were crumbling down, and moss had over taken what was there. There was some old steel equipment; a slide; a few swings; and one old, small pavilion. He figured out, though, why Lilly probably liked it here, for it did possess some of the most enormous, exquisite, old oaks he'd ever seen. The trees that were planted there many years ago now shaded nearly the entire park.

Lilly jumped into one of the old, flat-board-seat swings and kicked her feet back in the dirt as the swing moved back and forth, all the while talking to Peter, who was leaning on the post, watching her. This was a picture of the olden days. It did much good for him to see her like this.

"How do you like your job?" Peter asked.

"Oh, I enjoy my work," she said as drew with the tips of her shoes in the dirt.

Getting into Peter's world, she asked, "Do you like teaching?"

"Most definitely," Peter said, "especially when I have such great students." He grinned pointedly at her. He thought surely it'd be a year to remember with Lilly in his class. "I love to teach," he said while kicking at a pebble, in a serious mood.

"Well, someone has to have the brains in this world, or we might still be in the dark ages," Lilly said, laughing.

"One thing I'm learning, Lilly, is that wisdom comes in many different packages." He raised his eyebrows to her.

Lilly thought it was time to change the subject. She didn't like to talk about her lack of learning abilities with anyone, least of all her English professor. "I did want to thank you again for coming to breakfast and putting up with that shocking interrogation with my aunt. But I think she likes you."

It wasn't lost on Peter that Lilly had changed the subject, but he let it go. He didn't go back to school issues but instead went to safer territory. He said, "Speaking of meeting people, I want you to meet my cousin Willy. Willy, being the nosy guy he is, wanted to know where I was Monday night. So I kept him guessing a few days, but then he made me tell all. I hope that was okay without your permission."

"Oh, yes. That's fine. I know you use discretion," she said. Realizing that Peter might want to sit, she asked, "Do you want to go over there under that big oak and sit for a bit?"

"Sure. That will be fine," he said. Lilly flopped down and immediately began to pluck up blades of grass and twist them in her fingers.

"Ever since then, he's been driving me crazy about meeting you," Peter continued. "So it seems that we both have nags on our hands," he said, rolling his eyes. He was concerned that Willy would scare Lilly out of her skin.

"I'm looking forward to meeting him. It seems we at least have one thing in common," she said with a grin.

"And what possibly would be in common with the two of you?"

"You," she said as she tossed a handful of grass his way. "Why, you, Peter. We both care deeply about you."

While he brushed the grass off his shirt, he scolded her with his finger. He was quickly forming a plan. "Hey, how would you like to join me in a Bible study on Sunday evenings? The pastor is teaching in the book of Jeremiah. They have a worship team on Sunday evenings with a few extra instruments, my cousin plays the drums. Then, after the service, I could introduce you to Willy. We can get some pizza and head back to my apartment, where you and Willy can get to know one another."

Lilly was contemplating how to get there. "I'd really love to, but I don't want to take advantage of my aunt's generosity. She loans me her car for both school and work. She's let me live here without paying rent so I can save up to buy my own car," she said resolutely. "Maybe you can bring him by here sometime." Then her eyes got big. "But not on dirty-hands day," she said, thinking how embarrassed she'd be to meet this Willy looking like she had Monday.

Peter laughed out loud. "You don't know Willy," he said. "He probably would never notice." He snickered, thinking about his messy roommate. "He's a carefree kinda guy. I've been tempted to buy a spare pair of shoes and leave them in my car for all the times he's asked me if I know where he put his shoes," Peter told Lilly.

"He sounds like a very interesting guy."

"He's quite a character. But even though we are different in the way we do things, he has a golden heart. He actually reminds me a lot of you in many ways. He has a heart for the lost. He doesn't let compromise or legalisms get in the way of his devotion to God." Peter was very serious now. "He's continued to prod me about my own spiritual condition. He was the first person I talked to about my turnaround on Monday night, for I knew he would not only rejoice with me but pray for me as well."

"Now I'm really curious to meet this prayer warrior," Lilly said with bright eyes. "How can we make this work?" she asked out loud, trying to figure out a way.

"How about I just pick you up and that will solve the whole thing?"

"What about Veronica?" she asked, her head cocked. "Doesn't she come with you?"

"Um… she didn't want to do this particular Bible study. So I'll only be picking her up on Sunday mornings," Peter replied.

"Well, the morning was easy. I just rode the bus," she said, her forehead wrinkled in deep thought. "Well, I guess that'd be fine if you're sure you don't mind."

"What did you say?" Peter asked, not believing his ears were telling him the truth.

"Oh, just that I rode the bus to your church this past Sunday," she said, beaming. "I must say the whole morning was a delight. I did look for you but couldn't find you."

"I saw you. Third row from the front, piano side, was it?" he inquired.

"Yes, that was me. I like to sit up front so I'm not so distracted."

"Did you go to Sunday school?" Peter queried.

"Yes, I did. I went to the pastor's class on Revelation. I learned a lot just in the one class. I plan to keep going to it." Lilly smiled.

"Well, that explains the reason you didn't see me. I go to the college and career class. And I sit on the mid-to-back organ side.

But what I couldn't figure out is how quickly you disappeared afterward," he said, hoping to gain an answer from her.

"I needed to get to the bus. I didn't want them waiting on me."

"What do you mean by bus? Did you take the city bus to church?"

"Why, the church bus, of course." She flashed a big smile at him, knowing they both had lovely thoughts at the moment. "You know I'll never outgrow riding the bus."

"You are something," he said, thinking how perfect that was for her to do when she needed a way to church anyhow. And how much it must've meant to her, he didn't even need to ask. "Did you have a drive down memory lane on the bus, Miss Parker?" he asked, his eyes twinkling.

"Yes, Professor Collins, I did." She beamed up at him. "Guess who I sat by?"

"Who?" His eyebrows rose, his curiosity piqued.

"A lonely, little, nine-year-old girl," she said softly.

Their eyes were locked for several heartbeats, each taken back several years in time.

"That is no surprise," Peter said with a grin.

"And I had such a great time. Even after I get my car, I'll still ride the bus I think."

"You've such a heart for the lost and lonely," Peter said quietly.

"You would too if you had been in my shoes," Lilly simply said. She went on to say, "There's not a day that goes by that I don't think about that first knock on my door by Jeff and Jenny and that first church bus ride. It literally changed my life. So, naturally, it's very important to me. Speaking of, guess who I heard from this week?" she said, almost dancing around.

"Who would that be?" Peter thought he knew but played along anyway.

"Jenny," she squealed. "And Jeff too."

"Wow. That's great. I would've loved to have been there to see them open that letter of yours," he said, smiling just thinking of Jeff and Jenny going through the shock of hearing from Lilly as he had, seeing her again.

"Just what was that smile about, Petah?" she teased.

"Oh, nothing really," he said.

They talked for another two hours before heading back to the house. Peter set a time to pick up Lilly the next evening for church and said his good-bye.

"I better be off before having to stay for lunch and be cross-examined again. Don't know if I could take it twice in one day," he teased her. He tapped her on the nose and left.

"Good morning, Katherine. May I sit with you?" Lilly asked the little girl she had sat with the week before on the bus.

The little girl did not speak but scooted over, her eyes begging for love.

"I brought you a sucker," Lilly said as she handed her a red sucker. Lilly had bought a package to give away to kids as she met them.

The little girl quickly reached for it. Lilly noted her fingers were dirty and shaking. It tore Lilly's heart out. It was obvious that this little girl had learned at an early age not to trust others.

LORD, Lilly prayed, *help me love this little girl.*

Lilly continued to chat with her, and they sang bus songs together. She looked over at Katherine a time or two only to see that she'd twisted the stick of the sucker almost off and it was dingy from her dirty fingers and had practically melted in her moist hands.

Now I know what Peter must have seen. No wonder he fell hard, she thought to herself as she watched little Katherine.

Lilly was late when she slipped into the third row while the second song was being sung. Peter sighed in relief, for he couldn't help looking for her. Veronica noticed his odd behavior and that it looked like he was looking for someone but did not make anything of it until she saw that girl come in, late of all things. But what a little twerp like that had to do with Peter, she didn't know. She dismissed the whole thing from her mind and tucked her arm inside of Peter's.

CHAPTER 9

Peter opened the door for Lilly to get in. She was wearing a yellow summer dress that was simply refreshing after the afternoon he'd had with Veronica. They'd had an argument about his attending the evening Bible study. It had made for a miserable paper-checking afternoon.

"Hello, Peter. How was your afternoon?" Lilly asked.

"Oh, enlightening," he said as he pulled out into traffic.

"Why do you say that?"

How am I going to field this one? he wondered. "Oh. Well, I read a very nice paper today from someone I know." He merely avoided saying who he was checking papers with.

"Oh, that one. It was a hard topic, you know, Professor Collins!" Lilly teased. "I must say it's a very awkward thing to have you as my teacher!"

"Well, it's not easy for me to correct your papers either since I know your heart and what you want to say even if it doesn't come out grammatically perfect," he said carefully.

"Was it that bad?" Lilly asked with dread.

"Don't worry. You'll get better at it the more you do it. You have all semester. And by the end, you'll not even recognize your own work, it will have improved so much."

"Thanks again for picking me up, Peter," Lilly told him. "I hope it wasn't any trouble for you."

It was hard for Peter not to compare Veronica and Lilly, especially since the LORD had been showing him so much, and the changes God was making in him seemed to conflict more and more with Veronica. On the other hand, Lilly, though younger than Veronica, was so sweet. He shook his head. He had to quit comparing the two of them.

"I saw you were late this morning. Was everything all right?"

"Oh, I was checking on Katherine. When I peeked in the window of her Sunday school class, she was letting a boy have it." Lilly chuckled a little. "I immediately went in the room, even though the teacher had gotten right to the situation. I needed to know what was going on." Lilly paused and then continued. "Come to find out, a boy had tried to take away the sucker that I'd given her. It was a smashed-up piece of melted rubble, but it was hers. I'd no idea why the boy wanted to take it, but he tried. She yanked his hair and wouldn't give it up. So anyway, I went in to help the teacher and calm Katherine. So that is why I was late."

"She sounds like quite the uncharitable cherubim." He grinned.

"Oh, she just steals my heart, Peter," she said softly.

Peter noticed the softness in her voice. "Sounds like someone I know," he said tenderly and patted her hand.

"I must admit I did think of you this morning as I watched her on the bus. The longing to be loved in her eyes was more than my heart could take. I thought to myself it's no wonder you latched on to me when I was in that place," she said, looking at him, thanking him with her eyes one more time for pouring his heart out for her.

After Bible study, she followed Peter to the sanctuary and didn't know whether she should sit with him or not. This was when things were awkward and hard to deal with. This was when she wished she hadn't come and messed things up for Peter. Peter was almost to his pew and turned to let Lilly precede him, only to see no Lilly at all. He did a double-take. "She was just right here," he said to himself before he realized people were staring at him talking to himself. He cleared his throat and nodded in the direction of an old lady giving him a quirky look.

He slowly walked over to where Lilly was sitting and leaned close to her ear. "What are you doing over here?"

"I'm sitting here. What are you doing?" she teased, knowing he wanted a different answer.

Peter rolled his eyes impatiently at her teasing. "I know you're sitting there. Why aren't you over there with me?" he asked, assuming that it was understood she was to sit by him.

"Well, Mr. Collins, I didn't want gossip to knock at these people's doors about you having one woman in the morning and a different one in the evenings," she whispered with a sweet grin.

Peter seemed a bit slow on this one. When it finally dawned on him, he said, "Hmm. Well." She could tell he was struggling with what she'd said and the innocence of their relationship and the nasty thoughts of people gossiping about him all in thirty seconds. His face did quite a number. "Well, Lilly, I appreciate your love and concern for my well-being. That's very thoughtful of you." Peter crinkled his forehead. "But if you don't mind sitting with me, it would be my honor. Maybe this would be a good lesson for those who want to wag their tongues to change."

"Are you sure, Peter?" Lilly whispered, concern in her eyes. "I understand the dilemma you're in, and I don't mind sitting here. Veronica is your-your ..." she stuttered, "your girl, and she has the rightful place beside you. I have no business thinking that I can just sit beside you just because I see you. This is where things have to change, Peter," Lilly said, and she lowered her head so Peter couldn't see her eyes.

"Why do things have to be so complicated?" he asked her, his irritation showing, more to himself, not really expecting an answer. He knew that the music would start soon. "Lilly, come on. We'll deal with this later." He nudged her to get up. "I can't stand to see you alone when I can do something about it." They got up, trying not to make a scene, and went over to where Peter normally sat.

Lilly wanted to leave as much room between her and Peter as possible so no tongues would wag, yet she didn't want to offend Peter. It was nice to belong somewhere. Lilly remembered Peter's cousin Willy was the drummer, but because everyone was standing in front of her view, she couldn't see him. But she did enjoy the music along with the worship time very much. They stood and sang song after song, many of which Lilly noted were straight from Scripture. The songs brought much conviction to her soul. She longed in her heart to seek the face of God like she had never done before.

It wasn't until she saw this dirty-blonde, wild, curly head of hair coming toward them that she thought again of Willy. The singing portion of the service was over, and the players were going to their seats. He had a very boyish face with a big grin on it. He had big sideburns and peach fuzz where he needed to shave.

He's definitely good-looking, Lilly thought.

He was loosening his tie as he came down the side aisle. Lilly had to chuckle, for he'd worn it around his neck while wearing a white T-shirt and stone-washed jeans. He sat down by Lilly. She looked incredulously at his tie while he was shoving it in his pocket.

He grinned, leaned over and whispered, "It's a requirement." Then he got situated for the message, thinking this was going to be fun.

After the service was over, Peter did the introductions.

Willy said, "Well now, Peter. I was expecting Dorothy and her doggie, Toto. Not this, shall we say—" he looked Lilly over— "uh, the loveliest picture of serenity. Peter, man, you're holding out on me." Willy was really getting into this, and he could tell Peter was getting mad. "Why, you had me convinced that she was real young chick, not this lovely lady." Peter wanted to yank his ear off. Peter, through clenched teeth, proceeded with the introductions.

"Lilly, by now you have probably figured out this is my cousin and roommate, Willy McCollister. Willy this is the lady I told you about, Lillian Parker."

Willy held out his hand to Lilly. "It is nice to know you, Miss Lillian. It is miss, isn't it?" he asked politely.

"Yes," Lilly answered, not sure just where this creature had come from but all the while liking him too.

Willy knew Peter was after him, so he hit the pew, nearly scaring Lilly out of her skin, saying, "See ya. Pizza in a few." He skipped off down the aisle and jumped over the last pew and was out the door before she could blink an eye.

Lilly's eyes were huge. She turned to see a very disgruntled Peter. Then she let out a quiet laugh, realizing the two of them were as different as night and day. That had to be a hoot.

"I believe a reminder of what a special gift it is to have a close relative is due here." She laughed, remembering now his few comments about his crazy cousin that he'd made the day before.

Peter was not happy and rolled his eyes. "Come on. Let's go," he said to a giggling Lilly.

On the car ride home, Lilly riddled Peter with questions about Willy. Peter kept saying, "You'll see." When her questions were exhausted, things turned to a more personal level.

Peter admitted that lately he'd thought a lot about his life and about what he wanted in a wife and about marriage altogether. "I had begun to wonder if I am getting too set in my ways to think about a wife."

Lilly was quietly praying. Not sure how to respond, she said, "God will guide you, Peter."

"This is my, our, humble abode, Lilly." He had opened the door to the sound of drums. "Make yourself at home while I call in the pizza."

The room was a combination living-dining-kitchen, nothing fancy. The furniture was fairly new but not extravagant, and things were tidy—that is, minus the sock that she found in the corner of the couch cushion where she sat. She had her own prankster bucket turned over. She picked it up and waved it at Peter, holding her nose, while he was on the phone. He gave her the look she expected, so she laughed and wagged her finger at him all the more.

When he hung up the phone, she suggested, "Hey, Peter, how about a treasure hunt? There is sure to be more." Lilly was teasing Peter, getting ready to pull out the cushions.

"No," he said, thinking, *I'm glad Veronica didn't see that today!* He came over and got the rotten treasure and went to Willy's room and threw it at him.

Willy looked up, stopped playing, pulled out his hearing protection, and teased, "Glad you made it home, man."

Peter was not happy and wanted to make a point to Willy about the sock. He'd forgotten they had company. He said, "Willy, you promised not to leave anything in the living area. If Veronica had seen that today, I would've been very embarrassed."

"Okay. You're right. I'm sorry, Peter. I'll try to do better, and I won't tease you about Lillian anymore."

That's when they both stopped in dead silence, realizing that Lilly had heard all their conversation. Peter laid his head on the doorjamb. He seemed to go from one mess to another, he thought. Willy rescued him. He went right out to the living room to see Lilly. "Hey, what do you think you're doing taking the stuffin' out of the cushions?" he asked, laughing.

Lilly played along. "Some of the stuffin's need a washin'," she bantered back. Lilly really liked this Willy.

"Hey, Lillian, would you like to see my studio?" He motioned for her to get up and come over to his bedroom studio. She stepped to the door. "Wow!" was all she could say.

There were cables, microphones, speakers, and all kinds of things she had no clue about. Among the guitars there was the biggest drum set she'd seen. There wasn't a dresser, bed, or anything else.

"That's a cool studio, Willy," she said.

"Where do you sleep, Willy?" She sat back down on the couch.

"You're sitting on it," Peter piped up dryly.

She looked down. "Oh. I'm sorry," she said, standing up. "I didn't know." She was embarrassed and confused when the doorbell rang.

"I'll get the pizza," Peter said.

"Oh. Go ahead and sit on it. We do all the time." He was waving his hand at her to sit back down. "Well, that is as long as you leave the *stuffin's* alone!" Willy laughed, trying to make light of the whole situation.

"I see it's all making sense to me now," Lilly said. "Peter, you tried to sock it to me, but I just didn't get it." Lilly laughed at Peter, knowing the sock was a sore spot between the two of them.

Also, she didn't want Peter to worry that she knew Veronica had been over that very day.

While eating, Willy began asking Lilly a bunch of questions. From time to time, she looked at Peter to see just how much she should share. She kept it light and short. Peter had told him a lot already. But they talked about their interests and found they had quite a few things in common. Willy asked Lilly to share about her conversion, so she joyfully complied. Willy noticed how she lit up when she talked about God. He loved her already.

"Hey, there is an Imperials concert in Carlton just over the mountain," Willy said. "It's a Sunday night in a mega church. Tickets are only eight dollars apiece. Do you want to go? And it's on me." Willy slapped his chest.

They'd discussed mutual love for music already. But Willy hadn't told her where he worked. He'd only shared about his dream of being a drummer with a traveling Christian pop rock band. He felt this was his calling in life. It just hadn't happened yet.

Peter had been quietly watching the two of them. *They did seem to hit it off really well,* he thought. But he had to intervene here. "Willy, you're not thinking of taking her over the mountain in your, uh, grand chariot, piece-of-junk limousine, are you?" Peter asked in a stern voice.

"Well, Pete man, we could ride our bikes. You up to it, Lillian?" Willy looked at Lilly to see if she'd play along.

"Sure, I'm a century bike rider, didn't you know?" She laughed, enjoying the lighthearted banter.

Peter, on the other hand, didn't think it was so funny. "Come on, Willy. You can't take Lilly in what you call a car over the mountain. Something could happen!" He was furious. "You're getting way out of hand, Willy. You can be very young and foolish at times. You can be too outlandish for your own good," he said, barely controlling his temper.

The room got quiet, and all eyes were on Peter. Clearly, there was something going on here.

Willy, feeling as though he had been scolded, did not appreciate this fatherly part about his cousin. But instead of reacting like his flesh wanted to, he decided to be kind instead.

"Peter, are you offering to take us in your plush new vehicle? If so, I'd be happy to pay for the gas," Willy said.

Willy had him on this one. He had invited Veronica to this very concert and was surprised that she had agreed, so Peter couldn't take the two of them along.

"You know I can't, Willy," Peter said. He gave Willy "the look," hoping he would remember he had a car mate for the evening.

"Well, Peter, that puts me in a predicament. I tell you what. I'll make sure it's at least running." He laughed and looked at his cousin.

Peter's eyes narrowed.

"I mean running well. I will take blankets, water, and a flare, along with my tinker tools. How's that for making it safe for you to allow Miss Lillian to accompany me to the concert?" He flashed a big smile at Lilly from the floor where he was sitting, waiting for Peter to answer. While Peter hesitated, Willy added as tenderly as possible, "And really, I don't need your permission for me or my date."

The words were said lovingly, but Peter got the point. He wasn't in charge of Willy or Lilly. He just let his head get in the way and cloud his thinking, forgetting that these two people were adults.

"Point taken, both of you. I'm sorry I intervened in your affairs. Sorry, Willy, for saying the things I did," Peter said calmly. He then began to clean up. It was getting late, and he had to get up early in the morning, unlike his night-owl cousin.

Lilly didn't know what to do. She was uncomfortable with them having a squabble over her. She didn't want them to have words about anything, much less her. She gently said, "Peter, remember I probably lived and traveled every day in a vehicle in much worse repair. And God has taken care of me thus far," she pleaded, looking into his eyes. He was standing, holding the pizza box to throw it away, when she spoke again. "We have to trust," she said softly.

"Thank you for reminding me, Lilly," he said.

Willy noticed the tenderness there.

Peter went on in a more normal voice, "If you're ready, Lilly, I probably need to get you home."

"Thank you Willy, for your offer. I'll be glad to go with you," Lilly said with a smile flashing her heart into Willy's own. "It has been a joy to get to know you. I look forward to seeing what God has for you in the days to come," she said and turned to go but stopped, "And I hope I'm here to see it."

Willy went to the door and said, "It's about a two-hour drive including getting parked and such. So if you're up to it, how about I take you out for lunch after church and then we can just head on over, maybe stop at a Christian bookstore on the way and check out some albums to see what kind of beats we can drum up." He smiled and finished by saying, "And then on to the concert."

"That sounds great. I'll see you Sunday, Willy," she said and went down the stairs to Peter's car.

"That was an absolutely lovely time, Peter," Lilly thanked him. "It was the best fellowship I've had in a while," she said. "I haven't had a lot of that in my life, so I guess I'm really hungry for it and consume it like a starving child. Thanks for making that possible."

"It's all my pleasure, Lilly," Peter said. "Once again, I forget and take for granted the blessings of fellowship that have been at my feet and not so much yours over these past years."

"Your Willy is quite a guy! You were right. He is crazy." She was laughing. "But I mean a sweet kind of crazy, if there is such a thing."

"I tried to warn you."

"Yes, you did. But in all his crazy goings-on, he loves the LORD deeply, and you can tell. That is refreshing."

"Yes. I must agree with you there," Peter said. "Willy's heart for the things of God will bring anyone conviction," Peter went on to say, stealing a glance at Lilly. "I told you he reminded me of you."

"What I can't seem to figure out is his voice." Lilly was clearly frustrated, shaking her head. "His voice. I know that voice. But where would I have heard Willy's voice?" Before he could answer, she asked, "Is that dumb or what?" She was so confused.

Peter began to laugh.

"Why are you laughing?"

"Willy didn't tell you what he does for a living, did he?" Peter asked.

"Well, no, he didn't," she mused, thinking hard. "We talked about many things including what he wanted to do in the future, and we talked a lot about music," she said, forgetting that Peter was there when all this was discussed.

"Willy is the disc jockey for WAZE, The Ways of the Master Christian music radio station," Peter said, watching Lilly's reaction. "He works the night shift, three to eleven, Monday through Friday."

"That's it! That's it!" She snapped her fingers. She was so excited she could hardly stand herself. "That's where I've heard that voice. I listen to it every night on my way home from the restaurant and while I get ready for bed." Lilly was so animated that she'd found out what had been bugging her. "I've always had a love for the radio since I didn't have money to buy any Christian cassette tapes, nor did I have a tape player," she admitted. "So when I got to Farmington, the first thing I did was find a good Christian music station," she said. "Not all disc jockeys are easy on the ears, if you know what I mean."

He nodded.

"He's quite good at it, though. He fits the job perfectly with his energy and quick wit, along with his love for people."

"I agree with you," Peter said. "I think he enjoys his job, though he'd trade it for a touring band any day."

They were almost home when she asked about their living arrangements. How they worked things out was most curious to her. "So tell me, Peter, how is it that two of the most opposite people can actually live together and not have the apartment complex go up in flames?"

"Well, you got one thing right. We are different as night and day," Peter said with an exaggerated sigh. "I think what makes it work for us is the foundation being Christ. If we didn't have the desire to please God in how we live and treat each other, it wouldn't work. Though I've given him times to doubt my integrity." He went on, "Just like tonight, we have to, at times, remind each other of our territories and responsibilities." He was regretful in what he'd said. "We hold each other accountable too, and we have set some rules to help determine our lines."

"How do you have any time to yourself? It would seem being an English major and having a love for literature as you do that quiet time would be important to you," Lilly said.

"Well, we trade days," Peter said. "Willy has Saturdays, and I have Sundays. The person who does not have the day has to leave by nine a.m. and not come home until eight p.m.," Peter explained. "I'm thankful most days that I have Willy as a roommate."

Lilly now understood why Peter had seemed to have all day yesterday at the park and why Willy wanted to stay out all day next Sunday. It was all coming together now. They were pulling into the driveway at her aunt's.

"Thank you for sharing, Peter," she said softly. "This evening has been the tops for me. I'm forever indebted to you. I'm looking forward to next Sunday. Oh! I forgot I'll not be able to go with you since I'm going to the concert, but maybe the week after," she said in a hopeful voice.

"If you are interested in continuing the Bible study, I'll be here," he said with a smile.

"You're the best, Peter," she said, so full of joy. "Good night. See ya in the morning." Then Lilly looked sternly at him. "And no making fun of my bags!"

Back at the apartment, Peter threw his keys on the table. He then went to Willy's studio and leaned on the doorjamb while he watched Willy jam away. After a few minutes, he flicked the light switch to get Willy's attention. Willy hit the cymbals, stuck his drumsticks in his back pocket, and smiled at his roommate.

"Back already?"

"I didn't have to take her to the moon. What did you expect?" Peter asked.

"I'm just surprised you let her out of your sight for that long," he teased mercilessly.

"So what did you think of my Dorothy and Toto?" Peter ignored his teasing and asked.

"The only thing I want to know is when are you two gonna get married?" Willy asked, completely serious, with the biggest grin on his face.

Peter was stunned. "What are you talking about?" Peter questioned incredulously. "Are you nuts? She's just a kid," Peter said. "I'm not in love with Lilly." Then he said more calmly, "At least not that way. Besides, she's my student." He was rubbing the back of his neck.

"Yeah right. And does Veronica know about Lillian?" Willy wished to know.

"Yes and no," Peter answered.

"What do you mean? Man, you can't be seeing both of 'em at the same time," Willy admonished. "I might not be the smartest thing on the block, but you're asking for trouble." Willy let out a low whistle. "Gonna getcha in trouble, ol' Pete."

"Lilly knows about Veronica. But Veronica doesn't know about Lilly," Peter said.

They sat down in the living room, and Peter shared his heart with Willy. Willy was always a great listener.

CHAPTER 10

It was the Sunday, the day of the concert. Lilly had to put her hand over her mouth, holding back the laughter. She'd never quite seen the likes of this piece of work Willy drove. She wasn't sure how old it was, but she did know it was old. She thought it might be a 1970 or so four-door Chevy Nova. It had an old tennis shoe on the driver's side mirror and a upside down Coke can on the antenna. It was rusted in more places than not. And there was a pink-with-purple-trim hand mirror for the passenger side mirror that someone had glued on and let the glue drip down the side, whereupon it dried permanently.

"Sorry I'm late. I had to say good-bye to a little girl on the bus and get changed," Lilly said.

Willy held his hands open wide in a mimic bow. "Not a problem. Your chariot awaits." He began to open the door for Lilly, then he stopped. "You're not afraid, are you?" Willy asked, knowing she must be horrified.

Lilly was still laughing. "No," she said and got in. Towels covered the torn seats and the air vents were twist-tied open. He had a miniature drum and sticks that hung over his rearview mirror, along with two guitar picks on a string. Lilly didn't think she could hold in her laughter. She said the first thing that came to her mind. "Willy, this is so you."

"That it is, but I must say I don't get very many dates this way." He laughed. They were off to a good start for the day. "Not too many gals are as brave as you," he said with a wink.

"Okay, Willy. So tell me, since I'm sorta not so smart about these things, why in the world is there a tennis shoe on your mirror?" she asked with another giggle.

"Oh, that's easy," he answered. "I've a tendency to turn sharp when I park. I've almost taken off Peter's car mirror and hit my parents' mailbox three times turning into their driveway. So this was my solution. It's that simple. So tell me, Miss Parker, where do you want to eat lunch?"

"Well, it doesn't really matter to me, but good, ol' McDonald's sounds great," she simply said as though it were a steakhouse.

"McDonald's it is, then. That was easy," Willy said as he turned down the main road. "How was your week?"

"It was great. Especially after I found out what was bugging me last Sunday evening," she replied in an excited voice.

"Well, don't keep me in suspense. Spit it out."

"I think I should since you kept me in suspense," Lilly teased.

"What are you talking about, girl? You gonna drive me crazy," Willy retorted with curious laughter, thinking he really liked Peter's Dorothy.

"There's no chance of that happening," Lilly said as she rolled her eyes in laughter. "I think you've already taken that road trip."

"I thought I was bad. I bet you're a trip for Peter to keep up with." He laughed, thinking about his cousin. He shook his head. Yeah, Lillian would definitely take Peter for the ride of his life.

"Well, what I think I've really done is made a mess for him and Veronica," she said sadly. "At times, I wonder if I should just leave so Peter can go back to life as it was before I came," she reasoned, looking out the window.

"Oh now, girly." Willy was grinning and shaking his head. "I wouldn't think that at all. Peter does have some things to work through, but God bringing you here has been very good for him." Willy paused. "Trust me."

Lilly winced and looked at Willy. "I see what you mean," she said as she let out a big laugh.

Willy had parked *very* close to the car on the other side. Lilly could see just how handy the tennis shoe on the mirror was now. Both were still laughing as they went inside, Willy held the door for Lilly. He might be a bit strange, but he was a gentleman, she noticed.

"That was great," Lilly said as soon as they were back in the car after lunch.

"What? The food?" Willy was beginning to wonder if Lilly knew how to cook at all if she thought that was great. He scratched his head on that one.

"No, silly," Lilly declared animatedly. "The witnessing opportunity," she said, referring to the incident that had just happened inside McDonald's. "That's what we are here for," Lilly said with her heart showing through her eyes.

Willy saw what Peter meant now about being able to see into Lillian's very soul through those eyes of hers. She was a jewel. He said, "Let's just pray for them real quick." He proceeded to do so, Lilly joined in with her own prayers for those little boys and that lonely man inside.

They were well on their way when Willy brought up the subject again about the suspense Lilly was keeping from him.

Lilly laughed and repeated exactly what Willy said on the radio between songs: "Good evening. This is YoYo Willy on your drive home, bringing you up when you're down, coming at you with non-stop praise and ad-o-ray-tion, right here at WAZE, The *Ways* of the Master, the only Christian music station that rocks with the Rock. So fasten your seatbelts and set the cruise!" She had mimicked him so perfectly, even changing her voice, though she had a hard time not laughing.

"Am I being made fun of here?" Willy asked in plain innocence.

Lilly got a hold of herself and said, "Why, no Willy." She gave him a big smile. "Actually, I love hearing you on the radio. I was racking my brain on the way home last Sunday night. I finally asked Peter where I had heard your voice before. He told me. And sure enough, the light bulb clicked on and I knew I had been listening to you for over two months."

"What are some of your favorite hits?"

He wanted to catalogue some and play them for her in the future. He, of course, being very familiar with most all that was out there in the Christian music arena, knew all the songs she mentioned. They talked the rest of the way to the concert about different songs and their meanings. Willy shared about the singer's testimonies, if he knew. They had a great time.

Lilly had never been inside a church this big before. Willy saw her amazement and grinned.

"Big, huh?"

"Yeah," she marveled, moving her head in all directions, taking in the enormous building. The lights lowered thirty minutes before show time. By then, she could hardly tell it was a church. Lilly's eyes were huge, taking in all the instruments, cords, and amps. She leaned over and smiled. "And I thought your room was magnificent!"

Willy took the opportunity to bring Lilly into his world. He began with one piece at a time, telling her everything that was on the stage. Willy was enjoying every moment. He thought, not for the first time that day, what a delight Lilly was to be around.

"Wow!" was all Lilly could say. She still held that look of a little child in the candy store when the concert began.

If Willy thought he'd seen all there was to this creature, he was about to learn more. And so was Peter. For He and Veronica had arrived fifteen minutes before start time and were in the balcony. Peter had a bird's-eye view of both Willy and Lilly. He often found his eyes straying their way. What he saw was Lilly worshiping like he'd never seen. At first, she was clapping along with everyone else. At times, he saw her raising her hands in worship. It was clear she was moved by the words of the songs. He thought she might even have been crying once or twice. This was a side of her he hadn't contemplated before. It was like he was looking while she bore her soul to her Savior. He had to look away.

Peter was enjoying the concert too. He really liked this group. He glanced over at Veronica, who was trimming her nails. She smiled at him when she noticed his gaze. He returned the smile, but he didn't see the same heart he saw in Lilly. The words didn't seem to move her. At another time, he saw her slipping out her calendar and going over some pages. It was then that he glanced back at Lilly. At first, his heart jumped. He thought something was wrong. Then he realized that she was kneeling in prayer, her head facedown in her arms. He watched Willy kneel beside her. He assumed Willy was praying with her.

What a difference the two were. Here he was in casual dress attire, Veronica in her tailored red business suit. Both seemed a bit stuffy compared to Lilly, who was in a pair of jeans and had her hair in braids, being herself, and Willy, wearing what he always wore—both of them not caring what others thought of them but feeling free to worship their hearts out.

After some time, Veronica finally looked at her watch. Then she leaned over and asked, "How much longer, sweetie?"

Her closeness caused Peter to stiffen. He was appalled at Veronica's line of questioning. But he smiled and said, "I'm not sure, but it can't be too much longer."

It was clear that her heart was elsewhere. Peter made one final glance at his cousin and Lilly. Not too long after, the concert ended. Instruments were playing, and the lead singer was talking.

Veronica nudged Peter. "Hey, maybe we should leave now and beat the crowd," she said, gathering her things.

Peter was so embarrassed. "You mean right now?" Peter asked, hoping she would realize that she was being rude.

"Of course! If we wait, we'll be clobbered in the crowd and it'll take us forever to get out of this place," Veronica said in no uncertain terms. Peter reluctantly followed her out of the balcony, and out of the church. He was not happy about leaving. He wanted to be a part of what God was doing in that place.

As he maneuvered in traffic Peter decided not express his embarrassment but instead asked, "How did you like the concert?"

"Oh, it was nice but very crowded. I suppose I'll have to put on extra makeup in the morning to cover the dark rings under my eyes that I'm sure will be there," she fretted. She thought what a waste of time the evening had been.

As he was driving home, Veronica fell asleep. This gave him time to consider what might be going on, for he was confused as ever about what he felt for these two women that seemed to give his heart no peace. But after considering all that had happened since the beginning of the semester, he still came up empty. He decided to just pray. He prayed for God to show him what to do in these relationships. He prayed for Willy too. He was surprised at how quickly they got home and how pleasant the time was with Veronica asleep. The time with the LORD had been awesome.

On the other hand, Willy and Lilly were having the time of their lives. Willy had managed to get on stage and talk with the group, and of course, he brought Lilly with him. They stayed late. There were only a few people left when they headed to Willy's car. Willy cranked the car, only to hear the grindings of a dead car. Lilly's eyes got big with worry because it was very late. Willy did the funniest thing. He got out his two drum sticks, and went to the hood of the car and did a number on it. He put the sticks away, got in, and cranked the car. It turned over, and he put it in gear and pulled out of the parking lot.

Lilly had never seen the likes. Her eyes still big as saucers, she said, "Wait a minute, Willy. What just happened here? Am I to understand that the car doesn't start and then you get out and play a little tune and all of a sudden it starts?" she asked in total confusion.

"No, Lilly. I'm not superstitious, if that's what you think," he said calmly. "But I do believe in the power of prayer. So the drum playing on the hood was just to give me time to ask the LORD Almighty to start the car so that I could honor Peter and take you home safely." He looked over at Lilly. "And God was gracious to us both that we didn't have to walk."

Lilly couldn't take it all in. She had a lot to learn. She simply said out loud with her head bowed, "Thank You, LORD Jesus. Help me to trust like Willy does." She raised her head, in awe of the miracle.

"What was your favorite song tonight?" Willy asked to lighten the mood.

That did it. They were off, talking about the night's events all the way home.

Peter rolled over and looked at the clock when Willy came in the door. He'd been home and trying to sleep for almost two hours. He rolled back over, glad that Willy had made it home, which meant Lilly was safe at home too. Now he could sleep.

CHAPTER 11

On Saturday, Lilly found herself soaking in the approaching autumn at the park down the street. She'd taken her schoolbooks. She loved to get out and do her studies under the oaks. Looking around, she could tell the color changes were going to be upon them anytime now.

Peter just stood there, staring at Lilly. She was twisting her hair around her pencil as she was reading her text book. That she was concentrating hard was evident. He thought again about the surprise he was planning at Christmas. It gave him a smile as he walked over and took the pencil from her hair.

"How's my ragmuffin today?" he asked, surprising her.

"Oh!" Lilly almost jumped out of her skin. "You rascal, you like to have scared me half to death! What brings the most handsome professor that Shaftner State Community College has to a broken-down, long-forgotten park on the other side of town?"

He was still standing with one foot on the bench opposite where she was sitting. She was delighted to see him, and Peter read as much in her eyes.

"Oh. I was just wondering if the sun was as magnificent on the other side of town as it was on mine," he mused as he looked at the beautiful sky.

"Oh really," Lilly played along. "Well, I can assure you, Professor Collins, it's gorgeous over here. And now that you know, I guess you can be on your way," Lilly said as she innocently went back to her studies not really seeing the pages.

Peter, acting as though he thought she really didn't want company, walked away looking dejected and disappointed, hoping she would call him back. He was three steps away when he heard that ever-so-sweet voice beckoning him to turn around.

"Oh, Peter, please don't go. I was just being a tease."

Peter sat down.

"So tell me, Professor Collins, how are things going with Veronica?"

Lilly was looking so sweetly at Peter that for a moment, Peter couldn't look away.

Lilly always had a way of making Peter's day brighter. He wondered if that was not just the thing that had brought him over here to this dive of a park.

Lilly, sensing his hesitation, immediately looked down "I'm sorry, Peter. It's really none of my business," she said softly. "I'm sorry I asked."

The sad thing, Peter thought, was that Lilly really did care; yet his thoughts of Veronica were not so caring. It seemed that lately she really didn't care for him so much, or at least the things that were important to him. The changes in his heart that were overflowing into his life seemed to repulse Veronica. He wasn't sure what was going on there. He reached over and tipped Lilly's chin up to look at him.

"You are right, Lilly. It is my private affair. But I can also see how easy it is for you to ask about my life, seeing as our lives are so entwined," he said soberly.

"I do forget my place sometimes. Again, this is the problem of our unique friendship. I care about you. And she's part of your life, so it's natural for me to ask," she said as she tapped her pencil on her book.

"Ah, yes. My ever-caring Lil. What would I ever do without you?" he asked tenderly.

"It seems to me you were doing fine just a month ago, and now it seems I've caused you nothing but trouble," she said with a loneliness that tore at Peter's heart.

"Again, Lilly, I'll say that my professor side says it's none of your business, but the Lilly side of me can't refuse you." He sighed. "You've the most magnificent way of brightening my day!" He smiled at her. "And that's why I found myself over here, not to see if the sun shines brighter on this side of town. But to see you, knowing that being with you I'll have a joy-filled day, sent me right on over," he said, satisfied that he'd been so open.

"That's a tall order if I ever heard one," Lilly said, not sure how to reply. "I'm just me, nothing special." Changing the subject, she asked, "So, is everything all right?"

"Well, I just don't know what's going on these days with Veronica," Peter said. He went on as if he were in his own world. "It seems the closer my walk is with the Lord, the farther it gets from her." Peter shook his head. "I have been praying so much that God will go before me and that I'll honor Him in my relationship with Veronica. But it just seems the more I pray the worse it gets." He looked hopelessly at Lilly.

It pained Lilly to see Peter suffer like this. So she answered what she thought God would have her say. "I'm so sorry to hear of this trouble, Peter." She placed her hand on his. "If I've learned one thing, it's that God knows best," she assured him. "Whatever He has for you, He'll reveal it to you if you continue to seek Him. And remember that He uses all kinds of people, circumstances, and challenges, along with Scripture, to make His will known."

She patted his hand. "I'll pray for you about this, Peter," she said softly.

"You're a jewel, Lil. See how much you have encouraged me already?" He smiled. "It does seem like I've been seeing some answers. As God has convicted me about areas in my life and I seek to obey, it causes arguments with Veronica, which then illuminates more and more of her true colors, so to speak." He seemed saddened by this new revelation of someone he thought he knew. "It's as though I don't even know her," he ended forlornly.

Lilly wanted to offer some kind of comfort. "Well, it's for sure and certain that the Light, when shined, will reveal darkness. And that is what you are doing, Peter. And if she hasn't seen this before and your relationship was not built around spiritual values, then this is like blinding light in sore eyes or rubbing salt in an open wound," she continued. "It doesn't sound like she's changed her heart about you but that you have changed what is important to your heart," Lilly said, hoping to this would comfort Peter.

"I hadn't thought of it that way before, but I think you are right," Peter declared. It seemed a huge burden had been lifted, allowing his face to smile again. "Thank you, Lilly." He was quiet for a moment and then changed the subject. "So, by the way, I stopped by to see if you wanted me to pick you up for church tomorrow night."

"Ah, yes, that would be great, if it's no trouble," Lilly replied.

"Believe me." Peter chuckled. "It's no trouble."

He thought they both needed a change of subject. "So what are you studying so fiercely that anybody can walk up and take you captive before you look up from your book?" he teased.

"If you recall, Professor Collins, I have to study hard to make it. I was working on some ideas for my English paper."

Since he knew the topic—writing about your favorite literature piece—he also knew what she was thinking since they shared a mutual love for the same piece. It had entwined their hearts.

"Hey, we could read *The Hedge of Thorns* together again," he said before he knew what he was saying. He was staring at her, and for a moment, she couldn't look away.

Lilly moved and broke the spell. "I would love to, Peter. I don't think you have to ask. But what about Veronica?" she wanted to know. "How's she going to like you spending that kind of time with a female student?" Lilly asked, knowing she had to lay this one on the line, as Peter seemed blind to the fact that this might not help his situation with Veronica.

He rubbed the back of his neck. "I see what you mean. I think anyway." He was trying to think this through. He didn't like having restraints put on his and Lilly's relationship, for it was of the purest nature. But folks might not see it that way. "Well, you have a point," he said.

"Well, if it doesn't remind you too much of the olden days, you could call out these biology terms for correct spellings and definitions to help prepare me for my biology test? And if you're still not scared off, I'll let you give me advice for my English paper. You've heard that I have a harsh taskmaster in that class!"

Peter rolled his eyes. "If it reminded me of any day in the olden days, I would relish it." He gave her one of his special smiles. "And as for that mean English professor, I never heard of him."

Lilly had been at work for about two hours when they walked in. Lilly took a deep breath.

This time, she said to herself, *I'm not giving into my fears, L*ORD*. Help me!*

Alisha came around the corner and said, "Two in booth C, Lillian." She smiled. "And it's that guy of yours again." She went on to say, "And, hey, if you want me to wait on them, I'd be glad to. He was a great tipper."

"I appreciate it, Alisha. But this time, I'm not going to run in fear, for my God is not a God of fear." She went on cleaning her hands and grabbing her order pad.

Alisha was completely stunned that Lillian didn't get mad at her for trying to take advantage of her. *That Lillian girl is something*, she went off saying.

"Hello, Professor Collins. Hope this evening is going well for you and this lovely lady," she said as she squatted down table level to take their orders. "What can I get you to drink while you look over our selections tonight?" she asked sweetly.

"Hello, Lilly … Lillian." He stumbled over his words. "I'd like you to meet Professor Hughbert." He motioned with his hands. "Veronica, this is one of my best students, Lillian Parker." He twinkled at Lilly.

"Ah. It is nice to meet you. I am sure you are a great student because you have a fantastic English professor." She looked at Peter with longing eyes, trying to make a score with him as she squeezed his hand across the table.

Lilly, feeling like she was intruding on a private moment, said, "Yes, he's hard; but I'm learning so much." She ended with, "I really have enjoyed my classes at Shaftner."

It was clear that Veronica didn't want to carry on a conversation when she said, "Well, are you going to get our drinks or just stand there?"

Lilly, not accustomed to such snide and unkind behavior, softly said, "Oh. Yes, ma'am. Sorry about the delay. What can I get you to drink?" She took their orders and glanced at Peter, who had an unhappy look on his face. She scrambled to get the drinks back to them.

"This doesn't have enough ice in it," Veronica said. "Please redo it."

"Oh. I'm sorry I didn't get it right." Lilly grabbed the glass and went back to the kitchen, praying all the way.

Lord, help me. This is going to be harder than I ever realized.

She put as much ice as would fit in the glass even though that was not how she was trained. She put the drink down in front of Veronica. "Have you guys found a selection that tempts your taste buds tonight?" she asked, waiting patiently to take their order.

Veronica ordered something she'd never ordered before and asked for outlandish changes. Peter couldn't believe his ears. To say he was embarrassed was an understatement. He didn't know what had come over her. Peter knew Lilly was nervous and desperately didn't want to mess up. He wished they hadn't come at all.

The whole dinner was miserable. Veronica made Lilly take her meal back twice for no reasons that Peter could find. One of the times, it was just that she had changed her mind. The next was that the uneaten part of her dish had gotten cold so she wanted it reheated. Every time Lilly came to the table, Veronica seemed to have it in for her. However, Lilly remained sweet and gentle. Peter was disturbed and even mad at Veronica for being so unkind to his Lil. He'd even tried several times to talk about what he was learning in the Sunday evening Bible study, but she seemed disinterested. She just talked about the upcoming student body events and about the movie she'd gone to see without him. It seemed she was itching for a disagreement, but Peter didn't give in. He was glad when the evening was over. And so was Lilly.

She was like a damp rag when they left. Lilly went over to clear away the remaining dishes. There on the table was a folded one-dollar bill. But Lilly didn't know until later that it had a fifty-dollar bill wrapped inside. She didn't think she'd done a good job, and she didn't want to take Peter's money. She planned to return it when she saw him next.

On Sunday morning, Peter watched for Lilly to come in. As he looked around, he noticed her at the back, talking to a strange man he hadn't seen before. But then, it was a big church and there was no way of knowing everyone. But it concerned him. From where Peter was sitting, Lilly seemed quite friendly in her conversation with this strange man. She even patted the two boys with him on their heads and then took them off to children's church, he guessed. When she came back in, she sat at the front in her normal seat. He looked back to where the man was and saw Willy sitting there with him. He was determined to ask Lilly about it that evening.

The afternoon passed, and Lilly had just gotten in the car with Peter when both spoke at the same time. "No. You go ahead, Peter. I'm sorry," Lilly said.

"No. You go ahead. I can wait."

"Ah, Mr. Collins, with all due respect, elders first." Lilly giggled.

"You, missy, are gonna get it one day yourself. When that first gray hair comes, I think I will frame it," he teased right back. "But since I am older, I probably should go first so I won't forget." He got serious and asked, "Who was that guy you were talking to this morning?"

"Oh, that is Mr. Morton and his two sons," Lilly said. "Willy and I met them at McDonald's last Sunday." She went on to tell Peter the whole incident at McDonald's.

Peter was thrilled and laughed. "On your first date with my cousin, he takes you to McDonald's?"

"Well, don't be too hard on him. He did ask me, and I made the suggestion. Seeing the condition of his car, I didn't want to be accused by him of not being able to make upgrades or repairs."

"It's true that Willy don't make much, but what he does have he makes a lot of," Peter said kindly.

"That was sweet of you to say."

"He really is a great guy," Peter said. "Now, what were you going to say before I rudely interrupted you?"

They were close to the church now, but Lilly wanted to get this off her chest before she lost nerve.

She laid the fifty-dollar bill in the console cubby hole and said, "I need to return this. I didn't earn it. It doesn't rightfully belong to me." She'd done the transaction very quickly.

"Whoa! Wait a minute. Slow down." Peter was motioning with his hand. "What are you talking about?" Peter was sizing up the situation all right but wasn't about to take that well-deserved money back. He needed to handle this carefully. "First of all, let's get this straight," Peter said. "I was so embarrassed last night. I've not ever seen Veronica talk to someone so demeaning." Peter looked over to see if she was listening and taking all this in. "But I was angry that she would treat you like that. The only reason I didn't call her on the carpet right then and there was I didn't want to make a scene and harm your testimony or your employment status. And Veronica seemed to be in a mood to take on anyone or anything." Peter went on. "I hoped by my silence you were not offended at me or that you thought I didn't care that you were treated so disdainfully."

"Oh no. It was all my fault. For whatever reason, I didn't please her. She's the customer, and the customer always comes first." Lilly ended by saying, "Please. I will not take the money."

"To be sure, you will. And if you don't, I'll pull rank on you." Peter was being stern, and Lilly knew it. "I'm older, you know," he said. "And I disagree completely with you that you would think it was your fault at all." They were pulling in the parking lot now. "Lilly, she was all but a big brat!" Peter hissed out. "And of all things, I don't want us to argue about this," Peter said softly. "It's not like you don't need the money to pay for your schooling." He put the money in her hands and looked her in the eye. "I don't want to hear another word. Do you hear me?"

"Well, your car will look like Willy's if you keep giving your money away like this." She laughed and scooted out before he could comment.

They had a nice time in Bible study, both taking notes and learning so much. Lilly had to admit she liked sitting with Peter. She felt a sense of security. Plus, Willy came and sat by her on the other side. Not only was the singing and the message great. So was finally belonging.

CHAPTER 12

"Hello, James. It's a pleasure to meet you." Lilly was looking into the gray-haired, smiling face of her aunt's ex-husband. Lilly had just set the coffee cake on the table, thinking this time at least she didn't burn it. Her aunt seemed to be taking longer than normal to get out there, so she'd answered the door. Lilly almost cried when she spotted the flowers he had in his hands. "Here. Let me get a vase for those flowers." Lilly moved to do so he could release his treasured burden.

"Thank you," was his kind reply. "I hope she'll like them." Lilly looked up to see his face. He was grinning from ear to ear.

About that time, Aunt Maureen came in. "Good morning, James," Maureen said, "Did you meet Lilly already?"

"Yes. That must be the sweet young lady who took my bundle of flowers I brought for you to make them purty." James smiled at Maureen.

She looked away. She couldn't stand to see his care for her. "You didn't need to do that."

"I know, but I wanted to. Seeing as I missed so many other opportunities in the past, I don't want to miss this one." He said tenderly.

"I ain't promising anything. Ya hear?" Aunt Maureen was not falling for this kind gesture of his. This was all about his meeting her niece. Though she did wonder why she'd tried on four different outfits to find the right one. She wanted to make sure he knew his place. But when she went in the kitchen, she just raved over the flowers.

James and Lilly shared both their salvation stories. They shared about what they had been doing since their conversions. They even spoke about a few verses. James went on to talk about how much learning he'd done and how much God had changed his life. He wished he could do a lot of things over and do them right.

He looked over at Maureen, who had a single tear running down her cheek. She had been quiet so the two could get to know each other. But she hadn't reckoned on seeing James's heart so vividly. She was undone by all he'd shared. She knew he was speaking the truth.

Before James left, Lilly invited him to hear her speak at church the next Sunday evening. She'd already invited her aunt. She even went so far as to suggest he pick her aunt up, hoping she would not get kicked under the table. And to her great surprise, her aunt agreed. Lilly was thrilled beyond belief. She praised God for what He was doing in her aunt's life.

As the last student left, Lilly went to Peter's desk.

"And what brings my favorite student leisurely hanging around my desk?" Peter asked, brightened by her appearance.

"Yes. Professor Collins, I wanted to talk to you about two things. One is if you would read over this speech and give me advice, for I'm going"—she was switching her feet back and forth— "I'm going to share this Sunday night at church, and I want it to be perfect," she exclaimed.

"Really, that's great Lil." Peter was excited that Lilly had gotten this opportunity. "So let me see this speech."

She laid it on his desk and was pointing out some areas she wasn't sure about. He was leaning over her, but he couldn't get the smell of her hair out of his nostrils. He inhaled deeply, filling his senses completely. He mumbled something. He hadn't realized what that the closeness would do to him.

"Excuse me," Lilly said. "Did you say something?"

"Yes," Peter said dreamily. "Your hair, it smells lovely." He sniffed deeply. "What is it?"

"My hair? Are you talking about my hair?" Lilly asked in disbelief.

He nodded.

"I use the same thing I always have."

"Well, whatever it is, it is most intoxicating," Peter said, all smiles.

"Hello. Come back down to earth, Professor Collins. You've not heard a word I said about this paper!"

"Yeah. Right. What did you say?" Peter asked and went on to listen to Lilly's concerns about the possible problems in her speech. He read and gave his advice on the paper. "I'm really touched that you are going to share this." Peter stood back. "It'll be a blessing and an encouragement to many." He was so pleased and touched with what she was going to share.

"Are you sure you don't mind me including you?" Lilly looked him straight in the eyes. "I don't want to be an embarrassment to you in any way."

"That'll never happen." Peter touched her cheek briefly with the back of his hand.

She had to look away for fear she'd reveal all her thoughts through her eyes. She changed the subject. "Guess what," her big eyes telling him she had a secret.

"What is it, Miss Parker?"

"I met James yesterday, and both he and my aunt are coming!" Lilly said as she twirled around in excitement. "It was neat getting to know James." She went on and shared all that had happened. She ended with, "Keep praying for them, Peter."

"That is just wonderful, Lilly. I know you've been laboring in prayer and love for your aunt," he said. "I'll keep praying for all of you."

"Oh my, Peter. I've kept you way too long into your lunch," she said with guilt. "I better be off. Maybe you can catch up with Veronica yet," she said as she flew out the door.

"Likely chance of that happening," he mumbled. *She is going to make some man very happy one day,* he thought to himself, but he wondered how he was ever going to let her go when that happened. He ended up not even going to the lounge but read his Bible and prayed until his next class came in.

Lilly stopped by Peter's desk yet again on Friday. Peter, pleasantly surprised, gave her one of his raised-eyebrow smiles. He was stacking the papers they had just handed in.

"What can I do for you, Miss Parker?" he asked.

"Well," she said dryly, "you can put my paper on the bottom." She went on worriedly, "It will probably bore you to tears." She really didn't like the idea of Peter having to score her papers.

"Can't do that. Then everyone else won't benefit from your curve." Peter laughed. They both knew he was being more lenient with her grade than she deserved.

"That's one way to look at it. I guess I do the whole class a favor by going first." She laughed. "Makes everyone else do better! But that's not why I stopped by."

"You disappoint me, ragmuffin. I thought you just wanted to see me." He pushed back his chair and crossed his legs, waiting for yet another good story from Lillian Parker's life, his smile showing his pleasure.

"Quit calling me that! You would think I was a child," she teased, slapping at his pant legs, really wanting to make a point.

His eyebrows rose, saying what his lips would not admit. "And you're not?" they seemed to ask.

His grin split, and he said, "One look at you, Lilly, and there's no mistaking that you're not a child but a lovely lady." He looked her over in a sweet, understanding way. Then he continued. "Any man would be a fool to miss your elegance and beauty." He winked at her. "But you'll always be my ragmuffin. I got to go, Lil. See you Sunday," he said.

Slipping into his suit jacket while going down the hall, holding his briefcase was no small feat. But he knew he was already late and that Veronica wouldn't be happy. He slipped into a chair that was open across from Veronica, who was just finishing her salad lunch.

"So what's the excuse this time?" she asked unkindly.

He chose his words carefully. "Well, I don't suppose the reason matters so much as the loss," Peter smiled at her. "This is on me since I missed most of our lunch date. I'm sorry. Will you forgive me?" Peter asked sincerely.

"Let's just forget it. I have to go anyway." She got up, put away her trash, and turned to leave. "See you tonight?" she questioned with her pleading eyes, trying to understand what was happening to them.

"How about I grill out some steaks, bake some potatoes, and toss a salad together with all the trimmings and we can have an eat-in night. What do you say?" Peter asked. Veronica actually smiled.

"That sounds nice. What time you want me over?"

"Oh, how about six? That will give me time to make things special for our dinner," Peter said, giving her a smile.

"See you then, darling," she said and slipped out the door.

Peter was quick about his shopping so he could get the grill going. He'd been busy ever since the faculty meeting to make this a nice dinner for the two of them. He'd just lit the candles when Veronica knocked on the door.

Peter opened it to find that Veronica had dressed to the hilt. He wasn't sure why since they hadn't planned to go anywhere. Actually, Peter was caught off guard since Veronica was wearing a tightly clinging white, low-cut V-neck dinner dress.

Veronica flashed her eyes at him, her sequins sparkling on her dress. "Are you going to invite me in? I do have the right night, don't I?"

"Oh, yes. Yes. Come on in. I just have to pull the potatoes out, and we're ready." Peter was stumbling all over his words.

"Well, Pete, this is sure a nice setup you've done here. Why, you did all this for me?" Veronica questioned.

"Yes, I did," Peter said as he put the potatoes on the plates. "I hope you like it and that it will be a nice, relaxing evening for the two of us."

Veronica went to him and placed her hands on his chest.

Peter put his arms around her and kissed her and then backed up and said, "Welcome. Dinner awaits."

He was fully aware that she didn't care. She had other things on her mind. But that was not an appetite that Peter was willing to fill. With that, he pulled out her seat and she sat down with a sigh. She had thought for sure her provocative dress would get his attention, but it seemed to be failing.

They talked casually during dinner, both enjoying the nice food and companionship, though Peter longed for it to go deeper, to spiritual matters. He wanted to hear what God was doing in her life, but it never went there. And the times he shared on that level were pretty much ignored.

Dishes cleared and candles blown out, Veronica asked, "Hey, how about a movie? I hear there is a real good one. Oh, what was the name?" She paused, thinking. "I can't remember, but everyone has seen it. I hear it's action-packed." She flashed her manipulative eyes in his direction.

"Here, let me get the paper and we can check it out." Peter said as he got the paper and turned to the movie section.

Veronica, looking at it too, pointed. "Yes. That's it." She put her finger on the picture they had advertised for this film. "Have you seen it?"

With sinking dread, as Peter had feared, it was rated R. He knew this was coming. He prayed quickly that he would have the strength to stand firm for the LORD. He rubbed the back of his neck.

"Ah. No, I've not seen it." He was going to continue, but she cut him off.

"Oh goodie. I think we can even make the next-to-last showing if we hurry," she said as she was gathering her purse.

Peter caught her elbow. "Not so fast, Veronica. I need to explain something."

Veronica came to a complete halt, not sure of what he wanted to say but that he'd better be quick or they'd be late, and she couldn't stand to be late for movies.

"Veronica, the LORD has placed a conviction on my heart not to see those kinds of movies anymore. We need to pick something else out." He didn't want to condemn her, but at the same time, he needed to be steadfast with his conviction.

"Wh-what, just what, do you mean?" She blinked her eyes and stuttered.

Peter shuffled his feet, bracing himself for the blow. "It's not hard to understand. I just don't want to set things before my eyes that I will dwell upon that wouldn't be good." He was trying to make her see, but it was not working.

Veronica put her hands on her hips. "So what you are saying is that you are too good to go to the movie with me?" She was angry.

Peter shook his head. "No, I'm not saying I won't go to the movies. I have just changed my genre of choices," Peter looked at her, really wanting her to understand. "Here, let's look and see if there's another choice," he coaxed. He looked the page over. To his dismay, there weren't any other choices, so he was running out of options but still remained strong. "I've a great idea. I can go rent a movie or two and be right back. How does that sound?" He had put his arms on hers, looking at her angry face.

Veronica shrugged him off. "No thanks. I had my heart set on seeing this particular movie. Since you are obviously not going to take me, I will find someone who will. You know, there are plenty of offers that I've turned down for you. Perhaps I was wrong about you all along." She sneered and picked up her purse and went out the door.

Peter called after her, "Veronica, please don't go." Only to tossed his words to the wind.

She was in her car in just seconds, without a backward glance. She squealed out of the parking lot, leaving a much-burdened Peter in her wake.

Peter sat for a while and just prayed. Then he turned on the radio, hoping to hear Willy's comforting voice, and he was not disappointed. He then cleaned up the kitchen, praising God that He'd kept him faithful, though it had been hard.

Lilly sat on the front porch steps, waiting for Peter. It was already the beginning of October. The leaves were beginning to change, and there was beauty all around.

"What a picture of simplicity," Peter said to himself as he drove up and saw his ragmuffin sitting on the stairs without a care in the world.

She jumped up, her Bible, purse, and notebook in hand. She opened the screen door and called, "Peter is here, Aunt Maureen. Got to go. See you there." She let the door go and skipped down the sidewalk to Peter's car.

"Good evening, Miss Lillian Parker," Peter greeted with a smile. "I must say you are a very adorable ragmuffin sitting there on the porch!"

They had a nice time chatting on the drive to church. In the parking lot, he turned off the car and took Lilly's hand. "I wanted to pray with you before you speak tonight. I know we have Bible study first, but this will be the only time available, I'm afraid," Peter said.

"Thank you," Lilly said softly, touched by his caring.

Lilly sat up front in her usual morning spot so she didn't have too far to walk. She was nervous, as she hadn't ever spoken in front of a crowd this big. Yet she knew that for her LORD she could do this through His strength since it was His will for her.

After the singing the pastor got up and said, "Each month, we spotlight a ministry. This month, our spotlight shines on one of our hardest fields in this church. It's a ministry of faithful work of the heart, the bus ministry. To take a peek into this sometimes-difficult ministry is our newest member, who has jumped right in to serve in the lives of the children on the bus. Please open your hearts to Miss Lillian Parker."

Lilly walked up to the podium with wobbly legs. She adjusted the microphone haphazardly. Then she began with a squeaky voice, barely audible, but by the time she was through her first sentence, she was strong and clear. God completely took over, making this timid, weak vessel strong for His message.

"Good evening, to everyone both young and old," Lilly began. "I'd like to take you back in time a bit. I want to share this ministry from a victim's point of view. From the point of view of a child, I invite you to look into my heart. Journey with me, will you, to one very lonely Saturday in Arlington, Tennessee. There was a knock on my door. A little child of nine, still in my pajamas, opened the door, hoping not to wake my parents, who were still sleeping from a drunken party the night before. I poked my head around the door, with matted hair, a dirty face and sticky fingers, to see who was there. The couple who stood before me was nicely dressed and had smiles on their faces. They asked me if I wanted to ride the church bus with them the next morning.

"Now, understand, they had to wade through tall grass and beer bottles in the yard to the rusted trailer that was falling apart, in much need of repair. The front gate of the fenced yard hung half off its hinge, not exactly a safe-looking place to be. But here were people inviting me to go to church with them. The lady went on to tell me the time the bus would arrive if I'd like to come. The man asked if my parents were home. I said they were sleeping. He insisted that, of course, I should have my parents' approval. I said okay and shut the door.

"I was so thrilled that someone cared that I thought about it all day. As a matter of fact, I chewed the bubblegum she gave me for a whole week, saving it on my bedpost at night."

There were some "ughs" from the congregation, so she knew she had their attention.

"I met the bus the next morning at the end of the street so my parents wouldn't know what I was doing. I had not gotten permission, but then, they didn't really care what I did so long as I stayed out of trouble.

"I wore, if I remember correctly, rusty corduroy pants, even though it was summer; a pink velveteen pullover with three holes; dirty socks since that was all I could find in a hurry; and my old, torn-up tennis shoes, which I wore every day to school. I found out that I couldn't go to church barefoot, because I tried."

The congregation laughed.

"I don't want to focus so much on myself but to bring you to the real heart of the bus ministry, to take you to the not-so-clean *places*, to see the not-so-clean *faces* of people Jesus Christ came to save. I got on the bus that morning and sat by the window in sheer wonder. The couple never noticed my ratty clothes or uncombed hair. They just lovingly smiled and told me their names again. They also introduced me to a young teenage helper, none other than your very own church member, Peter Collins." Lilly looked straight at Peter and smiled.

Peter had forgotten about Veronica, completely taken in by the story, and smiled his biggest smile ever. He was so proud of his Lil. The old lady sitting behind Peter reached up and patted him on the shoulder.

"These three people loved me. They took me into their very hearts. They taught me so much about Jesus. They taught me about lying too. So by the time three weeks had gone by, I had to tell my parents, or they refused to let me ride. I say this unreservedly. They were the hands and feet of Jesus to me. I didn't miss a Sunday, for it was a haven for me. My mom was abusive and didn't care so much for me. My father was a drunk much of the time. Poor Peter more than once helped me lug my father up the steps and into the house. My parents argued a lot. There was no peace in my home. I spent as much time outside as possible. I called Mr. Collins 'Petah' because I had such poor speech. And, well, the cute nickname just stayed with me.

"They gave me a Bible. They truly spent their lives out for me. As years went by, I began to really understand what all these Bible stories had in common: a God who wanted me as His daughter. I couldn't believe it at first. I didn't understand. But Jeff and Jenny, the bus team leaders, and Petah, the helper never tired of showing me the way to Christ. When I was twelve years old, I cried out for Jesus to be my very own Papa. I was baptized and continued to grow and learn.

"I'll never forget that first bus ride. I'll always treasure in my heart all that I learned on the bus. For if it wasn't for the bus, I would have never taken the ride that leads to heaven. So even though the kids might drive you crazy and some might come from unloving homes, go to them. They desperately need you. This story has many twists and turns that has found me riding the church bus again right here to Grace Community Church and loving it. I've left out many details so that Pastor can feed us tonight." She chuckled. "But take this with you: Whether you give your money, your time, or your energy, it can make an eternal difference in the lives of children on those loud, gas-hoggin', big buses out there. I ask you to give your heart to this ministry both in prayer and action. You never know what life God will change through your endless, week-in-and-week-out labor in the bus ministry. I thank God for every Petah out there."

With that, she stepped down and went to the very back. Needing to be alone, she went to the last pew, which, thankfully, was empty and knelt and covered her face in her arms and wept tears of praise. God indeed had been so good to her. It was well into the message when she got up off her knees.

Lilly had spoken boldly and with much passion. It was like nothing Peter had ever heard. Even though he'd read her paper, it wasn't the same as putting fire to it. She completely missed the people standing, one at a time. Then, before she was to the back, everyone was standing and clapping and blowing their noses. She missed it all. But she was glad, for all the glory belonged to God alone. He had done marvelous things.

The pastor spoke, "I'm not sure there's an appetite left to feed."

There were several amens to that.

"That was a glorious testimony. I feel filled up already. I challenge you to take these words to heart. Just like any ministry, it's not the *program* but the *person*. Let us not ever lose sight of our command to love others with all our being in any and every ministry we do." The pastor then prayed a heartfelt prayer and preached a sermon on servant hood.

Peter had never been so glad that Lilly hadn't sat with him. Veronica had slipped in and had snuggled up against him. What a mess it would've been if Lilly had been there. Wondering about Veronica and why she'd shown up and where Lilly was going to sit took some of the delight out of his listening.

Veronica smiled at him. He smiled back in surprise. She was trying to make up for the argument they'd had on Friday night. She hoped her showing up would make a difference. But it seemed to her he was completely caught up in this girl's speech. Then she began to listen and realized that she was talking about her Pete. And this was the same girl she had read that paper about at the beginning of the semester. It was all coming together now. The one she'd seen Peter with after class a few times and the ditzy waitress were one in the same. She seethed inside. She wanted answers, and she would get them.

The service was over before Peter was ready to deal with things.

Veronica leaned over and whispered under her breath sarcastically, "You got a lot of explaining to do."

People were already headed his way, and he was immediately surrounded with hugs and slaps on the back, everyone wanting to know why he'd been holding out on them. But he hem-hawed around and snuck out the back just in time to see Veronica get into her car. He ran over to her.

"Hey, can we talk?" he asked breathlessly.

"What's to talk about?" Veronica asked and started her engine.

"For one, I need the chance to explain," Peter begged. He knew he owed her an explanation. "Hey, how about us going to McKenzie Park? It's well lit, and it's not too cool yet," he suggested. He couldn't take her to his apartment with Willy there. And he never went to her apartment since she lived alone. That, he had found out a long time ago, wasn't wise.

Veronica finally agreed. "I guess if it's not too long. I need my sleep, you know."

"Yes. I'll do my best to be quick." He gave her a quick kiss and said he'd meet her there. He jumped in his car and went right over, completely forgetting he'd left Lilly high and dry.

Inside the church building, Willy had already given her the biggest hug. "How about pizza? Our place?" he asked.

"Oh, that sounds great," Lilly said. "And if you don't mind giving me a ride, I'd appreciate it."

Willy looked around. "Where's the old man?" he asked, looking under the pews.

"Oh stop it, Willy!" she said. "Something came up." Several church folks came and hugged Lilly. They had tears and words of encouragement and lots of questions about the rest of the story. It was no time before Aunt Maureen meandered her way to her precious Lil. When Lilly saw her aunt, she grabbed and hugged her fiercely. Her aunt's face was wet with tears.

Lilly asked, "Is James here?"

Her aunt nodded and pointed, all the while blowing her nose. She moved toward him.

"James, so glad you could make it and that you brought the loveliest lady in town with you," Lilly said as she shook James's hand and winked at her aunt.

"I wouldn't have wanted to miss this for the world," James said. "Lilly, it was glorious to see how God used a simple means of man to do His will in your life as He has many others. Praise God for His unfailing love for us!"

"I will certainly amen that," Lilly said. "By the way, I want you two to meet someone special." Lilly called to Willy, who was leaning up against the back wall just watching all this transpire, enjoying every part of Lilly's sweet heart. "Willy, this is my Aunt Maureen, who took me in when I came here a poor, destitute, homeless bag of rags. And her friend James." Lilly left off the last names so as to not embarrass them.

What they saw was what Lilly was coming accustomed to: Willy in a nice, clean, white t-shirt; puka shell choker around his neck; clean, though not new pair of jeans that had his two drumsticks in his back pocket; and beige skateboard shoes with the wide rubber tops and soles.

"Aunt Maureen and James, this is Willy McCollister, Peter's cousin. They share an apartment over on Jackson Avenue."

Willy reached out his hand to greet them. "It's my pleasure to meet you. Any chance you're wanting to get rid of a boarder? I would much rather have Lilly for a roommate than Peter any day." He was getting them to laugh. "Are you sure?"

When Aunt Maureen could quit laughing, she said, "I'm quite sure. Though Lilly would be a great room boarder, I ain't givin' her up." Her aunt's fire was coming forth. "Besides, I'm an ornery old nag. You just don't know what Lilly has to put up with."

"Course, I better stay and keep that old geezer of a cousin of mine in place since evidently Lilly hasn't applied for the job," Willy said, and all eyes swung to Lilly.

"Willy, what has come over you?" Lilly was red faced. "It just so happens I like my job where I'm at. And besides, it pays more," Lilly said with a teasing toss of the head. Then, on a more serious note, Lilly looked into her aunt's eyes. "Thank you for coming, Aunt Maureen. It really meant a lot to me." She hugged her aunt again, and they left.

CHAPTER 13

Things were falling apart at the park. As soon as Peter got to the bench and sat down with his arm around Veronica, she jumped up.

"I just don't get it. What do you see in her?" she spat.

He tried to answer, but she steamrolled over him.

"I am more educated than she is. That is obvious. I make more money than she'll ever make. I have better taste in fashion. Why, she wears those, those housewifey-looking things. Her makeup is outdated, and she could use a haircut." Veronica was being hateful and pacing as she blasted Lilly in her anger. "Did you hear all the things she said? And that she still rides the church bus like a kid! How ridiculous!" she said. "I can't believe they'd even let someone like that speak in front of all those people." She sat down and looked at Peter with her steel eyes. "Just tell me, Peter, where do you fall into this picture?" She was tapping her foot. "Something tells me there is more to this student-relationship than you are letting on," she demanded.

Peter let out a big sigh. He was furious that she would speak about Lilly in such a way and totally blown away that Veronica didn't see how God had worked in Lilly's life. Actually, Peter, for the first time, saw things very clearly.

But due to his brief hesitation, she bellowed, "Are you going to answer me?"

"Yes, Veronica, I am," Peter said quietly. Peter had decided that Veronica wasn't worth his sharing the whole story, its miracles of God woven all through it, for her eyes were closed and her heart hardened to spiritual things. "I'm sure things don't look like what they really are. And I would never want to hurt you in any way," Peter said. He put a hand on the top of hers. "My whole world changed the first day of this semester when, yes, this Lillian Parker walked into my class."

"What do you mean?" Veronica was being obstinate and impatient. She withdrew from his touch.

Trying to keep it down to as few details as possible, he went on.

"Just as she shared tonight, we became very close friends. We were probably best friends over those four to five years. Then, after I went off to college and due to unforeseen circumstances, we lost contact altogether. So the first day of class was the first I'd seen her in five years. That's probably why I've been so distracted, especially the first few days, as I've had to process all this."

Veronica was actually listening for the moment.

"Why didn't you just tell me?" she questioned, feeling like he was hiding something.

"I didn't think you would understand. And really, I didn't think it really mattered, as we're just good friends," Peter said, though listening to his own words, he wondered, not for the first time, what exactly his feelings for Lilly were. He shook his head. "I wasn't hiding anything from you. We were and are just friends. We were catching up on time that we'd missed. Actually, she was the one to mention that our friendship might come between you and me." Peter said this more as a question than a statement.

"And has it?" she challenged, looking in his eyes.

Peter moved a bit and rubbed the back of his neck. "Yes and no," he said.

"Don't play games with me, Pete," she said coldly. "I'm not a Barbie that you can just use and toss out."

"Honey, please don't think that," Peter patted her hand. He leaned forward, elbows on both knees. "What I mean is that Lilly, I mean Lillian, when she came back into my life, showed me what was lacking in my own walk with God. She reminded me of those days long ago when I was so on fire for God. Actually, not but a few days into the semester, I rededicated my life to the LORD; those are the changes you are seeing in me." He looked at her. "Do you understand?" He really wanted her to.

"Do you love her?" was all Veronica asked.

"I do love her, but it's not what you think," Peter went on. "She is like a beloved little sister to me. I care deeply what happens to her. But I don't love her as in the romantic fashion you might assume."

This was not enough for Veronica. "I've got to go, Pete." Veronica had heard enough of this weird arrangement. "It's either her or me. You decide and let me know." She gave him one last, longing glare that said she felt she had been duped and walked off.

Peter put his head down and just prayed.

Oh, LORD, did I do the right thing? You're making things so clear to me. Even if Lilly wasn't in the picture, thank You so much for showing me that Veronica's heart does not belong to You before we married. Help me say and do the right things to honor You. I do not wish to hurt Veronica, but I know now that it's not Your will to continue in this relationship. Give me the strength to end this before more damage is done.

He went on to pray some more. Then he headed home.

He walked in the door, tossed his keys on the table like he always did, and looked over to see two silly adults singing, sitting around some pizza boxes. That was when he realized he'd forgotten Lilly at the church, but before he could say anything, Lilly spoke up.

"Peter, I'm worried about you." She had on the most serious face she could get. "I didn't realize Alzheimer's could set in so fast." She was barely stifling her giggles now. "You forgot that you came to church with a passenger and left without one! I think, Willy, that Peter isn't telling us the truth about his age." Lilly hoped to get a smile from him.

Peter wasn't taking the bait. He'd just had one of the hardest days of his life. He was in no joking mood. "I'm indeed sorry that I forgot you. I see my sweet cousin wasted no time in filling my shoes," he said dryly but shot Willy a thankful glance.

"Well, I had to beat all the guys off her. And in the end, she said she liked my car above all the others and she went home with me."

Willy was being Willy, and he and Lilly cracked up laughing. Peter was envious of their lighthearted banter, but he just couldn't join in tonight.

"I'll be in my room. I'll take you home when you're ready, Lilly. Just knock." With that, he turned toward his room.

Both Willy and Lilly looked at each other, wondering what was going on in that professor's head. Willy spoke up.

"Hey, bro. We saved you some pizza. Why don't you grab a piece and join us?" Willy asked, hoping to find out what was going on.

"Thanks, but I'm not hungry," Peter said as he went to his room.

As soon as the door was shut, Lilly grabbed Willy's hand. Both were sitting on the floor. "We have to pray for him," Lilly said in desperation.

Willy wholeheartedly agreed, and they prayed their hearts out for Peter, who was really hurting.

Then Lilly said she better go so Peter could get back and get some sleep for work in the morning.

"By the way, Willy, I've loved your special notes on the radio when you play my favorites. That's so kind of you." Lilly was very close to him and was smiling in his face.

"It is my pleasure, Miss Parker." He smiled and jumped up to help Lilly up off the floor.

"Thanks for the evening, bringing me here from church and getting the pizza. My heart is always encouraged in our time of fellowship in song, Word, testimony, and laughter. You're really a special guy," Lilly said and went and knocked on Peter's door.

Peter opened it. "Are you ready?"

"Yes, if you don't mind," Lilly said softly.

Peter looked so tired. She even wondered if he'd been crying.

"Let me get my keys," Peter said and headed to the door.

"Good night, Willy." Lilly waved and was out the door.

Peter had been completely quiet. Lilly couldn't take it anymore and laid her hand on his arm, trying to see his face. "Are you okay?" she asked.

He knew she was worried. But he didn't want to talk about Veronica with Lilly right then, so he said, "I will be. Don't worry about me, ragmuffin." He was trying to set her at ease while his heart broke in two.

Lilly didn't know what to do. She knew that something terrible was wrong with Peter; however, it was also very obvious he didn't want to talk about it. So she decided to remain quiet.

Peter was sad about the fact that this all had to happen on this very special night of Lilly's. She'd been just beautiful up there on the platform. He remembered her voice, strong and sweet at the same time. Her heart in her eyes was seen by all. His heart overflowed for joy just thinking about all Lilly had shared. He was proud to be her Petah, which was why, all the more, he was sickened at Veronica's thoughts of the evening.

"Hey, look at me," he said while he glanced her way. "I was so proud of you tonight."

She was about to protest, but he raised his hand to finish.

"I'm giving all glory and honor to God, for He alone can do as He pleases and has blessed me tremendously by allowing me to be your Petah. I just wanted you to know I do not have the words my heart wants to say about all you shared." He went on. "I don't believe I was the only one touched either, listening to all the sniffles. You just let God fill you up and speak through you. It was awesome to hear your heart's passion and the challenge you gave people like me to get out of our complacency and to get involved in others lives. Thank you," he said softly.

Lilly was astonished at Peter's words. She wasn't sure what he'd thought. "Thank you for what?" Lilly asked.

He looked at her again as he pulled into her aunt's driveway. "For being you," Peter said. "For still being that same ol', loving ragmuffin I met on that first bus ride." Peter about had her in tears, and he knew she could take no more. "Scoot. This *old* man needs some sleep."

Lilly did not have any words left. "You're the best," she said, and she went into the house.

Willy was playing his drums when Peter came back in. But he was purposefully watching out for him. He stopped just as Peter reached his bedroom doorknob.

"Hey, Peter? You all right?"

He continued going in his room but replied over his shoulder, "Yep. I'll be just fine." He had a tone of pain but resolution that God had led the way and he'd followed, though it hurt terribly.

Willy jumped up, put his drumsticks in his back pocket, and was leaning against the doorjamb as Peter took off his shoes and placed them neatly in his immaculate closet. "Lilly was awesome tonight, wasn't she?" Willy said with a huge smile, his arms crossed like he had all the time in the world to talk.

Peter perked his ears but just looked at Willy, trying to see where he was going with this. "Yes, she was," Peter said wryly. He didn't elaborate on his thoughts about it. Willy had this look on his face that Peter couldn't put his finger on. Peter had taken off his socks and put them in the clothesbasket and then leaned back on the headboard. "You're not falling for her, are you?" Peter hadn't given this any thought until now. They had only met, but they were sure fast friends and enjoying themselves so much that Peter began to wonder.

Willy let out a howl of a laughter that shook his whole body. Still leaning on the doorjamb, he said, "To tell you the truth, it would be easy to do. She is the most heartwarming, people-loving, God-worshiping woman I've ever met." Willy was looking right at Peter to see if he was listening. "But she's too close to family to even make her a consideration for anything serious." Willy shuffled his feet. "I can see what a magnet she must have been for you and why you fell so hard for her." Willy was pushing for all it was worth. "But what about now? She's not a little girl anymore, Peter." Willy wasted no time in the punch. "If you don't snatch up this precious jewel, someone else will."

This shot Peter up out of the bed. "What do you mean, Willy?" He didn't even let Willy answer. "Is someone else hitting on her?"

"Peter, I don't know. It's not my business, nor is it yours!" He knew that was a low blow, but Peter needed a reminder.

Peter sat back down on the bed. "I know. I know it's not any of my business. I was just... uh... uh... wondering. That's all. I sorta feel responsible for her," he said lamely.

"Whoa, Peter," Willy said. "I've never known a more complicated relationship. But you're not her father or caretaker. In the end, she'll not appreciate your oversight of her life." Willy went on so that Peter could get the full picture. "You better prepare yourself. I know guys are already looking her way, and it won't be long before some of them want to get to know her better."

Willy could tell Peter's feathers were up. He didn't like the sound of that.

"Well, they'll have to be approved by me," Peter said, jaw line tight.

"No they won't, Peter," Willy said quietly. "Lilly is a big girl. She has a good head on her shoulders." Willy was determined to stand up for his new friend. "If Lilly finds love, Peter, don't stand in the way." Willy was done.

Peter was scowling at him.

He turned to leave the man alone but mumbled as he left, "'Course, you could just marry her yourself and remove all the others out of the line."

Peter picked up a pillow and threw it at Willy as he was leaving.

"And besides, Lilly doesn't love me that way," Peter said to himself as he picked up his pillow and shut the door. The morning would come way too early, and he had an assignment that he wasn't looking forward to.

Peter spent his entire drive to work in prayer. He was very quiet in class, serious in his teachings. Even to Lilly, he seemed distant. She was worried about him. He didn't give her his usual special smile. He didn't even say hi or bye when she came and went. Lilly went to her car and prayed for Peter. She knew he needed prayer right then. She stayed in her car the whole lunchtime until her biology class began in prayer.

Peter slipped in the chair opposite Veronica in the lounge. They sat in the same seats practically every day.

"How are you, Veronica?" Peter whispered as he got his lunch situated.

"Tired since I was up late last night," she said sadly. She went right to the matter. "Have you made up your mind, who will it be Pete?" she demanded.

The other professors in the lounge had just left, so he felt like this was a gift from God to do it now. So he began. "I didn't get much sleep either. I spent a lot of time in prayer over this." He didn't want to hurt anyone, much less a woman. "I just feel like we're on different pages. Our lives are going down two different paths." He could tell she was about to cry. Peter went on. "I'm at the age of life where I'm looking to settle down with a wife and family. I've had to really take a look at what that means, and what the LORD has been showing me is that it is very important for my prospective wife to share the same scriptural principals and values that I hold important and precious. And it's very obvious that lately we've argued more about those very things than ever before. It showed me that we're definitely not on the same page, maybe not even in the same book."

"I see," came her icy reply.

"So, you see, I'm not really choosing but realizing I can't join your path and you don't care to join mine; thus, there's no sense in continuing to see each other," he said and sat back, almost letting out a big sigh of relief. He was prepared for her wrath, thankful that he'd actually done this at work so she couldn't give full vent to her feelings.

"Well, I was going to break it off anyway," Veronica jeered. "You're just too … too … well, too churchy for me." She was getting up and gathering her things. "I just hope you don't lose your professionalism in the process of getting this girl out of your head," she spewed out, turned, and stomped out of not only the lounge but Peter's life as well.

Peter was glad to be alone for a moment. He bowed his head in praise that God had seen him through.

Thank You, Lord. I'm so undeserving of your grace. So what's next, Captain? Your servant is waiting.

He prayed and got up and went to the office. As he went by the window, he saw Lilly coming from the parking lot. She was so graceful. She smiled at others. She stopped once to pat another student on the back. Peter was sure she was encouraging them. He smiled just watching her. His heart felt freer than it had in a very long time. He actually wanted to run out there and tell her, but he didn't. It would have to wait until later. But then he had an idea. He put his trash away and ran out the door, almost bumping into the librarian.

Lilly was almost back to the building area when she saw Peter coming her way. She would've been worried, but he was smiling.

When he reached her, she said, "Hello, Professor Collins. Is everything all right?" Her forehead was crinkled in worry.

Peter had to be quick. "Yes, Miss Lillian Parker. Things couldn't be better, unless you'll have dinner with me tonight." He beamed at her.

"Well, I'm free. I'd be honored to join you," Lilly said.

"Pick you up at six," he said and turned to go. He knew he had to be careful with his personal involvement with a student, and this was very public.

Lilly wondered at his jolly mood but just thanked the LORD that it seemed her prayers on his behalf were answered in a positive way.

"Where, my ragmuffin, do you wish to dine?" Peter asked as they drove out of the driveway.

"Hmm. Let's see. Since you called me ragmuffin, I guess McDonald's." She was smiling impishly. "That's where most kids love to eat."

"Let me try again," Peter said. "My lovely Miss Parker, my favorite student, my very adult student, where will I keep my sanity while dining with you?"

"If I had known you wanted to keep your sanity, I wouldn't have agreed to dine with you, Professor Collins." Lilly continued. "See, I can be very wild; and I just think it's boring to have to restrain myself to life ordinary." Lilly was holding in her laughter. "Especially if my very handsome English professor is going to grade his dinner partner's every move." Lilly laughed.

Peter crossed his fingers. "I promise to not be Mr. Professor, but I'll take the good looking anytime. Be yourself, Lilly, which is what I love about you." With that, the evening was off to a great start. He decided he'd just take them to Round the Corner. Lilly seemed to like it there.

Peter had ordered their drinks and looked over at Lilly. She was lovely in the sage-green color. He noticed her necklace lay lovely against her neck and shined as it dangled on her shirt. She really was the picture of sweetness every time he saw her.

"How was your biology quiz?" Peter asked as he took a sip of his raspberry tea.

"Oh, well, thanks to you, I got a B." The waitress came, and they ordered the same they had last time.

"That's great!" He smiled. Lilly, changing the subject, said, "My aunt has been asking me a lot of questions about church lately."

Lilly looked up to see if she should say what else her aunt had asked about. "She also asked me who that lady was sitting with you." Lilly looked at Peter to see his reaction.

He raised his eyebrows and asked, "What did you tell her?"

"I told her that it was your soon-to-be fiancée, Veronica. I told her that she's a professor at the college as well."

"You know, Lil, I thought you were past that," he said in a pretend angry voice and sat back against the booth and crossed his arms with a very stern face.

"What are you talking about?" Lilly asked, completely taken back at his sudden foul mood.

"Was it not the third week I'd known you when we discussed lying?" Peter asked, his eyebrows raised, his father tone quite apparent.

Lilly was all but a puddle of humiliation. "Yes," she said, "I learned not to lie and have tried my very best to always be truthful."

"Until…" Peter let the word hang.

"What are you talking about?" Lilly was getting a bit fired up. "This is simple, ol' Lilly here. Don't play games with me. Speak plainly." She sat back. "If I have lied, tell me the truth!" She wanted to laugh at her own puns, but this was too serious of a time.

"Okay, okay!" Peter raised his hands. "Don't go and get all upset." Peter had enjoyed pulling one over on Lilly for a change. "You lied to your aunt about Veronica and me," Peter admitted.

"Peter, I tried to answer her giving as little information as possible. But you know how my aunt is nosy." Lilly shrugged. "What was I supposed to say when she saw Veronica sitting rather close? It was obvious your relationship was more than friends." Lilly didn't want to talk about this anymore. They'd gotten their meals, and she dug into her burger.

"Veronica and I are over," Peter said in a voice that could dry up the Great Lakes and took a bite of his burger so he didn't have to say anything else and could just watch her reaction.

Lilly choked on her food and her eyes bulged out. She liked to have shared parts of her burger with Peter as she tried to talk with a mouth full.

Peter howled in laughter at the sight. He pretended to wipe his hands and burger clear of the debris. "Hey, keep your burger to yourself. I have plenty, but thanks for sharing." Peter was really having a wonderful time, actually quite out of his normal box.

By then, Lilly had gulped the food left in her mouth. "What did you say?" Lilly asked.

Peter smiled. "You heard me. Are you deaf?"

"Peter Collins, you will tell all and right now!" Lilly demanded.

Peter even thought if he didn't hurry up he just might see steam come out her ears any moment. "Well, since you already had your turn at sharing, I'll share what happened. Maybe not every detail, as it's painful. But I knew you would want to know how God had been answering your prayers for me." Peter went on. "Let's just say that God has made it abundantly clear over the past couple weeks, and then the past couple days confirmed that it's not in my best interest to continue a relationship with Veronica. We are certainly on different pages, quite possibly different books entirely." Peter chuckled at that, knowing just how true it was. "Even though it might seem very painful right now, I think that God saved me from even greater pain and possible danger in the future." Peter looked at Lilly.

She had a few tears trickling down her cheeks. "I'm so sorry, Peter." She touched his hand. "I hate to see you in so much pain. It breaks my heart to see you suffer." She went on. "But it's as you said. We were praying for direction, and God gave it. But God never promised that obedience would be pain free." She sighed.

"Yes, indeed," Peter agreed. "It's far from pain free."

"Is this what was going on last night?" Lilly quietly asked.

"Yes, and that's why I forgot you at the church." Peter took a sip of tea.

"Don't worry about me, Peter." Lilly was adamant. "I was just worried about you. And even more so this morning when you were so distant."

"Well, I didn't exactly break things off until lunch today," Peter said. "So you had me well pegged, my dear."

"I went to my car to pray for you at that very time you were probably talking with Veronica today," Lilly said, in awe of how God had prompted her to go and pray, not even knowing why.

It all made sense now. Peter was thinking of when he'd seen her from the window, leaving the parking lot and coming back to the campus buildings just before he went to her for this dinner invitation.

"Thank you, Lil. You'll never know how much that means to me." Peter was looking at her with such sincerity that Lilly had to look away before she cried again.

"How did Veronica take the news?"

"I'm afraid, not so well," Peter said. "But then it was that very character of ungodly affections that showed me that this isn't what I desire or what God would have for me in a wife."

Lilly grabbed Peter's hand. "We have to pray for her right now."

Lilly bowed her head and began praying fervently for Veronica. Peter didn't know what to do. He was struck by Lilly's compassion for Veronica's soul that he was speechless. Lilly was not overly long. Peter prayed briefly too.

Lilly sat back and looked Peter in the eye. "We must never forget to pray for the lost." Lilly was baring her heart, which is what Peter loved so much. "Never can we forget," she whispered, holding back tears of compassion.

Thankfully, the waitress came and refilled drinks and offered dessert. Both declined.

"So tell me, what's the perfect wife profile for you, Professor Collins?"

"At one time, I thought I could tell you," Peter said. "But all that has changed, so I really can't answer you. But this I know: I'm not going to take my eyes off Jesus, and who He points to is who I'll marry." Peter hesitated. "I just hope He does not wait until I am an old man." Peter chuckled.

"I don't know. It better be soon." Lilly was teasing. "You'll be a whole year older in just over a week!" Lilly put her hand up to her ear. "Wait. I think I hear them, yes, getting louder. Wedding bells; they are getting closer!" Lilly laughed.

Peter threw a French fry her way. "You, my ragmuffin, are going to get it!" Peter said, loving every moment of the evening. "I enjoy your company so much."

"There's not a day that goes by I don't thank God for getting to see you again," Lilly whispered, being completely honest.

They locked their eyes together for a moment.

"I have an idea, Peter," Lilly said, twisting the corner of her napkin. "Remember how we used to study the Bible together from time to time? I was wondering about asking Aunt Maureen if she would join us for a Bible study." Lilly went on. "She has been asking questions I can't answer so well. And I just thought with you knowing the Bible much more than me that, well, you could come on Monday evenings and we could maybe go through the book of Romans. What do you think?" she asked with hopeful eyes.

"I think it's a great idea!" Peter said. "Not that I doubt at all that you, my Lil, could study to find all her answers. But maybe coming from someone else besides you will help," Peter added. "So next Monday it is. What time you want me there?"

"Let me ask her first. She might turn me down flat," Lilly said with a frown. "I'll let you know this week."

CHAPTER 14

Peter was actually whistling Monday morning as he went through the office to get his work mail and any announcements he needed to know about.

He went to his office to prepare for class when he spotted the notice: "Professor Collins to the dean's office after last class."

He wondered what was up. He wasn't sure what this was about, but he didn't fret over it and went to his first class. Peter waited leisurely outside the door, hoping to ask Lil about Bible study that night. He was rewarded momentarily with her bright smile. Peter grinned at her as she approached.

She came close and whispered, "She said yes. Be there for dinner at five." She said it all so quietly and briefly no one would've known they'd spoken.

He grinned, nodding for an answer. She flashed him a big smile from her seat that made his morning even better.

Peter's smile and whistling disposition died after he went to the dean's office.

Dr. Whatley said, "Please, do come in and sit down, Professor Collins."

Peter came in and sat down in the stately, leather, wingback chair opposite the dean's desk. Dr. Whatley was a rotund man in a three-piece suit, screaming to get out, bald with curly hair on the edges. But what he didn't have in looks he made up for in a tight-run, strict-ruled college campus.

Peter asked, "What, sir, can I do for you?"

Dr. Whatley took off his glasses and began, his deep voice serious and accusing. "It has come to my attention that you have directed your attention to a certain young student in your class." He was tapping his glasses on the desk in stern disapproval. He didn't wait for a comment but went on. "Professor Collins, we run a very respectable college here." He gave a grim look. "And I intend to keep it that way. Am I making myself clear, or do we need to review the rules?" He ended by saying, "I believe the name that came to me was a Lillian Parker."

Peter was so taken back he stumbled over his words. "I… uh… I… uh…" He couldn't believe this was happening. It suddenly dawned on him that the only person who would've done this was Veronica. He didn't know how she could stoop so low. Peter was shaking his head, anger filling him that she'd accuse him of breaking the rules.

Dr. Whatley wasn't so patient. "Excuse me, and speak up!" His eyes shot daggers through Peter.

Peter cleared his throat, sat straight up in his chair, looked the dean right in the face, and said, "Yes, sir, you do run a fine and well-respected college here, one I'm proud to be associated with, which is the very reason that I would never jeopardize my position here by breaking the rules. I love my job and uphold the rules, tenets, and values of this college with the utmost high regard."

Dr. Whatley raised his eyebrows and said, "Well then, can you explain if this is true why such a complaint has found its way to my office?"

"Well, I'm not sure exactly of the accusation," Peter said, looking the dean square in the face. "However, if you wish to know what probably is being misunderstood, I can explain clearly," Peter finished.

"I don't have all day. Spit it out, Professor Collins," the dean said hastily.

Peter knew better than to take up the dean's time in sharing every detail, but he had to share enough to clear his name and defuse this accusation for Lilly's sake as well as the reputation of the college.

"I have to admit I've never quite had something of this magnitude happen before. And so, by nature, things might seem bigger than what they are," Peter said and then continued telling the dean the entire story, beginning with the first day of class.

Peter didn't want to discuss the level of friendship they had, for the dean probably wouldn't understand. Peter wasn't sure he did. He hated to do this, but he had to drive the next point home in order to make certain the dean knew he hadn't broken any rules.

"Dr. Whatley, I understand the relationship rules very clearly. They only prohibit an ongoing personal relationship with a direct student. It doesn't prohibit professors dating one another or other students as long as they're not in the professor's direct class." Peter looked at the dean. "It does state that all behavior is to be above reproach. My relationship with Lillian Parker is only, and I repeat, only friendship. If I thought there was a problem, I would have asked her to drop the class." Peter sat back a bit. "As a matter of fact, I've been dating Professor Hughbert for the last nine months, and if I miss my guess, this came about because we have chosen to take different paths and she saw this as a way to get back at me. It's a completely false accusation. Where's the proof of me doing such a thing as breaking the rules?" Peter asked. "I realize you have better things to do than sit and listen to someone's private life. And it's no one's business what Veronica and I do or don't do as long as we maintain our reputation as above reproach. This breakup of ours had nothing at all to do with Lillian Parker, but that still doesn't prevent Professor Hughbert from retaliation of the lowest degree," Peter said and sat back for the pink slip.

The dean, feeling as though he had just heard a love story if ever there was one, couldn't let that be known. Instead, in his sternest of voices, he said, "Professor Collins, consider this a reminder of the rules. Be very careful of your position with this student. Your career here hangs in the balance. If I were you, I wouldn't leave any doubt in others' minds that this friend is not a friend this semester but a student. You may be dismissed," he said and went back to his work.

Peter left the dean's office with the wind out of his sail. He really needed to pray, for right now he was so mad at Veronica he hoped he wouldn't run into her. He wasn't sure he could be kind at the moment.

"Well, hello there, Mr. Collins. So glad to have ya here," Aunt Maureen said.

It seemed that after the night she went to hear Lilly speak, the dam wall she'd put up against religion had busted and she'd flooded Lilly with questions. She seemed as open as the hole in the dam. So she was actually eager to have this Bible study.

"Good evening, Maureen. And please call me Peter." He had said the last part with quiet sincerity. "Mmm! Something smells delicious," Peter said with a lick of his lips, anticipating a great meal both of physical food and spiritual food.

Peter was taken back to see Lilly. Something about watching her at the stove just seemed right. He loved to watch her move around in the kitchen, but tonight, the food was ready and everyone took a seat. "This looks wonderful, Lil. You really don't have to go through all this trouble just for me," he said as he looked at her sweet face.

She had prepared a roast, mashed potatoes, gravy, green beans, biscuits with jam, and of course, cold iced tea to wash it all down.

After the meal, Peter began the Bible study in Romans 1:1, but they only got as far as the first seven verses. Aunt Maureen had many questions. It was like telling someone the Gospel for the first time. Peter did his best to answer her questions only to have more pour forth. They prayed with Maureen when they finished.

Maureen put her hand on Peter's. She had a single tear in her eye. And with a wobbly voice, she said, "Thank you, Peter. I didn't know." She got up and said, "I have a lot to mull over. I think I'll turn in for the night." She then quietly went to her room.

Lilly began to stack the dishes to wash later.

"Here. Why don't you let me help you with these," Peter said, rolling up his sleeves.

"Oh, how kind of you. I was going to do them later."

"Actually, I'm wired after such an open, awesome, exciting Bible study," Peter said. "Besides, I need to talk to you about something. How about you wash and I'll rinse," he offered.

Lilly finally yielded to his help with the dishes, as they might as well do them if he was going to stay. "Okay," Lilly said quietly. She was worried over what he needed to talk to her about. "So how was your day?" Lilly asked as she prepared her soapy water.

"I've had better," he said as he rinsed the glasses she handed him.

"Oh? Care to share?"

"Well, that's what I wanted to talk to you about," Peter said with a sigh.

He knew this was the time. Trying to choose his words carefully, he continued to rinse the dishes she handed him, though he noticed she had slowed down her washing. This told him she was worried.

Peter plunged in. "I had an interesting slip in my mailbox at work this morning. To make a long story short, so as to not bother you with the details, I had a reprimand from the dean."

Peter took a breath to continue, but Lilly interrupted.

"What?" Lilly asked, nearly dropping the plate she was handing him. "What in the world for?" she asked, completely stopping her chore.

"Well, that doesn't matter nearly as much as what I need to say because of it," Peter went on.

Lilly splashed her water in frustration. "Out with it, Peter!" she said. "I want to know every detail. Don't you dare even think of sparing me the details!" Lilly had momentarily forgotten her place, as it really was none of her business.

Peter thought for a moment. This was when it was hard. He was older, and he was her teacher. She was the student, yet she was Lilly. Did he share everything even though they were the closest of friends? Before he could form his answer, Lilly spoke up.

"Well, am I gonna have to rinse too?" she asked, handing him a plate.

"Well, I certainly don't want to lose this job," Peter said, coming back to planet Earth. "I can find another teaching job, but I don't want to get fired from doing dishes with you. You might not invite me over to eat again." He was trying to get her to loosen up and process what he'd say.

"What are you talking about, Petah? You're always welcome here. Now tell me what happened today, please." She'd let out her water and was drying her hands. Lilly walked into the living room and sat on the couch.

Peter plopped down beside her. He grabbed her hand in between both of his, and he began. "Somehow, it got to the dean that I was having a relationship with a certain student of mine named Lillian Parker."

Lilly jumped off the couch. "What?"

Peter patted the seat beside him. "Come, my little ragmuffin. Sit," Peter commanded.

"Who'd make up such a lie?" Lilly asked.

Peter hadn't wanted to say this, but Lilly needed to know. "I think it might quite possibly have been Veronica." Peter looked at Lilly.

"But why would she do a horrible thing like that?"

Peter shared very quickly what had transpired.

"I wouldn't have even told you all this except to ask you to help me from even the slightest bit of anyone thinking that accusation is true."

"I knew I should've dropped your class. Now look at what kind of mess you are in," Lilly fretted. "That's it! I'll drop it ASAP in the morning," Lilly said determinedly.

Peter, in his bold, professor voice, "No, you will not, Lillian Parker! That's out of the question!" He looked at her with raised eyebrows and a determined look that said he expected obedience. Peter went on. "But what it does mean is that we cannot even talk anymore on the college campus. Not that it should come to this." Peter was looking at Lilly. She had a sad look, but she was also nodding her head. "I mean, we both know that we don't have the kind of relationship we've been accused of, but I don't want to even give anyone the idea." Peter continued. "Lil, I want to be above reproach in this, not only for myself but for you too and for God's glory," Peter finished.

"Yes. Of course," Lilly agreed.

Peter went on. "This is what I think we should do. We cannot talk to each other outside of class at all." Peter laughed. "This will be hardest on me—" he was shaking his head and grinning, knowing how hard it would be for him to do this— "which is why I want you to help me," he said.

"What do you mean?" Lilly asked, her head cocked to one side in confusion.

"Well, if I forget and begin to talk to you outside of the classroom period with students in the room, meaning nothing other than being your professor, I want you to walk on by," Peter said.

"You're silly, Peter," Lilly said. "I can't do that."

Peter was serious. "Yes, my ragmuffin, you can. Our reputations and my job are at stake," Peter said with tenderness.

Lilly was rebuked. "Yes, Peter. I'll do as you ask."

Peter gently turned her face to him and softly spoke. "Like I said, I know you would have no problem with the restraint. I'm the one who'll have the problem. That is why I asked for your help."

"Okay," was Lilly's quiet reply.

"Now, I better be going. It was a lovely evening, Miss Parker," Peter said. He messed her hair up a bit, rose, and left.

On Friday morning, Lilly had decided to go ahead with what she had planned to do for Peter's birthday. At times it seemed silly to her, and she almost chickened out. But she finally gave way, and with determined steps, she placed the hand-decorated bag underneath Peter's classroom desk before his first class.

Peter came into his class right as students were arriving. As he scooted up to his desk, his foot rattled the bag. He looked under his desk and saw it was a gift of sorts. He smiled, its contents would have to wait to be revealed, for his classes awaited his instruction. Even Lilly's class came and went before he was able to see just what lay hidden at his feet. And true to Lilly's word, she was staunch in her resolve not to speak with Peter. She even went so far as to not even look his way or smile at him. He had to admit he wasn't sure he could endure the rest of the semester that way.

Peter sat at his desk, looking at the adorable, handmade bag. Even the flowers had buttons in the middle. Below, in the grass, was written: "With love, your ragmuffin." His lunch long forgotten, he looked inside. He pulled out its contents to find, indeed, more than his heart could take.

He pulled out five cards. On each envelope was written a year. He opened the earliest dated year, the year Lilly had disappeared. Inside, he found a lined piece of paper folded in half like a card. On the front was written, "Happy Birthday, Petah," in red crayon. He looked inside and found, "October 23, 1981," in the upper corner. Then he read:

My dearest Petah,

It seems silly to make you a card since I'll probably never see you again. But you will always live in my heart. I have cried most of today just thinking about you on this very special occasion. I miss you so much at times I think my heart will just stop beating. I'm putting my trust in God, as you always taught me to. But when my mom screams and hits me, I feel weak and want to waver in my faith. But God upholds me when I can't take any more. I prayed for you today that, wherever you are, you are having a wonderful birthday and God would bless you and keep you.

All my love,
Lilly

Lilly had colored hearts all over the card. It had a book laying on one side with, "The Hedge of Thorns," written on it.

Seeing the dates of the other envelopes, Peter knew. He plopped back in his chair, completely overcome with emotion. She'd made him a birthday card every year they'd been apart. He was completely undone by this gift. He no longer tried to choke back the tears. He let them run freely down his cheek as he said, "My precious Lil, will you ever quit astounding me with your love?" He truly felt so unworthy.

He wiped away his tears and opened the next year, 1982. On the front was a beautiful rainbow with a little ark under it. Written on it was, "May your birthday be one of promises fulfilled." Inside, she had drawn little animals all around the edges and colored them in with pencil. In the middle, it read:

My Dearest Petah,

I prayed for you today. I prayed that, wherever you are, all the promises you know or have read from the Bible will come true in your life. Though you may have questions, may you be like Noah and not have doubts. May you do the same this day and forever. Trust as Noah did in God's promises for you! I know I'll never see you, but I'm learning about the power of prayer. And throughout this past year, when loneliness creeps in—and often it does—I climb into the ark for protection, read my Bible, and pray the promises therein.

All my love,
Lilly

The next one he read was 1983. It had a gold cross on the front. Under it were the words, "You *crossed* my mind today. Happy Birthday!" On the inside, she had written:

My Dearest Petah,

I couldn't get you off my mind today. Though I know I'll never see you and you'll never get this card, it helps me to make them anyway. I've been centering my mind and heart on the cross this year. I've had such sorrow, such pain. It's gotten so unbearable. And when I think I can take no more, I read about the cross. I read about my Savior and the suffering of the cross that He endured for me. When I get discouraged, I think of you, how you pointed me to Jesus and the cross. I remember the first time I began to understand the sufferings of Jesus. You were there beside me. So I just wanted you to know how much the cross means to me. And I'm ever so thankful for the short time our paths crossed!

All my love,
Lilly

The last one was 1984. He slowly opened it. She had put a big shield on it. Written above the shield was, "Happy Birthday." Below the shield was written, "Ye Soldier of the Cross!" On the inside, she had drawn arrows with flames, a belt of truth, a helmet of salvation, shield of faith, and a sword of the Word. On the left side of the card, she had neatly handwritten Ephesians 6:13–20. On the right side of the card, she had written:

My Dearest Petah,

I'm praying for you today that you're being the soldier of the cross that I've always known you to be. I'm so thankful for this portion of Scripture and have committed it to memory. We're soldiers of the cross, and there is a real war out there. I know for me, my war rages all around me, outside my home and inside my home. I often go to my room to escape the fiery arrows. This is where I arm myself for war. I read, meditate, and memorize Scripture. I pray, pray, and pray. Know that wherever you are, I pray for you. I often have inner war with my heart, not wanting to love those who want to take advantage of me. So this warrior card really meant a lot to me. Just thought I would share it with you on your birthday. Wherever you are, Peter, fight hard!

All my love,
Lilly

Peter was so overcome. He closed his eyes in guilt, remembering just how far from a fighting warrior he'd been during those years; yet here was his faithful friend, praying for him.

Thank you, LORD, for Lilly and her faithful prayers. Thank you, LORD, that you have brought me back to your heart, Peter prayed.

Peter reached for the last one, this year's card. He turned over the envelope in his hand. It was obviously made out of a paper sack. He opened it. On the inside was a paper sack card. On the front was a heart with these words: "Faith, Hope, Love." On the bottom, she put, "Happy Birthday." He slowly opened the card. In the middle, she wrote:

My dearest Petah,

It seems strange to be writing you a card that you will read after so many I made that I never dreamed you'd ever see. I seem so suddenly out of words now that I see you face-to-face. But know this: you have always had my heart! I hope that this birthday will drive your faith to love Him more next year!

All my love,
Your ragmuffin, Lilly

Peter closed the card. *Lord, just what is going on here? She's so precious!* Peter thought again about the surprise he was planning for Lilly. She was sure to be delighted. Too bad he had some more teaching to do. He would have loved to see his ragmuffin right then. He had a plan forming.

Peter waited until about 8:00 p.m. to walk into the Stuffed Goose. It seemed weird to come here alone. He'd always been with Veronica. But tonight, he'd a special surprise for Lilly. He asked to be seated in Lillian Parker's section. He actually had gotten used to calling her Lillian to everyone, save Willy and, of course, her aunt.

Lilly was surprised when Alisha came by, a big, teasing grin on her face. "Looks like Mr. Right is back again," she said and batted her eyes. "Only this time alone!" Alisha put her hands on her hip and said, "D-three, unless, that is, you need me to do the honors."

Lilly knew she was teasing her.

"Hey, hey, hey, where's his date?" She was whistling now. "Here's your chance, Lillian girl! You betta snag him while ya can. He's sure the best catch I've seen lately," Alisha said.

Lilly playfully threw a towel at her friend. "Oh, hush. We're just friends," Lilly said and went out to the floor to take Peter's order.

"Sure he is. I've heard that before," Alisha said.

As Lilly went past her, she rolled her eyes at her coworker.

Lilly walked slowly to Peter's table, calming her nerves. "Why, fancy meeting you here, Professor Collins," Lilly said as she smiled into his eyes.

Peter looked back at her. "Why, yes, it is. I came here, for it's my understanding that you could help me with a dilemma I have."

"Why, Professor Collins, I'm quite sure I don't know what you're speaking about." Lilly replied, confusion written on her face.

Peter pointed to the table. Lilly had been so taken with greeting the customer she didn't notice what he had displayed on the table. It was all five of the cards she had made him.

Peter whispered in a husky voice, "Which one do you like best?" he asked. "I simply can't decide."

Lilly looked at him. Peter looked right back.

After a moment, Peter said, "I'll never be able to tell you with words my heartfelt appreciation for this gift that no price tag could ever be placed upon. Lilly, I'm so touched. I had to see you." He reached and touched her hand for a moment. "I will cherish them always."

"I love you, Peter. I always have. I always will," she whispered and quietly slipped away. She had to get back to the kitchen.

She leaned on the counter, fanning herself for a moment. Emotions riding high, she needed a moment to cool off. The effect Peter was having on her was making her melt in her shoes, and she had work to do. She splashed some water on her face and wiped it dry. Alisha came to the back right at that moment.

"Girl, what's goin' on with you?" she inquired, seeing Lillian's flushed cheeks.

"Oh, nothing really. Just trying to keep my head on straight," Lilly said and went to fill Peter's favorite drink just the way he liked it. She took it back to him.

He smiled at her. "So, do you have an answer? Which is your favorite?" Peter was distracting her terribly.

Lilly was so serious. "I really don't know, Peter. They all mean so very much to me. They were my connection to you when I never thought I would see you again. I didn't have much, and I wasn't able to bring much here. But I brought those, for they were like manna in the desert."

Lilly was so quiet Peter thought she was going to cry. He hadn't meant to do that, but he had to see her.

"If I had to pick one, it would be the last one, the one that I didn't have to put under my pillow and cry myself to sleep after making." Then she walked away.

Ten minutes later she brought him a salad. "Here you are, a fresh, loose-leaf salad with honey mustard dressing. Enjoy, sir," Lilly said in her sweet voice.

"Hey, I haven't even ordered yet," Peter replied.

"I knew what you wanted and just did it for you since you seemed to be without words." She winked at him.

"You're something, you know it?" Peter said as he dug into his salad.

"No, I'm not, but He is," she said as she pointed heavenward. She went off to leave him alone and wait on other customers.

He was enjoying his evening. Just watching her work gave him pleasure. She was graceful to everyone. Even her coworkers were a recipient of her kindness. She brought him his meal, and true to her word, it was exactly what he liked. She'd remembered well. That was just it—she was always thinking of others.

Peter had ordered dessert and coffee but was still there. Finally, Lilly asked if there was anything else she could get him. He said no. But after some time, he still had not left.

Lilly mustered up the nerve and asked, "Peter, are you going to stay here all night? They will be closing in about an hour."

"Well, that depends," Peter said, looking at Lilly.

"On what?" Lilly had to know, noticing how strange Peter was acting.

"Whether or not I can see you after work."

"Well—" Lilly gulped— "I'm usually pretty tired; and I have the bus route by nine in the morning. But sometimes I go to McDonald's with Alisha for a chat and a burger, but you've already eaten," Lilly said.

"McDonald's it is, my ragmuffin. I'll leave shortly. I'll wait in the parking lot, and you can follow me over. Will that work for you?" Peter asked.

"I think so. See you later. Let me know if there is something else I can get you before you leave."

"You've given me more than you know already," Peter said. "See you later."

He left not too long after that. She cleared his table and noticed he had written on a napkin, "I love your heart!" and had left another fifty-dollar bill. Lilly shook her head.

"What am I going to do with you, Peter Collins?" she mumbled to herself.

It was not overly crowded at 10:00 p.m. in McDonald's, but there was a young gal in front of her who had a baby on the hip, and her three-year-old was trying to carry the tray they had just ordered. The little girl tilted the tray too far, and the little girl's drink spilled over, soaking all their food. Lilly immediately went into action.

"Here, honey. Let me help you," Lilly said, grabbing the tray for her.

The little girl was crying. The mom had her hands full and was trying, but she could only do so much. She was upset that her daughter had made a mess. To say they were on the less fortunate side was more than obvious. Lilly took the tray and laid it on the counter and told the McDonald's worker to redo their meal. She handed her a twenty to pay for it.

Lilly then proceeded to squat down and took the little girl in her arms. She sat in the nearest booth and consoled the little girl. When the order was ready, Lilly walked over, took the tray to a table, got a highchair for the baby, and looked at the mom. The mom was standing there like a stone. She'd never seen such kindness. She didn't know what to say. Lilly sized up the situation.

"Come."

She motioned for the mom. Lilly took the baby out of her hands and put her in the highchair. She put her hand on the woman's shoulder and simply said, "Enjoy your meal," and walked away. She had laid a twenty-dollar bill on the tray along with a simple Gospel tract.

She walked back to a speechless Peter. All this took place in less than fifteen minutes, but what Peter witnessed he'd remember for a lifetime. Lilly didn't feel like eating now but went ahead and ordered a simple hamburger and a glass of water, all of about a dollar's worth of food. Peter raised his eyebrows at her when he looked at her tray. She ignored him.

They sat down in a cozy corner. "Are you sure I can't get you something?" Lilly asked.

Peter was shaking his head.

"They make great soft-serve ice cream," Lilly said.

"How is it that it seems every time I'm with you I'm learning something new?" Peter asked with a quizzical smile. "Some great professor I am. Somehow, when we are together, our teacher-student arrangement gets confused and I end up learning yet another side of this sweet ragmuffin that I thought I knew," Peter confessed.

"Well, I hope I haven't presented anything that is a false picture," Lilly said around small bites of burger. "If there's anything good that you see, it's all because of God—" Lilly smiled and was serious— "for I don't have to look very far to see what I'd be without God in my life," Lilly ended.

"But your heart is like none I've ever known," Peter went on honestly.

Lilly didn't know what to say. She was just herself. "Perhaps, Peter, it's simply this. You're harvesting, or rather the recipient of the harvest that was sown in me many years ago. The biblical principal that you reap what you sow is indeed true whether you sow evil or righteousness." Lilly took a drink. "Please don't elevate me. I've been through a lot, and God has been very patient with me. I mess up all the time. But when you've experienced such sorrow, wickedness, and pain, it makes you really appreciate every breath," Lilly finished, hoping she had gotten through to Peter.

"I get the feeling that I got a tiny glimpse of your suffering today when I opened my birthday gift. I must say that I don't think I really understood the depth of suffering you had to endure when you first shared with me," Peter said. "Did you really sleep with those cards under your pillow?"

Lilly put her head down. "Yes," she said. "After a while, I thought they'd get destroyed, so I put them under my mattress. But since I slept on the floor on a flimsy mattress, it was still like it was under my pillow. Every time, for about a week, they would stay under my pillow so I could pull them out and read them again." She couldn't look at him. It somehow was too vulnerable. "Maybe I shouldn't have given them to you. I mean, they're not even store bought. They look like a kid made them," Lilly ended with a shrug of the shoulders. She was questioning how stupid it must have been to Peter, a college professor, to get such hand-made, crayon-colored, simple cards from a pest.

Peter had closed his eyes at the very thought of her living conditions. He wasn't sure he wanted to know any more. But he was very sure he was glad she'd given him the cards. How could he convince her so? "I've received many gifts over my lifetime. Not to mention that I came from a more well-to-do family and they have also lavished me with gifts. Really, to tell the truth, I lack nothing." Peter looked at Lilly to be sure she was listening. "But nothing, and I repeat, nothing can hold a candle to the gift that came in the most adorable paper sack I have ever seen, made by hands of love, from the dearest person I know," Peter said. "I will cherish them forever, my love."

Feeling the need to change the subject, Peter asked about her bus route. "Who do you go out with, and is it anything like when you were a kid?" Peter inquired.

"Well, I can't really say since the comparison would be from two different points of view," Lilly tried to answer, "but this is what we do. On Saturday, we go to the church for breakfast at 9:00 am. Then, after we eat and have a short Bible devotion, prayer, and announcements, we head out and knock on each kid's door. We've not exactly knocked on any new doors yet," Lilly ended with a frown.

They continued to talk about the bus ministry, comparing the two timeframes and viewpoints in which both were involved until Lilly mentioned she needed to get home.

When she got to the car, she turned to Peter. "Thank you for dining with me!" She smiled. "I hope you kept your sanity," she said as she got in the car, thinking he didn't really like McDonald's. "By the way, happy birthday, my dearest Peter."

Peter chuckled at her and said, "Thank you for the best birthday ever."

He closed her door and went to his own car. He was well on his way home when on the radio he heard Willy doing his DJ stuff.

"Signing off for the night, I want to play two more songs. I want to wish my cousin and crazy roommate a happy birthday. You're the best! This first song is for you. And to my Lady Lillian, to make you smile, coming at you with one of your favorites. Until next time, remember, in all thy WAZE, give Him praise! Good night to all my friends!"

CHAPTER 15

The weeks seemed to fall into a pattern of sorts. Peter came every Monday night for the Bible study. The studies had been going great. Her aunt was opening up more and more. James was coming around a lot more often, and Maureen was softening her heart toward him. A lot of times, they all three played a rousing game of Scrabble after Bible study. Both Peter and Lilly were having a wonderful time making up for lost years.

Peter still picked Lilly up for Sunday evening Bible study, and they sat together during the evening service. Even though Peter now sat alone on Sunday mornings, as Lilly rarely sat with him he loved watching her. She sat in many different places, actually. She would sit with Alisha, if she came, or a youth in need. If a visitor she had invited came, she would sit with them. At times, Peter would find her sitting with Willy.

When he did, he would shake his head, thinking, *They do look good together.*

They usually had their heads together in some funny joke or teasing and playfully goofing off. And there were those times that Peter found himself at the side of the very woman who had turned his world inside out.

He often asked for her attendance on Sundays since she was off, but many times, Willy had beaten him to it or she was spending the day with her aunt and James. If it was either of those two, she would invite Peter to join her. But when she was counseling youth or going to another's home, he wouldn't think to impose. But each Sunday night, she'd come back to the apartment, and she, Peter, and Willy would have a great time. Then he'd take her home.

Lilly and Peter had kept true to not speaking on the college campus. They'd ended up leaving little notes on assignments turned in and assignments returned. It turned out to be a fun little thing they did. Lilly looked more forward to the bottom or end of a paper rather than seeing what grade she'd made. Peter was experiencing the same. When her paper came to the top of the stack, he always went to the end to see what comments or questions she had. He was checking papers by himself now. But he didn't seem to mind since he knew he would get to see Lilly through her paper.

Just a few weeks before Thanksgiving, Lilly was absent from class. Alarm hit Peter full in his chest. It was Wednesday, and he was sure he didn't remember Lilly saying anything about not being in class. So he was worried that something bad had happened. Due to keeping their agreement, he didn't think it wise to call her aunt's house and inquire about her. He'd just have to wait. He went all through the rest of the day, praying for her when he had the chance.

Peter went home and plopped his keys on the table. That was when he noticed the note written by Willy, his handwriting barely readable. He'd always had sloppy handwriting; great words but messy handwriting. The note read:

Lilly gave this to me today, asked me to give it to you. She was really awe inspiring. You should hear her sometime. Have a great evening!

Willy

He then opened the folded piece of paper underneath that one. It looked like it had been run over by a Mack truck, probably not Lilly's fault, but the mail carrier's. It was torn and dirty and had something sticky on a portion of the outer corner. That wasn't Lilly but definitely Willy. Peter had to laugh. Little did he know that the note would have him howling in just minutes. It read:

Dear Peter,

I've been looking up quotes for my speeches. I've been reading in several different books. I keep coming across this one author named Anon. Have you ever heard of him? What are some of his other writings? It seems he has some very interesting quotes! I know you are much more learned than me. Can you help?

Unquoted but very devoted,
Ragmuffin

After many moments of uncontrollable laughter, Peter began to think of how he was going to answer her without belittling her or making fun of her naïveté. He had a plan forming.

Friday after class, Lilly went to her car to leave. She found a note on her windshield. After she got in the car, she opened it. It read:

You are a sweet lady. You're kind and compassionate. You put others first. You love little kids. You're a prayer warrior. You're a great writer. You are a fabulous encourager. You're free spirited and a hard worker.

Signed,
Anonymous

Lilly put her head down on the steering wheel and just laughed until the tears came. She couldn't believe it. *Anon* was short for Anonymous. She had had no clue. She felt pretty stupid. How humiliating. But she was thankful that at least Peter had cared enough not to tell her in person. He was so kind and thoughtful. But she burst into laughter again as she started the car, saying to herself, "Who would have ever known?"

Lilly was watching Willy skateboard. It was Sunday afternoon, and Willy had invited her to join him. He did this every Sunday afternoon from about 2:00 p.m. until church time. Different kids from the neighborhood would come and skateboard with him. He'd talk with them, skate with them, counsel them when there was an opening, and pray with them if so led. This was yet another area of ministry for Willy. Lilly thought it was a great idea. She watched Willy. He amazed her with his ability and balance. He had two ramps that he did all kinds of tricks on. She asked him at one point when he was by himself how he managed to get the church to give him this fenced-off area for skateboarding. It was a good-sized area. She was just shocked the church had agreed to such a thing.

Willy laughed and skated around one more time and popped up his board with his foot and caught it in his hand. Even that trick amazed Lilly.

"It wasn't always easy. I was met with much resistance." Willy was breathing hard, as he leaned on the fence. "I used to just come and skateboard in the parking lot. Then one day, the parking lot Nazi—that's what I called him—came to inform me I wasn't welcome with those kinds of wheels. I really had to do some praying. I went to the church staff with the problem. And they, in turn, prayed about it with me. I shared with them my heart, that I'd been developing friendships and Bible studies that were making a difference. A proposal was then brought to the church on the condition that this would actually keep the skateboarders off the parking lot, thus keeping the parking lots intact. So it was voted to do it, and I'm in charge of it, and it has kept skateboarders off the parking lot. The really cool thing about it is the parking lot Nazi paid for the ramps himself and apologized for his insensitivity." Willy said all this with much enthusiasm. "It's been a great ministry! Most of the guys are faithful about coming."

"Thanks for sharing, Willy. And thanks for inviting me," Lilly said. "This is so cool!"

"You're great, Lillian. Whoever snags you up better know what he's got, or I might just have to tell him!" With that, Willy took his great smile off to skateboard some more.

Lilly had been on the outside of the fence to stay out of the way. But she'd been hanging on it this whole time. She was so enthralled she didn't hear Peter approaching.

He grabbed her sides and yelled, "Gotcha!"

Lilly screamed and jumped out of her skin. "Peter Collins, you ever do that to me again and I'll... I'll... I'll..."

"You'll do what, Lilly?" Peter had the biggest grin.

Lilly stomped her foot and turned back around only to see that Willy was standing, hand on his hips, hiding his smirk.

"Willy, no laughing!" Lilly said in her stern, teasing fashion.

Peter put his arm around her and leaned close to her ear. "I'm sorry I scared you. I just couldn't resist the moment." He chuckled. "I missed you on Wednesday."

She leaned back but didn't look at him. "Thank you for my *anony*mous note on Friday," she said.

Peter had all he could take. "So where were you Wednesday?" Peter beckoned for an answer. "Your seat was lonely."

Lilly knew Peter was probing, and for a moment, she didn't want to give him an answer. She didn't owe him one really, so she said, "I had a really hot date with a wild and crazy guy I just couldn't resist!" She tossed her head as though that was all the answer he was going to get. She turned and watched the skateboarders again.

He decided to try another approach.

"Well, don't you want to know what your assignments are?" he asked.

"Oh, I'll just call Jill; she can fill me in. I'm sure it's nothing real important," she said, not giving Peter the information he wanted.

Peter was getting irritated that she'd think so flippantly about her studies. Peter switched his feet back and forth in frustration. "You know, there is more to life than fun and games. And you shouldn't be so frivolous about missing class."

She could tell he was a bit ticked.

"And, Professor Collins, there's more to life than learning."

She spat out clearly, leaving Peter with nothing to say and no answer to where she'd been. He'd even thought he would ask Willy about it, but they'd missed each other the entire weekend.

Peter decided to drop it for now. If he didn't watch it, he'd be doing the father thing again.

Willy was finishing up with a guy and then getting ready to close down shop anyway.

"Thanks again for the day, Willy. I had a blast! I'll be praying for you. See you later!" She put both thumbs up at him and went off with Peter inside the main church building.

Why does it seem that she is so free with Willy? Peter wondered.

They went on to Bible study and then church. But it seemed that some of the wind was out of Lilly's sail.

After the closing song, Peter asked, "Is my ragmuffin still mad at me?" It was said with care and for her ears only, as they were still in church.

"I never was," Lilly softly replied.

Peter knew there was more to it than that. He asked her, "Are you up to coming to the apartment for our ritual of pizza and craziness?"

"I'm not sure I should. Remember, you said yourself that there was more to life than fun and games," she said getting her point across.

Peter knew he had stuck his foot in his mouth this time. Only, when he took it out, he left the shoe.

"Come, Lil. Let's go," he said as he led them out the door.

She didn't stop to talk to very many people, as she was worn out. Peter put her in the car and took off.

"So what is it that I did that has made you so put out with me?" he begged.

Lilly didn't want to talk about it, because she was about to cry. Peter's approval meant so much to her, and he had crushed her by his line of questioning and assumption that she wasn't a serious student. She knew she had to talk this out, for she couldn't stay distant from Peter; it hurt too much. Lilly licked her lips.

"Peter, you have power over me that I rebel against at times."
She was trying to explain, but she could tell Peter was lost. "I do
cherish everything you tell me, but when you treat me like I'm still
that little, nine-year-old girl who can't even make a proper decision, it makes me feel dumb and a like child to you." Lilly went on.
"It hurts me deeply that you think I was out partying and that I'm
not concerned and careful about my classes." Lilly ended. "It's not
like I'm not working my fingers to the bone just to get the money
to go," she whispered. "I want you to think of me as a levelheaded,
responsible, studious woman, not a bimbo-brained, careless nit-
wit!" Lilly ended with slumped shoulders.

What Peter hadn't known he now understood. As he thought
about it, he realized that he didn't think that at all. She would
have known that if she'd been able to read all his thoughts, yet
he did treat her that way sometimes—he knew it—just as he'd
done today. Really, it was none of his business where she'd gone.
Because he was older and had been the mentor for so long, he
found himself overbearing at times. It was like she said. She *was*
an adult. What could he say to make this right he was not sure.
But he'd better do something.

"Actually, there's a lot more to Lillian Parker than I ever antic-
ipated." Peter looked over at her with a romantic smile and said,
"And I, for one, love every bit of it. And I'm dreadfully sorry that
I ever made you feel otherwise."

Lilly was overcome by his words. "I do know that I hate dis-
appointing you," she admitted. "I try so hard to always make you
proud of me; and it seems at times I can never live up to your high
expectations, like today."

Peter thought his heart would break. What a difficult place to
be in. Peter took her hand in his. "Lilly, you are beyond precious
to me. I don't know how to get you to understand I love you just
the way you are." He squeezed her hand. "I have no expectations."

Peter went on to confess, "There are many times I wish I were more like you."

They were at the apartment now, so she let it drop. Willy greeted her with a hug and a huge smile. Willy was so cheerful and fun, quite opposite of Peter's serious nature. Peter ordered the pizza and then sat in the lounge chair, watching Willy and Lilly banter back and forth.

"So did you tell ol' Peter how great of a speaker you are?" Willy jabbed her in the side with his elbow. "Come now. You did tell him, didn't you?" Willy was joking around but soon stopped.

Lilly put her head down. "No," came the faint reply.

Willy, sensing that there was something amiss, took over. "You should've seen her, Peter." Willy looked over at Lilly. She gave him the "don't fuss over me" look, but he ignored her. "I've never seen a more graceful yet strong speaker in one. She got up to the podium in front of, oh, say, probably four hundred students and teachers and gave a speech that was funny, serious, tear-jerking, down to their level, truthful, and challenging all at the same time." Willy continued as he looked into Peter's stunned face, "It's obvious that I got to hear her bare her heart about a passion that hits close to home. In her speech, she shared part of her childhood. I'd no idea, Peter. Did you? Lillian's Hands to Hearts and Feet to Friends speech was awe inspiring. It was more than clear, that this is her calling: to share with other children, teachers, parents, or really anyone who will listen about child abuse; how to see it, report it, and help it. She really cares for kids who might not have any way out." Willy was beside himself as he remembered Wednesday when Lilly had knocked his socks off. He looked over at Lilly. "There seems to be a whole lot more to that lady than I thought."

"That," Peter said as he moved to get the door for the pizza, "is what I'm coming to learn very quickly." Peter gave Lilly a wink. He put his hand on the doorknob, looked straight at Lilly, and said very sweetly, "Every time we are together, I see another side of my ragmuffin that I haven't ever seen before." He raised his eyebrows at Lilly. "She's anything but boring." He opened the door and missed Lilly's bright red face. But Willy didn't miss a thing. He looked over at Lilly and raised his eyebrows in a "caught ya" look. The rest of the evening was spent in joyful fellowship.

But throughout the evening, Willy noticed they didn't take their eyes off each other. Willy silently cocked his head.

"In love, nothing," he said to himself.

On the drive home, Peter did apologize. "Lil, can you forgive me?" Peter asked softly.

Lilly, completely at a loss, asked, "For what, Peter?"

"Ah, my Lil, you have such a big heart," Peter sighed. "For being so harsh with you about missing class and here you were on a mission from God. Who am I to get in the way?"

Lilly waved her hand at Peter. "Not a worry. I had already forgiven you."

"What am I going to do with you?" Peter asked, shaking his head.

"Hopefully keep me," she said, more as a question. "You don't mind me tagging along in your life, do you? You're not getting tired of me, are you?" Lilly paused. "I can be a nuisance."

Peter, hearing her insecurity, had to make it clear she was going nowhere if he could help it. "You, my love, are not a nuisance. I love having you in my life and would be devastated if that were to ever change." He looked over at Lilly and brushed her check with the back of his hand. "Do I make myself clear?" Peter inquired softly.

Lilly's quiet reply was, "Yes."

"So, my Lil, what are your Thanksgiving plans?" Aunt Maureen asked just twelve days away from the tasty American family holiday.

"I was meaning to ask you the same question. Peter and Willy invited me out to Willy's family farm, but I told them only if I could bring you along," Lilly finished with a smile, looking at her aunt for an answer.

"I hate to disappoint you, Lil, but I can't." Lilly was concerned. "What do you mean you can't? I won't go without you."

Aunt Maureen figured Lilly would be over with the guys for the holiday, so this was no surprise. Peter seemed to be in the picture more and more, so she expected this. What she hadn't expected was that she'd be inviting James over and actually all their kids and families were coming as well. She had a big day planned.

Aunt Maureen said in her old, feisty voice, "Oh yes, you will! You'll go and have a good time with Peter and Willy, and I'll just be on tacks waiting to hear all your stories," her aunt said, laughing.

Lilly was rolling her eyes.

"But what about you? I can't leave you here all alone on Thanksgiving!" Lilly was adamant.

"You won't be." Her aunt said with a twinkle in her eye.

"Okay! Out with it!" Lilly demanded. "Just what are you up to?"

"Well, James is coming over for the entire day. All three of our children and their families are coming too!" Her aunt beamed with excitement.

"Oh, Aunt Maureen, that's so wonderful!" Lilly hadn't ever seen her aunt so exuberant.

"I'm not even sure we have all been together since our divorce. So this is really a big event. I hope everything will go good. I want it to be special," her aunt went on.

"It will be. Can I just pray for you right now?"

Her aunt nodded. Lilly prayed the most heartrending prayer on her aunt's behalf. Her aunt had to wipe away tears when she was finished.

They went on to make up a menu, Lilly promising to make four pies on Wednesday before she left, along with making rolls that could be frozen and then baked fresh that day. It was a special holiday, but for her aunt, this was extra special. And Lilly didn't want her aunt worn out. Her aunt said as she watched Lilly run out the door, "Have I told you lately how thankful I am you came and knocked on my door?"

Lilly turned and smiled. "I love you, Aunt Maureen."

CHAPTER 16

Lilly was flustered when she heard the knock on the door. She flung open the door. "Come on in. I ain't ready yet," she grumbled as she moved back to the kitchen.

"Ready for what?" came a reply.

Lilly backed up. "I'm so sorry, James. I thought it was Peter. How rude of me." She hugged him. "Happy Thanksgiving!" she said, trying to keep her floury hands off his back.

James grinned. He was delighted to be there, and the anticipation of this special occasion was written all over his face. "Hey, I was wondering if it would be all right to ask Maureen if I can join your Bible study on Monday nights. She asks me a lot of questions, and I just thought perhaps I could learn too and get to know the Word a little better. I'm sure I'm not as smart as Peter, but I can share what I do know. What do you think?" James ended with a hopeful smile.

"I think that is a wonderful idea!" Lilly gave James a grand smile.

"Hello, James," Aunt Maureen quietly said, her eyes mirroring how glad she was that he was there. Lilly had to get out of there before she began to cry. That would be a mess, tears mixed with flour and the other Thanksgiving pie ingredients. "Where do you want this bird, Maureen?" James asked as he brought in the big

Butterball. After parking it, he asked, "Now, how can I help you? Put me to work!"

"I didn't know you were gonna have help. I would have given pie-crust-makin' to him," Lilly teased.

Lilly was putting the latticework on top of the cherry pie when the knock came at the door. Lilly looked up at James.

"Here. Let me get the door for you," James offered, having sized up the situation.

Lilly's look was all the thanks James needed. It was obvious she didn't want to be seen with Thanksgiving all over herself.

She came out to the living room with her hair put up in a French twist, wisps of loose hair hanging down the sides. She looked breathtaking. She had on a lovely, forest-green dress that had autumn leaves falling down the front of it. Peter could barely drag his eyes away from her. He had never seen her with her hair up. Both James and Maureen knew a couple in love when they saw one.

Peter finally cleared his throat. "Are you ready?" he asked.

She kissed her aunt good-bye, and said, "Have a wonderful holiday full of new and precious memories."

Peter got Lilly settled in the car and was well down the road when he spoke. " I had planned to go out for lunch, but I'm afraid I might have to make a change of plans," he said in feigned contrition, shaking his head.

Lilly, thinking it was because she'd caused them to be late, said, "I'm so sorry Peter! I tried to not be late, but those pies were not cooperating! I don't know why I even volunteered. I don't even make good pies."

Peter chuckled. Beneath all that beauty was still his simple, sweet, adorable ragmuffin.

Lilly, trying to look indignant, asked, "Are you, Professor Collins, making fun of me? If I'd known you were going to be such a difficult traveling partner, I would have ridden with Willy."

"Whoa, whoa! Now you wouldn't really do that, would you?" Peter played along but really wondered if she meant it. "Do you mean to tell me that you would trade this Cadillac for his metal bucket horse and buggy?" He went on, shaking his head. "You disappoint me, ragmuffin; and I thought you had better taste than that!" He got more serious and said, "I'll tell you why you volunteered to make the pies: because you have a tender heart." Peter looked at her. "And," he went on, "the reason I considered a change of plans for lunch is not because we got a later start than planned, for we have plenty of time to get there, but because I didn't bring my bat to beat off all the eyes that will be on you if I take you *anywhere*." He looked over at her, his look encompassing all of her. He quietly said, "You look breathtaking, Lilly."

Lilly's breath caught in her throat. She wasn't sure what was going on, but he was looking at her in that weird way again. "Would you rather I change?"

"Um, I don't think so. I rather like the view myself!" Peter said. "I just don't like sharing."

He needed to rein in his thoughts, so he said, "And by the way, Miss Parker, you will not call me Professor Collins this weekend. Let's leave college and work behind us for the next few days."

"That sounds like a fabulous idea, Mr. Collins," she said, bursting out laughing.

"If I weren't driving, I'd pull you over my lap and give you a good whuppin'!" Peter said in the most outrageous voice he could muster up without laughing himself. "I can certainly tell this will be a weekend to remember."

"Is that a fact?" Lilly went on, teasing. "I agree with you that I think this will be a weekend to remember, but as far as the lap and the whuppin', I'd like to see you try!" she said, stealing a challenging glance his way.

"Well then, I don't suggest you find out," Peter said as they pulled into the parking lot of the quaint little café for lunch.

It seemed strange that Lilly had not met Willy's family. But with two different services, it was hard to get to know people. As well, the McCollisters had been doing some mission work and had missed a few Sundays. So somehow they just kept missing each other, which made this weekend even more special.

Willy grabbed Lilly in a bear hug when she got there and twirled her around. He left his arm hanging over her shoulder with a big smile and said, "Mom and Dad, I'd like you to meet Lillian Parker to most, Lilly to me, ragmuffin to Peter, and Lil to her aunt." Willy was being silly, hoping to make Lilly feel at ease. He knew she'd be nervous.

Lilly reached out to shake hands. Willy's mom shook her hand and then reached and gave her a hug. "Please call me Wilma. Welcome to our home."

His dad hugged her too and said, "I'm Douglas. Really, Lilly, make our home yours. We're so glad you're here."

Lilly thought he was the picture of quiet strength.

Willy's mom asked, "What do you want us to call you, my dear?"

Lilly tilted her head in the most adorable way. "Oh, it don't matter. Just please call me for dinner."

They all laughed.

Willy's mom looked over at Peter. "I'm surprised you even let her out of your sight." She smiled at Peter.

He'd been quietly watching all this, enjoying Lilly being fussed over. He knew she'd just love it here. He most certainly did.

"Welcome, Peter. It's always a pleasure to have our fondest nephew with us. How are you?" She'd gone to him and hugged him, bringing him into the little group.

"These days, with Willy driving me crazy and Lilly making sure he doesn't miss a beat, I'm growing old quickly," he teased as his eyes speared them both. "Really, I'm having the time of my life." He looked over at Lilly. "God has used the miracle of bringing Lilly back into my life to completely change me around. The direction of my life had gotten so far from its Captain I have literally had to do an about-face. I'm now walking the opposite direction, but it's the direction that pleases God," Peter said. "At least that is my desire. And I must tell you, your son was a huge instrument in praying for me and being a general thorn in the flesh about my heart condition." He looked at Willy. "I'm deeply touched and thankful for his love and longsuffering with me. He is truly a man after God's own heart," Peter ended, feeling very blessed indeed.

Wilma was the picture of country itself. She took off her apron and said, "Well, let's get you to your room. We have all weekend to chat, and I do plan on getting food in and info out!" Lilly laughed, knowing who Willy had inherited his antics from.

Just as Lilly left the room, Willy's nine-year-old twin sisters came bounding in. "Uncle Peter! Uncle Peter, can you play with us?" Though they were cousins, due to the age difference, they'd always just called Peter "Uncle Peter."

"Why, I've been waiting all day to play with you girls," Peter exaggerated to delight them. "What shall it be," Peter asked, "dollies, checkers, or Hide and Seek?"

"Hide and Seek," they both chorused over and over.

Peter thought about changing his clothes but decided against it, hoping he wouldn't regret that decision. Surely he wouldn't be rolling around on the ground.

Soon, they were well into the game and it was his turn to be it. So he counted.

"Ready or not, here I come," Peter called out.

Off he went in search of the girls. He'd spotted one of them and was running fast around the back of the house when he ran smack into Lilly. She'd come down the garage apartment stairs, heading to the kitchen. She would've hit the ground had he not suddenly grabbed her, keeping her from falling. After tumbling a bit but not actually falling, Lilly found herself wrapped in Peter's strong arms, their faces close together. Peter was breathing hard.

"Are you all right? We hit pretty hard!" He was finding it hard to take his eyes from her lips.

She thought she was fine from the collision, but his holding her was doing strange things to her. She just kept staring at him.

"Oh. There you are. Why are you holding this strange woman, Uncle Peter?" One of the girls asked.

The moment was lost, and Peter and Lilly immediately up righted and let go of each other. Lilly was fixing her hair and rubbing her head where she'd actually run into Peter.

"Susan, this is my friend, Lillian Parker. I brought her here for the weekend. Unfortunately, when I was chasing after you girls, in my haste to catch you, I ran right into her."

Peter looked at Lilly. She was smiling in pure delight at this little girl. Susan had her hand over her mouth, her eyes big as saucers.

"Are you okay?" she asked.

She was worried she had caused trouble.

Peter was about to answer when Lilly squatted down. She straightened the bow on the little girl's dress.

"I'm going to be fine, thanks to Uncle Peter, who caught me from falling to the ground after we crashed into each other." Lilly looked back at Peter to see if what she thought she saw was still there. Yes, he was smiling that special smile at her.

"Are you gonna marry Uncle Peter?" Susan was confused.

Susan heard Uncle Peter clear his throat, and she saw his disapproving look. "Oops! I better be going. Nice to meet you, Miss Parker Lilly. And, Uncle Peter, we can play later." Off she ran.

Both Peter and Lilly were laughing with their heads back. However, both were also thinking on what the girl asked, neither willing to say anything about it; but it remained on each of their minds the rest of the day. They'd walked a little past the back patio area where there was a huge, old oak stump just the right size for sitting. Lilly meandered over there, and Peter followed. She took in the full view of the place. It was a rolling forty acres, a hilly, rich pastureland dotted with cows in the distance. The color changes of the big trees were just magnificent. Wilma had a nice, big garden plot to the right. She also had a grape arbor that was well established. Lilly also thought she saw twelve to fifteen fruit trees planted around. Off to the front was a homemade but well-built swing/sandbox play set. Opposite that was a sand area with a volleyball net.

"It's wonderful out here, so peaceful," Lilly said, beholding what Peter usually took for granted.

After a moment, Lilly looked over at Peter to see what he was looking at, only to find his eyes on her. Both were thinking about the closeness and how wonderful it felt to hold each other. Lilly finally broke the spell.

"Well, I was on my way to see if I could help Wilma when all this Hide and Seek craziness happened. I better get in the kitchen and keep up my room and board. I'd hate for her to kick me out on my ear the first day."

Lilly had begun to get up, but Peter put his hand on her shoulder and sat her back down.

"Listen, ragmuffin. You're not here to work. You do not, and I repeat, do not have to work here. Wilma and Doug aren't like that. I want you to have a relaxing and fun time while you're here." Peter looked down at her. "And fat chance you'll get kicked out no matter what you do!" Peter grinned. "As for the rest of what you said, I wouldn't call it crazy." He whispered the last part and leaned closer to see her eyes.

Lilly licked her lips. She looked up at Peter and asked, "Just what would you call it, then?" A gentle breeze blew.

Peter was honest when he said, "I don't know, but when I find out, you'll be the first to know." Peter, looking at her lips, continued. "But I wouldn't call it craziness!" And he walked off.

Lilly thought her head would burst. She didn't know what to think about Peter lately. He was so attentive. It seemed as though he was looking at her more and more. She didn't know what to think about the fact that she'd nearly stopped breathing when he caught her and held her longer than necessary, so she thought. She remembered his breath on her face. She had the feeling perhaps their relationship was changing, but she didn't know what she thought about it. She needed some time in prayer and in the Word, which always seemed to sort things out for her. But for now, she was headed in to help Wilma. She just couldn't sit around.

In the kitchen, she found Willy up to his elbows in cookie dough. He was putting them on pan after pan.

"Wilma, what can I do?" Lilly asked after aggravating Willy by saying, "You missed one."

Willy was asking, "Where? Where?" before he threatened to throw a spoonful of dough at her.

"Let's see," Wilma said. "I have already done the potato salad. How about getting the baked beans going? Here is a recipe and other ingredients. After that, you can put the different chips in a bowl. I'm going out to get the cooler with the hotdogs ready." Wilma was quiet for a moment. "Lillian, there was something else that I wanted ask you about."

Lilly turned from what she was doing. "Sure, Wilma. What can I do for you?" Lilly was more than happy to help.

"Douglas and I had talked about asking you to share your testimony tonight." If she had looked at Lilly, she would have seen her go white as a sheet. "We both listened to the tape of when you spoke at church a while back, and we are simply dying to hear more. And so is everyone else, I'm sure." Wilma added, "Not to mention Willy has told us all about your school speeches, and it just seems right." Wilma paused. "Will you do it?"

Wilma looked at Lilly then. She was wide-eyed.

"Lilly?" Wilma asked.

"I'll do it," came the soft whisper.

Wilma went and hugged her, as a single tear had slipped down her cheek.

Wilma squeezed Lilly's shoulder. "How come I get the feeling there is a whole lot more to this ragmuffin that Peter has brought home to me?"

She smiled the most loving smile that just melted Lilly's heart. It was times like these that she wished her life had been different and that she could've had a mom like this. She scolded herself immediately, for that was being ungrateful for the plan God had for her. It was the very life she lived that God had used to mold her into what she was today.

Lilly's only reply was, "I'm always humbled that God would not only choose to save me. But to allow me to be a vessel for Him is just too much sometimes." Lilly smiled at her and then went back to her recipe. After she was through, she slipped into her room and got down on her knees.

LORD, *I'm undone before You. Why You would use a simple, sinful person like me is more than I can understand. But You have given me this opportunity, Father, and I don't want to mess up. I want You to be pleased with my heart and words. LORD, if there are any hearts You wish to touch, use me, oh LORD, as a drink offering; pour me out on Your altar of grace.*

After she prayed for a while she got out her well-worn Bible and read the account of Joseph with tears running down her cheeks. She had completely lost track of time. She looked at her watch to find the hands read 4:30 pm. Lilly jumped out of bed. She fixed her hair, dressed for the hayride, and scrambled down the stairs.

Lilly mingled with the youth and college students, chatting with many of them. Lilly was talking with a guy when Peter noticed her. He'd been watching for her but must have missed her when he put a few more bales of hay in the wagon. He actually chuckled out loud, his hands on his hips. What he saw was the cutest thing. Lilly had on overalls that had been made into a dress somehow. The bottom was just above her ankles, where it was fringed. He had never seen anything like it, but it was so adorable. It was just what his ragmuffin would do. She had done her hair in pigtail braids lying over each shoulder in the front. To finish the look, she had worn a white turtleneck under a red-and-white, small-checked blouse. The only thing missing, to Peter's view, was a straw hat and a long piece of grass hanging out of her mouth.

Wilma bumped into Peter as she was passing by. "She won't appreciate your laughter!" She was smiling.

Peter controlled his laughter. "You're right on that one. But isn't she so cute?"

"Well, from the looks of things, you're not the only one with that opinion," Wilma said, having noticed all the male attention Lilly was getting. Not that she had drawn attention to herself in any way, but she was just that sweet kind of girl that was easy to like. Wilma noticed the smile faded from Peter's face and his jaw was set. Wilma was not sure she should say this, but she did. She placed her hand on Peter's arm. "Remember, she's not yours," Wilma said with love, "and if you're interested, you better get in there and stake your claim." Peter didn't know what to think. Wilma had sized things up nicely. But he just wasn't sure what was going on in his heart. He just hadn't thought about his ragmuffin falling in love. It was beyond his comprehension, yet it was a very normal thing to do. Why was it okay for him and not her? His mind and heart were doing all kinds of crazy things, yet he still couldn't get this out of his mind. *Do I want to claim her; and if so, would she even want me? You're quite a bit older, Peter.* The last question lingered in his mind all evening.

Peter approached Lilly. "Good evening, Chad. Good evening, Lillian," Peter said congenially. "Hope you're both having a good time. I just came over here to ask Pippi Longstocking where she left her straw hat and freckles!" Peter just had to say that, but he didn't count on how embarrassed Lilly would be.

Lilly was crushed. She wasn't mad but *very* embarrassed. And it was clear to her that Peter thought her a child and didn't like what she was wearing. She gave Peter a look. But to Peter's surprise, it was a look of sadness. Peter, seeing the depths of his cruelty, didn't know what to do.

Fortunately, Chad saved the awkward moment. "Well, Mr. Collins, I think there is a whole lot more to this adorable woman than overalls and braids. Hopefully she'll let me find out," Chad said with a questioning grin at Lilly.

They called for everyone to get on the wagon at that very moment, causing Peter not to be able to reply. Chad grabbed Lilly's elbow.

"Come, Lillian. Let's go."

They went off to the wagon, Lilly glancing backward at Peter with sad eyes.

It would have been easy for her to let that spoil her evening, but that wasn't the way Lilly was—at least she tried not to be. She noticed that when she got on the wagon, hay was already everywhere. The wagon filled up fast. As it lurched forward, Lilly almost fell into the lap of the guy next to her. Everyone was being bounced around. That was part of the fun. But Peter didn't like it. He wasn't happy about the conversation with Chad. He didn't like how close the guys were sitting around Lilly, not that any of them had ill intentions; and it *was* overly crowded. Peter really was jealous of Lilly's laughter and joy that she was sharing with others instead of him.

That's really wicked, Peter thought. *The truth hurts.*

Some of the younger teens began to throw hay, and it was getting out of control when Peter gently but firmly put an end to it. Lilly caught his eye. He looked at her. She had hay all in her hair, and she was basically almost buried in it. They smiled at each other, caught in their own world. Then a huge, devilish smile spread across Lilly's face and she picked up a handful of hay and threw it at Peter. He threw a handful back, and then a full hay war broke out. Shortly thereafter, Lilly stopped and raised her hands and, even in her quiet nature, actually got everyone to stop throwing hay. She took one more sheepish grin at Peter. But Peter had to admit it had been fun to act crazy for a moment.

Willy had started some praise songs, and everyone joined in. Lilly loved to sing to the LORD. It was just something she hadn't always had, and it was a treasure she never tired of. On they bounced and sang. The night was cold, though no one seemed to care. Lilly thought the sky filled with stars was magnificent. Lilly didn't know when she'd had this much fun. Perhaps never. She didn't know how long they were on the hayride, but she often found Peter's eyes on her when she looked his way.

Finally, Douglas pulled back into the driveway and everyone hopped off of the wagon. Chad helped Lilly down. She thanked him.

He smiled and said, "The pleasure was all mine." Everyone was getting coffee or hot chocolate and roasting hotdogs. Peter keep a close eye on Lilly. He wanted her to have the freedom to get to know people, though he had females in mind, not fellows. With her work schedule, she didn't get out much.

He was praying and asking God to help his sinful attitude when Willy began to speak. "Our family wants to thank everyone for coming out tonight. I don't know about you, but I've already had a blast." He was smiling his Willy smile. "I want to say thank you, Mom and Dad, for loving us and for the heart you have for the young people here. I'm indeed a privileged son." He was looking over at his mom and dad, who were standing in the background.

"As I stand here thanking my parents, I'm reminded of the most wonderful home growing up anyone could ask for, I realize what a treasure that is." Willy looked over at Lilly. "Not everyone has been this blessed. Perhaps even some of you will be able to relate to what is shared tonight. Many of you have meet Miss Lillian Parker. Some heard her speak not long ago at an evening service. We have asked her to share the whole, unabridged story and the most current ending." Willy laughed a little, thinking what a hoot that was right now. He looked over the group and said,

"I've never met a more fascinating lady. Please welcome Miss Lillian Parker." Everyone clapped. Willy went over and helped Lilly up from the log she was sitting on and moved her to the middle of the crowd, close to the bonfire, so she could be heard. Willy leaned and whispered in her ear, "Glorify the King! You can do it!" He kissed her cheek and sat down.

Lilly smiled at him as soon as he was looking her way.

"As Willy mentioned," Lilly started out, her voice strong and clear yet humbled, her heart evident, "not everyone gets to have the pleasant family life that Willy and his sisters have enjoyed." Lilly went on, tears threatening. "I know some of you right here will be able to connect with my story. Some of you might have great heartache and sadness in your home this very moment. You might have hatred, discord, or abuse. You might think you're never going to live through it. Some of you might be angry at God for making you suffer this way." She went on. "If there's one thing I'd want you to take home from this evening, it is this: whatever situation you are in with your family, God has allowed it for His glory and His purposes. Don't allow yourself to ask, 'Why me?' any longer, but turn to God. Call out to Him! If you don't have a relationship with Jesus, let me encourage you to begin there. It'll make all the difference to your ending. If you're a Christian and you still find much of this story relating to you, then listen carefully. God has something for you to hear tonight. May all of you leave tonight knowing just how awesome God is!" Lilly sighed. "If you're one who can't relate personally with what I'm about to share, then look around. There are broken hearts all around you. Find one to minister to; embrace them as Christ would." Lilly cleared her throat, trying to stem the tears that threatened, and with a raspy voice, said, "If someone had not done that with me, I wouldn't be here today."

Lilly looked over at Peter. His hands were folded together under his chin, elbows on his knees, smiling at her.

So Lilly began with the day Jeff and Jenny knocked on her door. She spared no details, including the living conditions. There were gasps when she spoke of her mother's hatred and abuse. There were tears on faces, and Lilly could tell by the looks on some faces that God was working on their hearts. She even had a few laughs at the hairbrush set that was her first Christmas gift and that Jenny had brushed and fixed her hair with her new gift so she would remember to brush it thereafter. She spoke tenderly about all the times Peter had befriended her as the years went on. She also spoke about their treasured relationship and some of the things Peter had taught her about God. Everyone was so captivated by the story that when she yanked herself out of the town with the story of her departure, people nearly yelled out loud.

She proceeded to share almost exactly what she had shared with Peter about the years she spent in Farmington, Nebraska. She choked up a few times as she shared about those very dark days.

"This was the hardest time of my life," she told them.

She emphasized God's sovereignty over her life. She described every experience she'd had during her time away with such vividness it made people shiver. She tore her heart wide open for all to see this Lillian Parker. There wasn't a dry eye sitting around the fire.

Lilly actually broke down too. With a trembling voice and tears streaming down her cheeks, she said, "That is why the story of Joseph means so much to me. I've read it over and over, its truths written on the tablet of my heart." She then quoted Genesis 45:4–5— "'Then Joseph said to his brothers, 'Come close to me.' When they had done so, he said, 'I am your brother Joseph, the one you sold into Egypt! And now, do not be distressed and do not be angry with yourselves for selling me here, because it was to save lives that God sent me ahead of you,—' "and Genesis 50:20: "'You intended to harm me, but God intended it for good to accomplish what is now being done, the saving of many lives.'"

She then shared about her arrival in Shelbyville, North Carolina. She stole a glance at Peter when she began the next part. He, of course, had a grin ear to ear, knowing what she was about to share.

"Then on the first day of college…" Lilly began, and she shared the rest of the story up to that very night.

"My life now has a new page in its book, so to speak." Lilly was wrapping it up. "There's really no way for my heart to express what it was really like to have that first bus ride that forever changed my life; nor the heartbreak at having to leave Peter, Jeff, and Jenny; nor to convey those dark days that followed. But this I can tell you: I have absolutely no doubts that God was in every detail of my life then, as He is now. And He forever will be," Lilly emphasized. She ended with this: "So jump on the bus, and take the ride God has for you!"

Willy began to sing. All joined in. Lilly closed her eyes, tears streaming down her face, and raised her hands, praising her Father. After a wonderful time of praise and adoration, Willy had the group break up into groups of four to five wherever they were sitting to join hands in a time of prayer. Then, as people finished they left. Lilly, however, knew none of this, as she had left when they'd regrouped for prayer. She climbed the apartment stairs, changed, and got in bed. She cried herself to sleep as she praised God for allowing her to be His child.

Peter was looking frantically for her afterward when Wilma noticed him.

"She went to her room, Peter," Wilma said. She noticed Peter calm down. Wilma said, "I don't think I have ever heard such a fabulous story in all my days." She put her hand on his shoulder. "I can certainly see why your world has been turned upside down."

"That's the understatement of the year." Peter chuckled.

Wilma probed a little further. "So do you love her, Peter?" Wilma knew she was pushing the envelope of personal matters, but this was a special case.

Peter looked at her in shock then looked away and began to speak. "I think I'm going crazy. Before Lilly came into my life on the first day of the semester, my life had been going fine. Well, not really fine as God would see it, but it was orderly. I knew what I wanted and what I was doing, even though none of that really included God." Peter raised his hands and let them fall in exasperation. "Now I don't know which way is up!" He looked off into the night. They were practically the only ones still outside. "I cannot imagine my life without her, yet I don't know if I could handle losing what we have in order to find out if there's any more for us. Does that make sense? And I cannot stand the thought of her with someone else! That makes me a mean, old tyrant, doesn't it?" Peter looked at his aunt. He hadn't even allowed her to answer the first question, so she tried to hit them both.

"My dear Peter, love has a price. It sometimes costs one dearly to love. But the value of love comes in what you are willing to lose to gain it." She said this and gave him a hug and said, "Good night."

Peter went to his room, which was Willy's old room. They bunked together anytime the apartment above the garage was in use. Lilly was its occupant this weekend. Peter was readying for bed, as was Willy.

"Do you ever think you will tire of hearing that story?" Willy asked.

"Nope," Peter said as he put away his clothes.

"Me neither," Willy said, tossing his clothes on the chair, half falling to the floor.

"Course, Lilly is an awesome lady." Willy chuckled as he climbed in bed, leaving his clothes scattered.

"That she is," Peter said as he fluffed his pillow.

"One thing is for sure: we aren't the only ones who think so," Willy said, thinking of all the male attention that had been directed her way. He thought Lilly was completely unaware, but he had noticed it.

Peter's head came up off his pillow so fast Willy thought he might fall out of his bed.

"Just what do you mean?" Peter asked, in great distress.

"Come on, Peter. You can't tell me you didn't see that several of the guys were taken with your ragmuffin. Even her braids and overall outfit didn't discourage them." Willy was getting comfortable. "I can't say as I blame them. She's the most incredible woman I've ever met. If I were in a different place, I'd be asking her out on a date myself."

"She's got a date?" Peter asked incredulously.

"I don't know for sure. Why is that such a big deal to you?" Willy pushed for Lilly's sake and those poor guys who didn't stand a chance.

"I don't know," Peter said as he laid his head back down on his pillow.

"Look, Peter, take some advice from someone younger than you for a change. If you're not going to take her for your own, let her free. Let her love and be loved. Don't keep that from her."

"It's not that easy," Peter said and rolled over.

"Peter, I'm a simple guy," Willy said. "The two of you are literally a match made in heaven, and I don't mean that flippantly either. God has brought y'all back together; and as far as I can tell, ya don't exactly hate each other." He was hinting around. "Good night, Peter. It was an awesome night. God is more than good to us to call us His sons."

It was after 8:00 a.m. when Lilly made her way from the apartment. Breakfast was ready, so Lilly joined everyone at the table and after prayer dug into her pancakes.

All were eating when Willy spoke up, "Hannah, I saw you sitting awfully close to Leo last night."

Hannah turned beet red. "I'd be tending to my own business, big brother. You had enough trouble of your own," Hannah teased right back. "I thought Elizabeth would spill her plate watching you walk past her."

"You're crazy! She's only fourteen." Willy shook his head. "That makes me six years older than her." He gave her a disgruntled look. His hair was wilder than Lilly had ever seen it. It was obvious he hadn't showered yet. She giggled at his looks. He had on flip flops, a pair of raggedy, cutoff jean shorts that went just past the knee, and a wrinkled t-shirt.

Peter, sitting across from Lilly, spoke up. "Well it might seem strange when one is at that young of an age, but when you are older, the age difference doesn't seem to matter so much." He looked right at Lilly, for that was what he was quickly discovering.

Lilly looked right back at him. "Yes. I'd agree with you," she said quietly.

There was an awkward silence, so Doug spoke his thoughts, "Lillian, I was so touched last night. What an awe-inspiring story. I couldn't help going to bed praising God for the work He has done in your life."

"Thank you, Aunt Wilma, for the delicious breakfast," Peter said as he wiped his hands clean. "I'd like to do the honors of cleaning up for you if I can snag my ragmuffin to help me." He gave Lilly a hopeful look.

"Well, I don't know. I have twelve interviews with prospective dates. They should be arriving any minute, so I might have to let the twins help you." Lilly was trying to do her best to tease, and everyone at the table had a good laugh on that one, save Peter, who gave Lilly a disgruntled look.

"Mom, can we?" the twins chorused.

Wilma shook her head no.

"I think Uncle Peter will be up to his elbows in trouble as it is," Wilma said as she winked at Peter.

He didn't like being made fun of, especially in that way. But he laughed and said, "I can save you the hassle. Send one guy at a time to the sink. After I suds him down, wash him through, and wring him out, I'll send whoever is left standing to you for an interview," he bantered back.

"You'll do no such thing, Mr. Collins," Lilly said. "But because I love Wilma, I'll join you in the dishes."

Doug and Wilma just looked at each other, both thinking about what they had discussed as they lay in bed together last night. Both had smiles on their faces. Willy shook his head, mirroring the thoughts his parents were having.

At the sink, Peter was looking at Lilly as he rolled up his sleeves. "Now don't be too hard on me, or I will spray you." He flicked the handle of the sink sprayer toward Lilly. He was being really playful and fun for Peter.

"On a day like today, there is nothing in my heart but thanksgiving," she said with zeal. "There's so much to be thankful for, Petah. I think my heart will burst."

Peter noticed she had used his nickname without even realizing it. He loved it when she did that. It was just the sweet reminder of their beginning. He noted that she most often did it when she was nervous or extremely excited about something. Peter had filled the sink and decided to wash everything by hand so he could talk with Lilly longer. He hadn't even thought about the fact that this was the first Thanksgiving away from her mom and sisters. He wondered what all was going on in that little head of hers.

"Yes. You are so right. Why, everyone can be thankful for something on this occasion."

Peter was convicted about how much of his life he lived every day without a thankful heart. Lilly was a constant reminder of his complacency. She had a huge heart, and she lived life through the eyes of thankfulness. It made all the difference in the world. Perhaps that was even why Lil was so loving to others: because she was thankful for them first. Peter was really beginning to see more into that heart of hers.

Peter went on to say, "It'll be fun this evening when we all sit with cider and pie and share what we are thankful for."

"Thanks for the heads up. I might as well go take off my makeup now, for I'll be crying again," she said with a sigh.

"You shouldn't be embarrassed to cry, ragmuffin," Peter said. "And as far as makeup, you look lovely with or without it."

Lilly rolled her eyes in disbelief. "Let's see if all twelve of my dates agree with you," she teased.

Peter stopped washing. "Are you serious that you have a date?" He was looking intently into her eyes, not ready for her to go out with anyone else.

Lilly flicked her rinse water at him, barely getting him sprinkled but teasing that she would douse him any minute. "You, Mr. Collins, are a worrywart," she accused. She went on. "As a matter a fact, I was asked out three times last night." She didn't give any more information but asked in mock frustration, "Are you gonna wash or not?"

Peter went back to washing, slowly though, as he said, "And?" Peter was dying to know if she'd found someone special. It was driving him crazy.

"Why, Peter?" Lilly rinsed off the last dish. "Why do you need to know? Why is this so important to you?" She dried her hands, turned and leaned against the sink.

Peter ran his hand behind his neck in frustration. "I don't know, Lil. It's just that I'm not ready to think about it." Peter looked away for a moment. "I know you have a life of your own to live. And believe me, I want you to have what you've always wanted," Peter said as he looked back at her. "I'm just selfish. I don't want that life to be without me."

She was looking back. His face was intent as he looked at her lips. He was thankful that, at the moment, they weren't alone, for he had a desperate desire to kiss her. He was falling fast for Lilly. But how did he let her know that? He was not completely sure of what he wanted himself, yet he didn't want to let her go.

Lilly looked right back at him and softly said, "It doesn't have to be." Lilly could not believe the warm sensation she was having at his nearness.

Peter broke the spell with a laugh and raised eyebrows. He motioned outside with his arms. "I don't think those guys are gonna like me holding the lantern on your dates."

"No. I don't suppose they'd appreciate that." Lilly laughed.

"So what did you tell them?" Peter tried again, not being able to let it go.

"It just so happens, Mr. Collins, I told them I was taken." She tossed her head at him.

Peter's eyes got so big Lilly thought for a moment they were going to fall out of his head. His eyebrows raised, and his eyes bulged.

"You did?" he asked, utterly crestfallen to think that even before last night she already had someone special. "By whom?"

Lilly tossed her head and said with a smile, "You." Then she walked off.

Lilly had not anticipated it, but Peter grabbed her arm with a strong grip that she had to stop.

"Whoa! What do you mean?" Peter was confused. He just couldn't let her walk off.

"Peter, it's really simple. I work most every night at the Stuffed Goose." Lilly sighed. "The only nights I have off are Sunday and Monday. Sundays are at church, and Monday nights are taken with you and Aunt Maureen." She shrugged her shoulders as though that was easy enough. "Though I did tell them I'd love to get to know them more, just like I do everyone, but it'd have to be in the mornings on my off school days or Saturday or Sunday afternoons," Lilly said. "But I'm usually with my two favorite guys on the weekends, so I doubt they'll be seeing much of me." She smiled and walked away.

The relief Peter showed was great. He hollered behind her, "Hey, how about a walk later?"

"That will be great. I promised one of the twins a game of checkers. See ya."

She also had a tea party with the twins. She sat on the swing outside with the two oldest girls under thick quilts, drinking hot chocolate. They talked about their dreams and how God was working in their lives. It had been a wonderful day, and there was still more to come.

Lilly moved from the table to the counter where Wilma was rolling out dinner rolls. "Wilma, how can I help?" Lilly asked with a soft voice, simply taken with this new view of Thanksgiving that she'd never seen before.

Wilma looked at Lilly and then at the table of youngsters playing Pit. "I'd love your help, but don't you want to join in the game?"

"Wilma, I don't know if you can understand this, but today has been one like no other Thanksgiving. And it'd be so special if you'd let me be in here with you."

Lilly began to cry. She turned away for a moment. Everyone at the table turned to see what was going on. Peter had begun to get up to come over. Wilma put her hand up to stop him and shook her head no. She would take care of this. Wilma went to Lilly and engulfed her in her arms. Between sobs, Lilly spoke.

"I'm so sorry, Wilma. It's just that I've never had a mama who did this kind of thing, and I just wanted to be near you. I know you're not my mama. I was just overcome with desire." She pulled back, found a tissue, and tried to clean up her face.

"Oh, Lilly. I know I'm not your mother, but it would be an honor to play house today. As you can see, my girls have long lost interest in what you would count a treasure," Wilma said as she patted Lilly on the shoulder.

Lilly sniffled loudly. "I know it seems silly, but could we? I would cherish it always."

"You betcha. Here is an apron, and melt that butter over there for the rolls."

Wilma crinkled up her nose at Lilly. Then they were off. Lilly and Wilma giggled their way through. Wilma taught Lilly several tricks of the trade. Lilly, in her excitement to cook in the kitchen with a real loving mother, made some silly mistakes. There was much laughter when Lilly dropped eggshells into the sweet potato casserole and when she lifted the beaters out of the bowl of mashed potatoes while they were still on, only to have them go everywhere. But Wilma was patient, actually loving it, as she prepared Thanksgiving dinner with the most thankful person there.

Lilly prepared the table. She had the twins collect some leaves, acorns, and pinecones, and she spread out God's own natural decorations down the middle of the table. Then by each plate she set a name card. Under each name she wrote what each person meant to her.

Finally, all was ready. The dinner bell rang, and Doug, at the head of the table, prayed the most heartfelt Thanksgiving prayer Lilly had ever heard. And then the clatter around the platter was riotous. The food had to have been wonderful, but truthfully, Lilly was too lost in the family to have ever noticed what hit her taste buds that day.

After clearing the dishes Lilly went to her room. She had to get away and to her Lord. She fell on her knees.

Lord, I'm overwhelmed at your gift of today! I'm undone before you. I would have never dreamed of a day like this, much less a family focused around you. You are so great! Why, Lord, do you show your favor to me? Oh, Father, I love you so much. May my lips be singing to you praises now and always, no matter what tomorrow brings. I have just had the time of my life; and I owe it to you, oh Lord. Thank you!

She prayed and cried tears of joy and thankfulness. She also, with a heavy burden and through tears, prayed for her mom, sisters, father, stepfather, nieces and nephews, and her Aunt Maureen. Then she feasted in Psalms.

After she had her fill of true feasting, she left and went back to the living room. Peter looked up from his book. "Ready for that walk?" Peter asked.

"Yes." Lilly smiled.

"I can see where today would be an incredibly emotional day, perhaps draining too," Peter said, looking at Lilly to see signs of strain. "I sometimes forget that you just left a most difficult situation, and that leaves scars. A lifetime of scars probably bared their ugly heads today, if I'm not mistaken."

"Such thankfulness is grown from soil fertilized with suffering," Lilly said very quietly. "So it's the dark days that make this one so exceedingly bright."

"Have you thought a lot about your mom and sisters today?" Peter asked, touched by her words.

"Not a moment has gone by that she wasn't on my mind," Lilly whispered. If she wasn't careful, she'd be in tears again.

They continued their walk, Peter helping her to talk through her emotions about the day. Then they prayed as they came back to the house.

Everyone was around the living room with their pie and cider when Doug started the evening off. "I, for one, am extremely thankful to be head of this wonderful family." It was evident he loved his family greatly. "If absolutely nothing ever happened in my life, I'd still be the most blessed man ever." He went on to share more and then started the sharing around the room.

When it got to Lilly, she was already overcome with emotion. But, clearing her throat, she said, "I don't mean to sound like a broken record, but I can't come to this day without being thankful for my salvation." Lilly's voice quivered, and her tears threatened. "Even though I shared my story last night, I want to say, rather shout, my thankfulness for my salvation because I have spent a lot of time today thinking and praying for my family, all who are lost and have no hope. So there is nothing more valuable, more precious to me than the gift of salvation. Well, it just leaves you undone." Lilly was crying again, but they were tears of joy. She looked up to the ceiling. *Lord, help us to never take this for granted.*

Several others shared. Then it was Peter's turn. Peter cleared his throat and looked around the room.

"I must admit I'm ashamed to think that I have come to many a Thanksgiving day with a lack of gratitude, with a heart of complacency for my very blessed life. It has humbled me to see Thanksgiving through Lilly's eyes. It's reminded me just how blessed I am. I pray that God will continue to open them from the expected to the unexpected. I pray that from this day forward, as in the old days, love will be the main course and zeal and fervor will be the complementary side dishes so that I will not forget those forgotten." Peter couldn't help but look at Lilly. It started her tears afresh, but he wasn't sorry.

After all had shared, Willy got out his guitar and led them in some singing. Then, after a time, all joined hands and took turns praying. It was a time like Lilly had never known.

After people refreshed themselves, they all came back and started sharing old family stories. Peter had purposely made his way to the couch, where one of the twins had been sitting by Lilly, and stole her seat so he could be near Lilly for the rest of the evening. No one noticed, or so he thought. The rest of the evening was a whirlwind. At one point, while Lilly was intently listening, Peter took her hand and held it. He smiled at her and raised his eyebrows. She knew she'd been unconsciously picking at her fingernails and tearing them up. He hated to see her lose all her hard work. She rolled her eyes at being caught outright. But he still didn't let go of her hand, which was sending all kinds of feelings spiraling through her.

They had a wonderful time laughing until they cried. Lilly noted that this indeed was a precious family to have grown up with—not perfect, but they loved one another. Finally, Wilma sent the twins to bed. Not long after, both Doug and Wilma said good night.

"I think I'll turn in as well. I still need my beauty sleep, unlike the rest of you adorable people," Lilly said as she took her cup to the kitchen. She turned just before leaving the room, and with tears said, "I never knew what it was really like to have a family who loved one another. Thank you for letting me be a small part of that today. I didn't know my heart could be this full."

"I'll see her to her room and be back." Peter said and hopped up.

Peter, holding Lilly's elbow, went out and around to the apartment stairs. At the foot, Lilly turned.

"Petah, I'm at a loss for words."

Peter was looking into the loveliest face he'd ever known, even though Lilly's cheeks were still wet with tears and her makeup was smeared. But her eyes held a beauty he couldn't describe. The moonlight shone brightly over her face, illuminating her soft skin. Peter leaned down close.

"Then that makes two of us," he whispered. He needed to get away before he kissed her. He bent lower and placed a kiss on her forehead and said, "Get to bed, my ragmuffin. I'll see you in the morning."

CHAPTER 17

"Good morning," Lilly greeted Wilma and Doug as they came in. Lilly was curled up on the couch with a throw, her Bible, and a cup of the strong morning brew.

"Did you sleep well?" Wilma asked.

"Yes, I did. Thank you." Lilly smiled, "How about the two of you?"

Both Wilma and Doug looked at each other with a special smile.

Doug put his arms around Wilma's waist and said, "We always do whether we are awake or asleep." He winked at Wilma.

Wilma playfully jabbed Doug. "Douglas, not in front of company." She gave him a frown, wiggled out of his grip, and went to the kitchen.

But before she could get away, Doug popped her on the bottom and Wilma squealed.

Lilly giggled and looked back at Doug, who smiled back at her. "Being married is so much fun. You ought to try it sometime. I highly recommend it."

Lilly simply smiled at him and said, "Up until recently, I didn't have much opinion on the truth of that, but you and Wilma have definitely given me something to think about."

Both Wilma and Doug greeted Peter. He was already show-ered and dressed, hair in place, as he sat down close to Lilly, he leaned over like a three-year-old, and looked into her cup.

"Is there any more?" His voice, belying his appearance, begged for coffee to wake him up.

Lilly, quite taken with him, said, "Yes, there is more. But to wake up a sleepyhead like you might take a river. I'm not sure Wilma and Doug can afford that much coffee." Lilly was sucking in her cheeks, trying to hold a serious face.

Peter growled and gave her his meanest early morning face he could muster. "You ragmuffin. How dare you?" He was threaten-ing to tickle her. "If I recall correctly, you were the first one in bed last night." He went after her, almost spilling her coffee.

"Stop it, Petah. You're going to spill my coffee!" Lilly said as she pushed him away.

"The things I have to do to get a sip of coffee around here!" Peter teased back

Both Doug and Wilma decided this was a good time to exit, to give this couple, obviously in love, some privacy.

Lilly tilted her head. "Do you always wake up this grouchy?"

Peter laughed. "Nope! I left him in bed." He said referring to Willy.

"Something tells me that Willy doesn't have a grouchy bone in his body," she said, looking at Peter.

Peter asked, "Why do you think that?" Peter had put his arm on the back of the couch and let it rest on Lilly's shoulder.

The closeness was not lost on Lilly.

Peter had done some major computing last night, and there simply was no denying he thought the words *love* and *Lilly* were coming mighty close together. He wasn't sure what to do about it, though. It wasn't just that he loved her as he always had, but a new love had joined the other love. He'd gone to sleep very late, thinking about all these new feelings for Lilly. He thought about his feelings toward Veronica and his desire for a wife. And he kept coming back to Lilly. He smiled even in the darkness of the night. Yes. He was definitely falling for that ragmuffin. He'd been searching out what he wanted in a wife, not that it was just a list. He had told Veronica his wife had to love the LORD and hold to similar convictions and beliefs as his own. He racked his brain to deny that Lilly fit that description, to a tee. Plus she was fun, loving, and extremely beautiful too.

Peter had to confess as he lay under the covers that he had been in falling for her for some time. He just hadn't recognized what was happening. Even the passion he had for Veronica paled in comparison to what he was holding in check for Lilly. He chuckled as he thought, *We are as different as night and day in personality.* But he thought how much they complemented each other. And the gap in age didn't mean a thing to him, but he wasn't sure Lilly felt that way. One thing that held him in check was the woman herself. He didn't want to lose what they did have. She was way too precious to him. He realized this would be a journey of trust in God, but he was willing to go down that road. He planned to start today, letting Lilly know how special she was and, little by little, his intentions. He knew Lilly would give him a merry chase, but would they marry at the end of the chase?

"You didn't hear a word I said, did you?" Lilly had her arms crossed. "I'm worried about you. Not only are you grouchy and in much need of coffee, but you've lost your hearing too." Lilly clicked her teeth together and shook her head. "Such a shame," she teased mercilessly.

Wilma brought Peter coffee.

"Thank you." Peter laughed, "Apparently, you need to pour it on my head."

"What were you reading this morning?" a more serious Peter asked Lilly. Lilly read to Peter what she had been reading in the Word and then went on to give her thoughts on the section and ask a few questions. They were enjoying this time of study. They prayed together about the things they had read and discussed.

Then they sat back in comfortable silence. Peter had his arm around Lilly as she began to mischievously swirl her now-very-cold coffee remains. She began to swirl it more and looked at Peter with a quirky smile.

"Hey, are you still not awake?" Lilly asked as she continued to swirl her cup his way.

"You wouldn't," Peter said, beginning to raise his hands and scoot away. "Would you?"

He began to have serious doubts when she was quiet and kept swirling her coffee and looking at him as though she really was going to toss the entire remains in his face.

All of a sudden, she hopped up, "Nope. I wouldn't do that to Wilma, but I did want to see if you needed any more help waking up," she taunted and laughed as went way out of the room.

Peter tried to snag her but missed. "You just wait, my ragmuffin. You just wait."

"Wait for what?" Willy wanted to know as he walked into the living room.

The fact that he'd just gotten out of bed was obvious, or else he'd combed his hair with a pitchfork. Lilly covered her mouth to stifle the giggles at Willy's appearance. Lilly even saw wrinkles on his face where he'd slept hard.

They ignored Willy and all headed to the dining room, as Wilma had rung the breakfast bell.

Lilly breathed deeply the cool autumn air as she walked around the grounds, looking for a quiet place to study. Eventually she meandered into the barn and had the extreme curiosity to climb up into the loft. She'd never been on a farm before, much less in a barn. They'd always lived in the city. She carefully climbed up the ladder, holding her books under her arm, her notepad under her chin, and her pencil between her teeth. She got to the top and crawled to the middle. As she sat on her knees, she thought how magnificent this was. She closed her eyes and inhaled deeply the pungent smell of hay. She shoved her hands deep in the hay and then began to toss little pieces here and there. Laughing at herself, she began throwing big handfuls high in the air like a child in a candy shop. This went on for some time, Lilly thinking she was alone, having the time of her life, while Peter watched on, having the time of his life. Peter had snuck in quietly and had been watching her from the loft ladder, his head just over the top where he could see her. Her back was to the ladder. She was positioned just as she had crawled in, her shoes kicked off.

Peter knew he could not stay on the rung of the loft ladder much longer, so he cleared his throat and spoke. "Well now. I thought my ragmuffin was much more dignified than this that I should find her playing as a child up in the animal food storage loft," he teased as he climbed on up the ladder.

She closed her eyes upon hearing his voice, for she had thought herself to be alone and was embarrassed.

He came around and sat in front of her, very relaxed.

He's so good looking, she thought. "I guess I've been caught red handed, Professor Collins," she said and tossed a handful of hay his way.

"I should've made a higher wager for saying Professor Collins while here on break." His eyes were twinkling.

"Now just what kind of wager would that be, Professor Collins?" Lilly said playfully. She'd have taken her tongue out if she'd known his next words.

Peter knew he was about to be in treacherous water, but he jumped in both feet anyway. He sat up and moved a good deal closer to her so she would know he was serious. "If you say 'Professor Collins' one more time, I'm going to kiss you," he said. Fully enjoying the look of terror on her face, his grin reached ear to ear.

Her mouth opened in the most unfeminine way and then closed again. Her head went up in the air, her arms crossed, and then she looked at him.

"If I know anything about you, Professor Collins, it's that you don't break the rules. So, knowing this about your character means you just lied, for you aren't to be in a serious relationship with a student, remember? Therefore, you were bluffing just now." She said this with all the serious sauciness she possessed and then said, "Professor Collins," again just to prove her point.

All smiles drained from Peter. He lay back on the hay, sprawled out, defeated. "You're right." Peter sighed. "I can't wait until you're not my student anymore." Peter's thoughts were going wild about their future, not realizing how his comment sounded to Lilly.

Lilly was very quiet. She was hurt by his words. His approval meant so much to her. "I've never been very good in school, but I've really tried," she whispered. "I should've dropped your class, and then you wouldn't have to put up with such a brainless wonder."

Her voice was so sad that Peter's heart was cut like a knife. He scared her when he jumped to a sitting position so quickly.

He couldn't take that look. He brushed her cheek with the back of his hand. "You've got it all wrong, my love." He had moved very close to her face. He looked into her eyes with all the love he

had. "You're right about not breaking the rules. You got me there."
He wanted to take her into his arms to finish the explanation,
as if there would be a need for one after that. "Where you're all
wrong," he continued softly, "is why I can't wait until you're not
my student."

They were in a world they'd not been in before, so completely
aware of one another, emotions riding high.

"Why is that?" Lilly asked breathlessly.

Peter made no bones about it. He looked at her and smiled
all the love he had for her. "Why, so I can break all the rules." He
grinned, not moving his eyes from her face. "But until then," he
said, looking at her lips, "keep me an honest man and don't call
me Professor Collins again." He had come close to her. He now
leaned over until his face was right near hers.

Panic seized her heart as she felt his breath.

"You have a piece of hay in your hair." He said and plucked it
out and sat back.

All Lilly could say was, "Oh!" Her world seemed to be spinning when Peter was around.

Peter knew he needed space and a change of subject to get his
mind off kissing her. "What are you studying, even though you
were supposed to leave school behind you?" he asked with raised
eyebrows.

Lilly, fighting for control, said, "Well, unlike you, Pro…
Peter—" she put her hand to her mouth at her near mistake— "I
have finals coming up. You ought to know that it takes me a lot
of extra work to pass. So I brought along a bit of studying to do.
Plus, my English professor gave me a ten-page contrast paper to
write for my final. Can you believe that?"

"Well, it sounds like you have a ruthless, mean, geezer for a
teacher." Peter laughed. "Perhaps if you gave him an apple he'd
give you an A."

Lilly threw hay at him.

"Better yet, his favorite cookies might do the trick," Peter coerced.

Lilly pulled her knees up under her chin. "What are your favorite cookies? There's so much I don't know about you," Lilly said. Then she realized how that sounded and blurted, "Not that I would ever consider bribery!" She laughed. "But I just realized that there is so much I don't know about you after all these years. Yet I feel like our hearts are so much the same. How can this be?" she asked her thoughts awhirl.

"There is a lot about you that I don't know either," Peter said with a twinkle in his eyes. "And what I don't know I plan on finding out. I want us to really get to know one another much better."

"Well, let's get to it." She said all businesslike, "What's your favorite cookie?"

Peter licked his lips. "My favorite cookies are currant cookies," he said as though he were eating one at that moment.

"Currant cookies? I've never heard of them." Lilly wrinkled up her nose. "I know. I can do my contrast paper on cookies and title it: Old Dough in a New World." She had Peter laughing. "I thought you'd be just an ordinary, old chocolate chip fan."

"You might think I'm just an ordinary Joe," he said as he put his arm over his propped-up leg. "I'm sure that most of the time, my serious and orderly life means I only live in a box." He smiled at her. "But lately, my box has been overflowing."

Lilly gave him her most winning smile. Peter spoke up again. "I'll tell you what. I will break my promise and help you study if you promise to spend Christmas with me," Peter said with a mischievous grin.

Lilly leaned forward. "I can't think of anyone I'd rather spend that most precious season of all with other than the handsome Professor Collins from Shaftner."

Peter lay back on the hay, looking at the ceiling, for his heart couldn't take any more looking at Lilly. It was just too tempting.

They talked for a few more moments. Then Peter helped her with her studies. Before they knew it, the others were back from their horseback ride and all went inside for some cider and hot chocolate. The rest of the day was spent in absolute delight. They played games on into the night. Lilly crawled into bed just after 2:00 a.m. She knew she would regret it in the morning, but it was such a fun day. She hadn't wanted it to end.

The drive home was rather quiet. Lilly broke the silence and asked, "Why do the McCollisters call their place Barnabas House B and B?"

"It's actually very simple. And after I tell you what Barnabas means, you'll agree that it's indeed most appropriately labeled." Peter continued. "Barnabas, in the Bible, means 'son of encouragement.' They want their place to be a haven of encouragement to all who come there."

"There's no mistaking their hearts. I've never met a family quite like them," Lilly said, remembering what a sweet time she had just had. "I see what you mean about it being a perfect name for their family farm. Peter, thank you so much for inviting and bringing me to the Barnabas House B and B." She flashed him a very meaningful smile. "I'll cherish the memories forever."

They drove on home in companionable banter. Both were enjoying each other's company, neither one wanting the weekend to end. But way too soon, they pulled into Aunt Maureen's driveway. They looked into each other's eyes for a moment. Then Peter leaned over slowly toward her face. Lilly's eyes shut in anticipation, but Peter simply kissed her forehead. Lilly looked at him in confusion.

He whispered, "I had the loveliest weekend, my ragmuffin."

Lilly was converged upon as she went into the house. "Oh, Lil. You are home." Aunt Maureen beamed as she came over to hug Lilly.

Lilly noticed she was like a new person. *Something is definitely going on here,* Lilly thought.

The second week of December proved to be one of the biggest challenges that Lilly had faced since coming to North Carolina. Her finals week was upon her. She was a nervous wreck, so she prayed a lot. She asked God to help her remember all she'd learned and to go before her.

She'd asked her aunt to help her find a currant cookie recipe. Of course, her aunt knew of a good recipe and gave it to Lilly. She baked them early in the morning and put them in a clear cellophane bag, tied it with a cute ribbon, and put on the tag: "To my favorite teacher. Love, your ragmuffin." She placed them in a nice gift bag she had made with some tissue paper and slipped it under his desk early that morning before class. She had one exam that morning, and then she just had to turn in her English paper.

She'd finished her speech exam. She now sat in Professor Collins's class. He cleared his throat and addressed the class.

"I just want to say that this was by far the best class I have ever had." He was looking straight at Lilly. She was smiling back. "If I currently had a cookie for every great writer in here, I'd be a fat man," he said, hoping he had adequately conveyed his thanks for the cookies. She got the message. Peter went on. "I hope you have enjoyed this class as much as I have. I hope you go away with more knowledge and a deeper appreciation for literature. You can simply turn in your papers on my desk. You don't have to stay. Have a wonderfully meaningful Christmas. Your grades will be posted in one week."

Lilly was the last to leave. She was done for the day and was in a jolly mood, having completed two of her four exams for the week. She meandered up to his desk. Peter was looking at her with a big grin and raised eyebrows. She sat on the corner of his desk. She swung her booted foot without a care in the world. Peter was glad the semester was over, yet he would miss seeing her in his class.

"Just what is that smile all about, Miss Parker?" he asked with arms crossed, curious to know what was going on in that head of hers.

"Well, currently, I'm wondering if you'll eat all your cookies and your eyes will get so fuzzy that you cannot see all my run-on sentences and comma splices." She grinned, teasing him. "Just so you know, I'm hoping to do better than a *C* for *cookies* on my paper, Professor Collins."

"You, Miss Parker, aren't making brownie points by teasing me when I can't get near you. That, my dear, is teacher cruelty. Didn't you know that? And it's against the law."

Lilly put her hand to her mouth to stifle the giggle. "Oh my. Perhaps I should've made brownies. They would've given me a *B* for *brownies* instead of the *C* for *cookies*." She made a contemplative face.

"Ah. I think not. But I think I might need more cookies to convince me of your love for my class." He winked at her, holding up his bag. "For these are half gone already. And, I might add, very tasty," he said as he moved his head as close to her as propriety would allow. Then he got serious. "I'm going to miss you in my class. I'll be ever so lonesome to see your beautiful face." He thought his class would never be the same without her; however, since it meant he could more fully pursue her, he felt it a better deal. He touched her cheek ever so briefly. "There are times I wake up and wonder if it was all a dream that my ragmuffin actually was sitting in my class at the beginning of the semester." He was intense. "These last few months have been the best, and I look forward to where they go from here."

Lilly, feeling a bit insecure, asked in wobbly voice, "Petah, is this the end? Will I never see you?"

Peter knew she was upset, for she'd used his nickname.

Peter grabbed her hands into his. "Oh, Lil," he said breathlessly, "what an inappropriate place for me to convince you that just the opposite is true."

Lilly's eyes got big, and she seemed to calm down.

"What I'm afraid of is that you will get sick of me."

"That'll never happen." Lilly said as she looked into Peter's eyes.

Peter released her hands and patted the leg on his desk and said, "Well then, indeed, I'm looking forward to all that this next year brings with great eagerness, Miss Parker."

Lilly said, "Well, I'm done for today." She hopped off the desk. "It's a great relief to have two classes out of the way. I'll see you tonight, Professor Collins," she teased as she stuck her head back around the corner.

He gave her a teasing frown and a finger wagging. Peter said to himself, *It won't be long till I break you of that habit.* He stuck his papers in his briefcase and went to his office to start grading their finals. That night, he'd call Jeff and Jenny to confirm and talk one more time before the big Christmas gift.

CHAPTER 18

This Sunday was the first showing of the Christmas pageant to which Lilly had invited Aunt Maureen, along with several other people. It was that very morning as she sat next to Aunt Maureen that Lilly noticed her crying, which brought a torrent of tears to Lilly's eyes. There really was no way to watch the birth to resurrection of Jesus and not shed a tear. Lilly handed her aunt a tissue and patted her hand.

Having just arrived home from the bus route, Lilly found her aunt in a puddle of tears when she walked in not an hour after church. Though Lilly's stomach was growling ferociously, but she went straight to her aunt.

"What is it, Aunt Maureen?" Lilly asked.

Aunt Maureen turned to Lilly and said, tears running down her face, "That's what it's about, isn't it? I've been proud and thinking I'm something. Here Jesus came to be a human, to live and die for me, because of my sin." She put her hands on Lilly and was shaking her in desperation. "Tell me, Lil. I—my sin, my willfulness, my lack of acknowledgment of God—nailed Him to the cross. Am I right?" she pleaded, even though she knew the answer.

Lilly nodded her head yes. Her aunt went to her room and didn't come back out for a couple of hours. Lilly spent time in prayer for her and made them a simple lunch. She was glad that, for once, she'd not planned to be anywhere or do anything that afternoon. She was sitting on the couch with her Bible when her aunt emerged from her room, her eyes swollen from crying.

She sat down beside Lilly and asked in a quiet voice, "Are you for sure He would want someone like me?"

Lilly's smile stretched over her face. "Oh yes, Aunt Maureen, I'm sure."

"Well, I don't know iffin I know how to be a good Christian like you, Lil, but I asked God if I could be his daughter too, like you. I begged Him to save me as I repented of my sins. I told Him I wanted to do whatever He asked me. I told Him I believed He was real and that He was God and I needed a Savior." Lilly could tell she was excited. She went on. "I've never been so happy! I feel so free. I want to tell everybody!" She jumped up. "Why, I have to call James!"

Lilly laughed at her as she as she went to the kitchen to dial his number. She closed her eyes and praised God for saving her aunt.

The doorbell rang, and Lilly's head popped up from over the stove. "Who could that be?" she wondered.

"I'll get it, Lil." Maureen said as she left her bedroom. "It's probably James. I invited him to breakfast. Oh, I'm sorry I forgot to tell you," she said on her way to the door.

She opened it to find Peter with his hands in his jean pockets, freezing, his breath steaming in the frosty air. He smiled, stumbling over his words. "I was … um … I was coming over to give Lilly a test."

"Do come in, Peter. Get out of the cold," Maureen said. "We were just fixing breakfast. Would you like to join us?" She was hanging up his coat when the bell rang again.

"Well, I do know who that is," she said as she went back to the door and welcomed James in. "Well now, we'll have a nice breakfast this morning. You guys get yourselves comfortable in here." Then she was off to the kitchen.

"What's going on out there?" Lilly wanted to know as she flipped pancakes.

"Here. Let me help you make some more batter for those hungry guys out there," her aunt said as she prepared another batch of pancake mix.

Lilly turned from the stove. "What do you mean by guys?" she asked incredulously. "How many are out there?"

"Oh. Just two. James and Peter," Aunt Maureen answered.

"What is Peter doing here?" she wondered, worried she'd forgotten something.

She had the strong urge to go out and see what he wanted, but now she needed to double up and cook up some more sausage and make some more coffee. Her aunt helped, and twenty minutes later they were all seated around a homemade blueberry pancake breakfast.

Maureen said, "Let's pray." She bowed her head and prayed, "Dear God, thank you for letting me be your daughter. Amen."

Peter gave Lilly a questioning look. Lilly had been so totally blessed by her aunt's prayer that it took her a minute to notice Peter's bewildered look. Her aunt's prayer had been spoken from the heart with such a wobbly voice that Lilly thought she would cry.

She looked over at her aunt. "Share with Peter your good news!"

And she did just that.

"Oh. That's the best news one could ever share," he said as he got up and hugged her and kissed her on the cheek. "Welcome to the family," he said as he sat back down to enjoy the delicious breakfast.

"By the way, why are you here?" Lilly tilted her head in curiosity.

"He said something about a test for you," Aunt Maureen piped up.

"What do you mean a test? Did I not do so well on my exam? Not that it wouldn't surprise me," she said, discouraged.

"What's for dinner?" Peter asked.

Lilly, confused and a bit irritated, asked, "What do you mean what's for dinner? We're just finishing breakfast! And what in the world does that have to do with a test?" Lilly tapped her toes impatiently.

Peter laughed, figuring he better fess up before he was in the doghouse. "Yes, I brought you a test. But, seeing your foul mood, perhaps I should bring it back at a better time."

She gave him a stern look. "Are you accusing me of being grouchy, Professor Collins?"

Peter was all but laughing at her by now, and she didn't take it too kindly. Before he could answer her, she spoke again. She was shaking her head. "You came here too early and caught me without my makeup on. My hair is all over the place. At least I did shower, but you can tell by my clothes I was not expecting company. This is the real McCoy."

Peter laughed slightly, wishing they were alone, but Maureen and James seemed to be enjoying the entertainment. Peter cleared his throat. "My dear ragmuffin, you forget the nature in which I first met you. If I recall, you had on no makeup, your hair was a riot, and I don't think you had had a shower for some time. And I had no problem falling for you then, so you see, you are quite lovely to me no matter what you look like."

Lilly was caught up in his gaze and sweet words. Peter went on.

"It really isn't complicated. I'm the test."

"What? What do you mean?" She was confused.

"Remember last Monday when we talked and you said you'd never get sick of me?" Peter explained.

Lilly nodded, her lips almost a pucker.

"I decided to test you on it." He smiled. "So I showed up bright and early and plan to stick around all day to see if you are a lady of promises kept." He took a sip of coffee and just looked at her.

She scooted back her chair. "I think I'll do the dishes now, if you all will excuse me. James, it was good to see you again."

Seeing they needed some privacy, James and Maureen went outside.

"My, you're suddenly quiet," Peter said, thinking his coming was a mistake.

When she still remained quiet as she washed the dishes he said, "Lil, if you'd rather me leave, I will. I just thought perhaps you missed me half as much as I missed you already." He was drying his hands on the towel, getting ready to get his coat.

"Please don't leave." Her squeaky voice stopped him.

"Are you sure?" He turned around.

"Yes." She giggled under her breath. "I don't want to flunk my test."

He walked back to her. He put his arms around her backside as she was facing the sink, hands deep in suds. He was very close. He looked at the side of her face, her eyes not giving away anything. "Are you sure? This test can come back if you want," Peter said. "I didn't know it would be such a big deal."

Lilly sighed at his closeness. "I'm so sorry, Peter. I'm still vulnerable at times about my past." Lilly licked her lips. "It makes me feel all yucky that you think of me like I remember me." She paused. "Does that make sense?"

Peter tried to explain his heart to Lilly. With sweet tenderness he showed her his vision of the nine-year-old Lilly and his completely different view of the here-and-now Lilly. He was as descriptive as he could be and still keep all propriety. Lilly listened quietly trying to take it all in.

"So tell me, Professor Collins, how hard are you going to make this test?" Lilly asked, so completely lost in thought of all that was happening that she didn't realize her mistake or what was going to happen next.

Peter, wet hands and all, reached up, turned her face to his, and brushed her lips with his own. Lilly's eyes closed. She didn't know when she'd felt so warm inside.

"It depends on whether or not you're going to quit calling me Professor Collins," he said with a wink.

Lilly was bright red, her eyes revealing her heart. Peter thought it not fair that he could read her so well.

"Though I don't like to hear it, I really enjoy the consequences," Peter confessed.

He was thinking how lovely it had been to kiss her, even though it was ever so briefly. And from what he could tell, she hadn't hated it.

Lilly was breathless. "I guess I better work hard at passing this test, for I try to always keep my promises." Lilly let out the dish water. "And it's true that I could spend every moment with you." She gave the true confession.

"Well, as the test goes," Peter said with a big smile, "I'll be over here every day during break until I see for myself that you're not going to get sick of me, then I will know for sure if you have passed."

Peter wished he had a camera, for Lilly's eyes were so big and her mouth was wide open.

"Are you serious?"

"Why, of course," Peter said. "If it was easy, it wouldn't be a test."

"But what about Aunt Maureen?" Lilly questioned. "She—"

"What about me?" Her aunt had just walked in and heard her name.

Lilly gulped. "Uh … uh … Peter wants to know if he can hang around us, well, me, all day every day during break." She was stumbling over herself.

"Of course. He's welcome anytime," she said and winked at Peter.

"Well, I guess there is no getting out of this test now, my ragmuffin." He crossed his arms in satisfaction of winning. "I guess you're stuck with me."

"Here I was, thinking I was out of school!" She flopped her arms in the air in mock despair.

"How about we go to the mall?" Peter suggested. "I love to people watch, and I'll treat you to lunch too to make up for showing up this morning unannounced," he persuaded.

Lilly thought it a great idea, so that's what they did. As they drove to the mall, Peter's mind was on two women. He thought how Lilly's makeup revealed who she was, yet Veronica hid her true self under the layers of stuff. He shivered just thinking about the mistake he'd almost made.

The whole week was spent just like that. The second morning he came with three bags of groceries to help out Aunt Maureen. Lilly wasn't caught again naked faced and was always ready by the time Peter came over, which was by nine every morning. Peter thought this was the best school break he had ever had, test included.

CHAPTER 19

Christmas Eve dawned with magnificent beauty. Lilly stretched with joy as she got up. She had busily worked on a scarf for Peter and had finished it late the night before. She had planned to spend Christmas Eve here with Aunt Maureen and James. James had asked Lilly to come to his house to help him wrap gifts. Why he waited so late, Lilly didn't know, but still she wanted to keep her word. So she was ready by 9:00 a.m., just as James was ringing the doorbell.

Lilly couldn't believe how the time wrapping gifts had flown; it was just over three hours later that she noticed Peter's car when she arrived back from James's place. She was looking forward to every moment that stretched before her. But what she wasn't prepared for was Peter's Christmas gift.

Lilly opened the door. She was not two steps inside the living room when she heard a very loud, "Surprise!"

From the hall and the kitchen doorway came Jeff and Jenny. Peter leaned against the wall, soaking in the entire scene. He wouldn't have missed this for the world. She just stood there, her mouth gaping open, the look of surprise written on every fiber of her body. Then Jenny opened her arms and walked slowly over to a very stunned Lilly. That movement was all it took. Lilly nearly tripped over herself in a rush to get to Jenny, a very pregnant Jenny. Peter didn't realize two people could hug that long.

Finally, Jeff said, "Hey, what about me? Save me some!"

Lilly jumped back. "Oh. My manners. I've lost my head. I'm just so … just so … um …"

She went to Jeff, and he bear-hugged her. He did the same as Jenny had done. He couldn't believe he was actually seeing their Lilly once again.

Peter finally had mercy on everyone and said, "Hey, can I have one?" He was still leaning up against the wall grinning.

Lilly pulled away from Jeff's embrace, turned to Peter, and with all the scowl she could muster on such a happy occasion, wagged her finger at him. She knew this was all his doing. It had to be. She put one hand on her hip, pointed her finger at him, and said a big fat, "No!"

Peter howled with laughter. He was indeed enjoying this. She turned around Jeff had his arms around Jenny. Lilly walked up to Jenny and put her hands on her round tummy. "When … how … I mean when … you didn't tell me." Lilly kept feeling her tummy.

"Well, at your age, Lil, we won't talk about the how," Jenny teased. Lilly realized her mistake in her excitement and turned ten shades of red. "But we found out about this little miracle in May, and we are due to see the little fella—"

"Or baby girl," Jeff corrected as he winked at Lilly.

Jenny cleared her throat loudly and winked at Jeff. "Or baby girl in February."

Jenny was smiling brightly. They'd tried for over nine years for this moment, and Lilly knew it had been a source of tears, yearning, obedience, trust, and faith all in one.

Lilly hugged Jenny again with more tears. "I'm so excited for you both. I know you've desired this for a long time." She went to Jeff again. "Are you not just the most excited man on earth?"

It was Jeff and Jenny's turn to blubber.

Jenny said, "Look at you. Just look at you. You're so grown up! Peter did his best to tell us all about you, but still, seeing you from child to adult is a little mindboggling. Turn around for us," Jenny went on and looked Lilly over again. "Wow! I just never thought we'd ever get this opportunity. Indeed, God is to be praised, for only He could've done this miracle!"

"Peter, you better keep a good eye on her. She's going to snag some man's heart and take him for a bus ride he'll never forget," Jeff said.

Lilly hugged everyone once more. She finally noticed her aunt and James in the corner, tears in her aunt's eyes.

"Oh. Mind my manners," Lilly said. "Aunt Maureen, this is the couple I told you about—"

"I know, honey. I've already met them," her aunt interrupted.

"This is just crazy. I think I'm going to wake up and find this all a dream," Lilly was saying as she sat down on the couch and then looked back up in the faces of her most dearly loved friends in the entire world. "Wait a minute. How long have you been planning this?" she asked Jeff and Jenny.

"Well, since about the second phone call Peter made to us," Jeff said.

Jenny piped up, "That's why we didn't write to tell you about the baby; we wanted to surprise you."

Lilly was putting the pieces together. She spoke slowly as she went through each puzzle piece. She looked at James. "So that's why you drove so slowly, like a snail, I might add. Then you made me rewrap three gifts and design a basket twice. You took forever to decide who to give what. Then you didn't help me wrap a thing. Here I was, thinking not-so-kind words about you." She laughed and pointed a finger at him. "You were stalling for time so they could get here, weren't you?" James just smiled and said not a word. She turned to her aunt. "You were in on this too, weren't you?" Her aunt only smiled.

Then Lilly got up and slowly walked over to where Peter was leaning up against the wall, smiling. She looked up and whispered the sweetest heartfelt words. "You planned all this, didn't you? You're my hero," she said. Then she stood up on her tiptoes and kissed Peter on the cheek and softly said, "Thank you."

He looked down into her beautiful face, thinking what a sweet kiss that was, and he knew what a sacrifice it was for her to do such a thing. He'd not stopped grinning since she walked in the door, but he stared at her and said, "Merry Christmas, my love." He didn't say anything else. It was a priceless moment indeed. He was more than glad he'd thought of this some months ago and acted upon it. It was the best gift he'd ever given anyone.

After lunch, James said, "Now y'all go in the living room. Maureen and I are going to do the dishes." Lilly tried to protest, but he said, "Scoot. I'll not hear another word about it."

Lilly thanked them, and she, Peter, Jeff, and Jenny all went to the living room to catch up on the missing five years.

They talked, with Peter filling in at times. Jeff thought he'd not seen the man this excited in a long time. He could also tell that Peter and Lilly were in love with each other but wondered why no announcement of wedding bells had been declared. It seemed perfect that the two of them become a team as he and Jenny were. Lilly could not believe her ears when her aunt came in and told them it was time for dinner. She'd prepared a delicious Christmas dinner. Lilly thought she'd outdone herself, though it was very touching. Before they knew it, it was time to go out to the Barnabus House B and B.

"Have you met Willy before?" Lilly asked Jenny as they headed out the door.

"No, I haven't," Both Peter and Lilly laughed as if on cue. "Just you wait and see."

They enjoyed their drive out. All was quiet when they got to the farm. Wilma said everyone one was in bed in anticipation of the next day. Jeff and Jenny were introduced to Wilma and Doug. And Jenny got to see firsthand the love they both had for others.

"Lilly, I have you in the room with Olivia and Hannah. Do you know where it is?"

Lilly shook her head no. Peter offered to show her since it was down a few doors from where he shared with Willy. Wilma went on to explain, "I've set Jeff and Jenny in the guest apartment over the garage. Is that going to work? I mean, there are stairs. Are you okay, Jenny?"

"Oh yes, ma'am. That will be great," Jenny said, truly thankful they would have some privacy.

Doug spoke up. "Here. Let me show you the way." Taking their bags, Doug led the way, being the perfect host.

All went to their rooms. Peter pointed to Lilly's room door. The whole day had been way too much for Lilly. She'd begun to cry. Peter sat the bags down and took her into his arms. He smoothed her hair. "It's okay. What is it, my love?"

She pulled back from him. "Your gift to me has just so completely overwhelmed me. I'm afraid I'm going to wake up and find it's all been a dream," she said. "Why would you care to do such a fabulous thing for me?"

Peter brushed away her remaining tears with his thumb. He kissed her cheek. Avoiding the answer, he said, "Get some sleep, my love. Tomorrow is a big day." He then picked up his own bag and headed to his room. Lilly went in the room with the girls. They were awake, reading. They got up, hugged her, and pointed to the other open bed in the room.

The same was going on in Willy's room. "Hey, man! Glad to see ya made it!" Willy was slapping Peter on the back. "How's the test going?" Willy had climbed back in bed. "What was Lilly's reaction when you surprised her with Jeff and Jenny?" Willy wanted to know everything.

"Ah. I would tell you, except you tease me so much about being an old man. I just don't know if I can stay up that late," he teased. Peter put away his things and readied for bed.

Willy threw a pillow at him. "You better! I waited up for you so you could tell all. Especially since I've not seen a lick of you since you started this test with Lillian."

Peter gave in, pulled up the quilt around his neck, and told Willy everything. Willy did enjoy a love story, and he was sure hearing one. It was all he could do not to laugh listening to Peter go crazy about the woman he loved.

After Peter was done, he asked, "You love her, don't you?"

Peter was quiet for a moment.

"Oh, come on. Your secret is safe with me. And if you say no, I'll laugh at you!" Willy was already laughing.

"What's not to love?" Peter asked, evading the real question.

Willy sat up in bed. "You're a hoot, man. Just say it. While it's true everyone who ever gets to know your Lilly will love her, that's not what I mean, and you know it!"

"What are you afraid of?"

"I want to be sure my age does not repulse her," he said.

Willy howled out loud and then put his hand over his mouth when Peter threw a pillow at him.

"Be quiet, or you will wake the girls!" he said.

"You two crack me up," he said. "She's in love with you but thinks you think she's just a kid. And you love her, but you think she thinks you're too old for her." Willy was really laughing now, though quietly. "When I fall in love, it ain't gonna be this complicated. It'll be a piece of cake. I'll say, 'I love you,' kiss her, and propose," Willy said straightforwardly. "There won't be any of this miscommunication going on."

This time, it was Peter's turn to laugh. "Sure, Willy. And I promise to remind you about this very night when you're up to your ears in love with a woman and don't know what to do," Peter said with an experienced snicker.

"Well now, am I actually getting a confession out of you that you do indeed love Lillian?" Willy asked.

"Ah, yes. I do love Lilly," he admitted.

Willy went on. "It's not like you have never dated. Don't tell me you don't know what to do." Willy was teasing him without mercy. Peter rolled back over to face Willy. "That's where the mystery is," Peter said. "I really have no idea what to do. She's so special, I find myself at a loss." Peter was feeling much better actually having talked to Willy about all this.

Willy, being an excellent listener and friend, listened with all his heart.

"Now I feel things for Lilly that I never experienced with Veronica. Ah … so much more! I feel all the desires a man is supposed to have, and I feel like it's right this time, unlike anything I had for Veronica. But yet, because it's my ragmuffin, I'm all the more scared of messing things up." Peter sat up on his elbow. "Does any of that make sense?"

"Clear as mud, dude," he said, smiling.

Peter plopped back down on the bed in defeat.

"I'm just kidding. Of course that makes sense. Sorta anyway." He shot another teasing grin at his lovesick cousin. Willy asked, "Have you kissed her yet?" He was dying to know.

Peter said, "That is none of your business." He crossed his arms and said, "I haven't asked her yet." His forehead crinkled.

Willy fell back on his bed in laughter. "Man, do you mean to tell me you are gonna ask her if you can kiss her?"

"Why, of course. It's the only proper thing to do," Peter said.

"Whoa, whoa, whoa. Do you realize just how unromantic that is, Peter? You don't just ask, 'Can I kiss you?' like it is a business deal." Willy was laughing, yet he really wanted to help his friend out. "Did you ask Veronica?" Willy wanted to know.

"Why, no," Peter said indignantly. "But this is different," Peter insisted.

Willy got comfortable for sleep and said, "Well, one thing is for sure. Veronica and Lillian are two different people. I must say that Lillian Parker is a rare jewel if I ever saw one, and I can see how different it must be. Well, actually, it's probably completely different." Willy stopped and decided maybe he didn't know as much about romance and girls and complex situations as he thought. So he let out a big sigh. "Well, Peter, I don't know what to say. This one is too hard for me." He paused. "But you might try not calling her ragmuffin anymore."

Peter chuckled. "Yeah. There certainly isn't anything raggedy about her anymore. But if you had seen her as I did, a scared, filthy, unloved, poor nine-year-old, you would understand how the nickname fit."

Willy laughed, thinking he would've fallen just as hard as Peter had if it had been him. "I'm sure you are right. Good night, Peter. I'm glad you are here. But if you're going to keep chasing that ragmuffin of yours, you better get some sleep."

Lilly was glad she wasn't the last to the table. When she got there only two seats were left: hers and Willy's. Willy was the last to join them. Peter stood and went to pour both of them a cup of coffee.

Willy looked up. "Hey. Thanks, man. I usually don't drink the stuff, but since my roommate kept me up till all hours of the night, I might need to have a few cups." Willy grinned at Peter.

"Thank you, Peter. I should've done that," Lilly said.

"My pleasure," he said and winked at her. *She is beautiful this morning*, Peter thought.

Lilly, feeling very curious, spoke up after the blessing. "So what in the world kept you two up so late?" Lilly was looking back and forth between Willy and Peter.

Peter was tightlipped, but his eyebrows sent Willy a "better not spill the beans" kind of look.

Willy, in his light banter, said, looking at Peter, "One thing is for sure. Who needs a movie when bunking with Peter is much more entertaining?"

Willy was teasing Peter to the hilt, and Peter was glaring back at him.

By now, Lilly was really interested in their party secrets. She put one hand on her hip. "So, guys, what did you talk about that was so interesting?"

Just as she asked that, Hannah passed the basket of muffins to Willy.

"Why, muffins," Willy said as he took three out of the basket and put them on his plate. "Why we talked about all kinds of muffins."

Lilly let it go. She looked at Peter. "I must confess that I didn't want to go to sleep last night either."

"Whatever was the problem with my ragmuffin?" realizing a bit too late that he'd called her *ragmuffin* again.

Right at that moment, he locked eyes with Willy. He gave a nod of understanding. All this was lost on the rest of the occupants of the table.

Lilly spoke up with a bright smile, looking over at Jeff and Jenny, who were both watching her. "I thought I'd wake up and find this all a dream. I still can't believe I'm sitting here at this table with the only three people who loved me when I had nobody." She quit talking then as she gathered control of her emotions.

Jenny grabbed her hand. "Oh, Lilly, it's not a dream." She squeezed her hand and continued to soothe the girl. "We are truly here. And hopefully, by God's design, we'll never be parted again."

"How silly of me, sitting here crying like a nine-year-old, not exactly convincing you that I'm not still that little brat you found so many years ago, but a disciplined and respectable adult now." She cleared her face and put on a smile.

"Lilly, believe me," Jeff said, "tears never leave the lives of females." He looked over at his dear wife, whom he had witnessed many tears from, especially over this ragmuffin. "We don't think of you as a child. But I must say, no matter your age, you'll still be our ragmuffin," he said with all the love he had for this girl.

Jeff spoke, "I know everyone probably wants to get into the living room. But if we're not in a hurry, I'd like to share with you all that very first meeting."

Doug agreed readily for the family.

Jeff plunged in. "That particular Sunday in July was high-attendance Sunday. If your bus got sixty kids on it, the whole bus got ice cream sandwiches. It was just what we needed to get us to do more, go longer, knock harder, and even go places that we wouldn't normally go." He looked over at Lilly. Jeff felt the heat even as he spoke. "It was hot. We were pouring in sweat, glad to be about done. We had climbed back into the car, and I had begun to take my tie off when Jenny pointed to a trailer sitting off the edge of the last street. I really wanted my tie off, but one look into my lovely wife's face and I knew it was no use in even loosening it. We drove slowly up. We got out and walked to the gate that went to the sidewalk. The grass was almost knee high, weeds everywhere, some so tall they reached the broken windows near the front door. We looked at each other, both scared to death. Then I took Jen's hand and walked up to the door."

"There was a tree that hadn't been pruned in many years in the front yard. Under it was an old, rusted tricycle in the yard and some other rusted items. There were enough cigarette butts to have mulched the whole yard. There were beer cans and bottles strewn everywhere. There were what appeared to be two bags of trash just outside the door, but evidently, some dogs or other animals had taken the trash out already that morning. There was only one remaining shutter on the windows. The screen door was missing, torn up, and lying in the yard. The trailer itself was, I'm guessing, about twenty-five years old. The skirting looked like the teeth of a beggar in bad need of dentures. If I hadn't seen the torn curtain move, I would've thought it unoccupied, as it was in such disarray and so trashed. We walked up the wobbly cinderblock stairs and knocked on the paint-peeling door."

"Very quickly, the door opened just a peep. The most heart-wrenching little face peered around the door. Her matted, dirty blonde hair was a riot. The tiny little hand that held the door had bleeding, ripped-up nails. The little girl was only showing her face and her arm that opened the door, but I could tell she was in a thin, worn-out night apparel of some kind."

All eyes had been on Lilly as she let wet drops fall into her plate.

Jeff said, "Lilly, look at me."

Lilly slowly obeyed and looked up at Jeff.

"That is the moment I fell in love with you." Jeff's voice had gone very soft in controlling his own emotions.

Peter hadn't been there, so this memory was very dear to him.

Jenny grabbed her hand. She had been crying. "Me too. That little girl stole my heart, so now do you realize how special it is to see you again?" Lilly slowly nodded.

Jeff clapped his hands together loudly, making most at the table jump. "Now I shall keep you all in suspense about that ragmuffin of a girl so I can keep my manhood and not blubber all over everyone. And I know of some girls itching to go to the other room for a while," he said with a smile at the twins.

He also needed to give Lil a break. He hadn't anticipated how emotional he would get himself, so this was a needed break for both of them.

"A splendid idea, but we'll all be waiting anxiously to hear more," Doug said with a smile.

They all went to the living room. Lilly took off her shoes and curled up on the end of the couch, Peter quickly took up residence next to her, and Willy plopped down on the other side of Peter. He jabbed Peter in the side.

"Hey, buddy, you could pop the question right now. No one will hear ya."

If looks could kill, Peter would have been arrested. "You just wait. I'll keep a record, and play it over and over again when your time comes, drummer boy," Peter said, wanting to take his playing fingers and twist them into a pretzel.

Lilly leaned over. "What was that?" She looked at Peter. "Did you need something?"

Well, I do need something, he thought. *To lay a kiss on you that you'll never forget and a roll of duct tape a mile long to wrap my cousin up in.* But he said, "I just need to see if you are okay. That was quite a story in there. You better drink a lot of water this weekend. The way you've been crying, you might dehydrate."

"I hate that I can't seem to stem the flow. It seems like that's all I ever do anymore," Lilly said with a wobbly smile.

Doug quieted everyone down and welcomed them. "I would like to read the beginning of the redemption story as we focus on the gift above all gifts. Then we will pray and Willy will lead us in some Christmas carols." He put on his glasses and read with a fervent voice the first two chapters of Matthew and Luke.

After prayer and a wonderful time spent in singing their favorite Christmas carols, Doug led out again. "As has been our tradition for many years, we go from the youngest to the oldest in gift-giving. Let's begin!"

The twins went first and then on through the older children, and soon it was Lilly's turn.

"Lilly, you're next if you have anything you wish to share," Doug said.

Lilly got up and picked up a big bag and began to hand out little things from within. She'd given each person a gift that was specially thought out for them. For Willy, she had a gift bag with a twenty-five-dollar gas card for his beast; guitar strings; some picks; and a pair of socks that had "Couch stuffin'" written on the wrapper. He howled with laughter, and Peter joined in. She reached in her bag and brought out a regular-sized gift box she had wrapped for Jeff and Jenny. On the front, she had made a card. On the outside, it read: "For the teachers of the Teacher." On the inside, she wrote:

> I have no other gift to give but to let you peek into my heart, to see just what your investment in me did; what kind of impact your time, money, and energy did for one simple, poor child. I've never shared these with anyone.

When you're done, there is money for you to mail them back to me. I have nothing to give you but my heart.

She then wrote this verse:

A student is not above his teacher, but everyone who is fully trained will be like his teacher.

Luke 6:40
I want to be like you, Jenny.

Inside were spiral school notebooks, fifteen of them, in which she had handwritten like a diary. Jenny was crying, so Jeff spoke for his wife. He grabbed Lilly's hand and looked up at her.

"Lil, we are honored more than you know. We'll take special care of these for you. There could be no better gift than this open book into your life."

Lilly was crying too, and so were a few others in the room.

Lilly walked over to Peter and pulled out a smaller package. It had been wrapped carefully. Peter raised his eyebrows at Lilly, for he hadn't expected anything. Peter carefully unwrapped a scarf. Peter thought it was beautiful. An attached note said, "Made with hands of love, with every stitch made, for you, I've prayed. May this keep your heart warm today and always. Love, Lilly."

Peter put it around his neck. He smiled up at Lilly. "You made this for me?" he asked in sincere astonishment.

"Yes, I did." Lilly giggled. "I stayed up every night and took my old, ragged garments and spun them into yarn, which you have around your neck, so that you could carry a part of your *ragmuffin* with you wherever you go."

"You're a big tease. You know that?" Peter laughed out loud. "Besides, I can't believe that outlandish story, for the colors would have never matched. And between the bubblegum and the lollipops, you wouldn't have needed to crochet it, for it would've just stuck together!" he teased right back.

Even Jeff and Jenny laughed out loud on this bantering.

Jeff asked Peter, "Is she always like this?" enjoying seeing this new Lilly.

Peter rolled his eyes mockingly. "You don't know the half of what I've been through these past four months," he teased. Then turned romantic eyes on Lilly and said, "But I wouldn't change one minute of it."

Peter went next. He gave everyone a well thought out gift. Wilma and Doug finished up by giving each a gift as well. Joyous sighs could be heard by all. Everyone just sat back, contented. After a bit, Willy started singing "Silent Night." All joined in. They sang for a while, spontaneously worshiping. When all seemed complete, Wilma and Doug set out a huge buffet of delicious finger foods.

As everyone was settled, eating, Wilma asked, "So what did you do when that little ragmuffin answered the door? What did you say?" Wilma only expressed what everybody else wanted to know.

Jeff looked at Lilly, and then he looked at his lovely wife. "Jen, would you like to fill in?"

"Sure. I'd love to, honey." Jenny situated herself better. "It went something like this: Jeff asked, 'Is your mommy or daddy home?' She said yes but that they were sleeping. And you could see fear in her eyes, should she wake them up. So I asked her name. She answered, with a bit of quiet pride, 'My name is Lilly Beckler, and I'm nine.' I giggled at her and told her, 'My name is Jenny Singleton, and this is Jeff Singleton. We go to First Baptist Church Arlington. We drive a bus out here to pick up kids who want to go with us to church. We wondered if you would like to join us tomorrow.'" Jenny chuckled at the memory.

"And then she pointed to Jeff and asked if he was my brother. Again, I had to stifle a giggle. I told her he was my husband. Then she asked if we had any kids, which surprised me. 'Well, Miss Lilly, we just got married and we don't have any children yet.' She spoke up with pride about a cousin of hers who had had two kids and she wasn't married. The little girl said the story with such a complete lack of understanding that I was dumbfounded. At that point, Jeff jumped in to the rescue by telling her again we would love to have her on the bus and that we would be there about nine in the morning and if she had her parents' permission, she could join us on the bus. She called Jeff *mister* and said she'd come. Then I gave her a piece of bubblegum. Then she shut the door. Jeff and I turned around. Jeff put his hand on my back and told me to keep walking. He knew there was nothing we could do. He pushed me along, soothing me as streams of tears silently ran down my face. He put me in the car and turned on the air conditioning full blast. We were speechless. Then we held hands and just prayed for you." She was looking at Lilly. "I really didn't think you would show up, but I was wrong."

Everyone in the room was on the edge of their seats, wanting more. Jeff and Jenny looked at each other and grinned. Jeff shrugged his shoulders and said, "Go ahead. It's the most captivating story."

It was hard for Peter to see the pain and heartbreak as they shared, but he also knew she would praise God for every word spoken. Peter took her hand in his, leaned over, and whispered, "You still captivate my heart just like the first day I met you." He was smiling. He wanted to say so much more, but he didn't. Peter said, "Go ahead, Jen. Tell them about the next morning." Peter grinned at the remembrance.

"The next morning, I couldn't believe it, but there was the little girl two streets up from where she lived. We stopped the bus and she hopped on. She was dressed in a tattered shirt that was too tight, along with pants that didn't match and were in about the same condition. She was no cleaner than the day before, her hair untouched, and she was barefoot. But she smiled at both of us and said, 'Good mornin', mister,' to Jeff. She evidently had never been on a bus, for she touched every seat as she walked down the aisle. I followed her. I went down on a knee and removed a crumb from her cheek and asked, 'Lilly, where are your shoes?' She replied, 'Oh. At the house. I never wear shoes except to school.' Her face, cute as a button if you could see past the dirt steaks, was smiling adorably at me. 'Lilly, you have to wear shoes at church.' Lilly was literally crestfallen. Then she perked up and went to Jeff and said, 'Hey, mister, can you wait a minute?' Jeff squatted down and said, 'Yes. I sure can.' Then Lilly said she'd be right back."

"She hopped off and ran all the way back home. She left a stunned bus crew in her wake. It couldn't have been five minutes, and we saw her running back as fast as she could, a shoe in each hand. She hopped back on the bus, a smile nearly stretching off her face. She looked up at Jeff, holding the shoes in her hands, and said, 'Now can I ride, mister?' Jeff ruffled her hair and said, 'Sure you can.'" Jenny looked at Peter. "Why don't you pick up the story?"

Peter said he would and squeezed Lilly's hand and gave her a smile. "I watched her closely. As each kid got on the bus, they'd look at her and keep on moving. I thought my heart would break in two. I went over and asked if I could sit by her. She said yes. Then she asked my name. I told her it was Peter. She repeated, 'Petah,' with the cutest smile." Peter put his head back at the memory. It was too much for him. "Then she said, 'I like that name, Petah.' Then I gave her the villainous lollipop. Her eyes got so big that I had to resist giving her the whole bag. The bus was very crowded, as we'd not only met our goal but exceeded it by three children.

After a bit, I had to get up to let two more kids have my seat. But Lilly was so enthralled with the bus that she didn't notice the prejudiced attitude of those now sharing her seat."

"I'd taken Lilly to her Sunday school class. I could tell she was a bit scared, but she went right on in." Peter chuckled and shook his head. "If I'd known what was going to happen next, I would've stayed with her. Jenny told me in church that after she'd got her group of kids to their classes, she was walking past Lilly's class to go to her own, when she heard a ruckus. She stopped and peered into the class. Lilly had a boy in a headlock and was pulling his hair and saying, 'That's my sucker, not yours,' over and over. The teacher was in there but was not quick enough before Lilly had taken things into her own hands." Peter looked at Lilly and smiled. "You certainly had a mind of your own." He squeezed her hand.

Jeff went on to finish what happened that morning. "When all the kids were back on the bus for the ride home, we passed out the ice cream sandwiches. What a mess, with sticky wrappers everywhere and the hot, July sun melting the sandwiches like a patty melt." He continued. "Lilly had taken her sandwich and held it. I asked her if she was going to eat it. She smiled up at me and said, 'I wanna give this to my papa. He doesn't smile much, and this will make him happy.' This melted my heart. This girl wanted to give what she had to make her dad smile. What could I say? I knew it would melt before she got home, but I hadn't the heart to tell her so."

Jeff went on to share, "It wasn't fifteen minutes later that more than my heart melted. Yeah. You guessed it. So did her sandwich. Big tears rolled down her cheeks as she held the dripping sandwich in her hands. It had leaked out all over her clothes. I called Jen over to help her, for I just couldn't do it. Jen threw it away, got out some wipes, and cleaned Lilly up best she could. All the while,

Lilly silently cried. Even if we had had more sandwiches in the cooler, they would've been melted, for it was a scorcher of a day."

Jenny picked up the story. "I hugged her and tried to comfort her. She looked up in my face and said, 'It's okay, missus. I'm just glad you let me ride your bus. It was real fun!' She threw her arms around my neck and then sat down for the rest of the short ride home. She said as we neared two streets away to stop and she would get off there. We thought it strange, but she was insistent. So we did. She hopped off, slipped off her shoes, and ran the two and a half blocks home." Jenny sighed as though she'd just really relived that day.

Hannah asked, "Did she keep riding the bus?"

Jeff and Jenny both laughed out loud. "Yes," they chimed together.

Jenny said, "This scenario happened for three more weeks, this picking her up two and a half blocks away and dropping her off at the same spot. She did remember her shoes, never any socks, though. Each week, she only wore them at church and took them off on the bus."

Lilly looked down at her feet. She had slipped off her shoes when she sat down. She smiled. *Some things never change,* she thought. She silently slipped her feet back into her shoes, embarrassed that she'd be caught outright.

Peter noticed, and whispered, "It's okay, Lil, if you don't want to wear your shoes." He winked at her.

She realized he'd caught her thoughts and actions.

"At least I have learned to wear socks," she whispered dryly.

She didn't take her shoes back off, Peter noticed, but she wiggled her feet now and again. He was sure they were uncomfortable.

Jenny continued. "Each week, she'd meet us in the yard and talk to us over the fence. It actually appeared that she was waiting for us on Saturdays."

Jeff interjected the big but. "We had the growing suspicion that her parents didn't know where she was each week. So I had to address this with her, which was no small task. After the third Sunday when she got off the bus, I followed her out to have a bit of privacy. She was about to run off when I called to her. I went to her and hunkered down to her level. I asked her if her parents knew she was riding the church bus each Sunday. Lilly nodded her head slowly. I just waited and looked at her, and then her head began to go sideways in a no. 'Lilly, thank you for telling me the truth,' I said, 'but you must understand that we must have your parents' permission. Now—' I took her hand— 'if we don't talk with either parent next Saturday, you'll not be able to ride the bus anymore.' Big tears welled up in her eyes. I had to turn away. She wiped them with the back of her hand, which made a smear of mud. She said, 'But, mister, my parents don't care where I am so long as I ain't in no trouble. And I promise to be real good on the bus, and I ain't fought with nobody since the first time. Hadn't I been real good, mister?' She was patting my shoulder. I sure wish someone else could have done that job. I certainly did some quick growing up myself during those first few weeks and months. 'Yes, Lilly,' I said as I put my hand on her shoulder. 'You've been real good. But if something were to happen, we still want your parents to know where you are each week so as far as the bus and church are concerned. Do you understand? We must have that parental permission.' She nodded her head and was about to turn to run. I spoke again. 'Lilly you're very special to us. And we hope with all our hearts that you get to keep riding the bus with us.' She said she hoped so too and ran off."

"I got back on the bus. Of course, my dear wife wanted to know every detail. And Peter was looking over her shoulder, ears perked up like a puppy dog. That little ragmuffin had stolen our hearts on that very first bus ride. We didn't know what we would do if she didn't tell her parents."

Jeff, left the story hanging off a cliff so to speak. Then the twins jumped up and down together, chorusing, "Finish the rest! Finish the rest!" their eyes begging. "Did she get to ride the next week?"

After a long drink, Jeff told them what happened the next Saturday.

"When we turned onto her street, she saw us and immediately ran into the house. By the time we got to the gate, there was a big, grumpy man waiting on us."

Lilly spoke up. "Were you really frightened of my papa, Jeff?" She went on, teasing him. "Why, he'd just awakened from a night of heavy drinking. He had a bad hangover. He hated his sleep to be interrupted, not to mention he had tripped getting out of bed and almost slipped on a beer bottle when I turned on the light, nearly blinding him. Plus, he couldn't find his pants and he had put his shirt on wrong side out. And you were scared?" she teased mercilessly. "Why, every fiber in his being spoke of gentleness!" Lilly was laughing.

"Yeah. You laugh," Jeff said. "Man, my knees where knocking so loud. You introduced us and asked permission to ride the bus. All your dad said, or rather growled, was, 'You better take good care of 'er, or you'll pay.' And he walked off, back to the door with permission granted."

Lilly was thinking, *And he turned out to not be my papa at all!* Lilly spoke. "I loved my papa. Even finding out he wasn't my real dad didn't change my love for him. He'll always be Papa to me. And in his own gruff way, he loved me, and I accepted that." She wiped away tears. "He was all I had."

Jeff was thinking how sad it was to defend such a man, yet she loved him. He still had a lot to learn.

Peter took a turn. "I remember the next day, she showed up in a spaghetti strap, skimpy dress. But she was so proud because her dad had gone to the thrift store that very day and bought her something proper to wear, she told me as she did a curtsy to show her Petah. She had actually gotten two dresses that day, and she took turns wearing them. Both were out of date, scanty, stained, and too short, yet she felt like a princess in them." Peter was shaking his head. "I was so humbled. Here I was, living in the land of the plenty, complaining if I didn't have the most fashionable pair of jeans."

"Well, a few weeks later, it was another blazing Sunday in August. We met Lilly running up to the bus in long sleeves and pants, wrinkled like they had been shoved in a drawer." Peter paused, not sure he could go on. "I'd been sitting with her, somewhat out of protection for her, and I was quickly becoming very attached to this ragmuffin. Naturally, I was curious about the attire for the day. I knew something was wrong. She looked out the window with sad eyes when I questioned her. Sweat was pouring down her face. Her hair was wet from the smothering heat. So I suggested she pull her sleeves up to cool off. She immediately became defensive and said no and that she wasn't hot. I told her not to lie, that I could see she was hot. Then I offered to help her and went to reach for her arm, she jerked away from me and almost curled up in a ball. She put her head down and covered her face, as she didn't want the other children to see her crying and make fun of her. 'What is it, Lilly?' I remember begging her to tell me."

"Only after I promised not to tell anyone and expressed my friendship did she pull up her sleeves. I remember gritting my teeth so that she wouldn't see my reaction to the horrible sight of her arms. There were deep gouges in her arm on the inside skin in several places and then some scabbed scratch marks too. This was someone's evil fingernails. I thought they might need some treatment to keep from getting infected it was so bad. Lilly then put down her sleeves and said she'd fallen on her bike. I couldn't believe she would protect her attacker. Her eyes were so sad I couldn't take it. Who in the world would do that, I had no idea. I asked Lilly who was taking care of the open sores and if she'd told her mom. She shrank back and whispered, 'No. There's no need.' A single lonely tear ran down her cheek, and I realized without Lilly saying it that it was her mother who'd done this to her."

"I got close to her face, holding back my anger, and asked Lilly if her mother had done this to her. She didn't respond, which said more than an answer. I will tell you, my ragmuffin, many times you had me, Jeff, and Jenny not knowing if we should have called in the authorities on your behalf. I've never been in those kinds of situations. Even today, I question whether we should've intervened more."

"I second the thought," Jeff agreed.

"There were many times we cried; we knew you were abused. I hope we did the right thing. It is so hard to know. What if it made things worse for you? Oh, you just don't know how we struggled over this time and again whether we should call in Child Protective Services," Jenny said.

Lilly smiled and spoke up quietly. "There are many times I have wondered that myself. Even as I now speak up for children in such cases as I found myself in, I advise them to seek help. Evidently, God didn't take me out of it but carried me through it and has used it to help mold me into who I am. I don't look back and blame anyone; and I wouldn't change anything, for these were the times I drew closer to God. It's what drew me to fall in love with my bus captain, his wife, and their helper." She sent a sweet smile their way. "Please don't ever look back with regret," she reassured them. "I can't thank God enough for each of you. At different times you were the shoulder God sent me to cry on, the hands to help me up, and the heart to keep me loving my family. You were Jesus to me, so I wouldn't change anything."

It was as though everyone had journeyed back with them and didn't want to leave. Jenny spoke up.

"I don't think I'll ever forget the time I brought over some fresh bread and cookies. You'd not shown up to ride the bus that Sunday. So on Tuesday, Jeff and I went to check up on you. I knocked on the door. You were so surprised when you answered it. The look of surprise on your face made the trip worth it. I can still remember every sound made by your enraged mother after you shut the door. Oh, how I wanted to open the door back up, grab you, and run. I listened to her slap you and scream at you, accusing you of having a boyfriend visit. She shoved you so hard that it sent the bread and cookies to the floor. I heard you scrambling to get them. Then your mom shrieked, 'That's just fine. You take the bread. I'll take the cookies. I don't want to see your face until tomorrow.' By then, you had scrambled to obey your mom. I ran from your trailer then almost falling in my haste to get away. When I got to the car, Jeff was all freaked out by my screaming for him to leave. We were almost home when I calmed enough to tell him what happened. I actually had nightmares after that. I just don't know how you did it, Lil," Jenny said.

Lilly pointed her finger to the ceiling and looked up. "Only by God's mercy and grace did I survive."

Peter leaned his head back on the back of the couch, his eyes shut. He wasn't sure how much more he could take. He knew there were often unexplained marks on Lilly, but she never told anyone about them. But as the years went by, Jeff, Jenny, and Peter knew. He remembered seeing a handprint across Lilly face on more than one occasion. It was no wonder to him that she loved coming to church so much.

Peter spoke up. "Remember when we went to the lock-in and I brought you home and you nearly tripped over your father lying in the yard near the walkway, completely passed out, drunk. Your father was no small man, as I remember. It took both of us to get him up into the house and onto the couch. I can remember that was my first time inside your home. There was trash everywhere. You had to clear off the couch before we could heave your drunken dad up there. Food and dirty dishes were everywhere, along with dirty clothes and magazines. I remember your words to me as you saw me taking in everything: 'Sorry about the mess. With me gone this evening, I didn't have the chance to clean up. Thanks for helping me with my dad. Poor guy. At least I didn't have to sleep outside this time.' You said all that without preamble. I asked what you meant about sleeping outside. I can only imagine what my face must have looked like. You shrugged and said, 'I usually don't have help. So I get up in the night to check on my father. If he passes out outside, I get blankets and pillows then I sleep next to him in case he needs something, just as I'll sleep on the floor right here,' and you pointed to a little piece of floor showing. Then you opened the door. 'Thanks again, Peter. I really had the time of my life tonight.' I left, no longer tired, and drove around town for a bit, trying to get my mind off all I had just witnessed. I'd already become very protective of you; but that night, my heart was ripped open to the core. I've never seen such love for someone as you had for your dad. God used that to convict me sternly about my own lack of unconditional love."

Wilma smiled and sighed loudly. "I must go to the kitchen, or we'll have to eat Christmas dinner the day after Christmas." She chuckled. "I've been honored to listen to all that God has done, and I look forward to more. I can see why you have a more tender heart for others. It encourages me to seek that too." She smiled and went over and hugged Lilly.

Jeff turned to Jenny. "You, my love, are taking you and the baby to bed for a nap."

Jenny gave a longsuffering look. Jeff stood firm.

Lilly started to rise, but Peter grabbed her hand.

"Hey," he whispered, "where are you going?"

"I thought I would go help in the kitchen," she said quietly.

Peter, getting up, still held her hand. "I know it is cold, but would you take a walk with me?" Peter wanted a more private moment with Lilly to see how she was really doing.

Lilly looked toward the kitchen.

Peter, reading her mind, said, "They have enough help in there. And I haven't had enough of you. Please," he coaxed.

"Sure," Lilly finally agreed.

They were walking out on the hillside when Peter asked, "How are you, Lilly? Has this all been too much for you?"

Lilly was looking down, watching her step. "I can't say that it has been easy, Peter. Some of those memories make me so vulnerable. They are so vivid it is like I'm that little girl all over again. Hopefully I won't have nightmares."

"Do you usually have bad dreams?" Peter asked concerned.

"Yes, I do. Often if I've concentrated on the past too much. Or if someone is heavy on my heart, it seems to affect me in the night," Lilly confessed.

"I'm sorry, Lil. I never dreamed this would be so painful."

Lilly stopped walking. She put her hand on Peter's arm and said, "Please don't be sorry. In a strange kind of way, it's the path of healing to talk about it. And, well, with Jeff and Jenny here, it's our connection. And no matter how bad things were, you three came into my life. And that is the God part of the story. And without the bad parts, the good parts wouldn't be so grand. Does that make sense?"

Peter's love for this woman just swelled. How'd he ever think he could live without her? He looked down in that face, wanting to tell her he loved her.

But he put his hands on her face and whispered, "It makes beautiful sense."

Then they began to walk again.

Lilly went on more lightheartedly. "I was thinking about the night we went to the lock-in." She looked over at him, smiling. "For me, that was like Cinderella going to the ball. I mean, I really don't think you know just what that night did for me."

"It was like I was a princess, being invited to the most wonderful ball with the best-looking knight." Lilly was trying not to blush, but it was not working; and Peter noticed. "Of course, I had never been to something like that before."

"It meant more than I can explain that you, being so handsome, could have had any girl go with you but you chose me." Lilly paused, trying to gain control of her emotions. "That you'd ask me, a poor, ratty-looking ragmuffin, instead of a hot date, well, it spoke words of love that there are no words for," she said and looked up at Peter. She had a single tear on her cheek.

Peter reached over and wiped away her tear. "I had the best time ever because of your view of the evening was like that of a ball; yet you were humble and kind, which a lot of girls wouldn't have been. And that is something I still love about you today."

"Well, you get what you get with me," she laughed. "I have no hidden agenda, no pretense."

"Ah. What I love. A woman who doesn't have to play games," Peter said. He was thinking of girls he had dated in the past and of Veronica, who was a master at manipulation.

"That night, you took me away from the pain and abuse to the land of love and miracles. Do you remember any of this, what I was wearing, what I looked like?" Lilly asked.

Peter remembered it all very clearly. It had torn his heart out. He could tell she had done her best. And her hair was clean and brushed. But the fact that she still didn't own matching clothes and her pants were high waters, along with the holes in her shoes, made her the center of talk. He saw the teasing giggles. He heard the unkind words. He watched the girls get up and move when she came to sit on the bleachers. Yes, he remembered. But did she?

Lilly noticed the disturbed look, almost fierce, and then the shaking of the head. *Maybe this is not a good memory for him,* Lilly began to think. She said, "I'm sorry I brought it up," her smile gone. This was indeed one of her most memorable times with Peter, but perhaps it wasn't one of his.

Peter stopped and faced Lilly. He said, "Please don't be sorry. It's one of my special memories of you." Peter chose his words carefully. "I thought that you were the most beautiful girl there. I couldn't have been more proud to have you as my date. And should you have left your shoe, I would have searched far and wide to find its owner."

"Petah, you always know just the right thing to say." Lilly shivered and continued to walk. "It was hard at times since I was neither blind nor deaf to what others thought of me. Yet you seemed to be so different. Why?"

"Lilly, it's hard to explain. Even though I was seventeen and in the midst of the glory of teen hood, it's sick to watch wickedness. And where there might have been a very good-looking girl, what you might call a hot chick, it isn't so hot when spewing cruelty. It's hard to call something like that beautiful. One might have looked like a cheerleader, but what she cheers for can make a difference in what she looks like to me. Does that make sense?"

They'd finished their walk but not their talk, so Peter suggested they head to the barn to get out of the chilly air and finish their chat. Closing the door behind him, Peter turned on the light and leaned on a support beam. "Lilly, look at me," Peter demanded. "I'll admit I don't understand the ways of girls. I'm sure there is a certain amount of built-in desire from God to want to look pretty. I don't know how else to explain it." He rubbed the back of his neck. "But what most girls don't realize is that when it's overdone, it outshines the beauty of the heart; then they're not so attractive." She hadn't been able to maintain eye contact, and he didn't push her. "I'll say that this is at least the thought of most Christian guys. Since the day you walked into my class-room, you are—" he stepped back and looked her up and down, clearing his throat— "very lovely to look at. There isn't a thing unattractive about your looks at all." He raised his eyebrows and crossed his arms. "Which is one reason I get jealous when I see you talking with other guys, because they aren't blind to what I'm looking at either." Peter whistled and looked her over again. "I need to quit calling you ragmuffin, for you're no longer a ragmuf-fin by any stretch of the imagination. It's only a priceless term of endearment, and most certainly not how I view you. Even in all your outward beauty, your heart still outshines it. So you're a great package, beautiful on the inside and gorgeous on the outside!"

"It's my observation after seeing you again that even if your childhood had offered you more opportunity in the areas of fash-ion, you still would've stayed more on the simple side of things because that is just who you are at heart." Peter said. "And, Lilly, those are the very things that I adore about you. I love your simple ways of everything, from the inside to the outside. I wouldn't want you to change one thing."

She looked up at him.

"I'm hoping my opinion matters to you," he said.

They stared at one another, Peter wishing he could kiss her.

Lilly pulled away and dug in her pocket. She handed him the somewhat-smashed gift. "This is for you."

Peter grinned and tore open the package, watching her all the while. "Lil, you didn't have to do this. Just your presence with me is the best gift."

His smile was huge, for in his hand he held a leather-bound book. He whistled as he turned it over in his hands. On the front was embossed "The Hedge of Thorns." Peter spoke, a bit breathless. "I don't know what to say. I'm so touched. It's so beautiful." Peter opened the inside cover and read what she had written there.

> To my Petah. May our hearts be ever entwined as much as our love is for this piece of literature.
>
> Love, Lilly.

Peter looked at Lilly. He was speechless. Lilly looked back at him with a sweet yet impish grin and said, "I was hoping we could read it together again, Professor Collins."

He went toward her, and she felt the strong desire to bolt from him. But before she could, he saw the fire in her eyes and grabbed her wrist as she made her attempt.

Peter dragged her back. "Not so quick, Miss Parker," he said. He was tapping his fingers on the book, debating what he was going to do next.

Lilly was enjoying this way too much. "Aren't you gonna punish me?" she asked, breathlessly teasing.

Peter came closer. "That depends," he said, his eyes riveted on her face.

"On what?" she asked.

Peter thought this was not exactly where he wanted to do this. "It depends on whether or not you understand my intentions."

"I think I do," she whispered.

"Well, then you deserve my most sincere punishment, Miss Parker," He put his hands on her face, slowly bent his head, and kissed her tenderly, sweetly, and as long as he thought he should. He was smiling when he came up from such pleasantries.

Lilly closed her eyes and said, "I never knew punishment could be so wonderful." She opened her eyes. "I might just have to be naughty again to see if you're a consistent disciplinarian," she teased.

Peter came close and put his arms around her waist. "You can call me Professor Collins all you want. I assure you punishment will come," he said with a smile. He looked into her eyes. "Boy, am I ever glad you're not in my class!"

"I'll miss being in your class, Professor Collins," she said as she pointed to his chest. She just wanted to feel those lips on hers one more time so she wouldn't think it was all a dream.

Peter looked into those eyes, thinking he would never tire of kissing the woman of his dreams. Just before their lips touched, the door opened and the moment was lost. It was Doug.

"Sorry for the interruption. I just needed to get some feed for the animals and a couple more things," he said as he began to fill his arms. "Sure is dropping off outside. You two finish your walk?"

Peter wagged a finger and whispered to Lilly, "I'll get you later. I won't forget!" Then he walked over to help Doug. "Yes sir. It was beginning to get cold and we still had some things to clear up, so we came in out of the wind. Hope that wasn't a problem."

"Naw. It's not a problem. Ya just might come out smelling like hay!" Doug looked at Peter and noticed the book. "What ya got there?" he asked.

Peter smiled. "Lilly gave me this." He handed it over for Doug to see.

"That's real nice," said Doug.

"Yeah. It's both of our favorites." Peter looked over at Lilly. "I actually gave her a copy when she was a kid. A few months later she admitted that she didn't like it because she couldn't understand it. So thereafter, I made an effort to read it to her once a week after school. And before long, she loved it. So it became her most cherished literature piece, it was already mine." He smiled at Lilly, who had come to stand by him. He put his arm around her and said, "That was actually what she said in her introduction in my class that made me look up into the eyes of a very grownup ragmuffin!"

Lilly piped up, "Professor Collins—" she looked at him, knowing he wouldn't kiss her right then— "as a way of introduction, had everyone go around the room and say their name and their favorite piece of literature." Lilly flashed Peter a teasing glance. "Professor Collins started in the back of the room. I was the second person to speak. Of course, I was speechless, already having seen my Petah. Poor Professor Collins. His mouth opened like a trout out of water." Lilly had been emphasizing *Professor Collins* every time. She knew she was in big trouble, but the game was worth it. "Then, after what seemed like forever, Professor Collins ordered me to his office. I walked in a daze to Professor Collins's office. Poor Professor looked as though he'd seen a ghost. When I did get to Professor Collins's office, he was so befuddled that not much was accomplished. Professor Collins said he had to get back to class but he couldn't believe I was there." Lilly had mercy on Peter and said, "For that matter, I too was in a cloud not believing that my Petah was my literature teacher, Professor Collins," she said, getting one more dig in and smiling big, rocking back and forth on her heels.

"Here. Let me help you, Uncle Doug," Peter said, laying aside the book. He then turned to Lilly, raised nine fingers, pointed at her with a wink, and left to help his uncle.

Lilly laughed all the way back to the house. In her conversation with Doug, she had purposely called Peter 'Professor Collins' as many times as she could, teasing him, as they talked about the book and their first meeting. It sure had been fun, Lilly thought. When she came back in dinner was ten minutes away. She felt bad, but she did enjoy her time with Peter.

The meal was fabulous and the company great. Jeff and Jenny noticed the closeness between both Peter and Lilly that wasn't there before.

The rest of the weekend was a whirlwind of Christmas spirit because it was the Spirit of God that brought their hearts together. It was a sad Lilly who said good-bye to Jeff and Jenny Sunday afternoon. But though she had tears, she was so glad she had gotten to see them at all.

CHAPTER 20

Peter sat, turning the big, shiny apple in his hand. Then he picked up the note that said, "To my favorite teacher! Have a great first day!"

Peter just sat there and smiled. It was Monday, the first day of class for the next semester. He'd arrived early whereupon he found that his Lilly had already been there.

He wondered if there would ever be a day she didn't surprise him. He definitely was in love, and it was so different from anything he'd ever experienced. Lilly was so beautiful, both on the inside and outside. She was caring, transparent, fun, and easy to love; and her zeal for the LORD was infectious. He was sure going to miss her not being in his class, but then his smile grew. But it did have its positive side. His students began to come in and he was forced to set aside his wife-to-be for the remainder of the day.

It was a Sunday afternoon in February, and Lilly had gone to the living room to visit with James and Maureen. They looked at each other and smiled.

"Should we tell her?" James asked with a huge grin.

Maureen's smile was big, as she nodded her head.

Lilly had stopped to witness this exchange. "Tell me what?"

Aunt Maureen said sheepishly, "Lil, I want you to meet my husband, James!"

Lilly's mouth was wide open, her eyes huge. "You're kidding me!" She pointed her finger from one to the other. "You mean you two got married?" she yelled as she pranced around the room. She put her hands on her hips. "Wait a minute. When did this happen?" Her eyes twinkling. "Just what have you two been up to? And why was I not invited?" She had a lot of questions.

The two of them were obviously in love. They just looked at each other.

"Go ahead and tell her," James finally said.

Maureen smiled at James and took his hand, and told Lilly every detail.

Lilly took her aunt in a long bear hug. "Oh, Aunt Maureen, how I have prayed for this! God is so good to us." She then hugged James. "May the two of you have even a better marriage this time, as it is built on the foundation of Christ Jesus."

She was running behind for evening Bible study but was delighted at the news that had caused the delay. She jumped in Peter's car.

"I was just about to come in and get you." He sounded like he was teasing, but Lilly knew a hint of seriousness in his voice too.

"Well, you'll never guess what held me up. It's a wonderful reason."

"Oh really?" Peter said, now very curious.

She shared all that had just been told to her.

"Love is in the air, I suppose. What a lucky man to be married to the woman he loves." Peter smiled at her.

"That is marvelous, Lilly. I know you have prayed long and hard about these things."

The next Friday, there came a big snowstorm, and the bus driver who usually drove Lilly's bus fell on some ice and broke his hip early that morning, which was why that evening Peter found himself at the hospital, visiting the elderly man and asking him how to run the route. The staff member in charge of the bus ministry had called Peter and asked if he was interested in filling in for the man. Peter thought it was a great idea and was sure it would surprise the socks off the lady who occupied his mind constantly.

"Hey, I need a favor. Don't tell Lilly. I'll be there Saturday to go with her. But still stay quiet about me driving and about poor Mr. Owens. I'd love to surprise Lilly." The man, knowing Peter was in love, was all for it.

That morning Lilly was at the church by 9:00 a.m., sitting down at the breakfast table with fellow workers, when Peter came in.

"Hello, Miss Parker. Is this seat by chance taken?" he asked close to her ear, holding his tie back with his hand.

"Why no, Mr. Collins. Please, do sit with me." Lilly, more than a little curious, asked discretely, "What are you doing here?"

He had from time to time come and picked her up after she had finished with the Saturday visitation, but never had he joined her for breakfast.

"Actually, Mr. Owens was going to be out today, and he suggested I'd be a great fill-in, so here I am. You get to show me where to go and I will follow you around like a lost puppy." He smiled at her, helping himself to the delicious, hot breakfast. Lilly couldn't seem to calm the butterflies in her stomach at this news.

It was difficult maneuvering on some of the roads due to the ice. Lilly was glad Peter was driving. But she had to smile as she watched Peter interact with the children, especially Katherine.

Lilly thought, *He's just like me.*

She had warned him that she would steal his heart in a matter of minutes. And that was just what happened.

The next morning was bright and a little warmer, so the snow was melting fast. She arrived in plenty of time. Mr. Owens was normally ahead of her and had the bus ready and running. So it was a minute after she stepped on the bus that she was greeted with a warm, deep, and very familiar, "Good morning," that she froze.

Peter's grin was ear to ear, seeing Lilly's mouth drop wide open in the most unfeminine way. It had been well worth the secret for this very moment of surprise.

"Well, Miss Parker, are you going to get on so we can go and get the kids?" Peter had his hand on the big door handle, ready to close it.

Lilly was still staring with her mouth hanging open. Peter cleared his throat. "Lil, honey, you might want to close your pie hole and hang on. It might be a bit bumpy as I get used to driving."

Lilly was still shocked, but she did close her pie hole, suddenly very embarrassed that it had been hanging open. And hang on she did. Peter knew she had questions but just tried to concentrate on his driving.

"Petah, you got a lot of explaining to do." She was so outraged, she used his nickname. "Where is Mr. Owens?"

Peter, driving carefully and pulling up to the first stop, said, "Mr. Owens, my sweets, is in the hospital with a broken hip." He heard her gasp. "So I guess you're stuck with me for a while." He was smiling, trying to act as though it would be suffering to work with Lilly.

Lilly looked at their helper, a youth of sixteen, who shrugged his shoulders and had a smirk on his face, playing right along with innocence.

"How did Mr. Owens get hurt, and how did you find out about it?" Lilly asked as soon as she was back on the bus from getting the first child.

Peter grinned. "I'll tell you what. Since I need all the concentration I can muster, how about I answer all you questions over lunch today?" He thought that was a clever way to get her to go out with him.

Deciding to be amusingly difficult, Lilly said, "What if I have other plans?"

Peter, very evenly, hiding his snicker, said, "Well, I believe, ragmuffin, you were the one with the questions."

Lilly was frustrated but didn't speak of it again and put her heart in focus for the children's sake. She sang with the big books in her hands. It was kind of silly at times, yet these kids were learning truths of God through it. Peter enjoyed every bit of it. It almost brought tears to his eyes, for this was all very hard on his heart. It brought back memories that had been well tucked away.

Peter looked at the note on his desk. Lilly had left him a note and a bag of currant cookies. The note said:

"Lillian Grace Singleton, born 12:32 a.m. this morning. She is adorable, says Jeff. 7 lbs, 18 inches long. A head of light, soft, red hair. Jenny is doing great! Just thought if you hadn't heard you would want to know! Have a great day! Your ragmuffin. P.S. You're a great bus driver!"

Well, now he'd make his plans. He had wanted to make sure about the baby first.

That Saturday morning as they got in Peter's car to do the bus route visitation, there was a card in the passenger seat with her name on it. She looked at Peter. "What's this for?" she wanted to know, looking confused.

Peter smiled. "Open it," he coaxed.

She began to slowly open it.

"I know your birthday is not until later, but I found the perfect gift for you, and it just couldn't wait," he said as he glanced over at her. He had pulled out of the parking lot and was on their way to the first house.

Inside was the most beautiful birthday card. As she opened it, another something fell out. She picked it up from her lap. She squealed. "Plane tickets! Plane tickets!" She was waving them around. She was literally bouncing up and down.

Peter said, "I thought you'd want to see the baby." He was glad he had done this. It was so worth every penny just seeing her this delighted.

"Oh, Peter, yes I want to go see Jenny and the baby and Jeff too!" She looked at the ticket again. "What about my school and work?" she asked. All kinds of things suddenly came to her mind. "It's not so easy to up and go," she went on. "These tickets are for Saturday through Thursday." She was looking them over. "Boy, Mr. Bowman is going to be *real* happy," she said, thinking about having to tell him she would need some days off.

"As a matter of fact," Peter said with a smile, "he wasn't so happy when I told him you wouldn't be at work that Saturday but would be back in time for work Thursday evening." Peter stole a glance at Lilly, her mouth wide open again. He chuckled at the sight.

"You did that?" Lilly asked incredulously. "You talked to my boss?"

She was so animated Peter laughed out loud at her antics.

"Yes, ma'am," Peter said. "No easy task, for that guy can be intimidating."

Lilly snickered. "No kidding! I still shake when he comes around checking on us," she said. Lilly squealed again. "Oh, thank you, Petah! I just can't wait! " She looked at the card finally. It was very nice and well picked out, Lilly thought. And he had signed it, "Your Petah."

Lilly leaned over and gave Peter a kiss on the cheek. "Thank you so much, Peter. That is the most thoughtful birthday gift I've ever gotten." She was smiling as she got out at the next house.

"Well, for that kind of thanks, I shall find some more gifts," he said with his brows raised and his eyes twinkling.

She playfully slapped his sleeves and said, "You'll go broke buying kisses from me when no purchases are necessary." She'd knocked on the door, so he couldn't return a comment; but he gave her a look that made Lilly smile back and lift her chin in the air a bit. But she held her giggles as a little boy came to the door.

CHAPTER 21

Peter was there bright and early to take Lilly to the airport. Peter laughed at her excitement.

Lilly rambled about her week and about what was to come, combining information. She didn't realize that what she was saying was clear as mud, but Peter didn't care. He was thrilled at her excitement.

When they got there, Peter pulled out an extra suitcase. Lilly was puzzled.

"Will you check this with yours? I told Jeff I would send some things for them and the baby," Peter asked Lilly.

"Sure, but it looks like you went a little crazy," she said, noting that the size of the suitcase was bigger than a gift box.

Peter's smile was huge. "Well, there is nothing like a baby to bring out the crazy side of a person. They've waited a long time, and they are very special to me." He directed Lilly to sit down in the waiting terminal. "So what do you think about them naming the baby after you?"

Lilly sighed. "Oh I'm so humbled and honored that they'd do that. Words escape my heart realizing someone carries my name." Lilly had said all this very passionately, for she did love Jeff and Jenny so much and knew she'd just fall in love with this little baby of theirs.

At the first boarding call, Peter walked Lilly to the roped-off area. "I'll miss you," he said. Then he kissed her forehead and told her good-bye.

"I hope when I come back you can make a better aim at the pie hole." She winked at him. "I'll miss you terribly, but thank you again so much for this trip." As she walked away she turned and blew him a kiss.

Twenty-five minutes later, the flight was calling, "Last borders. In two minutes, the doors will be closed. All final boarders."

Peter said out loud, walking to the door, "That would be me!"

Knowing the surprise that awaited Lilly almost made Peter unable to find his ticket. He made himself walk slowly down the temporary corridor and onto the plane. He scanned quickly for his seat number. He noticed Lilly was intently looking out the window at the tarmac, watching everything going on outside.

Peter leaned over and asked, "Is this seat taken, ma'am?"

Lilly's head swung around. "Peter Collins, what are you doing?" Peter was situating himself and fastening his seatbelt. The pilot came on the air, giving his greetings and instructions. Peter, grinning the whole time, finally gave in to Lilly's begging eyes.

He leaned over and said, "I told you I would miss you terribly."

"Peter Collins, you will answer me right now," Lilly demanded.

"Well, if you're ready, I can try for the pie hole now," Peter said, knowing teasing Lilly might cost him some scowling looks.

"Are you coming with me?" Lilly asked, still in total disbelief at what was happening.

Peter laughed out loud. "Well, unless you want me walking out on the wings and jumping to my death, I guess I am. Let's see. I think I just saw a few clouds go by." Peter was trying not to call her unaware, but they'd already taken off; evidently, she'd not noticed.

"Oh, how silly of me. Of course you're not going to just get off the plane." She slowly turned her head. "Wait a minute. You planned all this, didn't you?" She didn't wait for an answer. "You bought your ticket at the same time as mine, didn't you?" She looked over at Peter, who was nodding his head yes with a smirk on his face. Lilly jerked her thumb backward. "So that luggage doesn't have baby gifts in it? It has your stuff?"

Peter held up his hands. "Now wait a minute. It does have a small little gift, but the rest is, well, something for Jeff and Jenny to look at while I hold their baby."

"Like what?" Lilly asked with sarcasm.

Peter, indignant but still playing with Lil, said, "Like my clothing."

"You, Professor Collins, are incorrigible!" Lilly wasn't mad. She was just so overwhelmed she didn't know what to say.

Peter leaned close and whispered in her ear, "Are you mad and wish I hadn't come? Do you wish me to change seats?"

She turned and faced him, their eyes and lips close. "No, I'm not mad at you. Just surprised. I'm glad that you've come. It was inconsiderate of me that you wouldn't wish to see your family and the baby on your spring break as well. And as far as changing seats, apparently, I need someone to tell me whether I am up or down since I thought you could walk on clouds a few moments ago."

Jeff was at the airport to pick them up. Lilly nearly ran to him and hugged him so long that he feared he might need a tank of oxygen when she finally let go.

"Oh, Jeff, it's so good to be here. Where are they?" She was looking around. When she looked back, Peter and Jeff were embracing.

Peter was congratulating him in person. Both were laughing at Lilly. She was looking around for them like a lost kitten.

Jeff put his arm around Lilly. "Come, Lilly. They're at home. Jenny wanted to come. I made her stay home so she could rest," Jeff was saying as he directed them to baggage claim.

Lilly snorted. "I bet she loved that." Lilly knew that Jenny did state her mind about matters.

Jeff patted Lilly on the back. "If I didn't know better, I'd think you two were related."

Jenny heard the car drive up. She had just put the tea kettle on, and set out some cookies and sandwiches. She'd planned a tea party for the girls: her, Lilly, and the baby.

Lilly jumped out of the car like her pants were on fire, ran to the door, went inside and met Jenny holding the baby in the living room. Hugs, kisses, and shouts of joy were heard. Peter had come in and shut the door, only to witness that Lilly had taken the baby and was sitting on the edge of the couch, cooing, talking to her, and cradling her tenderly.

Peter couldn't take his eyes away from this precious picture of Lilly with the baby. Peter finally made his way to the back of the couch and looked over Lilly's shoulder. The baby was absolutely precious. She had an adorable, pink outfit and a white, knit cap. Lilly finally looked up.

"Peter, isn't she just beautiful?"

Peter found his voice. "Yes. She takes after her namesake," he said softly.

Lilly caught the softness in his voice and wondered if something was wrong, but this was not the time or place to ask him about it. "Peter, do you want to hold her? She is quite a lovely fit."

"You bet I do, but I'll wait my turn."

"Well, I'm afraid you just won't get a turn," Lilly said, "because I'm not going to get tired. However, let's have pity on Peter, shall we?" she said, talking to the baby in cute, little baby voice. "I'll share. How about that, Peter?"

She got up and carefully placed baby Lilly in Peter's arms. Now it was Lilly's turn to have her emotions run wild. He looked sweet holding the baby.

That could be our baby, Lilly thought.

She loved Peter Collins with all her heart and would be honored to be his wife and have a bunch of cute, little babies like this one. That would be a dream come true.

Lilly went on to hug Jenny and ask about how she was doing. Jenny said to Peter, "When you get tired, we're going to have a girly tea party."

Peter handed her over, and the three of them went into the kitchen to the little party that she'd fixed. She took two trays loaded with goodies and cold iced tea back out to the men. Both guys had big smiles for her.

"I love you, Jen," Jeff said, taking a sip of tea.

"Me too!" Peter said.

Jenny smiled at both of them.

Lilly and Jenny had a sweet time. They'd been separated for so long, and every moment counted. Plus, tea parties had never been part of Lilly's life, so this was special. And that was exactly what Jenny had wanted. They talked about many things. They went from one topic to the next. A lot had happened since they'd seen each other. They ran out of tea long before they ran out of words.

CHAPTER 22

Jeff came and put his hands on Lilly's shoulder. "Lilly, we knew you'd want to see some folks, and there are a lot of people who want to see you while you're here. So we took the liberty to plan an evening at the Maxwells'. You do remember them, don't you?"

Jeff was looking into the face of a frightened little girl. Jeff looked over at Peter, who was watching Lilly intently from a distance. He'd known they were planning this and had thought it was a good idea, but now he was second-guessing himself.

"Why would people want to see me?" she asked quietly, her face giving way to fear.

Jeff looked over at Peter for help.

Peter came and knelt on the floor in front of her and took her nail-bitten hands into his. She was trembling.

"Honey, there are many people here in this church who remember you well. We weren't the only ones whose hearts you captured when you made that first bus ride."

Lilly was thinking. Peter went on.

"I mean, you had Sunday school teachers. And even the kids in your classes, why, they're all adults now. They remember you, I'm sure. And who wouldn't?" He tried to calm her fears.

Jeff dreaded the next thing he had to tell her. Knowing this, Jenny joined in to try to help.

"Lilly my dear, we're sorry this upset you. We wouldn't have done it if we'd known it would upset you. Do you remember the kid you kicked in the shin for trying to take your sucker? He especially wants to see you. While some of the people have married, most are either in college, getting ready to, or are in steady jobs. We only invited folks we thought you would remember. Aren't you a little curious about what happened to all those people who were your world when you were here at the church?" Jenny asked.

Lilly looked up, on the verge of tears. "I'll be so embarrassed," she said, holding back her emotions.

All the adults looked at one another helplessly. Peter spoke up.

"Why would you be embarrassed?" He hadn't realized the depth of emotions and struggles that coming back here might evoke in her. He was only thinking of the baby.

"Well, they probably all made something of their lives, and look at me!" She had to look away. The dam holding back the tears threatened to burst at any moment. "I'm nothing," Lilly fretted. "Why, I can barely make it in my classes. I can't make it on my own. I'm just a mess. I just won't measure up." With that, she buried her face in her hands and cried uncontrollably.

The baby eventually cried, and Lilly looked up and actually laughed and hiccupped, putting all the adults at ease a bit.

"Here I am, crying like a baby, when Lillian should be the only one allowed to do that."

Peter sat down on the couch beside her and spoke. "My sweet ragmuffin, the things that you're all about aren't measured by degrees, wallets, houses, and cars." Peter looked at her, willing her to understand what he was saying. "I don't think people are going to be sizing you up. However, if they were to get out their measuring sticks, you're right. You'd be on the bottom of the success ladder by the world's standards. But I wouldn't take anyone, no matter how successful they are, over the woman I'm looking at right now, who probably has the biggest heart of all the people that'll be there tonight put together."

Lilly was trying to clear away the tears, while Peter finished.

"You see, things of the heart aren't easily measured. Your love for God and others blows all earthly success out the window. And you're the most thoughtful person I know. That's why you're so special to me. Even your college goals are to serve others. I'd be so bold as to say we could use a lot more Lillys in this world."

Lilly had herself together and looked at Jeff. "How many people are we talking about?" Lilly asked, thinking she could do this for God if He wanted her to; she knew He'd help her through. She'd just had a moment of weak flesh.

Jeff twisted his hands together. His face looked tormented. "Well, it started out small, but it grew. And before I knew it, probably a hundred people," Jeff said anxiously.

"A hundred people?" she shrieked. "I don't know whether to run and hide or beat you first."

"What can I say? You're a popular woman," he said. "As you mingle and get reacquainted with folks you know as well as I do, you never know how what you share with them might help them in their own struggles," Jeff encouraged.

Lilly wanted to be upset, but she just couldn't any longer. Seeing this as an opportunity to express God's goodness, she agreed.

She jumped up. "So what are we waiting for? What can I do to help?"

Everyone went into motion. With the four of them working, things got done in record time and off they went to the Maxwells' place.

Peter kept a good eye on a very nervous Lilly. They had arrived after several folks had gotten there, two of which were Peter's parents.

"Mom, Dad, remember Lilly Beckler?"

Lilly found herself suddenly shy.

"Though she has a different last name, you all knew her as Beckler," Peter explained.

"Why, of course we remember you," Cindy Collins said, reaching out to give Lilly a slight hug.

Cindy was one of those professional-looking women, and it made Lilly pale in comparison. She'd worn her overall dress, though not the pigtail braids.

Ralph Collins smiled, stuck out his hand to shake Lilly's. "How was your flight, Lilly?" Lilly smiled at the man who was an older version of Peter. "It was filled with a few surprises, but after I got over them, it was fabulous," she said as she smiled at Peter.

Peter smiled back.

It didn't take long for Lilly to be captured by a flood of people. Jeff and Jenny had seen to it that everyone wore a nametag. If they had married, they had both maiden and married names on it. This helped Lilly a lot. It didn't take long for her to be lost in the evening. She was having a wonderful time, seeing how people had changed, how God had grown them or the challenges that they were presently in. Her fears melted away. Even Peter, who kept looking her way to be sure she was all right, was having a wonderful time.

There was hot chocolate and a small fire for warmth and roasting marshmallows. It was a cool night, so Lilly often found herself by the fire. Indeed, Lilly had found herself sharing most of the night, individually or in small gatherings, what all God had done in her life, encouraging them to run hard after Jesus. The time in fellowship went by so quickly she couldn't believe two hours had passed when Peter showed up at her side with hot chocolate and chili dogs.

They somehow had gotten separated again when the singing started around the fire. But it didn't take long before Lilly found Peter. His eyes were staring through the fire, warming Lilly's heart. She returned his smile. Though they were separated by space, their gaze was unbroken. Their hearts were completely entwined. There was more fellowship around the fire. Even though both were in separate conversations, they managed an unspoken dialogue with each other.

People kept questioning both her and Peter about their future together.

Lilly's standard answer was, "I'm not sure what God has for us. I'm just taking one day at a time and am confident that whatever God has for us will be the best no matter what."

Peter's answer was, "We've certainly been on a wild bus ride, but as to where that bus ride will end, I'm not sure."

Both would smile as they gave their answers. Neither one was willing to reveal the depths of their heart to anyone, especially since they'd not revealed so much to each other yet. As the evening drew to a close, Lilly was so thankful that she had gotten to reconnect with old memories.

While he walked her to Jeff and Jenny's car, he explained that he would be staying with his parents. She had figured as much. He brushed her cheek with the back of his hand and said, "Good night, my love. Sweet dreams. See you tomorrow for a big day." He then put her in the back seat next to the adorable baby Lilly.

Lilly laid her head down on the fold-out couch in the baby room. She was exhausted, but she couldn't close her mind. She replayed the entire evening, moving from one person to the next. As she did, she prayed for each one. She tried to forget the sight of other women hugging Peter. There were more than several lovely, unmarried ladies who were closer to Peter's age. Was this jealousy? She didn't know, but if not, why did it bug her so much to see a girl's hand on his arm while laughing? Perhaps this was the time that God would chose to answer Peter's prayer for a wife. Lilly fell asleep wishing it would be her.

CHAPTER 23

Sunday came all too soon. Lilly had awakened during the night with the baby a few times before Jenny could get to her. So it was red eyes that Peter looked into when he saw Lilly that morning at church. Peter watched her for a moment. He chuckled. She touched everything with such remembrance and quiet serenity. He wished he knew what she was thinking. He'd found her in the foyer and then watched as she moved to the sanctuary. Old memories, flooding her like waves, threatened to overtake her at any moment. She stood in the aisle and turned around and around.

It was getting late, so Peter decided to interrupt. There would be time for this later. He stepped in and said, "I hear there is a beautiful lady who doesn't know where her Sunday school class is," his arms crossed and smiling at her.

"Oh, Peter, it's so … so …" She turned around. "I'm so taken back in time," she said in wonder.

"Speaking of time—" Peter looked at his watch— "we're going to be late, Miss Parker. And as adults, we just can't do that."

Lilly wanted to stay right where she was; but for Peter's sake, she moved forward. He didn't like to be late.

"Please, please, Peter. Take me by the kids' Sunday school classes," Lilly begged in desperation.

Peter couldn't argue with her pleading eyes. They were quick, but the effect it had on Lilly left her swimming in tears by the time they'd made it to class.

Lilly had found herself sitting with Jeff and Jenny, holding baby Lilly during the service. Somehow, she and Peter had gotten separated, but that was okay. Though she didn't know very many people, it was still home. She soaked it all in. She didn't even allow all the female attention that Peter had gotten that morning to distract her.

He walked quietly so as to not disturb her thoughts. He said, "There's my ragmuffin." He put his arms around her for a moment since he'd made her jump. "I thought I might find you out here."

Peter was sensitive to her silent reflections. She watched every child get on. She watched every helper. Tears made a steady stream down her cheeks. She spoke not a word. She just stood by the brick sign of the church and let memories flood her until each and every bus had left. The buses had fresh paint, but they were painted the same. It was more than Lilly could take.

She was a limp rag by the time she began to walk her way across the church lawn and climbed into the car with Jeff and Jenny and baby Lilly. They were to have several of Lilly's closest friends over for lunch. Lilly looked forward to it, but she couldn't get the morning's events out of her head.

After everyone left and before evening services, Peter asked Lilly to join him in a short walk.

Peter put his hands up and cupped her face and placed a sweet kiss on her lips.

Lilly took in a deep breath. "What was that for?"

Peter smiled and rubbed the back of his neck. "Well, I wanted to be sure you didn't decide to stay here with some young chap and make me a lonely man," he said.

She started to walk off to get her sweater, but he grabbed her hand.

"Secondly, because I wanted to." He winked at her and let her go.

It was a lovely afternoon of sharing memories with friends. And her barefoot walk with Peter was so like old times that she didn't think she could get any fuller. She didn't have long to contemplate, as it was time to head back to church for evening services. She arrived early so she could meander around a bit more, this time going into rooms that were empty of people but full of memories.

She slipped in beside Jeff and Jenny just in time for the piano to start. Peter could see her, as he was in the middle section, toward the back, sitting with several of the single college and career adults and smack dab between the two women who had claimed him since he showed up in Arlington.

Church was over before Lilly was ready for it to be. She could hear the pastor saying after he had prayed the closing prayer, "Before you leave, I have asked a very special person, one of our own, to come and share her story with us. Many of you are new from the past few years, but I must tell you: expect to be blessed. This little girl came on one of our buses when she was nine years old. Please give a warm welcome to Miss Lillian Parker."

The applause was deafening in Lilly's ears. Up to the podium she went, her knees knocking. Peter closed his eyes and prayed for her.

Lilly started out, "I'm indeed honored to be here. I never dreamed this was possible; and I must admit I've been flooded with memories today, ones very dear and sweet. Please know, church family, that your work in the bus ministry is not in vain. Be encouraged tonight as I share what a bus ride from this very church did to change my life."

She went on to tell the whole story, from start to finish, not leaving out any details.

She ended by saying, "With all this, I praise God for the efforts of Jeff and Jenny on that one day they decided to knock on my door."

After church, Lilly was nowhere to be found. She had slipped out and was waiting in Jeff and Jenny's car.

Peter turned the tape over in his hand. It was labeled, "The Bus Ride, by Lillian Beckler Parker."

Peter smiled put it in his jacket pocket and went to the truck he'd borrowed from his dad for the week. He was whistling as he pulled out of the parking lot.

When Jeff and Jenny opened the back door to put baby Lilly in, they found a very sound asleep Lilly. Both Jeff and Jenny looked at each other and smiled.

Jenny said, "Poor girl. She is out cold. She must be exhausted." Jenny shuddered at the thought.

They put baby Lillian in next to sleeping Lilly and went home.

Jeff aroused Lilly and helped her in and took her to her room, whereupon Lilly crawled into bed, clothes and all. Jenny put the baby to bed. She noticed that Lilly had only managed to get her shoes off. She chuckled at how much she looked like that nine-year-old girl they had meet ten years ago.

Lilly slept until 9:30 a.m. She was so embarrassed.

Lilly's hair was quite a mess. She'd come right to the kitchen. "Good morning, Jenny. I'm sorry I slept so late." She snorted. "And I'm supposed to be here helping you."

The baby was in the basinet in the corner of the small kitchen. Lilly went over to see her.

"You were very quiet last night. I didn't hear a peep out of you."

Jenny laughed. "You, my love, were out cold," she said as she finished the flowers for the table. "Can I get you a cup of coffee, Lil?"

Lilly moved her hair out of her eyes. "Oh yes, please." She moved to sit at the table. "Let me guess. I slept through everything."

Jenny smiled at her as she handed her the morning brew. "Yes, including the need to get into your pajamas," Jenny teased. "Can I fix you some breakfast?

"Just a little something so I don't make a pig of myself at lunch." Lilly laughed.

Jenny gave her some muffins and juice and joined her for a chat. "How are you doing, Lilly?" Jenny asked with concern. "There were so many people touched by your testimony last night. It is just such an honor for both Jeff and me to have been the ones God chose to be used in your life."

Lilly was quiet as she reflected while eating her breakfast.

Jenny said, "I can assure you that Jeff will want to be here to hear every word about your visit so far." Jenny looked into Lilly's eyes. "We love you, Lilly, as if you were our very own. We want to hear what is going on inside your heart. I don't think any of us realized the roller-coaster ride your emotions would take in coming back for a visit. But I must tell you, Lilly, face them head on."

"Thank you, Jenny. You always know what to say," Lilly said.

Jeff came home after a few hours at work to visit with Lilly. Both Jeff and Jenny burst out laughing many times at Lilly's version of happenings. At one point, Jeff asked Lilly if she drove Peter this crazy. Her reply had them laughing all the more.

On a more serious note, Lilly did open her heart and told them, "I can't enjoy the sweet memories without the bitter ones riding tandem with them." Lilly was crying softly. "Yesterday, as I watched the children get off the buses lined up out front, every bus ride came barreling through my heart. The kids on the lawn took me back in time to when I was there. And even some of those memories are tainted by kids who made fun of me and fought with me." Lilly laughed a little at the remembrance in the early times of her rolling around on the plush lawn in a fight. "The classrooms are freshly painted and have different posters and decorations on the walls, but they are the same. I can't tell you what it did to my senses to look into every room. I even went into the chapel for a while. I don't know if you can understand what it's like to be back to the place where my life was changed. This was where the first people who loved me came into my life."

Jenny touched her hand. "You're right. We can't fully understand, but we're glad for you to have this opportunity, it might take you weeks to sort through all your feelings."

Lilly went on. "Then, to top it all off, seeing Peter with plenty of older, lovelier, women makes all kinds of other emotions join in the race to see which one will send me over the edge. Not to mention that there is not a moment that goes by since arriving that I've not relived the nightmares of my life I had here." Lilly just sat there and let the tears flow.

"I'm so sorry you're heavily burdened, Lilly," Jeff said. "But all I can say is that God knows. Keep your focus on Him, not on what's going on around you. Enjoy the sweet memories that God gave you, most of all, His gift of salvation. And when the difficult memories come, face them, don't run, and try to find something good and something to pray for in those bad memories."

"Jeff, you're the best," Lilly said.

Time seemed to speed by, so it was a surprise when there was a knock on the door and it was Peter, dressed and ready for their dinner date with the Fleddings.

"Oh my." Lilly jumped up. "I forgot." Lilly's hand flew to her mouth.

Jeff talked to Peter while Lilly readied herself. "Peter, I shall give you the once-over about patience. If you don't hurry up and pop the question, I'm gonna skin ya."

Both men had a good laugh over that.

On a more serious note, Jeff asked, "What's the problem?"

Peter laughed. "Actually, it's been a study of patience for me. But rest assured, I will ask soon. If you haven't noticed, Lilly is a very simple person but with a complex heart. I want to be sure that she's where I am."

They ended their enlightening conversation as the topic of conversation came in the room, ready to leave.

They were riding in the truck when Peter asked, "So am I to understand you forgot about our date at the Fleddings tonight?"

"No not on your life!" She grinned impishly. "I just forgot to keep track of the time!" Peter pulled into a park. They still had about fifteen minutes. Peter wanted to know how Lilly was handling all this. He reached in his shirt pocket and retrieved the tape from Sunday night and handed it to her.

"Thought you might want to keep it," Peter said.

"Thank you, Peter." Then Lilly asked, "You didn't by chance bring a ball and mitts did you?"

Peter cocked his head, not sure he'd heard her right. "No, I didn't think about it, nor would I have wanted to chance getting dirty before dinner tonight."

"Oh of course not. What was I thinking?" Lilly said.

Peter said softly, "I think I know what you were thinking, that a little girl is hurting right now and how much she used to love to come here and play catch with her friend Peter; that during those hours of play, the world was a happy place. So naturally, since that same little girl is hurting, no matter how old she gets, playing ball with Petah will always make for a happy time."

She burst out in tears. Peter pulled her over in the seat and just let her cry against him while he held her.

"Oh, Peter. I think I will drown in the pain. I don't think there's a worse abuse than to be unloved." She went on bawling.

He stroked her hair and just kept telling her it was going to be all right.

Peter started the truck some twenty minutes later, when all the tears were expressed, and drove to the Fleddings.

They were greeted by Wyatt, who welcomed them both in with hugs and took them to the living room of a quaint but nice home. He spoke to Lilly.

"Lilly, I've not had the chance to say how much your sharing has touched my heart. It's still so hard to believe you're that same little girl I used to tease as Peter's shadow. I must admit I didn't think of you much more than a little annoyance at the time. But because Peter wouldn't allow a single unkind comment about you from anyone, I had to watch my words carefully. But you were just a dirt bag of a kid, and I never saw what his fascination was with you." He smiled. "But now I see just how wrong I was." He ended in saying, "He is reaping his reward pressed down, shaken together, and running over, I would say." Wyatt stood and slapped Peter on the back and grinned at him. "I better see if Rachel needs any help." He went toward the kitchen. "Please make yourself at home."

CHAPTER 24

Peter was sitting in the living room, holding baby Lillian, when a grumpy-looking, hair-everywhere, barefoot Lilly walked through the room, headed to the kitchen. She was completely unaware of anyone else in the house. Jenny asked her if she wanted to have her coffee in the living room with Peter.

Lilly looked around everywhere. "What? Peter's here? Where?"

Lilly wrapped her robe tighter around her and walked back into the living room. Lilly stopped in her tracks to see his lap full of pink. It was such a lovely sight that it took Lilly by surprise. He was drinking coffee and just looking at the sleeping babe in his lap. He looked up to see Lilly's lopsided smile.

"Do you mind if I join you?" Lilly asked.

"I was hoping you would," he said as he patted the spot next to him. "I need a diversion to keep me from falling too hard for baby Lilly that I might just have to up and quit my job and move back here to keep her in line."

Lilly curled up on the couch like a satisfied cat, holding her coffee and looking in Peter's lap at the most beautiful baby she'd ever seen. Both of them were captured by the babe's sleeping sweetness.

"But," Lilly said, "if you did move back, you certainly would have no shortage of wife options."

"Just what are you saying, Miss Parker?"

"Oh, come on, Peter. I'm not blind. You know those twins, what are their names? They have swooned over you like a mama with a sick youngun," Lilly said, getting her hair out of her eyes and sipping her coffee. "All you'd have to do is say the word. I can already hear wedding bells in the distance." Lilly wasn't being unkind, just letting a little bit of the fear in her heart slip out. She took a quick sip. "And your mom would be delighted, to boot."

Peter had wondered if Lilly had noticed. He guessed he needed not to wonder anymore. Peter looked Lilly in the face and smiled. "Those twins' names are Charity and Hope Thomason, and I'm not interested in either for a wife." Peter looked at Lilly, but she looked away. He pulled her chin back to face him. "As a matter of fact, my two favorite ladies in the world are right here in this room." Lilly could feel the air leaving her chest.

Lilly said just above a whisper, "They'll be a disappointed set when you leave, for you, Professor Collins, are quite a catch." Wanting to change the subject, she asked, "So what are you doing here anyway?"

"Well, I came for breakfast so I could spend time with Jen, Jeff, and the baby. We're not due to leave until ten o'clock, a few hours yet."

As if on cue, Jeff came through the kitchen, dressed for work, and said breakfast was on.

"Oh, Peter, that was such a lovely morning, wasn't it?" Lilly was saying as she settled in the truck. "Jeff and Jenny are the best!"

"Yes, it was indeed a lovely morning," Peter agreed. Lilly was so excited it didn't matter what they did as long as they were together. The first place they went was to the park. Peter got out two mitts and a ball.

"Okay, ragmuffin. Loosen up your arm," he said as he tossed the ball into his glove. This was a sweet past-time memory they did often.

Lilly was giggling so hard that she almost tripped over a large branch. They played catch for how long she didn't know. Then he got out two sodas, and they drank them as they sat on the tailgate. Peter looked at Lilly. She had sweat pouring down her face and her hands were a bit dirty, but he was having the time of his life.

Lilly hopped down and began to walk. Peter joined her.

Lilly said as she kicked sticks in the dirt, "Remember when we used to come here and read *The Hedge of Thorns?*"

Peter smiled. "How could I ever forget?" He laughed, his eyebrows high. "I remember some ragmuffin throwing my book across the way, she liked it so much."

Lilly put her hand up to her mouth. "I know. I'm so ashamed to have done that. But I just couldn't understand the words." Lilly kept walking. "But now I cringe at the thought of throwing any book, much less my favorite one." She was lost in memory now. "Remember we used to lie on our backs and take turns reading a chapter at a time?" Lilly turned and faced Peter and walked backward. "Those are some cherished memories, my Petah," Lilly said with a smile.

Peter put up finger. "I promised you a trip down memory lane, so I will be right back," he said as he went back to the truck.

As soon as he turned his back, Lilly scrambled up a tree. There were some great climbing ones in this park, and she had climbed them often in the years they'd lived in this town.

Peter had retrieved a quilt and his copy of *The Hedge of Thorns* and went back to where he'd left Lilly, but she was gone. Peter didn't know what had come of her until he heard the giggles. Then he heard Lilly's voice.

"Professor Collins, in all your learned days, have you not learned how to keep up with a simple ragmuffin?"

Peter put his hands on his hips. "No. They don't teach such things as that in school." He looked up and finally found her.

Lilly looked down at him. "Would you care to join me? I can give you some lessons," she said, smiling.

"I'm not the young teen who used to chase you in these trees." Peter sighed. "Come, Lilly. Join me on the quilt." He held out his hand for her to come down to him.

All Peter could hear was fast scrambling. She plopped down right in front of him, leaves in her hair and tiny bark pieces on her shirt. "Really, Peter, are we to read together?" she asked, breathless from jumping down from the tree.

He picked the leaves and bark pieces out of her hair. "Yes, Lil. If you want to."

She straightened herself up. "I would love to read with you," she said as she helped him with the quilt. "What a beautiful quilt," she said. Peter began to lay it on the ground.

Lilly stiffened. "Oh, we can't use it. It'll get dirty." Lilly was trying to fold it up. "Hey, let's just read like old times. We didn't use anything then but a soft patch of grass."

"Lilly, we are older now. I do wish to use the quilt for added comfort," Peter said, hoping to win.

"And I want to feel the grass between my toes!" Lilly put her hands on her hips. "My, we are different!" But she gave in, and they used the quilt.

Down they went, their heads almost together and their bodies flared out. At different times, Lilly would roll over to her stomach. Peter got on his side with his head on his elbow as he finished the book and closed it. They stared at one another for a long time. Peter took Lilly's hand and put it on his chest.

"You do wild things to my heart, Miss Parker."

They just stared at each other, completely free to enjoy the view.

After a while, Peter said it was time to go. He drove to the church parking lot that was right next to the high school. They got out. Peter walked her down the front street and then onto the high school grounds.

Peter said, "This is often where I prayed for you." He laughed. "And where I told guys about my crazy ragmuffin shadow."

"You mean you told other people about me?"

Peter just nodded with a smile. "This place holds a lot of memories."

They soon left the high school grounds and crossed the street to the church. He directed her over to the bus yard, found the old bus they had ridden on, and open the door.

"After you, my love."

Lilly couldn't believe this. "What are you doing?"

She ran her hand over the church lettering on the outside of the bus. Then Lilly slowly climbed up into the bus. She looked all around. It was the same. Peter had sat down about middle of the bus, his back to the window, his legs stretched out along the seat. He watched Lilly go back and forth, touching each seat. Silent tears trickled down her face. He could tell she was reliving scenes, songs, and faces. She would occasionally look over to see a smiling Peter.

Peter wasn't sure how long she'd done this before she came and sat in the seat behind him. "Oh, Peter, this is too much!" She smiled. She looked around again from where she was sitting. "How will I ever repay you?" she asked with a smile.

Peter thought, *Well, I can think of one way. Be my wife.* But instead, he said, "Well, there is one small thing you could do."

Lilly was all ears, eager to please. "What is it? You name it, I'll do it."

Peter winked at her and pulled out a bag. "I have a PBJ, an apple, and some water for you to take off my hands."

"Peter Collins, has anybody told you how special you are?"

Both had their backs to the windows, legs stretched out. They spent the next three hours remembering sweet memories.

Finally, Lilly sat upright in the seat and faced Peter, her eyes mirroring her heart. "What's happening to us?" Lilly couldn't take the guessing anymore.

Peter brushed her cheek with the back of his finger. "I'm not exactly sure, but what I need to know is, are you going to run from it?"

Lilly thought she understood his meaning. She quietly said, "No. When I'm with you, there's no need to run away."

"Good. Then let me make my intentions clear."

He reached up with his hands and kissed Lilly and with all the passion he possessed. She kissed him right back.

When they were both satisfied, they laughed.

Lilly said, "Who would have ever thought?"

Peter said, "Do you wish to go back through the church again?"

"No. Really, I'm good. I'll go tomorrow night, and I think that's enough." Lilly cocked her head. "But thank you for asking. And thank you so much for doing this and sharing the best lunch in town."

Peter rolled his eyes. He still couldn't confess that he really disliked PBJs.

Back in the truck, Peter took Lilly to her old middle school, which, of course, wasn't open, but she peered into windows. It didn't hold great memories, but it held memories of Peter. After she had her fill, Peter took her to the elementary school, which was close to her trailer.

On their way, Peter went through town first, to all the places that might be of interest to her. Then he drove the old bus route as best he could remember. Then he came to her old place. Peter turned off the truck. Lilly was like a robot. She got out of the truck and walked slowly over to the fence, which was falling down even more. The trailer looked abandoned, windows busted through, and the grass hadn't been mowed. Peter had come to stand close but not touching her to give her privacy. But when she reached to go in the gate, he pulled on her arm.

"You're not going in there," he said and was shaking his head. No matter what her longing to do so was, he wasn't going to let her.

"But, Peter, no one is there," Lilly cried.

"I'm sorry, my love. It's not safe." He shook his head. "The answer is no."

All fight drained out of Lilly. She just stood there and stared at the shambles of what she'd called home here in Arlington. Silent tears streamed down her cheeks. She didn't make a sound or a move. Peter didn't touch her but left her alone to her own thoughts.

Lilly, from time to time, would shake her head and cry some more. Peter knew she was probably praying. He knew this would be hard. But yet, somehow, he knew this would be part of her healing. He suspected she would've probably come here herself if he hadn't brought her.

Oh, LORD, the pain is so strong. I don't think I can do this without You. I need Your loving arms right now. I'm so thankful You plucked me from sure destruction. Oh, LORD, I can never repay the debt of Your free redemption. Father, even in the cruelty and abuse, I want my mother to know You. I want my earthly father to know You, wherever he is. He was the only one who ever cared anything about me, but even that was so little. Oh, Abba, heal my heart. It's broken in two.

On she prayed her heart out to her God.

When she was spent, she turned to Peter, who was leaning against the front of the truck, feet crossed, waiting patiently. She was a limp ragdoll, her face downcast like Peter had never seen. He put his arms around her as she came near him, and he pulled her tight. It was her undoing. She thought she'd expired her tears for the day. She was wrong. She sobbed harshly with all the emotion that was pent up inside her, for all those years came bubbling to the surface. She didn't realize it, but she had two fists full of Peter's shirt and had drenched the middle with her unbidden tears. Peter was gentle as he waited.

Peter leaned close to her face. "Oh my ragmuffin, it hurts my heart to see you hurting. I just want you to know I'm here if you want to talk about it."

Lilly looked around, pretty sure that the people who had once lived here on her street no longer did. She kicked pebbles at her feet. They walked along the road, as there was no sidewalk. Lilly laughed.

"Remember when I used to skateboard for you right here in the middle of the road? I really thought I was something, and you, Petah, laughed at all my tricks," she said in bittersweet remembrance.

"Ah yes, Lilly. You were quite the sport at it." Peter was grinning at the memory. "You tried to get me to do it in my church clothes. You were very hard to resist, you know."

They had walked to the end of the street and were back to the truck. Lilly was suddenly quiet, he noticed.

"It is amazing at how much you treasure when it is all you know," she said with such sadness in her voice.

Peter, at such times, felt so helpless to understand this child of his heart yet woman of his dreams. He had finally figured out though that if he would nudge and be patient, he would learn more.

"What do you mean, Lil?" he asked as they headed back to Jeff and Jenny's.

"It just seems so silly, but it's like about the ice cream truck. That was my world, and I don't want to lose it." She looked over at him for understanding. "Does that make sense?"

Peter nodded. Lilly went on.

"The ice cream truck is one of my few happy memories, and I will always cherish that memory." She laughed. "Even now, if I hear a bell off a bicycle or something like that, I jump up to run to the door." She was laughing. "Well, mostly happy. I stole the money most of the time I was able to delight myself in ice cream truck assets." She wiggled. "I guess that part I'm not too happy about."

Peter smiled. "So I have an ice cream truck addict and a thief in my dad's truck? Should I be hiding my wallet?" He continued to tease her with no mercy.

Lilly was in her best dress. She had Jenny do her hair in a most magnificent style. Peter thought she was a sight to behold. He'd almost wanted tonight to be the night to pop the question, but he decided that perhaps with all the things this week had brought, he didn't want to throw her into more tumult. But he planned on the evening being special anyway.

They were sitting at the most expensive steakhouse that Lilly had ever been in. Lilly leaned over.

"Peter, this is quite the place. You didn't have to do this," she said politely. She was so nervous at being in such a high-class establishment.

Peter had already given the order while Lilly had gone to freshen up. His Lilly was going to have steak tonight.

"I know I didn't. I wanted to," he whispered.

He was absolutely the most handsome man she'd ever known, and his looking at her was making her melt. She needed to quiet her beating heart.

Peter reached over and gently brushed her cheek with the back of his finger and said, "I thought tonight would be a night of sharing old memories and beginning new ones." He was staring at her again.

The air left her chest so quickly she thought she'd faint. All that was in her heart was shining out from her eyes.

Peter liked what he saw. He smiled and began to chat. She relaxed a bit, but the intimacy of her own thoughts never seemed far away. The candlelight seemed so romantic, though Lilly wasn't a romantic kind of girl; yet this evening was challenging that.

Peter was having his own thoughts that not much longer and he could ask her to be his wife. Then he wouldn't have to fight so hard for restraint every time he looked at her.

When their meal arrived, Lilly couldn't believe it.

When she put the first bite in her mouth, her eyes got big and she chewed and then ate some more. Peter all but laughed out loud at watching her. She delicately but deliberately ate her entire steak without stopping once.

Embarrassed that she had downed the whole thing so quickly, she asked, wiping her mouth, "How did you know I'd never had streak?"

Peter smiled as he began to cut his and eat. "I pay attention, ragmuffin. You told me this when you thought we might have PBJs at the Valentine banquet, remember?"

She smiled and nodded. "Well, I can't think of a better person to share a first with than my Petah. Steak is indeed mouthwatering."

They talked on into the evening and had coffee and dessert, though Lilly was not sure where she was going to put it after all that food. But the day's excursions had given her an extra appetite. Then they went and sat on a bench overlooking a lake on the outskirts of town, the moon casting a beautiful shimmer over the water.

"Peter, this evening has just been lovely." Lilly smiled. "You make me feel so special. You planned this day with such detail for me I really don't know what to say," she said softly. "I wish it didn't have to end."

Peter wanted to say, "*Marry me and it won't.*" But instead, he said, "Everything in your world means something to me."

Lilly was shaking her head. "But why, Peter? Why?" Lilly searched his eyes. "This was a lot of trouble to go through for a memory of a dirty, ole, gum-chewing, tree-climbing, barefoot brat of a kid."

Peter scooted a little closer, put his hands on her face. Then he whispered close to her face, "Because I love you."

Lilly's eyes registered shock, her eyes growing wide, her face shaking. "No. You only love that little girl. That's all."

Peter had no other choice. He bent his head quickly and kissed her passionately. Lilly wanted to fight, but she couldn't. She was wrapped in his arms, and he was kissing her. She kissed him back with all the love she had inside.

Finally, after several kisses, Peter said, "Yes, I love that little girl who captured my heart so many years ago. But that's not the same kind of love I have for this woman in my arms," he said. He looked down at her lips. "And if you need more convincing, I can manage."

Lilly smiled. "Well, maybe I'm having a little doubt." She giggled and found his lips upon her again.

He whispered in her ear, "I love you, Lillian May Beckler Parker!"

"Oh Peter," she whispered breathlessly. "I would have to lie if I said I did not love you. I just never thought I would get to tell you."

Peter squeezed the arm he had around her shoulders and said, "Every day, I'm still amazed at God's abundant blessing in us meeting again. It really is a miracle, and one I intend on never forgetting." Not long after, Peter took her home, both feeling fulfilled in their love for each other.

CHAPTER 25

Lilly said her good-byes in a puddle of tears while Peter took her luggage to the truck.

Jeff followed and said, "Take good care of her. And let us know when the wedding is." He slapped Peter on the back and gave him a bear hug.

Jeff and Jenny both hugged Lilly for as long as they could. Jenny was crying too. Then Lilly held baby Lilly one last time. This about made Peter come apart himself. When she held the baby, it was such a lovely picture that he could hardly stand it—not only thinking how lovely they both were but also in anticipation of when he would look on Lilly holding their own bundle of joy. To Peter's guess, if he had not made her leave, they would still be there. Plus, he had one special stop to make.

She knew the moment they were headed toward the subdivision that was in front of the deplorable trailer park in which she lived half of her life. She began to get anxious. "What are you doing?" She looked over at him and then out the window. "I thought we were on our way to the airport."

Peter was quiet, and her anxiousness grew. She didn't know why he wasn't answering her.

"Are you gonna answer me?" she almost yelled at him.

Peter smiled and very politely said no.

Lilly sat back in a huff. Peter did all he could not to laugh. Peter went to the end of the street and turned around and parked the truck.

"Get out," Peter said.

He took her to the tailgate and let it down and hopped up on it. He put out his hand for her to join him. She glared at him but slowly obeyed. "I thought we would sit for a spell and read the story of Joseph like old times. Is that okay with you?"

"Oh yes. That would be just fine. That is my favorite story, but I don't want to be late for my flight," she fretted.

"I won't let you be late, my love."

They were more than halfway done when Lilly placed her hand on his arm, looking up in the air.

"I hear it. I hear it," Lilly said, and she looked over at Peter. It was coming closer. "It's the ice cream truck, Petah!" She had jumped off the tailgate and was headed toward the sound.

Peter smiled as he looked at her. He wasn't sure if his heart could take any more. She was so cute. He could just picture her doing this as a little girl. It was at the other end of the street.

"Hey, wait for me." Peter said as he hopped down quickly

The bell of the truck had always brought sweet memories even when she couldn't get anything. The tune that it played always attracted her to the window if not to the truck. When she got to it, there were about six kids there. And immediately, Lilly began to dig in her jeans pocket. She paid for each child's ice cream. They were astonished.

Each one said with big eyes and a smile, "Hey thanks, miss," and went off slowly to enjoy their treat.

As she looked around, there was a boy who hung around but not in line. Lilly knew the look. His eyes wanted the delicious ice cream, yet his pockets were empty. But just like her, he waited around the truck. She met his eyes and motioned for him to come and get something. He ran over in a huff of breath.

"Thanks, miss! That's real nice of you!"

Peter stood back, watching this whole scene. Grubby hands holding ice cream, tongues licking happily amid smudgy faces. His eyes had become moist when he saw what she was doing. *Ah, my ragmuffin, you do good for my heart,* he thought. He knew she didn't have much money, yet she spent it on these street scalawags.

He continued to watch. When she didn't get anything, he was surprised. He walked up next to her. All the kids were gone. She looked up into the eyes of the same man.

"Hi. My name is Lilly. I used to live down in that trailer many years ago." She pointed to her old place. "I used to be one of those little kids who came every day to your truck. Well, I know you probably don't remember me, but you sure brightened my day!" She dug in her pocket for a tract. "A lot has changed in my life since then. Jesus has saved me and transformed my life. Here is something to read while you make your stops. Thank you for putting smiles on kids' faces." She then turned and walked off.

The driver still had his mouth hanging open at her kindness. Whereas he didn't really remember her, her kindness today wouldn't be forgotten.

Peter immediately went into action. He stopped her not two steps away, the ice cream man watching. "Hey, Lil, what are you doing?" Before she could answer, he asked, "Why aren't you getting something?" Peter had brought her all this way for this very thing. He didn't plan to leave without accomplishing his goal.

Lilly looked away for a moment, swallowing her pride. Then she looked at Peter. She put her hands in both front pockets and pulled them out. "I'm all out of money!" Then she put her hands to her chest. "But my heart is full!" She smiled at him and walked past him down the street.

"Whoa there. Wait just a minute, young lady," Peter said. "You turn around right this instant and march back over to that truck and get your favorite ice cream treat," Peter said sternly with love. He raised his hands at Lilly's protest. "I don't want to hear one word out of you."

Lilly rolled her eyes. Peter twirled his finger in the air, indicating for her to turn around. She finally complied.

Back at the side bar of the truck, Lilly asked for a pushup.

Peter came up behind her and said, "Make it two please."

"Coming right up," said the smiling man. Having seen love many times, he knew what he was witnessing.

Peter paid the man with a ten-dollar bill and said, "Thank you for waiting. Keep the change."

The man said an astonished, "Thank you! Thank you so much!" His huge smile showing his gratitude.

They waved at the man as they walked off.

Lilly was already savoring her first bite. Oh, what memories poured over her as she swirled that creamy orange sherbet in her mouth. She opened her eyes and glanced over at Peter and about choked on her ice cream, laughing. Peter was intently trying to figure out how to get into his pushup, he'd heard Lilly call it. His frustration keen, he didn't have a clue as to what to do to get it to pop out.

Lilly had compassion on him. "See. If you'd been a street scoundrel like me, you'd know these secrets, my dear Peter."

Peter scowled at her. She laughed some more but took the pushup and opened it for him and showed him how to push it up to get more.

Peter thought he probably looked a bit silly, but he could see why Lilly liked them. He looked over at her. She was in total enjoyment. He chuckled at the sight. *Just like a kid and ice cream to make you forget the world,* Peter thought. But he said, "These are very good. I can see why they were your favorite."

"We better head to the airport. Thank you for letting me in your world. Some things I'm learning, there's just not words for," Peter said softly.

The departure at the airport wasn't easy on either of them. With Peter staying through the weekend to visit more with his parents, Lilly knew she'd be alone. This caused the tears to come easily.

"Scoot," Peter said as he turned her toward the gate. "You're going to miss your flight standing here, my ragmuffin." Peter pushed her in the right direction, which made her quicken her step.

She turned and silently mouthed, "I love you, Peter Collins," and blew him a kiss.

CHAPTER 26

To Lilly's surprise, the weeks fell into routine very quickly. It still seemed strange to have Peter as the bus driver, but she loved it. Three weeks had already passed since their trip. It was Sunday after church, and Peter was in the driver's seat. Lilly was on the stairs at the open door, waiting on the rest of the kids to get on the bus when she noticed a paper stuck in the windshield wiper. Peter had been watching her and knew just when she saw it. She looked at him.

"Go ahead and get that, will ya? I don't want it to blow off when we drive down the road," Peter said seriously, belying his heart beating out of his chest.

She stepped off, reached up on her tiptoes, and got the bright yellow paper. She opened and read it.

"Will you register next semester as Mrs. Collins?"

Peter was watching her face intently to see what she would say. She was biting her lower lip. Kids were getting on the bus, but they both had momentarily blocked out the noise. She looked up at him. Their eyes met. She couldn't believe he'd just asked her to be his wife. She was astounded. She didn't know what to do. She was still in such a state of shock.

He finally raised his brows and asked, "And what is your answer?" He had to admit he expected this to be easy. He didn't think it necessary to wait any longer. He loved her, and she loved him. *And* Jeff had threatened him.

Lilly shook her head slowly. "No."

Peter couldn't believe it. She'd turned him down flat. *What is going on?* he wondered as he turned the bus on. All the kids were on by then, and Lilly went to work, the question never far from her mind. Her heart was racing. She was dancing in her head.

He asked me to marry him!

But she still had a mission field, single or married, and she loved the kids on her bus route. So she gave them her heart and attention. She'd deal with Professor Collins later.

He, on the other hand, was going crazy. It took every bit of concentration just to drive, and he had to discipline himself not to get a bad attitude while waiting to talk to the woman whom he'd just asked to be his lifelong partner in marriage. He was sorely tempted to broach the subject on their way back to the church to park the bus; but the helper was still on the bus, and it was a very private matter.

Once there, the helper said good-bye and hopped off the bus. Lilly got up, got the broom, and went to the back of the bus to quickly sweep it out. Peter immediately went to her. They were alone, but other buses could pull up anytime. Peter wasted no time in repeating the question, wanting an explanation for her answer. He wasn't being very patient at the moment, and Lilly knew it.

She was humming a tune as she swept.

He took the broom from her and said, "Why?" He rubbed the back of his neck. "Why, Lilly, can't you marry me and be my wife?" There was a mix of tears and anger in his throat.

"Peter, Peter," Lilly said, putting her hand on his cheek. "I never said I wouldn't be your wife. That wasn't the question."

"Look, Lil. Don't play games with me." He switched his feet, defeat washing over him, pain coming on in fast waves. "What are you talking about?"

Lilly smiled one of her lovely smiles at Peter. "I can't be Mrs. Collins when I register for the next semester, for, you see, I'm going to take summer classes." She was smiling impishly. Then she continued. "And when I become Mrs. Peter Collins, I want the grandest wedding ever."

Peter was still staring, taking all this in. Then, in just a few seconds of computing all she had just said, his grin began from one ear to the next. He burst out like a school kid, "So you'll marry me?"

Lilly smiled. "Yes, I will marry you." She had her hand on her hip. "Now, if you don't give me my broom back, I might think about changing my mind," she teased. Peter handed her the broom and ran up to the front of the bus he was so excited. Lilly just stopped a minute and laughed, watching him. He was picking up trash like a mad man, though as a very happy mad man. Then he ran back to her.

"Um, will you go to lunch with me?" he asked breathlessly.

Lilly giggled. "I'm glad I didn't have plans. Someone needs to be sure you don't hurt yourself!" She really loved this out-of-his-box Peter. He was so cute.

Peter put his hands on her arms and said, "It does crazy things to a man when he finds out that the woman who has stolen his heart agrees to be his wife!" He went back to finish his job. "I'm almost done here. How about you?" he asked. They met in the middle, both having just finished.

They looked at each other, trash bag and broom slipping from their hands. Peter framed his hands on her face, and for the next few moments, Lilly could hardly breathe. Peter spoke breathlessly.

"You, my ragmuffin, have made me the happiest man on this planet." His own breath came hard. "And I love you with all my heart." He slowly bent his head, anticipating the enjoyment of her lips on his very own. When he had kissed her passionately, he pulled back his head and smiled. He wasn't sure he could contain his joy.

Lilly spoke into his loving eyes. "And I'm the luckiest woman ever to have you even consider me an option." She licked her lips and whispered, "I love you more than you'll ever know."

Peter hugged her one more time. "Well, let's go then, my wife-to-be," he said, smiling as he helped her down the steps and closed the door.

Peter had taken Lilly to Round the Corner and actually asked to be seated in a certain booth, the one they'd first sat in. And to Peter's delight, it happened to be available. Lilly had gone to the restroom upon arrival. He sat shaking his head. *I'm really going to be married!* He continued smiling, just thinking about the days ahead and about what it would be like to be a husband.

Peter had laid *The Hedge of Thorns* in front of her seat. He spoke as soon as she had returned and was comfortably seated. "I took the liberty to order our usual," he said as he put his napkin in his lap, acting nonchalantly. "I was wondering if you would read to me my favorite chapter while we wait." He pointed with his eyebrows to the book. "It's marked."

Lilly shrugged her shoulders. "Sure," she said. "Anything for you." She smiled at him and opened to where the bookmark lay. That was when she noticed it. The most beautiful engagement ring Lilly had ever seen was tied to the end of the bookmark. Lilly's mouth was agape, her face shining like Peter had never seen. "Why, Lilly, have you forgotten how to read?" Peter said.

Lilly was astounded. "Why—she breathed— "I guess I suddenly do find myself without words. Peter, it's beautiful. I'm just so … so …" She had tears trickling down her cheeks. "I just never dreamed …" She couldn't go on.

"Go ahead." He motioned. "Untie it, and put it on your finger, for I want the entire world to know you're mine."

Lilly's hands were shaking, as she fiddled with the knot, thinking for a moment she wasn't going to be able to free the jewel. When she got it loose, she looked up at Peter, who nodded with his brows up and all smiles. She carefully and slowly put the simple yet elegant diamond on her ring finger. She shyly held it up and looked at it. It was beautiful, even though she sighed at her nub-bitten nails, which looked horrible. Lilly flashed Peter yet another dazzling smile.

"How did you know the size? It fits perfectly?" Lilly asked.

"Let me see," Peter smirked. She put her hand over at him. He took it into his and placed a kiss on it.

"You look beautiful wearing it," Peter said.

"That is a strange compliment."

"Well, I just couldn't find anything that would compare to the rare jewel of my ragmuffin, so I had to make do." Peter said.

Lilly nodded, understanding. Then Peter went on.

"But it is a lovely match—beautiful, elegant, yet simple and not overly done, just like you," Peter said. "And as for size—" he chuckled— "that's what holding hands was all about."

"You rascal. Is that how it is?" Lilly teased. "You only held my hand to get my ring size?" She was still admiring the engagement ring and all that it meant.

"Well, that is at least the excuse I used in my head." Peter winked. "I kept telling myself I just wasn't sure so I needed to hold your hand again to be sure."

Their order came then, and they went to eating.

"So when shall we become Mr. and Mrs. Collins?" Peter asked around a bite of burger.

They spent the rest of their lunch picking a date and discussing wedding dreams.

CHAPTER 27

There was a knock on the door, and then it opened. There was Lilly, standing by the window, twisting her hands back and forth. Peter, so in love with this woman, went to her, knowing she was a nervous wreck.

Lilly caught her breath and tried to hide. "Why, Peter, you aren't supposed to see me before the wedding!" Lilly was frantic.

Peter went and put his hands on her upper arms. "My ragmuffin, it's okay. I thought you might need a kiss or two." He kissed her cheek. He looked into her eyes. "How are you really?"

She moved from his embrace, her dress swishing in the movements. She went back to the window. "I'm scared," she admitted. "I can only imagine that your mom will be shedding tears today, but not of joy." Lilly expressed her fears.

Peter knew this would be hard for her. "As much as I love my mom, she's not who I'll be sharing the rest of my life with. I'm so sorry that you've had to struggle with my parents. It was the last thing I expected. I do love them and must honor them, but as of today, my wife takes top priority over my parents." Peter had raised his eyebrows as he looked into her sweet face.

"I just don't want to disappoint you or your parents." Lilly was breathless.

He walked over and reassured her that that wasn't going to happen and that he loved her. Seeing she was playing with something in her hands to keep from biting her nails, he asked, "What is that?" Peter chuckled.

"Oh, this?" she asked as she held up a melted, twisted, bent sucker. She didn't know she'd done that to it. She sighed. "Oh my!" Then she laughed. She went on to explain, "I gave Katherine one of my suckers when she got here. She was nervous, and so was I," Lilly said. "Come to think of it, hers looked like this too."

Both Lilly and Peter burst into laughter, both thinking back in time to a little, nine-year-old girl named Lilly.

"Well, my love, I left the front, and I think I hear the music starting." He picked up her beautiful bouquet of summer wildflowers and handed it to her. And then he stuck the sucker in the middle of it. "For later," he said when Lilly gave him a queer look. He kissed her cheek and said, "Not much longer and you'll be my wife." Then he slipped out of the room and back to his spot on the platform to watch his bride walk down the aisle.

Jeff took his cue from Peter's return. Jeff leaned forward for Peter's ears only. "Well, Peter, shall I go get your bride?" he asked with all smiles as he quietly patted Peter on the back.

Through much dilemma, they made an unusual arrangement. They decided that Jeff would play two roles. He would be both best man and he would also give the bride away. Being there for both Peter and Lilly was a double delight.

Jeff knocked softly on the door and went inside. "Is there a ragmuffin in here who wants to be married to an old geezer downstairs? You look beautiful, Lilly." There were tears in his eyes. "Do you know how I've prayed for you?" Jeff paused. "God has more than abundantly answered." Jeff kissed her on the cheek. He bent his elbow out for her to take it. "There's a man waiting, if we are much longer, very impatiently for his lovely bride to come marry him."

Lilly had silent tears coming but she smiled and took his elbow, and they headed out the door.

"Well, we certainly can't have an unhappy groom on his wedding day, now can we?" she said sweetly.

Lilly was not prepared for the sight that awaited her in the sanctuary. She stopped Jeff, tears coming on strong. "Can you give me a minute?" She was so taken with all the wedding party standing up there, including Peter. The flowers and candles, the petals on the floor, everything was so beautiful. What took her back was how many people were there. They all cared. She was so touched the tears just poured.

Jeff knew he couldn't keep her much longer. He thought they had already played all the verses of the song twice. Jeff leaned over.

"If we keep Peter waiting any longer, he might just come after you." He smiled. "Are you ready to give your heart away?"

"You're right. The way Peter keeps looking back here, we better get on with it, or he might just do it." Lilly giggled.

Lilly took Jeff's arm and began to walk, but when everyone stood and turned to her and the wedding march music began, it was too much. The tears began in earnest, and her knees melted. She gripped Jeff fiercely. She decided to look straight ahead and watch the scene before her as she walked down the aisle. Mr. Morton's two boys, the man they met in McDonald's, were the ring bearers. At the present moment, they were wiggling around, about to get into a fight. Katherine was swinging her empty basket, her hair coming down out of the chignon Wilma had put it in. Lilly nearly laughed out loud. If she was seeing what she thought, there was a sucker hanging out of Katherine's mouth.

When she reached the front, Willy stepped out and sang "The Cornerstone." He did a fabulous job. Lilly was so taken watching him, and listening to him sing, tears kept coming. She glanced at Peter, and she thought his eyes were misting over too. After Willy slipped back into place, the pastor spoke.

"Dearly beloved, we are gathered here today to join in holy matrimony Peter Ivan Collins and Lillian May Parker. Who gives this bride away to be joined in marriage to this groom?"

"I do, with all my heart," Jeff spoke up as he raised Lilly's hand and kissed it then placed it in Peter's strong hand. Jeff then went and slipped back into his best man spot.

Lilly turned and handed Jenny her bouquet to hold. She had turned halfway when she reached back and snatched the sucker out of the top. Jenny's eyes got big, and she had to hold her mouth to keep the laughter in.

Lilly's eyes meet hers, and she whispered, "Just in case!"

Lilly and Peter were facing each other. Lilly's hands lay inside Peter's, along with the melting sucker. Peter smirked when he saw what she'd done. Their eyes locked together as Willy sang a song he had written for them. The words were so special, just like Willy.

After that, there was a short sermon on marriage being built on the Cornerstone, Jesus Christ, and what it meant to have Him LORD of your life. He included the Gospel message too. Then they pledged to each other. Lilly liked to have never gotten hers out through the tears but managed. Peter was strong as he shared his heart with Lilly, never taking his eyes off her.

When they went to light their unity candle, Peter did a double-take. Sure enough, Lilly had popped her sucker in her mouth, the ratty stick hanging out as evidence. She was totally oblivious to the improperness of such an act. But Peter just chuckled and wondered just what he was getting himself into in the years to come.

After the candle was lit, they held hands while yet another song was played, "The Wedding Song." When it was complete, they exchanged their vows.

"Rings, please," the preacher called.

Peter was looking at Jeff. Jeff squatted down and told the two boys to come. They came over, their hair was messed up now. It was obvious to everyone they were not used to being in church, much less in a formal activity as a wedding. They'd been quite the entertainment, which was why their hair was in such disarray. But Jeff gave a ring to each one and hoped they wouldn't lose it in transport.

Lilly said, "With this ring, I thee wed…"

After they finished their vows, the preacher announced them husband and wife. "You may kiss your bride!"

Peter had the biggest grin. He'd waited a long time for this moment. He came up from kissing *his wife* for the first time and asked, "It was cherry, wasn't it?" They were now facing the congregation.

"Yep." She snickered.

The preacher concluded, "Please join me in welcoming Mr. and Mrs. Collins."

They went down, hand in hand, in a roar of applause. When it was time to do the traditional cake-feeding to each other, Lilly's desire was strong to shove it in his face a little, but she didn't in effort to be kind to her beloved. But she nearly got it all over her dress because she was laughing so hard when Peter tried to feed her and kept missing. Everyone was laughing by the time it was all done. And Lilly desperately needed a napkin.

She was rolling her eyes when he pointed for her to come over to the punch bowl. She wasn't sure she could take another mess. They had special bride and groom goblets, and they had to hook arms and drink at the same time. Lilly didn't often enjoy a meal without dripping something on herself. She was horrified at the thought, for it was red punch. She also knew that with their height difference, he might as well pour it down her throat. With the gleam Peter had in his eye, Lilly found herself shaking her head no. Suddenly, she was no longer thirsty. But Peter was persistent in using his index finger to call her over. The whole room had stopped to watch the newlyweds. Lilly was frozen in indecision when she heard Willy in the crowd.

"What's this Peter? You already losing control of your wife? You haven't even been married that long!"

He was teasing of course, but Lilly knew submission was a serious thing; and Peter's mother flashed through her mind. The group roared at Willy's humor, but all were watching what Lilly would do.

She slowly propelled her way toward the huge, red punch bowl. When she arrived, she was rewarded with a kiss just missing her mouth.

Peter said out loud, "No. I rather think of it as gaining her heart. But as most of you know, that was done many years ago."

Lilly had a wobbly smile. Peter, having read all she was thinking through her eyes, turned to her, handed her the bride goblet, and said, "To my love." Then he toasted gently on her glass, turned back to the crowd, raised his goblet; and drank. Lilly was so relieved she almost spilt it on herself when she subconsciously slumped her shoulders in relief. Lilly quickly raised her cup with a nod and followed Peter's example.

Peter then said, "Please join us in the pleasantries of refreshments."

There was other fun to be had, but not too long after most of the festivities were over, Peter came to claim his wife, wanting to get away and be alone with her. He came up behind her and slipped his arm around her waist and whispered in her ear, "My ragmuffin, are we close to the end? I'm a most anxious man to not share you anymore."

His smile was huge, and all followed the delighted couple out to the parking lot. As soon as the door was opened, they were showered with rice from everyone. It was a surprise, even though it was expected. Everyone was cheering for them and throwing rice following them into the middle of the parking lot. About that time, there was a huge loud honk. Both Peter and Lilly looked up at whoever it was laying on their horn only to see Willy waving out the window of Peter's car. He was grinning from ear to ear, yelling congratulations as he drove off.

Peter actually was lunging forward when his car disappeared. He turned when the horror hit him. Sure enough, sitting in the middle of the parking lot was Willy's car, all decorated with cans and streamers and "Just Married" written on the back window with shaving cream. Lilly was covering her mouth's loud shrieks of laughter, for she knew Peter was not happy. Peter was shaking his head. He would get Willy for sure on this one. He put his hand on his hip and turned to Lilly.

"Did you know about this?"

Lilly straightened, for she was bent over, laughing. "I promise you I had nothing to do with this, my love!" she said. "Well, shall we stand here or get into our honeymoon Cadillac?" she asked for all to hear, hoping to lighten Peter's disposition.

The joke was not all that funny to him but hilarious to watch. He walked over and adjusted the shoe on the mirror, hitting it in frustration. He rolled his eyes and waved at everyone with a fake smile and opened Lilly's door, which he had to jerk open, for it was stuck. When he got in on his side, there was a note attached to the steering wheel that said, "She always did like my car better!" He had to crank the car twice before it started. Peter was by now thankful it had started at all.

Peter didn't calm down until they were at the hotel desk and Willy's car was no longer in sight. He wasn't going to blow their wedding day or honeymoon over this, but he wasn't about to let Willy off the hook. He took Lilly up to their room. It was late, and he was sure Lilly was tired. He sure was. He began to take off his jacket, vest, and tie. Lilly was frozen to the floor.

Peter finally noticed and went to her. "What is it, my love?"

Lilly turned her face away. She was embarrassed to admit it. But she wanted Peter to know. "I'm scared." She motioned toward the bed. "I don't know if I can go through with it," she said and turned sad eyes to his face. "I never had anyone to talk to about those kinds of things, and I'm frightened senseless. I want it to be right and perfect, yet I feel like I'll let you down." She was about to be in tears again.

Peter put his hands on her upper arms and leaned to look into her face. "Hey, hey. It's okay, Lil. It's okay." He pulled her to his chest, and she did cry then at his love and his caring. She didn't cry long, but when he thought she was through with her tears, he pulled her away from his chest and said, "Do you not think that perhaps I'm nervous about that too?" He wanted to say the right thing. "More than anything, I want this to be a most memorable, pleasant experience too. And I have to be honest, ragmuffin, I know as much as you do," he said to ease her conscience. "However, I'd be a cruel and inhumane husband to require of you what you're not ready for. And I won't do that." He definitely thought he was ready to be a husband in every way but wanted to be gentle with his wife. "If you are okay with it, let's just see what happens."

Lilly nodded. "It's not that I find you repulsive or that I'm afraid of you." Her face heated with her next statement. "It's not that I don't desire to be one with you as a wife should be." She licked her lips. This was so hard to talk about, but she had always been able to talk to Peter. "But I'm scared I won't do the right thing, as I don't really know what all is involved. I don't want you to be disappointed in what you have chosen."

Peter thought there wouldn't be any disappointment. "Lilly, my love, there's not going to be any disappointment from me. I love you. We'll keep at it until we get it right. And right now, your lips are looking very lonely," he said as he looked down at her rosy-red lips.

Lilly put her arms around his neck. "That is one sure way to drive the fear away." She smiled and then allowed her lips the companionship that both desired.

At about 7:00 a.m., Lilly woke up with her head laying on Peter's bare chest, with his arm around her. "What time is it?" she asked sleepily.

Peter had been sleeping lightly, his hand over hers that lay on his chest. Peter said, "Um, it is time to kiss my wife good morning."

"Last night was wonderful." Lilly said as she stretched her legs, wondering if it had all been a dream. She sighed contentedly.

"Last night? What was last night? I don't remember anything," he said teasingly. "I guess I need to be reminded!" He picked up her hand and began to kiss it, all up her arm, and before they knew it, it was 9:00 a.m.

At the breakfast table, Peter said, "I like starting out my day like that, Mrs. Collins. We should really consider keeping up the tradition!" Peter was in the lightest mood Lilly had ever seen him.

She smiled as she bit into a bagel. "I will see what I can do."

EPILOGUE

It was the first Saturday in October, and Lilly was dressed ready to go but nearly in tears. Peter had patted his leg, indicating he wanted her to sit on his lap. This was a common occurrence since they were married. Lilly spoke between her tears.

"I just can't do it!" She sniffled. "I just can't. Oh, Peter, I've tried, I'm just no good at it!" She was fiddling with her hands. "You're gonna wish you hadn't married me. I can't do anything," she fretted.

Peter shushed her. "Hey, sweetie, it's okay. Hush now. Everything is going to be all right. Just tell me what's going on."

Lilly twisted her shirttail, sniffled again, and took a deep breath to try to explain. "I've tried to be a good wife. I've tried to learn to quilt. I've been going each week to learn how, but I just don't seem to get it. I wanted to make a nice quilt for our bed, and I just can't seem to get this sewing thing down." She flopped her hands. "I want you to be proud of me and do the things wives are supposed to do, but I feel like an utter failure." She cried some more, having come clean with this confession.

Peter pulling her to his chest let her cry until she seemed finished. Then he said, "First of all, you're going to call and tell the ladies you'll not be in attendance today." He put up his hand to her coming protest and shook his head that he'd take no rebuttal on this. "Now, you listen to me, my lovely bride, you don't need to do anything to make me proud of you. I already am." He nuzzled his nose on her cheek. "Not everyone is cut out to quilt. Excuse the pun." He chose his words carefully. "You need to be sure this is what God is wanting you to be involved in because you already have your Hands to Hearts and Feet to Friends ministry; and that, at times, might take a lot of your time. And don't forget the bus ministry. If you schedule yourself to the max, you won't have time for the opportunities God sends your way."

"But I want to do those domestic things like the old ladies at church do."

Peter smiled. He could just picture her being like some of the dear old ladies that he just adored. "Lil, this will come in time, perhaps. But give yourself some space. There are seasons for everything; and right now, perhaps your season is working with needy and destitute children and teens," Peter said softly, feeling sure that was Lilly's calling, at least at the moment, not learning to knit or crochet. Even though those are fine and lovely arts, that was not how God had put together his Lilly. He brushed her chin with his finger. "You have a big heart, and there are kids out there who need you," he said and kissed her forehead. "Now, hop up and make that call, and then I shall take you out to lunch, my ragmuffin."

Lilly was standing in Willy's studio bedroom doorway this early morning. She didn't need to be at class as early as Peter, so they drove separately. But Peter hadn't left yet. He'd just finished his breakfast. He came and slipped his arms around Lilly.

"Miss him, don't you?"

He knew she did. Willy had been such a part in both of their lives. Even though he had gone on tour only three weeks before their wedding, it was now early November. Willy had asked if he could leave things the way they were in case this music tour didn't work out. They'd both agreed, knowing it meant that he would possibly move back in. But that was okay. They loved Willy. He just would have to figure out a way to sleep in his room and not on the couch. Lilly laughed at the memory.

Peter decided that Lilly's neck looked inviting and hoped his interest would take her mind off his cousin's absence, so he began to kiss her. She knew he needed to get to work, but she was beginning to think he had other ideas.

"I thought you needed to be off to work?" she questioned him in between kisses.

"Um, I do." Then he went back to what he wanted to spend the day doing. Peter said, "Who knows. We might have to boot Willy's stuff out if we need to replace it with a baby crib."

Lilly finally slipped out of his arms. "I do declare, Peter, you're going to be late for class. And then we won't be able to feed the thing!" she said, teasing. Not that she minded the attention, but she also knew she didn't want him in a rush to get to work because of it.

"Okay. You're right. I'll just start earlier tomorrow." He said and winked at her.

She walked over to him put her arms around his neck. "That will be fine, Professor Collins," she said as she gave him a kiss to last all day.

Peter said as he opened the door to leave, "You, Mrs. Collins, make it hard to leave. Did you know that?" He looked lovingly in her eyes. "See you later, my lovely ragmuffin."

The week of finals, Peter walked into his classroom and stood frozen at the chalkboard. In gigantic white letters was written, "Professor Collins is gonna be a daddy." Peter kept staring at it. Then a big grin from ear to ear stretched out across his face. He was about to go fetch her to see if it was true and to see if she was all right, but his first student walked in. He quickly erased the private message from the board but not from his heart.

At lunchtime, Peter went at breakneck speed as much as was dignified in search of Lilly. He found her in the library. Since it was cold outside, she had given up her favorite place under the oaks. He cleared his throat and whispered loudly and directly, "I need to speak with you."

Lilly looked up, smiling with a gleam in her eye. "Oh. I'm so sorry, Professor Collins. As you can see, I'm very busy at the moment."

Peter shuffled his feet impatiently. "Well, it's my understanding that expectant women shouldn't be too busy. They say they should take it easy."

Lilly kept up her shenanigans. "Well, then you'll be pleased that I have only volunteered to do the campus Angel Tree; Good Samaritan shoe boxes, you know, getting five hundred of them wrapped; and two parts in the Christmas play," she said, smiling at him like there was nothing special going on in the world.

Peter crumpled his brow and sternly said, "Lil, come with me." He turned on his heels and expected to be followed.

Lilly reluctantly gave up her game and with great excitement, followed in her husband's wake to his office, whereupon he hugged her and began to question her rapidly. He put his hand on her stomach. He said, "I don't feel anything. Are you sure you shouldn't lie down and rest?"

Lilly laughed at his hyper concern. He was funny to watch. "Why, Peter, of course you can't feel the baby yet. It is only probably five weeks old."

Peter finally sat down and patted his leg for her to sit on it. "Okay, ragmuffin. Out with it. Tell me everything."

Lilly sat in his lap and said, "I had a suspicion that it was a possibility, so I took a pregnancy test and it was positive." She was so excited she hugged him and kissed him. "You, my love, will make a great daddy."

Peter said, "I just still can't believe it. You really have a baby inside you?"

Lilly nodded.

Then Peter said excitedly, "We have to call my parents and Jeff and Jenny."

Lilly spoke up, jumping off Peter's lap. "I need to call Willy; he'll be so surprised." Lilly was walking away. "That is if I can find him." And off she went, leaving a very happy husband in her wake to see if she could find out what in the world Willy was up to.